SPECTACULAR
THINGS

SPECTACULAR THINGS

A Novel

BECK DOREY-STEIN

The Dial Press New York

The Dial Press
An imprint of Random House
A division of Penguin Random House LLC
1745 Broadway, New York, NY 10019
randomhousebooks.com
penguinrandomhouse.com

Hardback ISBN 9780593446287
International Edition ISBN 9798217155354
Ebook ISBN 9780593446294

Printed in the United States of America on acid-free paper

1st Printing

First Edition

BOOK TEAM: Production editor: Ted Allen • Managing editor: Rebecca Berlant •
Production manager: Maggie Hart • Copy editor: Muriel Jorgensen •
Proofreaders: Cathy Sangermano, Deb Bader, Adele Starrs

Book design by Elizabeth A. D. Eno

The authorized representative in the EU for product safety
and compliance is Penguin Random House Ireland,
Morrison Chambers, 32 Nassau Street, Dublin D02 YH68, Ireland.
https://eu-contact.penguin.ie

For my teammates, which is to say, for my family

Look, we are not unspectacular things.
We've come this far, survived this much. What
would happen if we decided to survive more? To love harder?

—Ada Limón, "Dead Stars"

OPPORTUNITY

2028

AN EARLY LABOR DAY

The bridge is up.

Of course it is.

The bridge is up and the baby is coming.

"Maybe it's a good sign?" Mia says from the passenger seat.

"Definitely," Oliver agrees, shifting the car into park. "Back to how it all began." He reaches over to touch Mia's knee, but only briefly. It's August and unbearably hot.

They sit. They wait. They sweat.

In the surrounding vehicles, tourists roll down their windows and hold up their phones to document the high drama of a drawbridge: how the road rises into a wave of asphalt that eclipses the sun.

"I should text Cricket," Mia says, closing her eyes as the next contraction builds. "Right? I should text her?"

"Sure, if you want—"

"I'm not going to." Mia leans forward and bows her head to ride out the pain. "She needs to focus."

"So do you."

"Worst-case scenario, we'll stream the game on my phone." Mia had a feeling this exact situation would occur: her labor coinciding with the Summer Olympics Gold Medal match between the U.S. Women's National Team and the Netherlands.

Game day for both Lowe sisters.

Oliver drums his thumbs on the top of the steering wheel. "This feels longer than usual," he says, looking past Mia and out toward the bay. "I don't even see a boat."

For summer people, the notion of a drawbridge is intrinsically romantic—an engineered nudge to slow down and enjoy the view. It's why they come here. Because like Maine itself, the bridge serves as a reminder that this is The Way Life Should Be.

Locals running late, however, tell a different story. Especially this time of year, in the high season, when just one ship can delay hundreds of cars, thousands of start times, and, as of twenty minutes ago, at least one woman in labor, which, for Mia in this moment, begs the question, *Is this the way life should be?*

Finally, the drawbridge comes together like clasped hands and settles back down into one unified road. The arm of the barrier gate lifts. The bell rings. Oliver steps on the gas.

At the hospital, there is no bursting through doors or rushing down halls or screaming out for drugs. Instead, there is only a long but entirely civilized line to check in at the front desk of the maternity ward.

"It's like an Apple Store," Mia jokes nervously, trying to summon her sister's sense of humor, strength, and capacity for pain. Cricket would be so good in this situation—her mind and body hammered into steel over decades of training. Cricket thrives on high stakes, loves high stakes, has made an entire career out of high stakes.

Mia, however, prefers reliable outcomes. She believes a surprise is called an upset for a reason: that a sudden change in expectations is indeed upsetting.

A nurse calls out her name. Oliver takes Mia's hand and follows her lead. He squeezes her fingers as they walk past a room with a baby crying, and then he squeezes again when they hear a mother sobbing.

"Oh, thank God," Mia says when they enter the delivery room, beaming at the sizable television mounted on the wall. Oliver grabs the remote and speeds through the channels until that familiar stretch of green consumes the screen.

"Big soccer fans?" the nurse asks, eyeing the husband and wife's matching U.S. jerseys. Mia's kit is stretched so tightly over her stomach that the nurse wonders if all that compression helped to induce labor and how, exactly, they're going to get it off.

"My sister is one of the goalkeepers," Mia volunteers just before doubling over. The contractions up until now have been relatively minor. But they are suddenly excruciating, walloping, and relentless. She doesn't want to do this. She can't do this, and she's about to say so to Oliver, but then she hears her mother's voice in her ear, reminding her, just as she always has: *No pain, no gain.*

Mia knows there is only one way to meet her baby, and it's through this gauntlet of agony. She is a Lowe, not a quitter, and so Mia closes her eyes and channels her mother's resilience, her sister's stamina. She remembers to focus on this moment just as the nurse jabs an IV into her forearm.

"To be honest, I'm more of a hockey guy," the nurse says, and then, recalling a provocative Super Bowl commercial that penetrated every corner of the globe, he looks at Mia with sudden intrigue. "So your sister knows Sloane Jackson?"

COMPETING FOR HARDWARE

Sometimes Cricket thinks of her adult life as driving as fast as she can while circling a full parking lot. You can't force a spot to open up—you just have to put your head down, grind in your highest gear, and hope for fate to break your way.

Hidden from view in the mouth of the players' tunnel, Cricket watches the Jumbotron as she shifts her weight from foot to foot. The thousands of children chanting in the stands look like little warriors, manic from soda, bug-eyed with adrenaline. The game hasn't even started, but they've already smeared the flags painted on their cheeks and screamed their way to a second wind. *Get up, get up, it's coming, it's coming*—the young fans shove their hands in the air as The Wave goes around the stadium again and again and again.

Every step to get here has been a battle, but Cricket and the U.S. Women's National Team have advanced to the Gold Medal match of the 2028 Summer Olympics in Los Angeles. Now they have ninety minutes to prove they are still the greatest women's soccer squad in the world. Their reputation has been challenged before, criticized, dismissed, and kicked in the teeth multiple times over the years. They are not immune to the comments of sportscasters and cynics who say dynasties are destined to crumble.

In just a minute and right on cue, Cricket will enter the arena with the other "game changers," which is what the coaches call reserve players, or substitutes, which is just a nicer term for dispensable backup. It's what Cricket has always been on this team. When she crosses the field and heads for the sideline, the fans will clap but keep their eyes trained on the players' tunnel. The starters, not the game changers, are why the fans are feral, waving their homemade posters for the TV cameras while gleefully straining their vocal cords.

"Game changers! Let's go!"

Cricket jogs past the starters, who are lined up inside the tunnel and holding the hands of young kids in shiny red shorts that contrast nicely with the white U.S. uniforms. Locally sourced from nearby club teams, the children have been plucked from obscurity to represent the future faces of the Beautiful Game. Today is a day they will all remember, and several years from now, one of them will even cite this match as the reason why she chose to pursue a career in professional soccer.

Sloane Jackson stands at the front of the line. When Cricket runs by, she forces herself to say, "You got this." Because the outcome of the game is more important than their mutual resentment. Because a win is a win and gold is gold. Even if they're no longer friends.

The starting goalkeeper gives Cricket a solemn nod back, already deep into her own meditation and ignoring the small pigtailed girl holding her hand. Adrenaline bounces off the tunnel walls as the U.S. coaching staff claps and teammates yell, "LFG! Let's fucking go!" The starters stand shoulder to shoulder with their adversaries, the imposing Dutch, who bark their own encouragement, "Laten we gaan! Kom op!"

Taking the field with the other game changers, Cricket blinks in the bright lights and catches the sonic buzz of the fans. She's actually, finally here. She's made it. This is what her entire life has revolved around for as long as she can remember. Even if she's just cheering from the bench with the other reserves, her presence proves what her mom always said: She's a Lowe, not a quitter. And if she can make it this far, then it's entirely possible that someday her time will come and her parking spot will open up.

Searching the stands, Cricket finds the designated Friends and Family section, full of familiar faces, even though none of them are her friends or family. Mia was too close to her due date to fly across the country. Like the team sports psychologist first encouraged her to do years ago, Cricket imagines she can see her sister up there. She waves, and Mia waves back.

A loud hissing surrounds the stadium and then a deafening *KA-BOOM*.

Fireworks dazzle overhead as the starting players emerge from the tunnel amid strobe lights, drones, and vuvuzelas. There's a deafening uptick in screams as the fans identify the eleven worthy of taking the field in this Gold Medal match. As they have done for every game in this Olympics, thousands of fans start chanting the name that haunts Cricket in her dreams. To the same tune as they yell *U-S-A*, diehard National Team supporters profess their allegiance to *SLOANE JACK-SON! SLOANE JACK-SON!* Faces disappear behind phones to capture their queen in pixels.

"Hands in!" team captain Gogo Garba commands. They are gladiators immune to mercy inside this arena. They are not the nice ladies from the Volkswagen commercials or the silly dancers on TikTok. Instead, they are a pack of hungry wolves tracking their prey. These women are here to win at any cost, under every circumstance.

"OOSA-OOSA-OOSA-AH!"

The starting eleven take the field.

A whistle blows.

The match begins.

Destiny bares its teeth.

A SPIKE

"Oh nice," Mia's obstetrician says candidly, glancing at the television in time to see the starting Olympians emerge from the tunnel. "I forgot this was on—should be a great game."

"Dr. Elliott?" A third-year resident throws out some numbers she reads off the monitor. The OB shakes her head and tells the resident to adjust the sensor before asking Mia to scooch down to the edge of the bed. "I'm going to use my fingers to measure how dilated you are—you'll feel a bit of pressure."

Dr. Elliott inserts her hand and Mia breathes in through her nose and stares at the TV screen: Gogo passes to Speedy, who carries the ball to the far corner and crosses it. Mia grinds her teeth through the cervical exam and continues to name each player as she sees them on the field. This game just might prove to be the perfect distraction.

"Five centimeters dilated," Dr. Elliott announces, looking up at Mia. "Great start."

"Same numbers," the resident says quietly, staring at the OB, who stands up to see for herself. The silence between them only draws more curiosity.

"Everything okay?" Oliver asks.

"Mia's blood pressure is a touch higher than we'd like," Dr. Elliott explains. She takes a step closer to Mia. "We're going to keep an eye on it, and hopefully it drops as you adjust to being in the hospital and preparing to give birth to your first child—there are plenty of reasons why blood pressure can spike."

Oliver looks for where he put the remote. "We've got to turn off the game," he says. "Your body is reacting to it."

"Hell no," Mia says without looking at him, eyes glued to the screen. Occasionally, the camera zooms out for a wide shot of the pitch, and Mia glimpses the floof of Cricket's high blond bun, the neon green of her long-sleeved goalkeeper jersey. It's enough to carry her through the next contraction.

An hour later, Mia buries her head deep into her husband's chest. At some point she ripped off her skintight soccer jersey, or rather the seams gave up on her and the shirt more or less popped off on its own. So here she is, slow dancing with Oliver in a nursing bra and maternity underwear, grunting and moaning with abandon. The pain is so all-encompassing that she has been stripped of clothes, speech, ego. That is, until Gogo scores in the seventieth minute of the game. "Holy shit!" Mia yells before puking down the front of Oliver's shirt.

"Now they just need to keep the lead and kill the clock!" Oliver says, removing his vomit-covered USA jersey.

"Put on mine," Mia says, and Oliver knows better than to argue with her.

In the seventy-fifth minute of the game, the resident checks Mia's vitals again. "Your levels are still high," she says, reading the monitor. "But the baby looks good, so Dr. Elliott says we're going to stick to the game plan and let you take your time, as long as you're comfortable."

"*Comfortable?*" Mia scoffs.

"Relatively comfortable, I mean." The resident blushes. "Anyway, you're doing great! Just let the baby lead the way!"

"Is it bad," Mia asks Oliver once the resident has left, "that when I hear 'baby,' I still think of Cricket? Like, I still think of my mom calling Cricket the baby, but now—"

"Totally normal," Oliver reassures her, running a damp washcloth along her hairline. "And I think that's all about to—"

"Oh my God!" Mia shouts, pointing at the television. "Oh my God!"

A STALK OF CELERY

In the eighty-third minute of the game, the United States still up 1–0, Cricket hears the scream and knows it's Sloane.

Whistles blow, flags fly. Down the bench, players gasp. In the stands, children mimic adults by holding their crossed fingers in the air and whispering, *Getupgetupgetup*. There are seven minutes left—still plenty of time and infinite possibilities for the Dutch to neutralize the scoreboard. The coaches yell at the refs while players catch their breath and silently will Sloane to find her feet like she usually does. From the nosebleed seats fans yell at Sloane to shake it off, and from the sideline Cricket feels a rush of shame-laced excitement as she thinks to herself: *This is it.*

The ball rolls toward the end line and then out of bounds. No one chases it down. Instead, the referee closest to Sloane approaches her and visibly dry heaves at the sight of her leg.

Medics rush the field.

Teague, the U.S. head coach, joins the team doctor at Sloane's side and takes a knee.

The ten starting U.S. field players encircle their felled goalkeeper, and through their legs, Cricket glimpses Sloane writhing on her back, begging and crying up to the sky, "*Please no, please no, please no.*" But Cricket knows from experience that such prayers arrive too late and almost always go unanswered, so she looks away and waits.

The Jumbotron replays what happened in slow motion. Cricket gulps down image after image with everyone else in the stadium. The Dutch corner kick. The lofted ball. The fight inside the box. Sloane's bright red goalkeeper gloves appearing over the fray, flying like two angry stop signs above every matted ponytail and slick forehead—all except for Mila Visschers, tenacious darling of the Netherlands, who is known for her offensive acuity and vertical leap.

Footage from multiple angles documents what happens between the goalposts, but even as Cricket watches gravity yank Sloane and Mila down into a mashed-up heap of bones and muscle, the physics of the collision seem impossible. It's a cartoonish brutality designed for video games. Under Mila's boot, Sloane's leg bends backward. Frame by frame, her quadricep folds in like rubber. It's an optical illusion, a sadist's magic trick.

Emma, the third-string keeper, takes a step closer to Cricket and squeezes her forearm to convey what they both know is about to happen. It's Cricket's turn. Here's her parking spot.

The fraught buzz of the stadium escalates to an aggravated hornet's nest when Sloane tries to sit up. She screams and the crowd reacts in kind. Two more medics sprint onto the field, carrying a stretcher, but Sloane's agony-soaked wails serve as its own diagnosis. She is the best goalkeeper in the world, a woman known for her intimidating bark, her unrelenting bite, her fearless physicality—it's what makes her so good and how the United States got this far.

On camera, in tailored blazers and with scripted notes, network correspondents discuss how one moment can sabotage a team's chances. In the postgame wrap-up, the talking heads will poeticize the barbarity of that moment between Sloane and Mila. They will echo what one U.S. defender told NBC Sports—that Sloane's femur breaking sounded like "a stalk of celery snapping in half." But what the sportscasters keep to themselves—and off the air—is the same thing Sloane's teammates repeat in the inner sanctum of the locker room: You can't forget a scream like that.

But that's later, and right now, all eyes are on Teague, the U.S. National Team's head coach, marching back to the sideline with a general's consternation, as if her career depends on the next seven minutes, which it does. Anders, the goalkeeping coach, calls Cricket's name from down the bench and keeps his back to the pitch as medics load Sloane onto the stretcher. "She's done," Anders tells Cricket, his electric blue chewing gum running figure eights in his mouth. "You're up."

Ignoring her vibrating hands, Cricket puts on her lucky gloves. No time to warm up. No time for anything except this. Seven minutes plus stoppage time. On the Jumbotron, a sudden streak of fluorescence catches her attention before Cricket realizes that's her on the screen, in her long-sleeve goalkeeper jersey, looking like a terrified human highlighter. She tries to neutralize her face as she visualizes what comes next and hums the first song on her gameday playlist to calm her nerves, "Get Low, Fly High."

Medics wheel Sloane off the field to a standing ovation that makes the entire stadium quake. U.S. and Dutch fans alike cheer for Sloane, but also for the game itself: Regardless of players' battles on the field and each country's struggles off it, soccer endures. The game is a show, so of course it must go on, even as an understudy takes center stage with an Olympic gold medal on the line.

This is not just the last seven minutes of a match, but also the next decade of Cricket's life if she plays the way she knows she can. This is her shot to step up and into the spotlight. It's the chance she's dreamed of since she was a child; the beginning of her storied career as the starting goalkeeper on the U.S. Women's National Team.

Everyone knows that one player's loss means another player's opportunity—it's the unflinchingly cruel yet eternally hopeful nature of the game. The never-ending twists of a forever-evolving story. It's why everybody loves an underdog.

And it's why more than sixty thousand fans watch Cricket Lowe sub in at center field and wonder what will happen next. She steals a glance at the Friends and Family section, squints, and gives a quick nod of recognition when she sees Mia and Oliver in her mind's eye. This is what they've always wanted. Even if they aren't really here, Cricket knows they are watching.

Sprinting onto the field and into the goal, Cricket touches each aluminum post for grounding. She is accustomed to the thunderous noise from the bench, but on the pitch and under the lights, the fans are so loud that the sound overwhelms her senses. She can't see straight or hear herself think or get her legs to stop shaking. The adrenaline surging through her nervous system makes her bones twitch and her eyes stretch. This is the experience she has chased with dogged tenacity since she was a kid—to be so anxious and simultaneously so empowered, holding the fate of the match in her lucky lime-green gloves. This is where she belongs, Cricket tells herself. This is where she is meant to be, where she has dreamt of standing since she first learned to run.

"Tonight is Cricket Lowe's first-ever international appearance!" a commentator announces. The stadium sucks in its breath, flabbergasted. A dirty secret unleashed, the weakness of inexperience. The Dutch players look at one another like sharks catching the distinct scent of fresh blood. Nevertheless, Cricket's muscles remember what to do here. She continues to jump in place, trying to warm up her legs in record time.

"And that's compared to Sloane Jackson's sixty-four caps!"

Cricket absorbs the collective shock that rumbles like a groundswell, like this announcement has just cost the United States the game. "Let's give Cricket a round of applause!" the commentator directs. The stadium obediently erupts with noise, filling the air with Cricket's name—tinged with pity, doubt, and fear—as the referee draws her whistle to her mouth.

The game commences.

Seven minutes to win it all or lose everything.

This is entertainment. This is sport. This is tribalism in its purest form. This is so much bigger than just Cricket, and yet the commentators keep repeating her name. All the cheering and jeering and chanting from the stands funnel into Cricket's eardrum and course through her bloodstream. There is an undercurrent of us versus them buzzing through the stadium that distracts her until Cricket sees Mila Visschers accept the ball in the midfield and head to goal. With the ball at her feet,

Mila loses her defender and charges Cricket with ankle-snapping speed and one clear intention.

The Dutch star looks up at the goal, and so Cricket looks at Mila's boots, her hips, the ball, and here it comes. Nothing exists except this shot, which is going toward the lower left corner of the net. It might be wide but it's going to be tight.

Cricket doesn't think before she dives. She can't afford the time. Instead, she chases her instincts, even as she questions whether she can get there. The world slows down until the milliseconds stand still and Cricket hangs suspended in the air. The ball rotates in place.

She's not going to get there.

She's not going to get there but she's got to try to—

Yes!

There it is at her fingertips.

Cricket absorbs the force of a twenty-eight-inch ball traveling seventy miles per hour and knocks it away from the goal, then scrambles to throw her body on top of it like the ball is a grenade and she's a war hero in the making. She covers the ball before anyone else can get a foot on it, and the stadium bursts into astonished and then joyous applause, but all Cricket can hear is her own voice as she finds her feet and shouts at her defensive line, "Get out!"

Cricket hurls the ball so it lands on a platter for one of her midfielders, who passes it to Speedy up top. On a team of Olympians, how fast must one be to earn the nickname Speedy? She is a rocket ship strapped to a comet racing the speed of light in hot pink cleats.

Speedy takes the space and makes herself a threat by baiting the Dutch defenders, each one a Subzero refrigerator swathed in orange. She draws the defenders out, only to pass the ball to Gogo. They aren't looking to score so much as keep possession until—there it is. The referee's whistle. Two short beeps followed by one long exhale.

It's over.

It's all over.

Relief blooms in every atom of Cricket's being.

At the other end of the field, her teammates run toward one another and form a swarm before running toward the defenders, who join the mass and head toward their own goal, their own keeper. They pull Cricket into the heart of the huddle, just before the entire squad collapses on the grass.

It is euphoric madness in the middle of the heap. Cricket is covered in her teammates' sweat, with someone else's hair in her mouth and tears on her cheeks as they scream into one another's faces, camera crews hovering above them, failing to capture the heights of their highs as the four starting defenders make snow angels in the confetti with their eyes closed but all their teeth showing. In the goal net, two rookies embrace with full-body shakes as their lifelong dream becomes their 3D reality.

With their boom mics hovering, several camera crews surround the team captain as she gets down on her knees and kisses the grass, then runs over to squeeze Cricket. "You did it!" Gogo yells, lifting Cricket off her feet. They are Olympians, Gold Medal champions of the world. Everyone is claughing—that beautiful mix of tears and joy, crying and laughing and asking one another if this moment is really real.

By the time Cricket gets to the locker room, most details of the night will already be fuzzy, but now Speedy is cartwheeling through the confetti, and Taylor's kid is crashing the field, holding her arms out so her mom will pick her up, and Cricket aches to see her own. She once again squints at the Friends and Family section until she sees her.

Cricket runs to the stands. She blows kisses back to the five-year-old girls and mouths "Thank you" to their parents and claps with her hands over her head because this was a group effort. They won because of the support from the fans. They won because they played for one another. They won because they are winners, and because long before today, Cricket earned her place between the goalposts on the best soccer team in the world.

Soon enough, the team will get it together and warm down responsibly. Soon enough, they'll load onto a bus and exit the stadium. But until then, the cameras roll and twenty-two hearts beat together in a singular revelry, a collective sigh, a jubilant cry that can never be conveyed, only experienced, and it is this: They have just won it all.

PUSHA-PUSHA-PUSHA-AH!

"What a game!" Dr. Elliott declares. "Mia, almost time to start pushing."

"Here we go!" Oliver whoops, massaging Mia's shoulders like she's a prizefighter between rounds.

On the television and at full volume, sportscasters discuss the U.S. win and Cricket's last-minute save.

"I'll be right back," Dr. Elliott says, glaring at the numbers on Mia's monitor. "Just breathe and try to relax."

Mia promises she'll try just as her phone rings. Her sister.

"You did it!" Mia shouts. In the background, she hears the inebriated National Team chanting, *Oosa-Oosa-Oosa-Ah!*

"*We* did it! Cricket shouts back as champagne sprays the side of her face and someone licks it off her cheek. "How's it going over there?"

"I'm nine centimeters!"

"Hell yeah!" Cricket cheers. "What's that mean?"

Before Mia can respond, Taylor, one of the four mothers on the National Team, grabs the phone out of Cricket's grip and cups her hand around the speaker.

"Go Mia!" Taylor yells. "Nine centimeters? It's game time!"

"My sister's having a baby!" Cricket announces to the locker room.

Taylor puts the phone on speaker and yells, "Push, girl, push!" And someone in that squad of twenty-two Gold Medal Olympians, swaying together with arms interlocked, has the brilliant idea to change their chanting from *Oosa-Oosa-Oosa-Ah* to *Pusha-Pusha-Pusha-Ah!*

Thousands of miles apart, Mia and Cricket hear each other's silence amid all the noise as they both rub at their wet eyes, overwhelmed by the support from the team and wishing their mother were with them.

"You won a gold medal, Cricky!" Mia yells into the phone. "You did it!"

"And you're doing it!" Cricket shouts back. "I love you! Tell that baby I'm coming!"

Two hours of pushing later, Mia and Oliver are delirious from exhaustion when the monitor begins to beep and won't relent. The OB barely glances at it before turning her back to place two calls, speaking so quietly that Mia and Oliver can't hear what she says from only a few feet away.

She hangs up and turns to them. "We're changing the game plan," she says. "Mia's blood pressure is spiking, so we're going to stabilize you with magnesium while trying to really get moving toward delivery, okay? Okay." She does not wait for their reaction.

"Mia, I want you to focus on your breath, and since we're going to start increasing your levels of Pitocin, expect to feel the contractions intensify rather . . . expeditiously."

Twenty minutes later, Mia pukes for a second time from the pain. She hears plastic tearing and paper rustling and metal instruments clinking. A whole team is telling her to push, and she thought she was, but they're saying it's not enough. Oliver's eyes are bloodshot as he tells her to keep going, it's okay, it's okay, and between surges of torture she notices she broke the skin on his hand.

Finally, a nurse says, "One more push and you're going to be a wonderful mother," which makes Mia smile and she begins to say thank you but she can't quite get the words out. She can't quite—believe—how impossible—this is—and yet—she's still—pushing—

"Here she comes!" Dr. Elliott says, and Mia feels the head and shoulders dislodge and the slippery little body slide out and it's all so primal it's like she's the livestock in some farm documentary—and that's before she hears the piglet squealing in distress as Dr. Elliott asks, "Would you like to hold her?"

Mia nods, too exhausted to speak. Dr. Elliott puts a bundle of baby on her chest and when Mia looks down, she gasps with recognition.

This face.

She's known it her whole life.

Mia never thought she'd see eyes like these again.

"Look at her," Oliver says, laughing through his tears as he crouches down beside them. Mia nods against Oliver's unshaven chin. She's never been this tired or this proud, this happy.

"Okay, Mia, we need a few big pushes to deliver the placenta," Dr. Elliott says. "And then we'll clear the room for skin-to-skin and family bonding." Oliver takes the baby, and in several pushes, Mia delivers the placenta. But Dr. Elliott does not congratulate her or clear the room.

Instead, she tells her resident to call an emergency code.

Within seconds, the room floods with new faces. "What's happening?" Oliver asks Dr. Elliott, but she ignores him to direct the team as they wheel Mia out of the room and down the hall. "What's happening?" Oliver yells after them.

"We need to stabilize her in the OR," Dr. Elliott calls over her shoulder. "She's losing a lot of blood."

As Mia disappears within the scrum of medics, Oliver stands alone in the abandoned labor and delivery room. In his arms, the infant looks up at him, a concentration of hope and trust in her startling blue eyes.

MAINE RETURN

It is six long days before Cricket finally lands at Portland International Jetport. She has eighty-two unanswered messages when she takes her phone off airplane mode, and she ignores them all as she texts her sister a photo of the taxidermied moose at baggage claim. Her phone rings immediately.

"You're home!" Mia chirps, and Cricket smiles at the sound of her sister's voice—it's been too long since she's heard it. The last six days have been nonstop press events, parties, and networking opportunities. So much champagne. So many boat rides. So much Advil. "We're actually at the hospital," Mia says.

Cricket stops so abruptly that a fellow traveler rams into her from behind. "Is that normal?" she asks. "Is the baby okay?"

"Yup, just meet us here," Mia says cheerfully. "Did you bring the gold?"

Cricket laughs as she compulsively pats her carry-on bag and feels the circular outline of the medal. Her two goals for this visit are to take a picture of her newborn niece wearing her hard-earned hardware and to thank Oliver and Mia for their unwavering support. Without a doubt, it was a decades-long family push that propelled Cricket to the National Team. Oliver and Mia's encouragement—and Mia's steady string of sacrifices—paved the way for Cricket's achievement. *The gold,* Cricket will tell them, imagining Mia's tears of joy, *belongs to all of us.*

Entering the hospital, Cricket puts her phone on silent and pops into the gift shop on the first floor. She purchases a bouquet of expensive pink roses and a gigantic stuffed giraffe that costs more than a week's worth of groceries. But as her manager, Paula, keeps reminding her, Cricket is in a different financial place now than she was a month ago.

The Olympics changed her life. Those seven minutes in goal turned everything on its head, and for the past six days Cricket has been drinking from a firehose of publicity offers, sponsorship deals, and creative-driven collaborations. The numbers Paula throws around in contract negotiations aren't just surreal; they're silly.

Cricket tracks down Mia's room and knocks on the closed door.

"Yo!" Oliver says, swinging it open and enveloping Cricket in a hug so tight that the giraffe's stiff hooves dig into her leg.

"You're here!" Mia shouts from the hospital bed.

Cricket launches off Oliver and runs toward her sister, taking in her familiar face and the baby on her chest. "I brought you—oh wow, she's beautiful." Cricket squeezes herself onto Mia's bed and demands the sleeping baby in her arms. "She's perfect," Cricket says. "I know people always say that, but she really is."

"And her game stats are fantastic," Oliver boasts. "Ninetieth percentile for height, eighty-fifth for weight, ninety-ninth for head size because apparently that's a thing, and she's also managed to pee on each doctor who's held her, so I'd say that's one hundred percent goals scored for shots taken."

"Amazing." Cricket grins. "But what's her—"

"Elizabeth," Mia answers, scrutinizing Cricket's face as she delivers the syllables. "Sorry for ignoring your texts; I just really wanted to tell you in person."

"Oh," Cricket manages to say. The baby's face begins to blur as Cricket takes in the moment. "Oh wow."

History folds in on itself like an accordion and Cricket blinks back tears while trying to comprehend this brand-new North Star for their lives going forward. Her body floods with a grief-stricken joy only Mia could understand: their mother's name upcycled into this itty-bitty human, their blood running through her little limbs under her translucent skin. Admiring the baby's pink rosebud of a mouth as it tries to nurse the air, Cricket tells her sister the truth: "She'd be so happy."

Squished side by side in the hospital bed, Mia rests her head on Cricket's shoulder and asks, "You think she'd be okay with the nickname Betty? That's what we've been calling her."

"She'd love that," Cricket confirms. It's only when she reaches over to pat Mia's hand and sees the ID bracelet around her sister's wrist that Cricket processes the facts of the scene: that Mia is lying in a hospital bed, wearing a hospital gown, with an IV attached to her arm, six days after Betty's birth. "Why are you—"

Mia's dramatic exhale sounds more like an exorcism and puts Cricket on high alert.

"What's going on?" she asks, looking at Oliver, who keeps his focus on Mia, who stares at their infant daughter, curled up in Cricket's arms.

"We've had very different weeks," Mia finally says, forcing a meek smile as she faces Cricket. She gestures for Oliver to take the baby, and he does. Father and daughter walk the five steps to the window and examine the puffy clouds that seem to be moving at a clip across the sky.

"I started hemorrhaging," Mia says to Cricket. "Right after Betty was born." Her voice wavers as she remembers how scared she was and—if she's being honest—how scared she still is, in this moment. "I lost enough blood that it caused—everyone calls it an AKI, but it stands for acute kidney injury."

"Okay," Cricket says slowly, because she is intimately familiar with injuries, and although they always hurt, they always heal. "Are you better now?"

Mia looks past her sister at Oliver, so Cricket does, too. If she weren't so well versed in her brother-in-law's body language, she wouldn't know that the vein near his jaw twitches when he's biting his tongue.

"What?" Cricket asks him. They developed a shorthand long ago to cut through all the niceties and get to the point. Mia shifts in her hospital bed, visibly wishing they could talk about the weather.

"The AKI nearly killed her," Oliver says, his voice low and garbled, as if he were speaking from the bottom of a riverbed. He has never been this afraid or felt this helpless.

"It's super rare," Mia says, just before Betty lets out one long cry.

Cricket turns to face Mia. Still lying next to each other in the hospital bed, their noses are just a couple of inches apart.

"So you never went home?"

Mia shakes her head. "Apparently it happens to, like, one percent of women."

Cricket's mouth flaps open. Oliver and Mia look at each other like they're trying to synchronize their alibis.

"It's not as bad as it sounds," Mia volunteers.

"That's true," Oliver acknowledges, weighed down by sarcasm. "Because it's actually much worse." He shifts his gaze from his wife to Cricket and explains, "The AKI damaged Mia's kidneys so badly that she's had to have dialysis every day."

"What is that?" Cricket asks. "I don't even know what that is."

Oliver looks down at his sneakers. "She's treading water," he says, instinctively running a hand through his dark blond hair. Cricket sees that his fingernails are chewed down to nubs. "A machine does the job of her kidneys," Oliver explains. "It takes three hours of dialysis every day to clean her blood, just to keep her stable." He gives Mia a look, and she holds his stare. They are bracing for something.

"What are you not telling me?" Cricket asks.

"It's important to remember that I'm stable now," Mia says.

"And her numbers are good," Oliver adds.

The effort to assuage her concern only makes Cricket more nervous. Laying out all this verbal cushioning before delivering devastating news—they've done it to her before.

"Just tell me," Cricket says, feeling her heart rate quicken. "Please."

"She needs a kidney," Oliver says, reaching for Mia's hand. "To have any semblance of a normal life, Mia needs a kidney, and my diabetes takes me out of the running and—"

"Wait, what?" Cricket looks at Mia. "But I thought it was just an injury?"

Mia nods. "It was," she acknowledges. "But it was so violent that it developed into CKD—chronic kidney disease."

"So you need a kidney," Cricket murmurs. "And we have the same blood type."

"Yes," Oliver says. A ragged knot of silence pulls between them—a vague but undeniable tension that Cricket can't discern.

"Is that it?" she asks. "Do they need to run tests? Can I just give it to you now? And don't—I mean, is this a permanent thing? Don't laugh, but do I, like—do I get it back at some point?"

"You don't borrow a kidney," Oliver says, shaking his head.

"Okay, so you need it forever," Cricket concludes. "That's fine, let's do it."

"Cricket," Mia says, shaking her head, a faint wisp of a smile wiped clean from her face. "I love you, and I wish it were that simple."

"If you need a kidney, I'm giving you a kidney," Cricket insists, rolling off Mia's hospital bed and standing up, only to bend over and stretch her calves. Her muscles have been so tight from all the flying, and practice on Monday is going to come way too soon. "How is this even a conversation?" Cricket asks, her fingers grazing the hospital floor. "How did you go six entire days without—"

"You'd have to give up soccer," Mia interrupts. "You can't play with one kidney."

The room reverberates from the aftershocks of such an impossible statement. Cricket stands up straight. She faces Mia before looking at Oliver, who stares back at her with eyes sunken from exhaustion but alive with fear.

"Oh," Cricket says in disbelief. She opens her mouth but can't think of anything to add.

"We're not pretending it isn't—we understand it's a very difficult decision," Oliver says, swaying in place with Betty asleep on his shoulder. "It's a huge ask, especially right now, given where your career is going."

"Yeah," Cricket manages to say. She can barely formulate words, let alone complete thoughts. How can this be happening? And now, when she's finally seeing her dreams—all of their dreams—come true? But it's Mia. Of course she'll help. Except—quitting soccer? Who would she even be? She's only twenty-four years old—what would she even do with her life?

"We obviously don't expect you to decide right now, on the spot," Oliver says, but his focus on Cricket, his attempt at reading her, implies otherwise.

"Oliver—" Mia starts.

"You should have told me," Cricket says, guilt flooding her system as she thinks about the past week—the late-night shows, the tequila shots on some billionaire's mega yacht, the team's appearance on *Good Morning America*—all while her sister was bleeding out. "I would have been here sooner," she tells them, because fighting about the past is easier than considering the future. "You should have called me as soon as things—"

"She was trying to spare you," Oliver says. *"Per usual."* It slips out because he is stressed and dangerously sleep-deprived, but it slips out nonetheless. And as though the baby senses her father's anxiety, she starts to fuss.

"I'll take her," Mia says as Betty's cries become more insistent. Cricket watches her sister accept Betty and, fumbling with her hospital gown, draws her close to nurse.

"Listen," Mia says, speaking to Cricket but looking down as the baby struggles to latch on. "None of us want to be here, in this situation." She chances a glance up at Cricket. "I'm sorry we didn't tell you earlier, but I wanted you to enjoy winning without worrying about me."

Cricket stares at Betty's tiny feet.

"Asking you to give up your career is totally insane," Mia says and Cricket nods along with relief, because finally, thank God, there is a grown-up in the room speaking rationally. "It's not fair, I know that," Mia says. "But I can't figure out any other way"—Mia stops abruptly, experiencing an intense, sudden bout of déjà vu before she continues— "to make this work."

Cricket looks at her sister attached to a machine and tries to tamp down a spark of anger, a smoldering cinder in a mess of underbrush. She knows it isn't fair to feel this way when this is a question of her sister's life, but Mia and Oliver understand better than anyone that giving up soccer is a question of Cricket's life. She doesn't have a plan B. She doesn't have a partner or a baby. Ever since she graduated from college, she has trained eight hours a day, six days a week, because playing the game means working around the clock. It's not just a job but a lifestyle. Cricket has sacrificed everything to be a professional athlete, and she has done it for *them*. Not for herself. Because of Mia and Oliver, Cricket's life is soccer. Her worth is soccer. And now they want her to just give it all up?

"Isn't there a list?" Cricket asks. "Like of donors or something?"

"I'm on the national donor list," Mia says. "And I'm relatively young and healthy so—"

Cricket nods encouragingly.

"So I guess until they call me up"—Mia looks at Oliver—"we can just stick to the dialysis schedule and make do."

"That sounds good," Cricket agrees, ignoring Oliver as he paces in front of the room's one window. It's his pissed-off walk. She knows it well. "How long is the list?"

"A hundred thousand people deep," Oliver says dryly. "Give or take. And there's always a risk that the dialysis stops working—at any time, without warning."

"Which is unlikely," Mia says, shooting her husband a *tone-it-down* look. "But yeah, it's a long list—my transplant coordinator thinks it would take about two years."

Cricket's mind instinctively jumps to the soccer calendar. The next World Cup, what would be her first, is in three years' time.

"So if you get one from the donor list, we could still make it to the World Cup," Cricket says, attempting to sound upbeat, grasping at hope. "Betty would see me play." The idea of her niece—and everything continuing the way it should—lifts Cricket out of the moment and back to the way it's supposed to be. Back to their plan. Because this has *always* been their plan.

"Yeah," Mia says, gazing down at Betty. "That would definitely"—

she pauses, searching for the right words—"that is definitely an option."

"And waiting two years—I mean, it's less than ideal, but it's doable, right?" Cricket asks. Throughout their lives, Mia has masterminded ways to make impossible, untenable, significantly-less-than-ideal situations doable.

"You're not getting it," Oliver interrupts. "Mia's kidneys could shut down any second," he says. "She's dependent on a machine to stay alive."

"How bad is the dialysis?" Cricket asks. "Is it painful?"

"No," Mia answers honestly.

Oliver cuts in. "But even when she leaves here, even when she's considered 'stable,' she'll still have to sit in a chair three times a week, three hours at a time, which means she can't be with Betty or go back to work. She can't go anywhere. She can't do anything, let alone travel to see you play. Her life will be on hold until—I guess until her name comes up on the donor list—right? That's what we're saying?"

Cricket doesn't correct him, doesn't volunteer her own vital organ, because that's what a kidney is—a *vital* organ. "I could pay for a nanny," she says instead. "Or a housekeeper, or just, like, give you money? From endorsement deals, I'll give you whatever you need."

"That's really generous," Mia says, her voice soft. The baby has fallen back asleep on her chest, but Mia continues to watch her. She is thinking—Cricket can see her sister thinking—but Mia ultimately says nothing.

Oliver sits down in the visitor's chair, rubs his eyes with the palms of his hands. "So just to make sure we're all on the same page, you're choosing the next three years of anything-but-guaranteed glory over your sister's life."

"What? No—no!" Cricket stammers. "I just need—I think I just need to think it over? And talk to my team?"

"Sure." Oliver pulls out his wallet and walks briskly across the room. He presents Cricket with a business card like he's issuing her a red card for misconduct. "That's Wendy, the donor coordinator," he says. "She said to give her a call—her cell is on there, too, in case you—"

"Okay. Yeah, thanks," Cricket says, accepting the card. She cannot imagine calling this person. She cannot imagine walking away from her team, from this opportunity, from her parking spot. But it's Mia. Cricket's mind goes blank, unable to process. She slides Wendy's business card into the back pocket of her jeans. "I'll call her and let you guys know what everyone thinks is best."

"So right now your decision is no decision?" Oliver asks.

"I have to figure it out," Cricket answers, raking her hand across her face.

Oliver turns cold. "Sure, well, in that case, Mia needs her rest," he says, the vein by his jaw twitching. "And you might as well head home."

Cricket's stomach backflips, and Mia looks up from the sleeping baby. "He means home-home—Knickerbocker Avenue home."

But that doesn't seem to be at all what Oliver means, and his silence confirms Cricket's suspicion that he wants her gone. She nods, pulling herself together. "Yeah, no," she says, trying to reclaim some control. "I've got practice on Monday, so this was always going to be a quick trip, and since you're still in here—"

"Right," Oliver says. "We're still in here."

Cricket pulls up the handle of her suitcase. "I'll call you," she volunteers, "after I talk to Wendy"—Cricket looks pointedly at Oliver—"and everyone on my side of things."

Oliver moves to rub Mia's shoulders, protective as tears stream down her face. "Thanks for coming," she says, faintly, as Cricket bends down to give her a hug.

Cricket kisses the top of Betty's head and turns to leave. She says nothing as she closes the door behind her, the world on mute as she walks down the hallway, slogging forward in a murky slow motion.

Two years is nothing.

Two years is everything.

It's tomorrow and a lifetime away. She hits the elevator button and waits.

What just happened?

MONOMYTH

1989

MYTHOLOGY

Eight years old and still tasting blood, Liz Lowe hopes her parents remember her tooth after their night out with the Sweeneys. She tucks it under her pillow and prays they are too drunk to notice which bill her father withdraws from his wallet in the dark. They gave her a dollar the first time, then forgot twice, but then last time they slipped her a twenty during the power outage, which is why Liz has taken the initiative to unplug her Rainbow Brite night-light. Her parents are very generous when they can't see what they're doing.

In Highland Acres, a leafy suburb outside of Richmond, Virginia, cars are never locked. Sidewalk chalk rolls between driveways on windy days, yielding only for the front wheel of a tricycle or the wet nose of an inquisitive doodle. This is the land of full-time nannies and white-collar salaries. Here, neighbors volley complaints about delayed flights and the criminal price of boat paint as they wheel in their trash bins.

After their night out with the Sweeneys, Liz's parents do indeed forget to leave her money from the tooth fairy. "Is it because you hit the bottle too hard?" Liz asks the next morning, parroting Mrs. Sweeney, which makes her father laugh and her mother moan before they send her downstairs to fetch the pill bottle with the blue label. When they are still asleep at noon, Liz makes herself a cheese sandwich and presses her tongue into the space where her tooth used to reside. Across the kitchen, the wall calendar celebrates what she already knows: only one week until she leaves for overnight camp.

Up until now, Liz has spent every summer at the Highland Acres country club pool, under the heavy-lidded gaze of her mother and her mother's friends, who flip in unison from their stomachs to their backs every twenty minutes like a spit of rotisserie chickens heavily marinated in baby oil.

Lenora, Liz's mother, is the unspoken queen of the club; her status is earned and maintained in the seamless fit of her red swimsuit. Unlike some of her less disciplined friends, Lenora has bounced back from maternity in record time, thanks to a strict diet and *Jane Fonda's Workout* VHS tapes. Lenora's favorite compliment to receive is the one she most often repeats to her husband over dinner—that even in a tiny bikini, she still looks like she's never had a baby at all.

"But did you?" John Lowe asks every time, pulling his wife onto his lap at the dining table, both of them oblivious to their child poking at her green beans. Liz, like everyone else at the country club, knows her mother is unapologetically "one and done" with children. It doesn't matter that John still wants to try for a boy, Lenora tells her companions poolside. She wants her life back.

When Liz first hears her dad, a commercial real estate agent, explain "buyer's remorse," she immediately thinks of how her mother stares at her when no one else is around. Like she is last season's must-have accessory but in the wrong color and size, which, in a sense, she is.

A baby girl. Worse, everyone notes how Liz, tall and blond, takes after her mother. "Only without a single wrinkle," Lenora is quick to reply, swinging her daughter's hand with a glitchy smile.

"I look ancient compared to you," Lenora says most nights as they stare into the bathroom mirror, mother and daughter, side by side. Pulling the outer corners of her eyes up toward her hairline, Lenora adds, "And I'm supposed to just accept that you're the new version of me." Although Liz tries to sidestep the long shadow of her mother's ever-cooling interest, it only becomes more and more difficult.

She cannot wait for camp.

A week after school ends, Liz finds an empty seat on the yellow school bus that will take her a hundred and fifty miles away from Highland Acres. She watches as the driver loads her steam trunk full of bathing suits, Jelly sandals, and mosquito repellent to fortify her for eight weeks in a forest. Other kids Liz's age—the youngest accepted—only attend for two-week stints, but Lenora submitted a special request, along with a financial supplement generous enough to earn the Lowes a plaque in the canteen.

As the bus merges onto the highway and heads west, Liz has no idea what to expect, but never in a thousand years does she anticipate falling in love before entering the third grade.

This, however, is precisely what happens.

It is there, in a clearing between the woods and the lake, that Liz Lowe discovers soccer. She is drawn to it instantly and intensely—the physicality, the team mentality, the pending glory of a goal scored. But more than anything, it's the consistency. While her bunkmates change over every session, and her mother's communication vacillates between candy-filled care packages and radio silence, the game of soccer—with its rules, refs, and clean lines—remains the same, day after day, week after week.

Throughout the summer, the counselors watch Liz with awe and whisper among themselves. They assert she is a natural and even sign out the camp camcorder to tape her. Liz hears them on the sidelines, shouting out names that do not belong to any of the campers—names like Pelé and Maradona—whenever she has the ball at her feet.

On the last day of camp, several young adults wearing red lanyards and fresh hickeys around their necks go out of their way to introduce themselves to John and Lenora Lowe and tell them of their daughter's potential. "She's the most talented kid I've ever seen—and this is my fourth summer," one redheaded counselor says to Mr. Lowe's tassel loafers. It is there, standing in the gravel pen of the camp parking lot in late August, that Liz finally feels the coveted warmth of her mother's gaze. It's a sensation akin to riding a dolphin or scoring a goal at the buzzer. It feels like blossoming inside of joy itself.

"She could be a star athlete," Lenora tells John over dinner that night, her eyes bright with the possibility. Liz wordlessly navigates her plate of swordfish and snap peas, remembering that this is what family dinners are like—her parents speaking around her, even when it's about her. She already misses the sloppy joes and mealtime songs of camp. She longs to cannonball off the dock at sunrise and walk with friends to attend the weekly bonfire. But above all else, Liz needs to play soccer again. Under the table, her legs twitch at the thought.

Biting into his second ear of corn, Liz's father nods in agreement with her mother. "Of course she could be a star—she has our genes." Lenora tilts her head, puckers her lips at him. John wipes his butter-greased hands on his napkin. "Sign her up to play this fall," he says, leaning back in his chair. And then it dawns on him, the second-best option for a father without a son: "I'll ask around the office about travel teams. From the get-go, she should play at the highest level if she's going to be the best."

As Liz grows up, her reputation as a soccer phenom expands across the state, then the region, then the country. Lenora and John gladly pay for the private training sessions and the elite tournaments and the summer showcases. Busy as they are with their own lives, however, the Lowes themselves rarely attend these matches, which so often conflict with their social engagements. But Liz knows that if she scores enough times, her father will learn of it by the second hole, and her mother will grin as she insists to her tennis partner, "But I told her to go easy today."

Or rather, the Lowes are too busy until Liz becomes too good, the glint of her rising star too blinding to ignore. When the mayor of Richmond stops Liz on West Cary Street to congratulate her most recent hat trick, John and Lenora reconfigure their schedules so they can attend their daughter's games. Lenora dutifully writes down the time of every match and tournament on the kitchen wall calendar as soon as they are announced. She uses a black Sharpie so thick-tipped that there isn't space to write anything else.

Before Liz's sophomore year of high school, Lenora buys her daughter enough red ribbon to wrap around their entire town. "No one can miss you now," Lenora says. "Only the best player on the field can pull off a red ribbon." And although Liz has become increasingly aware that her relationship with her mother is, at best, complicated, she rolls out a fresh piece of ribbon before each game, tying it into a bow around her high bun.

On Halloween of that same year, three girls from the neighborhood ring the Lowes' doorbell in their matching Umbro shorts and jerseys. "You're soccer players!" Liz says, bending down to give them each a high five with their fun-size Snickers. She volunteered to stay home and hand out candy since she has a game the next day. Most of her teammates are drunk in the woods right now.

"We're not soccer players!" the smallest trick-or-treater shouts, spinning around to show Liz her red ribbon. "We're you!"

The following year, Liz hands out candy to at least a dozen miniature versions of herself. A group of moms geek out and ask for her autograph when she answers the door. "You're the next Mia Hamm!" one of them gushes, pushing past the kids she's supposed to be chaperoning. "I was in Atlanta for the Olympics last summer and I swear you are totally the next Mia Hamm."

As Division 1 soccer coaches begin reaching out to Liz, her parents find it endlessly amusing that respectable adults are sending their teenage daughter handwritten letters and plane tickets to come visit their campus, meet their team, tour their facilities. Their only child has become the gleaming mantelpiece they'd always dreamed of, the talk of their gated community, the headlining story of the local news when she leads her team in back-to-back state championships. In every article, there is mention of her red ribbon.

In November of her junior year, Liz verbally commits to play soccer at UCLA. To celebrate, her parents take her car shopping, and at the dealership John makes it clear that even the nicest vehicle on the lot costs far less than four years of out-of-state tuition. He springs for all the bells and whistles the salesman throws at them: the leather interior, the CD player and surround sound speaker system.

The first song Liz plays as she drives off the lot that day is the same hit pop song that kicks off her soccer team's warm-up playlist: "Get Low, Fly High." Liz adopts the song as her own anthem. Beaming in the passenger seat, her dad looks at her with anything but buyer's remorse.

The summer before her senior year, Liz travels with her high school team to watch the 1999 Women's World Cup Final in Pasadena. "It won't be long until we're all wearing Liz Lowe jerseys and shouting about how we used to know you," her teammates tease as they enter the Rose Bowl.

A few hours later, when the United States wins in a shootout and Brandi Chastain famously tears off her jersey, Liz is so overwhelmed that she finds herself crying and cheering simultaneously. That night, she uses her parents' credit card to order bottles of champagne for the team from the hotel bar. Her parents see the charges, but they don't mind. Room service is still far less expensive than four years of out-of-state tuition and they, too, believe a World Cup is reason to celebrate. They, too, believe their daughter will be the next Mia Hamm.

In the fall of her senior year, Liz is awarded First Team All-American and whispered to be in the running for Gatorade Player of the Year. In every photograph, she wears her hair up in a high bun with her signature red ribbon, which every opponent has learned not only to respect but dread. And after she scores the game-winning header in the state championship, Liz returns to Highland Acres and sees each house in the community has displayed the same sign on their front lawn: LIZ LOWE = OUR HERO!

Some nights, even at seventeen years old, Liz still stands next to her mother in the bathroom, both of them brushing their teeth in front of the mirror. And so it makes sense that Lenora, ever vigilant of their contrasting appearances, is the first to notice Liz's yellow pallor. Eyeing her daughter, Lenora diagnoses her in the same disappointed tone she implements whenever Liz sprouts a pimple or declines an invitation to the nail salon. Unfortunately, Liz has not been dabbling in bulimia, as Lenora had hoped. To her daughter's reflection, Lenora states with disdain, "You're pregnant."

Liz won't tell her parents who the father is or how she met him. When they ask and then beg for information, Liz only says that he will not be in the picture. But she wants the baby, Liz insists. It's her body and her life and she is keeping the baby.

Liz's refusal to simply take care of the situation is unfathomable to John and Lenora. It's also a betrayal. The mortifying shock of their new reality swings through the house like an axe at all hours of the day, every interaction ending in tears, swearing, or slammed doors, usually all three. "We gave you everything!" is her mother's favorite refrain, hurled at Liz's back as she retreats to her room. The joke is not lost on Liz that she worked so hard to earn her parents' approval only to flush it for someone else's affection. Her father has no choice but to finally call Coach Ellis at UCLA and inform her of the regrettable development.

In the spring of her senior year, Liz counts down the days until graduation before realizing the baby growing inside her will not honor the engagements written in Sharpie on her mother's calendar. When Liz feels her first contraction, she is still weeks away from receiving her diploma, and the next morning, by the time the first period bell rings, she has become a mother.

The baby is so profoundly exquisite in her smushed-alien-face way that Liz instantly believes they will be okay. She will make sure of it. It doesn't matter that every single college soccer coach rescinded their offer. It doesn't matter that they all but laughed in her face when she promised she'd be back in game shape by preseason. It doesn't matter because Liz is not a quitter.

After the nurse on duty badgers her about filling out the Acknowledgment of Paternity form, Liz tears the blank page into minuscule squares and makes a show of pouring the white confetti into the trash can. There will be no father on this new, undefeated team. Her second day postpartum, Liz shuffles down to the hospital post office, mindful of her stitches, to mail a letter. She expects nothing back, but Liz wants him to know their daughter's name.

In the sanctuary of their hospital room, Liz watches her baby sleep and flips open the atlas she bought for this very occasion. As soon as she recovers, Liz has decided they are busting out of her parents' house and starting over. "We're the next Thelma and Louise," she tells her newborn, whom she calls her best friend.

John and Lenora have not come to see her. When Liz finally breaks down and asks to call them, the nurse says they left a message the day before to let Liz know they would be in Europe through the fall. "They said to tell you congratulations and to please water the lawn while they're away," the nurse says, avoiding eye contact as she restocks the diaper cart.

Thumbing through the atlas, Liz imagines starting her new life in Charleston, or New Orleans, or Corpus Christi. She pictures her baby on a boat, at Mardi Gras, in cowboy boots. Ultimately, Liz decides to raise her baby in a tiny village on the coast of Maine. The reason is simple: She still believes she is destined for greatness, and this seaside town pinned beneath her finger is called Victory.

Four and a half months later, the day before her parents are due back from their extended vacation, Liz packs her car so full of stuff that she worries about getting pulled over. With her rearview mirror obstructed, Liz rolls down her window to see behind her, only to realize how rarely one must look back when forging ahead.

The soccer dream is not over, she writes in the letter she leaves for her parents. *I've just moved the goalposts.* Merging onto the interstate, Liz decides her future depends on her own positive outlook, and so she thanks her lucky stars for giving her everything she needs to push forward: a full tank of gas, a road map spread across her lap, five thousand dollars in cash from her parents' safe, a shoebox full of game-winning red ribbons, and her best friend asleep in her car seat.

TRAINING DAYS

Before she can speak in full sentences, Mia Lowe knows she was conceived the day the U.S. Women's National Team won the 1999 World Cup. Her mother reminds her every night at bedtime that she is named after the legendary Mia Hamm. "You, too, are destined to be a great soccer player," Liz tells Mia before she falls asleep. "And so that is what we must work toward."

Except for the coldest winter days when the temperature falls dangerously low, mother and daughter rise early to get a touch on the ball and a step ahead of everyone else. Most of the year, Mia returns home with wind-chapped cheeks, but in the summer she walks back from the beach suntanned and smiling.

Everything is better in the summer: They train barefoot on the cool sand at sunrise with the ocean as their captive audience. Liz brings her portable stereo and blasts the burned CD her high school soccer team played during warm-ups. Mia feels like an adult, breaking a sweat with her mother, listening to "Get Low, Fly High" while mimicking her mom's calisthenics.

When a disjointed army of homemakers and caregivers arrives on the beach, weighed down by ruddy-faced children and baskets full of battered toys, they openly stare at Liz and Mia warming up with high knees and butt kicks, Frankensteins and crab walks. "Cold muscles are as dangerous as great white sharks," Liz says, shimmering with sweat and oblivious to the women watching them.

The onlookers—tented in their husband's rust-stained work shirts, the collars stretched and buttons missing—take in Liz's toned legs and perky, twenty-one-year-old breasts, and pray to sweet Jesus that the new babysitter twisting herself into a pretzel is only a problem for some rich mother who can afford to be elsewhere right now. The handful of men traversing the beach this early in the day are always solo, unburdened walkers and joggers, although their pace tends to slow considerably when they clock Liz performing deep lunges across the sand in her high school soccer shorts, rolled twice at the waist band.

Once they finish their warm-up, Liz claps her hands together and tells Mia, "Let's practice first touches." She uses clumps of seaweed for cones, collects driftwood for goalposts. As Mia receives ball after ball from her mother, she doesn't complain that she's hot or thirsty, or that the slant of the sun is now blinding her. Instead, she uses her hand as a visor and tries not to get distracted by the other kids squealing at the water's edge.

"Good job adapting," Liz says, passing the ball back to her. "You'll face bad weather, lousy field conditions, and half-blind refs, but you've got to stay focused and play through every obstacle if you want to be the best, and you know how I know you're going to be the best?"

"How?"

"Because you're a Lowe, not a quitter."

Sometimes, after Mia passes the ball to her mom, Liz will flick it up from her foot and into the air, juggling as Mia counts each bounce. As talented as a trained seal, her mother is worthy of her own circus act.

"Keep going!" Mia pleads when Liz volleys the ball back to her.

"You try," Liz instructs. "You want the ball to feel like it's a part of your body, like it's as responsive to your brain as your fingers." But the ball doesn't float in steady bobs or graceful arcs when Mia tries to juggle. She can only string two, maybe three connections together before the ball bangs off her knee and lands in the ocean. As she runs to retrieve it, Mia notices a girl her own age wearing a yellow swimsuit and hunched in the sand, humming to herself as she inspects a mussel shell. She seems content doing absolutely nothing.

Mia feels the girl's eyes on her as she slides her mom the ball, now slick from the ocean. Liz begins to juggle once again. "It's all about practice," Liz says. The ball bops happily above her knees—left, right, left, right—as steady as a metronome. "You'll be doing this before you know it," Liz says, heading the ball once, twice, three times in a row. "You're still too young to practice heading, but when it's time, just remember: You can only use your head if you keep your eyes wide open."

After the beach, mother and daughter walk toward home, passing a long line outside the local bakery. The promise of fresh croissants lures groggy adults out their front doors and into the queue. Liz hands Mia the water bottle they share and reminds her to hydrate properly for a quicker recovery.

Everyone waiting in the bakery line looks up at Liz because she is tall, but they continue to stare because her face is the same irresistible invitation as a turned-down bed, a glass-surfaced lake—you can't help but fall into it. She is young and beautiful and magnetic. And while Mia frowns at the truck drivers that honk, the construction crews that whistle, and even the old ladies who bless Liz for her figure in the CVS checkout line, she delights in the captivated inquiries from strangers about Liz's arctic blue eyes. They are such a singular, startling blue that Mia once asked her mom, after reading a children's book on Alaska, if she was part Siberian husky.

"I've got the resilience of a sled dog," Liz had replied thoughtfully. "The tenacity, too."

It's true.

When she'd fled Virginia, Liz drove straight to Victory, stopping every three hours to feed Mia in the back seat. She pulled into a Hannaford parking lot just after seven a.m., and dreamt with her eyes open about sleeping forever. But it was the first day of her life in Maine, a big day, and so Liz snapped the hairband on her wrist, retied the red ribbon around her high bun, and approached a well-dressed woman unloading a cart full of bagged groceries.

"Good morning," Liz said with a small wave and a big smile as she held Mia against her chest. "I'm Liz Lowe, and this is my baby, and we're new in town, like brand-new—"

"I can see that," the woman said warmly, nodding at the infant. Her name was Sally Green and, as a mother of three, she recognized Liz's situation in her bones. Sally's oldest was in college, her youngest about to start middle school. Just then, Mia let out a hunger cry and Sally fought the instinct to pop a finger in the baby's mouth.

"I'm sure this is going to be the craziest interaction you have all day," Liz was saying, "but do you know of anyone hiring?"

Maybe Dr. Green said yes because she had grown up racing Siberian huskies in northern Maine and Liz's eyes bred instant familiarity. But more likely, it was the ambitious capability shining through those ice-blue irises. Even with breast milk stains on her shirt and panic in her voice, Liz Lowe was clearly a go-getter with something to prove and a desire to learn. Dr. Green hired Liz on the spot to work her front desk.

"And the baby?" Liz asked.

"Is adorable," Dr. Green smiled, reaching out for Mia while saying the baby could come to the office, no problem. Dr. Green had made the same accommodation for her last assistant before she'd moved home to Ohio the previous month. "There's even a chance," Sally thought aloud in the parking lot, "that we still have a Pack 'n Play buried somewhere in the storage closet."

After her first three weeks in Maine—and having grown tired of the less-than-reputable Victory Motel & Car Wash off I-95—Liz sold the luxury SUV her father bought her for UCLA. She used the cash for a down payment on a bungalow that was advertised as "full of potential." Dr. Green cosigned the mortgage, already understanding the strength of Liz's character and her determination to "win" at all things— whether it was fitting in one more patient before the holiday weekend or actively building her credit to attain a perfect FICO score. On a regular basis, Dr. Green found herself wishing that her own children demon-strated more of Liz's formidable can-do-it-ness.

Meanwhile, the bungalow provided mother and child an immediate safe haven. But it also gave them a mold problem and a leaky roof. On Mia's first birthday, the oven suddenly quit with Liz's half-baked cake inside, and then, just after Christmas, the refrigerator started gasping for its life. Liz shed tears of all kinds in those early Victory days—scared, frustrated, irate, self-doubting—as there are only so many home repairs a single mother can tackle with one hand mixing Jell-O for her sick kid and the other dialing dental patients to remind them of their upcoming appointments.

Within two years of moving in, however, Liz saved up enough to buy some time: She beat back the mold, replaced the oven igniter herself, and hired her neighbor's son to patch the roof for next to nothing. Together, Liz and Mia painted each room in the house a different hue of the same sunny optimism that had taken them thus far and outfitted every square foot of their space in well-loved wares from the local swap shop. The pink floral couch they rescued from a curb over in the nice part of town fit in the living room like it was custom-designed for the space.

Stepping back to admire her work, Liz knew that even her own mother would be impressed. Not that they'd spoken since Liz's pregnancy, and not that Liz cared about her mother's approval anymore—only her daughter's. While Lenora had treated Liz as the competition, Liz championed Mia as her first-round draft pick, her number-one teammate. In Mia's bright brown eyes and death-grip hugs, Liz recognized what she's yearned for all her life: the promise of unconditional love.

Which is why, four years after arriving in Victory, Liz continues to serve as the eternally grateful and fiercely loyal front desk receptionist at Dr. Green's dental office. On a daily basis, she expertly assuages the anxieties of cavity-prone patients and laughs off their personal questions that always dance around the same core argument: Shouldn't such a capable and beguiling young woman be the center of attention, not submitting insurance claims and scheduling teeth cleanings?

"I have a young daughter," Liz tells them, and the patients nod with understanding, because this makes sense—regular hours, health insurance, et cetera. But then Liz elaborates: "And I'm training her to become a world-class soccer player." At this, the nervous, nosy patients continue to nod with understanding, but only because they suddenly remember that the most beautiful people tend to be a little bit nuts.

FAIREST ONE OF ALL

To celebrate her middle child's high school graduation, Dr. Green hosts a party in her spacious backyard the last Saturday in May. The adult punch is unapologetically strong and the live band shockingly good for a trio of juniors whose matching bangs prevent them from actually seeing their instruments. Liz and Mia stay late, dancing on the makeshift dance floor, and that night Liz lies down next to Mia after tucking her in.

"My sporty Snow White," Liz slurs, cradling Mia's face in her hands. "The fairest one of all." Pushing Mia's mop of curly brown hair out of her half-closed eyes, Liz murmurs, "It's so crazy—you're all him."

Mia holds very still. Her mom never talks about her dad. The only thing Mia knows for sure is that she physically takes after him—dark features painted onto light skin that burns while her mother tans.

"It's like you're this perfect souvenir from a city that no longer exists," Liz says. Mia waits for more information, but the next sound from Liz is a nasally snore. In the morning, Liz doesn't remember calling Mia a souvenir, but it's a line Mia never forgets. If she is a beloved souvenir, then her value as a person is based on the memory of someone she's never met, just like her first name celebrates someone she will never be. But she is a child, and her mother's best friend, so she tries to be all these other people anyway.

A few weeks later, after a soccer training session on the beach and a pit stop at the bakery, Mia still has buttery flakes of croissant stuck to her cheek when she spots him from halfway down the block. The strong July sun warms the backs of her shoulders as the man rises from the rocking chair on their front porch and cautiously lifts a hand to wave.

Mia hopes it might be the handyman, finally, to fix the dryer, but then she notices the springy brown curls that match her own, the dark eyes against the fair skin. He looks like her, like a boy Snow White, short and lean with his kneecaps sticking out of his legs and his thick eyebrows now lifted in uncertainty as he waits for Liz to acknowledge him.

"What the actual fuck?" Liz asks, stopping abruptly on the sidewalk. Mia's mouth drops open. Her mother never swears.

"Hi there," the man says, ignoring the language that Liz usually reserves for the gas company when they accidentally bill them twice. He turns his attention to Mia and says hello, calls her by her name.

"Don't speak to her," Liz spits at him. "And get off my porch."

Mia gapes at her mom's uncharacteristic rudeness, but the man just keeps standing there, smiling pleasantly. When he says how beautiful Liz looks, Mia wonders if he is hard of hearing.

"We should talk," the man says. "Let me take you to breakfast."

Liz crosses her arms, says something that is stiff with resentment but not a no.

That day at her nursery school's summer camp, Mia forgets all about the stranger on the porch until it's time to go home and Liz is late. This is by no means unusual. One by one, the other parents swoop in and scoop up their children.

When only Mia is left, the two remaining counselors toss a coin over who will wait with her. Mia decides then, at four years old, that when she is a grown-up, she will show up early. She will never make other people change their plans on her behalf.

"I bet she'll be here any minute," the counselor who wins the coin toss assures the counselor who didn't.

Tires in the gravel parking lot, brakes screeching as she takes the turn too fast, a maniacal cackle. Her mother's soundtrack.

Mia and the counselor look through the office window: There's her mom—and the man from the porch. He's reclined in the passenger seat, one hand draped out the window, the other absently running a finger up and down her mother's swan neck. Mia watches as Liz cuts the engine and rests her head on his shoulder, closes her eyes. She is extremely late but not exactly rushing to retrieve Mia or apologize to the counselor.

From twenty feet away, Liz looks different, unknowable, as she leans into the stranger with her eyes shut. Staring at her mother's resting face through the windshield, Mia's stomach rumbles with concern as she remembers what her mom taught her on the beach: *You can only use your head if you keep your eyes wide open.*

THE Q IN QUESTION

The man's name is Q.

On the drive home, he reaches into the back seat to shake Mia's hand like she's an adult. "How do you do?" Q asks. His hand is rough but his smile is warm. He reminds her of the stray cat who sometimes sleeps under their porch—Q seems nice enough, but it's hard to know how he'll behave if they bring him inside.

After pulling into their driveway, Liz asks Mia to walk with her to the beach while Q prepares dinner. Passing the jetty where they usually train, Liz plants herself in the sand and pats the spot next to her. "Let's talk," she says, and Mia sinks down beside her, happy to fold under her mother's wing.

Liz opens by saying, "Q is for Quimby." Mia is still wondering if she should recognize that name when Liz adds in a swift pelting of words and information, "And Quimby is your dad." She delivers this news with the same resigned matter-of-factness as the weather forecast for a rainy weekend. "But I'm not sure how long he's staying, so it's probably best if you just call him Q like I do, okay?"

"Okay," Mia says, because the question feels like when her mother holds up her hand for a high five, and Mia never wants to leave her mom hanging. She has no idea if it's okay. She is not even a whole hand old yet.

Over the next week, Q makes Liz a different kind of happy than Mia has ever seen. Even if he weren't constantly suggesting bike rides and movies at the drive-in and all-day hikes with packed picnics at the summit, Mia would love him for the way her mom laughs when Q picks her up and throws her over his shoulder. For the way he calls her "Lightning Liz" when she and Mia race past the eight houses on their block after their morning training sessions. For all the cooking and cleaning he does when Liz is at work, and for the fancy cocktail he hands her when she walks through the door. It's clear to everyone that Q isn't going anywhere.

"He adores you, too," Liz tells Mia one night when she's tucking her in. "I hope you can grow to love him as much as he loves you." Mia assures her that she can, that she already does. The three of them go to Funtown Splashtown in Saco, and the beach, and on long drives up the Maine coast, which her mom knowingly refers to as "Downeast." They construct forts in the living room and devour pancakes at midnight and hold hands around the town of Victory as a trio that, Mia can't help but think, is not unlike a family.

In addition to being Mia's father, Q is also a full-grown man living in her house, which proves infinitely fascinating. He likes to fix things. Mia keeps Q company as he cleans out the gutters, sharpens the knives, replaces the lightbulbs, and paints the garage. He unclogs the kitchen sink, snakes the shower drain, wipes down the baseboards, and forbids Liz from entering the kitchen until he's plated the dinner he's prepared. Whenever Liz discovers something Q has mended, improved, cleaned, or concocted, she runs to him declaring, "Love of my life!"

Q mows the lawn and fortifies Liz's anemic hydrangeas with liquefied kelp he purchases from a fancy plant store in Kennebunkport. Mia goes with him on that errand, and in the checkout line he surprises her with a glass bottle of Coke, which he says came from Mexico and tastes better than the regular Coke in the grocery store.

"Your dad is right," the cashier says as she rings them up. Mia and

Q smile at each other. Anywhere they go, everyone assumes Q is Mia's father because they look so much alike. It's a welcome change from the eager parents who approach her mom at the mall, or Hannaford, or even the pediatrician's office, and immediately ask her what she charges for an hourly rate. They all assume she's Mia's babysitter.

On the ride home from the plant store, Q explains how the color of a hydrangea is based on its levels of pH—for example, pink hydrangeas have a higher pH than blue hydrangeas. Mia looks at him and thinks how lucky she is to have such a smart father. As he speaks, they pass the soda back and forth, not even wiping the bottle lip between sips because they have the same germs and, according to Liz, the same face.

Sometimes, when it's just the two of them, Q is extra goofy, almost a kid himself. In the car, he likes to do big loopy swerves when there aren't any vehicles coming in the opposite direction. He'll walk up to perfect strangers, introduce Mia as his daughter, and say she's going to be the best soccer player in the world, just wait and see. Out to lunch, he'll pretend to fall asleep right before the check comes and then tell the nervous server who wakes him that Mia is paying, which always gets a laugh. One time, he even gets kicked out of the arcade for climbing up the Skee-Ball lane and plopping the balls directly into the hole for one hundred points each. After Mia is forced to hand over her gigantic teddy bear to the same manager who then escorts her father off the premises, Q explains to Mia that sometimes adults lose their sense of humor. "Life is one big running joke," he tells her. "Don't forget that."

In early August, Mia takes a break from the neighbor's sprinkler in the middle of the day when she can feel her skin burning. Q's car isn't in the driveway, but the door to her mom's bedroom is shut, which means she's making phone calls for Dr. Green's office. *Mom is calling patients, so I must have patience,* Mia tells herself, delighted by the homophone. Her teacher recently called her "exceptionally bright" and "a sponge," but Mia isn't sure how those two can both be true because the sponge in their sink is dark blue. Regardless, Mia grabs the *Highlights* magazine Q bought for her and sits down at the table to attack the word search.

"Ladies?" Q calls from the front door, over the rustling of bags.

"In here!" Mia answers. She abandons the *Highlights* to help him unpack. Q has promised to grill the best ribs of her life, which shouldn't be all that hard to do because Mia has never tasted ribs before.

Decades later, Mia will see ribs on a menu or at a neighborhood cookout and still think of Q. That night, he does, in fact, grill the best ribs of her life. The sweet yet savory meat is unlike anything she's ever consumed, and so it's impossible to decipher whether it's the flavor or the novelty that makes them so memorable. It could have been the way Mia's mother laughed through the entire meal—bent forward, clutching her stomach, begging for mercy—as Q turned his stack of discarded ribs into fangs, fingers, and, most creatively, a scroll of revised Ten Commandments ("Thou Shalt Not Pee in the Pool!") that made the meal unforgettably delicious.

Regardless of why those ribs tasted so good, there's no doubt in Mia's mind why she never orders them at a restaurant, prepares them at home, or nibbles them off a paper plate during a block party. It's because that night, Q tucks her in and kisses her on the cheek. "I love you, Mia," he says. She says it back to him, her eyes wide open to find his in the dark.

It is the first time they say it to each other, and it feels like a satisfying completion of something they started, like when she and Liz fold multiple loads of laundry and, at the end, every single sock has a match. It feels like the double-knotted bow Q tied around her wrist at the Victory Summer Carnival so her balloon wouldn't float up into the sky and vanish. It feels like what they've been working toward all summer, and here they are. Finally.

But when Mia wakes the next morning, Q has disappeared, and so has her mother.

THE DARK DAZE OF HEARTBREAK

Q actually leaves. Liz doesn't. Technically, she's in her bedroom. But with Q gone, she's a different person. Not the mom she was before his arrival but a crying, lethargic mess who never wants to do anything. Sometimes, she'll call Mia's name through the closed door and ask her to come in, come cuddle. And Mia always obliges, holding still in bed and not mentioning the stale air or the sunlight just beyond the blackout curtains that Q installed.

Liz doesn't emerge from her bedroom until Mia's school year starts up, ten days later. During drop-off and pickup, Mia notices her mother's hair is greasy for the first few days, then matted, then hidden under the faded blue baseball cap Q left behind. "I'm sorry," Liz tells Mia every morning on the drive to kindergarten. Rimmed in red, Liz's eyes look extra blue in the rearview mirror. "I wish I were stronger," she says, using her sleeve to wipe the freshest batch of tears. From her booster seat, Mia tells her it's okay.

Unlike her mom, the adults at school never cry in front of Mia, or even seem sad. In fact, the only time Mia's two teachers sound down is when she overhears them talking about her mom, who has worn the same shirt every day that week, and it just so happens to be inside-out and visibly stained.

"She's younger than us, you know," says one teacher to the other. Through the classroom window, they watch Liz make her way across the parking lot. "Like, significantly younger."

The other teacher shakes her head. "Super tragic," she says in a tone Mia doesn't like at the time. Only later will she identify it as pity.

The teachers don't realize that Mia hears them—and that Liz does, too. Their voices carry through the open window and across the parking lot. Unlike her daughter, Liz knows exactly what pity sounds like because she's been subjected to it ever since senior year of high school after everyone found out she was pregnant. She will not be pitied, and she will not subject her daughter to pity, either.

Liz drives straight home. She tosses Q's baseball hat in the trash and washes her hair with three rounds of shampoo and conditioner. Three is her lucky number, and she is feeling lucky. Combing out the remaining knots in the mirror, she tells herself she is ready to begin again. She snaps the hairband on her wrist. It's time to reset and to reclaim Victory as her own, on her own, and so she will need champagne, her daughter, and sequins. Lots of sequins.

Liz throws a New Year's Eve party that very night, on a Wednesday in September. "We're not waiting for December thirty-first to start over," she explains to Mia on the drive home from school. "Tonight we're celebrating our new beginning—put this on." She hands Mia a purple feather boa and silver plastic crown that she procured from the Dollar Store. "At midnight, we jump in the ocean—it's called a polar plunge, and it's supposed to be totally life-changing."

"Okay," Mia says, because she doesn't like to leave her mom hanging.

That night it's sequins and glitter and enough rhinestones to make Elton John blush as Liz and Mia lower the lights and dance in the living room, each holding their own bottle of bubbles—cheap prosecco for Liz and Martinelli's sparking apple juice for Mia.

"It's almost midnight," Liz says, catching her breath between Britney Spears and Christina Aguilera. "Let's find your shoes and get ready to leave—we need to be in the ocean when the clock strikes midnight for the magic to work."

"Do I have to put my head underwater?" Mia asks, pulling open drawers in search of a pair of goggles they most likely don't own.

"Yes," Liz answers with a straight face. "For a full New Year's polar-plunge reset, yes."

"Are you going to put your head under?"

"Absolutely."

Before they leave for the beach, Liz pours boiling water from her tea kettle into two hot-water bottles, which she then wraps in the towels they bring with them—along with the noisemakers and sparkly scepters and a box of firework poppers they chuck at the sidewalk, laughing at the sparks.

At 11:59, stripped down to their bathing suits and holding hands, they scream as they run toward the black water at high tide, voices bouncing off the jetty. They sound strong as they count down before they both hold their breath and dip below the water's surface.

Time freezes.

Mia is only under for a second, and yet the water pricks her like a gazillion needles and the Earth buzzes with a high frequency, and even though her eyes are closed, she swears she can see her mother grinning down there, away from the world, the two of them keeping each other safe until they pop back up into the chilly night air, amid the dazzle of stars, the empty beach.

"Happy New Year!" Liz shouts. "Race to the towels!"

On the sand, Liz folds Mia into a terry cloth burrito and holds her to her chest as they admire the diamond-studded sky.

"Hot chocolate?" Liz asks.

The teenage boy working the window at Dunkin' Donuts takes one look at Liz and insists their drinks are on the house. Even with wet hair and eyeliner smeared down her cheeks, Liz is beautiful. Mia knows this for the fact that it is, and not the subjective bias of being her daughter.

"Do you feel reset?" Liz asks. Mia nods from the back seat, whipped cream tickling the strip of skin between her nostrils. She's unsure what a reset means, but if it involves hot chocolate at midnight with her mom when the rest of the world is already asleep, count her in.

SOCCER SURPRISES

The reset works. Liz wakes up the next morning singularly focused on enrolling Mia in peewee soccer. At four years old, Mia is one of the youngest players on the field: Her jersey drapes past her knees, and her shin guards are so big that they slip down the spindles of her legs and rub blisters into the tops of her ankles. The discomfort is nothing compared to the thrill. Like her mother before her, Mia falls instantly for the sport.

Liz attends every practice and game, cheering for her daughter and leaping to her feet whenever Mia wins the ball and shouting encouragement when she loses it. "Next time, Mia!" Liz yells after an opponent beats her in the midfield. During Saturday morning scrimmages, Mia pretends not to hear her mom when Liz yells, "Keep the width up top" because Mia has no idea what that means and neither do any of her teammates.

At halftime, when she sees other parents distribute sugar cookies and frosted doughnuts to the team in their huddle, Liz plays along, cooing, "Sprinkles! How fun!" But when it's her turn for snack duty, Liz uses it as an opportunity to educate the other parents on what's effective fuel by handing out halved bananas, and kiddie cups filled with her handcrafted rehydrating potion.

Mia dutifully gulps down the electrolytes and her mother's soccer dream because from the very first practice, she understands what the sport can provide: escape. With the ball at her feet and a defender on her back, it doesn't matter that Mia's father doesn't live with them, that Q hasn't called Mia once since he left. Instead, on the soccer field, Mia focuses on what she can control by running fast and going to goal.

Off the field, Liz teaches Mia to keep track of her team and personal stats in a red spiral notebook. When the Pinchers lose a game, which isn't often, it's helpful to see the breakdown and how the numbers add up to the outcome. Mia realizes the numbers always make sense.

Arithmetic, like soccer, presents clear expectations and distinct rules Mia finds easy to follow. She prefers the predictability of numbers and soccer matches to the ambiguous real-life muck that transpires beyond their boundaries. It's impossible to quantify how much she misses Q, but it's easy to tally up goals. And whether Mia scores or not, there is always a next time. Unlike people, the soccer field stays put, waiting for her. In that sense, nothing ever changes.

Until the first Saturday in October. Despite a two-goal lead at half-time, Mia's team loses. But the true upset occurs after the game, when Mia runs across the field toward the stands and sees her mom puking off the side of the bleachers.

QUEEN OF CAPS

Seven months later, Liz names her second baby after the most capped soccer player in the world, Kristine Lilly, who scored 130 goals during her 354 games with the National Team. Although lesser known than Mia Hamm, Kristine Lilly arguably won the 1999 World Cup for the United States when she blocked a sure-fire shot on the goal line, with her head, during sudden-death overtime against China.

"She became my hero in that moment," Liz explains to Mia as they sleepwalk on the beach in the middle of the day. The baby kept them up all night, again. "And why wouldn't I name both my girls after my heroes? Especially when my heroes are lifelong friends and teammates, just as you two will be?"

Mia looks at the newborn nestled against her mother's chest and then stares up to the cloudless summer sky with a million questions because why is the baby here? The beach is where she and her mother go to be together, to contemplate life and listen to the lapping of the waves. This is their place, away from it all, but now the baby is here, and even in this Atlantic sanctuary, the baby is as loud, irreverent, rude, and flatulent as she is at home. She hardly seems like the "built-in friend" Mia's teachers promised she would be. Rather, Kristine is a perpetual mess of liquids going in and coming out, a parasite who shamelessly gloms to their mother with a squid-like death grip.

Worst of all, the baby looks just like Liz. Everyone says so—even the women at the beach tip their sunglasses forward to coo that the baby is Liz's blond-and-blue-eyed clone, rather than the shrieking, leaking leech Mia knows her to be. And yet, Liz insists this midnight monster is a gift for Mia: "Q and I made you for us, but we made Kristine for you, because you deserve a sibling."

"I deserve *better*," Mia argues, but Liz doesn't hear her over the baby's hungry squawks. They stop near the jetty for Liz to feed Kristine and Mia checks her watch because this unscheduled break is going to make them late for Mia's playdate. Her mom never seems to even notice that they are always late for everything. When two teenage boys jog past just as Liz is tickling the baby's lips with her nipple, Mia considers joining them and running away from this hamster wheel of exhausting humiliation.

At Kristine's one-month checkup, the pediatrician stretches her long and says, "This is what I call a cricket baby—she's got legs up to her shoulders." And that's all it takes to rebrand a newborn. Kristine forever becomes Cricket, and Cricket is quickly deemed a physical phenomenon.

Breezing past milestones at such a clip that even the pediatrician appears stunned during their appointments, Cricket casually holds up her gigantic head at six weeks old. A month later, she rolls over with the ambitious control of a gymnast performing her floor routine. Cricket crawls at five months. She walks herself into the pediatrician's office for her nine-month checkup with such sure-footed confidence that the other parents in the waiting room openly gawk.

On the playground, Cricket's peers drool over their unsanctioned snack of leaves and woodchips as they watch Cricket hoist herself up and complete the monkey bars.

"What a weirdo," Liz whispers to Mia from the green metal bench where they sit close together. "I could never do the monkey bars that well." They do not need to supervise Cricket, who is preternaturally aware of her gross-motor limitations, but rather they serve as her audience and two-person panel of judges. "Seven!" Liz calls out after Cricket flies down the big slide that most kids are too scared to climb up—including Mia. "Stick the landing next time!"

The only thing Cricket fails to do as a toddler is actually toddle—she goes from walking to running in a day, a pint-size gazelle moving in one fluid motion. She follows Mia everywhere, tracks her, and anticipates where she's going. More than once, Mia will reach for a book and all of a sudden it's in Cricket's hand, her little sister beaming as she gives it to Mia and asks her to read it to her. It would be impressive if it weren't so annoying.

Things change—and not for the better—when Cricket is four years old. It's the summer, and that bleary gray before sunrise when Cricket takes the last thing Mia has been able to keep for herself.

"I want to train today," Cricket says, rubbing her eyes while looking for her shoes.

Standing by the front door, dressed and ready to go, Mia, now nine, cannot believe her ears. Cricket is not a morning person. In fact, Liz usually pushes Cricket in a stroller to the beach, where Cricket sleeps through the entirety of their practice.

Not today. On their six-block commute, the sidewalk is barely wide enough for a pair, and so Mia trails behind Cricket and their mother, confused as to why she feels like she's eavesdropping on their conversation when this is supposed to be her time to talk. Cricket barely notices when Mia steps on the back of her sneaker because she is too focused on practicing tight possession. Mia always carries the soccer ball under one arm on the walk to the beach, but Cricket has insisted on dribbling it.

"Nice control there," Liz says after Cricket expertly navigates her way around a broad-backed dog who pulls hard on the leash, desperate to sink her teeth into the synthetic leather. "For the next block, only use your left foot," Liz challenges.

During beach warm-ups, Mia tries not to notice how Cricket moves with notable quickness. At the house, she was barely awake, but now Cricket devotes her full attention to each stretch and every drill with a predatorial sharpness. Meanwhile, Mia asserts her dominance by juggling the way her mother has taught her.

As the sun rises above the water, Mia demonstrates all the things she's already learned from years of beach sessions. She can feel Cricket watching her, so she lets the ball drop from her quad down to the top of her foot and flicks it over to Cricket under the guise of a friendly volley. To Mia's shock, Cricket receives the ball with the inside of her left foot before bopping it back into the air with control.

"Like this?" Cricket asks as the ball obeys her for nine consecutive touches, now ten, eleven.

Leaving the beach and turning onto their street, Liz gives the command: "Ready, set, go!" Mother and daughters sprint past eight houses, Liz several paces ahead until she slaps the white mailbox standing guard outside 125 Knickerbocker Avenue and declares herself the winner.

"I respect you too much not to try my hardest," she explains to them. "So when you do beat me, you'll know you really beat me." Once Mia and Cricket catch their breath, the three Lowes step onto the front porch together, careful to avoid the weak spots in the floorboards.

"I'm going to beat you both," Cricket says. "Not yet, but soon."

Weeks pass, then months, and each morning on the beach, exhausted mothers look up from their phones and angle their heads down to peer over their sunglasses. Among them, there is a consensus that the older girl, Mia, is a gifted soccer player. They've watched her for years, and she's no doubt growing into a local talent with a splashy high school career ahead of her. But the little sister—who really isn't so little, not with those ski poles for legs—she's something else. Maybe it's the girl's uncanny speed, or the way she just always seems to *get there*. It's like she can manipulate space and time to accommodate her plan with the ball.

"The older girl, the pale brunette, she's very good," one local mother in a navy one-piece tells her friend, who is visiting from Massachusetts. "But the blonde—just watch her—that girl is a total freak of nature."

PRE AND POST

Six-year-old Cricket has never second-guessed the identity of the man in the large black-and-white photograph hanging above the toilet: It's her father. She's grown up on a diet of Disney movies so it just makes sense that one of her parents is dead.

"Good morning, Dad," Cricket says to him after her first flush of the day, every day. Muscular and mid-stride on a race track, the man frozen in motion in the Lowes' bathroom shares the same dark hair and determined look as Mia during morning training sessions. His bulging quads explain Cricket's own strength.

"Do you ever miss him?" Cricket asks her mom, who has stumbled into the bathroom. Hair still mussed from sleep, Liz gropes for her toothbrush.

"Miss who?"

"Our dad," Cricket says.

"Your dad?" Liz asks, her bleary blue eyes suddenly as bright and alert as high beams.

"Yeah," Cricket says, nodding up at the picture. "Him."

"Oh, honey," Liz says, unable to hide her relieved delight. "That's not—that's Steve Prefontaine, a famous runner."

"My dad's name is Steve?"

"Nope," Liz says, bending over to spit and rinse.

Mia's face appears in the doorframe, officially hitting the tiny bathroom's maximum capacity. "What are you guys talking about?" At eleven years old, Mia is average in height—she stands on the middle bleacher for school chorus—but she is only three inches taller than her sister.

Mia finds Cricket's height just one of several irksome things about her. Cricket's eyes and hair have remained as light as their mother's. She is a walking recessive gene and yet Cricket demonstrates her physical dominance on a daily basis; she stands on the side of the bleachers for her school chorus, only blending in with her classmates when they are given a six-inch advantage. She is the first pick for any game on the playground, whether it's four-square or capture the flag. The boys don't even feel self-conscious about picking a girl first—she's just that good, it would be dumb to go with anyone else.

"Cricket thought Steve Prefontaine was your father," Liz explains to Mia with restraint, a laugh tugging at the corners of her mouth.

"You thought our dad was in the Olympics?" Mia asks her sister, pointing out the rings on his white tank top just above three letters: USA. "And on a poster?"

"I thought it was just a really big photo."

In most households, the conversation would turn to questions about the girls' actual father, but Liz steers them headfirst into a Steve Prefontaine Ted Talk—the promise the runner had represented and the shock of his death from crashing his car.

"What's that say?" Cricket asks, pointing to the script below Steve's feet.

"To give anything less than your best is to sacrifice the gift," Liz reads. "Steve said that—pretty good, right?"

Her girls nod absently, their minds pivoting toward the day ahead, the fact that their mom is already running late, which means they are already running late.

"Steve Prefontaine may not be your dad, but he's one of my greatest influences," Liz says. "And that line"—she nods at the poster—"it's helpful to say whenever you don't feel like doing something you need to do."

Because Cricket cannot yet read, she repeats the line to herself on the walk to the bus stop until she has it memorized: *To give anything less than your best is to sacrifice the gift.* The next morning, she sets her alarm clock and recites the quotation as a prayer because as much as Cricket loves soccer, she is not a natural early riser like her mother and sister, who seem to effortlessly spring out of bed for sunrise training sessions. And unlike Mia, Cricket is not a school person. Or a load-your-plate-in-the-dishwasher person. But reciting Steve's words forces Cricket to understand what's at stake, and she'd rather battle the alarm clock than give less than her best.

Others have begun to expect the best from her, too, and not just her mother and sister. As Cricket's talent begins to draw a Saturday-morning spotlight, soccer coaches and teammates and the parents of teammates will approach her after games and let Cricket know that she was a shining star out there on the field, that she could really go places if she puts her head down and does the work.

In the years ahead, Cricket will write her adopted mantra in the margins of her homework and on the walls of heavily graffitied bathroom stalls. She will select it as her senior quote for her high school yearbook and write it on the inserts of her cleats. Cricket will live by these words, which she attributes as much to her mother as to Steve Prefontaine himself.

No matter what happens, she will give her best, and come what may, she will not sacrifice the gift.

WINNERS AND QUITTERS

"**D**o you know why I named you Mia?" Liz asks her older daughter, now fourteen, as they drive to pick up Cricket from the fancy indoor sports facility in Portland.

The coach of an elite soccer club, the Stallions, called Liz to invite Cricket to try out. He had heard Cricket's name multiple times from "trusted sources," by which he meant the overly invested parents of his current players.

"Because Mia Hamm is the best," Mia says, preoccupied with the notice from the power company in her hands. Eighth grade is hard enough without the extra work of trying to manage her mom's utility bills, which she has been doing for years. It isn't the math—numbers come easily to Mia—it's tracking down the bills themselves: She just found this one balled up in the glove compartment and already past due.

"Mia Hamm is the best, that's true," Liz acknowledges. "But what people don't realize is that Mia Hamm was also the ultimate team player." Sensing the gravity of the conversation, Mia sits up in her seat and devotes her full attention to her mother, who launches into yet another soccer speech about the famous '99er.

"Sure, Mia Hamm scored a ton of goals and was the nucleus of the National Team, the humble hero," Liz continues. "Oh look! It's eleven-eleven—make a wish!" She is talking too much and too fast—Mia feels her heartbeat pick up speed as she waits to see where this lecture is going.

"But she was also the leader in assists," Liz says. "Did you know that?"

Mia shakes her head.

"She sacrificed so much of her own glory to lift up the entire team," Liz explains. "And that generosity is why I thought she was worthy of naming my firstborn daughter after her."

"Mom?"

"I need your help with Cricket," Liz confesses, keeping her eyes on the road and flicking on her blinker. "If she makes this team, it's a big deal, but it'll logistically impossible unless I can count on you to step up."

"I'm fourteen."

"You're Mia Lowe," Liz says. "You're brilliant and you can do anything."

"But what—"

"There's this phrase, 'pay to play,'" Liz says as they drive over the drawbridge and into the city. "It's shorthand for the fact that a kid needs to come from money to make it in sports—most definitely for college and professional, but even in high school. I mean, look at this place." They take in the several stories of glass, the heated domes, the invisible millions that built the sports complex. They eye the luxury cars in the parking lot that stand guard like sentries.

"I don't want Cricket—or you—to ever lose out on an opportunity because of money."

"How am I supposed to pay for Cricket to play soccer?" Mia asks, barely hiding her repulsion. "I'm fourteen!" she repeats.

"I know you are, honey, and I don't expect you to pay for soccer, but I need to get a second job, at night, so we can afford more things in general, which means I would need you to pick up the pieces at home—dinner, laundry, making sure Cricket does her homework."

"Oh."

"I know," Liz says, merging onto the highway. "It's not fair. I know that and I'm so sorry. But I can't figure out any other way to make this work."

Mia flashes back to the thousands of diapers she's changed, the sleep she's lost and the hours she's logged comforting, entertaining, and indulging her baby sister. The electricity bill is still in her hands, her own soccer bag in the back of the car. "Will I still play? For my team?"

"I wouldn't ask if I weren't desperate," Liz says, either ignoring or not hearing Mia's question. Tears plummet silently from her cheeks to her lap. Three things about Liz Lowe: She never curses, she never arrives on time, and ever since their first midnight plunge, she never cries.

"I'll do it," Mia says, realizing what this implicitly means. Her own soccer career is over. There won't be time to play if her mom needs her to cover the home front.

Liz looks at her, nods until she's confident in her voice. "Thank you," she musters, and she sounds so fractured that Mia feels sick with shame that she attempted to resist.

Even if Cricket doesn't deserve her sacrifice, her mother does. Liz reaches over and squeezes Mia's hand. Staring at their fingers intertwined, Mia understands the inextricable braid between love and sacrifice. Then she looks at the clock and tells her mom what she always tells her: "We're really late."

Halfway through the Stallions tryout, the head coach asks Cricket, "What's your favorite position to play?"

"All of them," Cricket says. She is nine years old and revels in every aspect of soccer the same way she appreciates every flavor of ice cream, every kind of candy, every episode of *Friends* because of how much her mom laughs each time Joey enters a scene. Cricket is an equal opportunist—anything she is lucky enough to experience becomes her immediate favorite.

"What about goalkeeper?"

"I love it!" Cricket exclaims, oblivious to the weight of his inquiry. "I like coming off the line and surprising attackers," she says with a widening grin. "Because it's actually more like scaring them."

"Great," Coach says, offering Cricket a fist bump. "You have more sense than the rest of them." The previous season, which was Coach's first year out of college and first time with the Stallions, he didn't have an established keeper. Instead, he'd forced every player to take a turn in goal, which resulted in weekly tears and a middling record.

But Coach sees outsize potential in Cricket Lowe—not just for her own career but also for his. At twenty-two years old, he's meant to be coaching young men, not little girls. But here he is, doing more coaxing than coaching because Major League Soccer hired someone else. He'd made it through three rounds of interviews with the New England Revolution before he found out he'd lost the spot to a guy vaguely related to Ronaldinho.

Politics.

It always comes down to politics.

Coach has no choice but to stick with the girls for now, so he'll make them winners like any legitimate coach would. An undefeated record will help him negotiate the terms of his contract with MLS next year when a staff vacancy undoubtedly opens up. Standing in front of him now is the missing piece to his puzzle: a keeper.

"Want to step in goal?" Coach asks.

Five shots in, he understands what he has on his hands. Cricket Lowe is a talented goalkeeper in the rough. He smiles as he chips shots and tells her, "Well done," while she adjusts her movements to his critiques. It doesn't matter that Cricket is a nine-year-old girl. She's good, really good, and Coach is going to make her great. Herein lies the inherent beauty of coaching: seeing promise, cultivating it, and encouraging it, until you teach yourself right out of a job.

"I played goalkeeper through college," Coach tells Cricket as they wait for her mom to pick her up. They kill the clock with a goaltending exercise called the three-cone drill. "And we're goalkeepers, by the way, not goalies," Coach says. "Goalies are just children using their hands; goalkeepers are the conductors of the field, and I think you could make one hell of a conductor."

"Let me guess," Cricket says. She breathes heavily as she runs backward for the drill, but her panting does not diminish her audacity. "Because you need a goalkeeper? Or because I'm tall?"

Coach laughs with genuine surprise. He's not used to such bluntness from a third grader. The rest of his players speak to him with a little more reverence, a little less certainty. "Your height definitely helps, and we need a keeper," he allows. "But do you know what makes a great goalkeeper?"

Cricket shakes her head.

"An internal M-A-P—a map—which stands for Mentality, Adaptability, Patience. You're brave and agile and vocal and strong—all the qualities of an exceptional goalkeeper."

Cricket doesn't blush or shrink from these compliments but rather lifts her chin to meet them like a cat emerging from the shadows to sun herself.

"Most of all," Coach continues, "I get the feeling that you understand the responsibility that comes with the position, the sacrifice required."

Cricket nods, taking in this information and accepting her fate with pleasure. "So should I get my own gloves or what?"

Two days later, Coach calls to congratulate Cricket—she's made the team.

The day after that, Liz fills out paperwork for her second job and takes Mia on a tour of the two supermarkets within walking distance to show her which store has the best deals for what and how to maximize coupon codes. Mia goes a step further and creates a spreadsheet to help them keep track of their spending. Within a few weeks, however, she notices she's the only one who inputs her receipts.

Cricket, too, must step up. Liz makes it clear to her younger daughter that she is responsible for securing rides to and from the games and practices that coincide with Liz's work schedule. It's an easy ask compared to Mia's but still a daunting task for a nine-year-old. Nonetheless, Cricket makes the calls, even when it requires talking to dads on landlines.

Together, they rally. Together, they forge ahead. Together, they pay for Cricket to play because they're Lowes, not quitters.

Except for Mia, who unceremoniously stops playing soccer. According to her former teammates, she is the epitome of a quitter. In the school hallways and cafeteria, they stick out their bottom lips and beg her to come back. "We need you!" they say after their first Saturday game, which resulted in their first loss of the season. When their charm offensive doesn't yield results, the girls stop trying to recruit Mia and instead cast her off. They remove her from the team email. They block her on Gchat. They ignore her at the lunch table. They treat her like she left them to play for another team, which in a way, she did: Team Lowe.

Mia gets through the social ice-out by summoning the strength of her namesake. Mia Hamm gave up her own goals to make her teammates look good, and that's what she is doing, too, because family is the ultimate team anyway, and she will lead in assists. Exiting the cafeteria alone, Mia reminds herself that Cricket's success and her mother's happiness are only possible through her sacrifice.

NIGHTTIME ROUTINES

Six nights a week, Liz waits tables at Primo Bistro, an Italian oasis in nearby Portland with fresh pasta, award-winning desserts, and a shamelessly pricey wine list. While her mother collects menus and drops checks at Primo, Mia tidies the bungalow and cleans up from dinner. At ten p.m., Mia coaxes Cricket into bed by reminding her she can only continue to grow tall if she sleeps. Thanks to the Stallions head coach, Cricket is already obsessed with becoming a professional goalkeeper. She knows she needs every inch she can get because the taller the keeper, the smaller the net.

Most nights, Mia falls asleep on the pink floral couch and wakes to the familiar screech of worn tires pulling into the driveway. She turns off the TV and stumbles out to the kitchen, then fills two glasses of water. With the only usable knife in the house, Mia slices lemon wedges.

"Hi you," Liz whispers through an exhausted smile. Mia watches her mother as she locks up, slips off her clogs, and holds out her arms. She envelops her older daughter who has worked all day for precisely this. In the briefest of seconds, the whole kitchen smells of garlic bread and Liz's end-of-shift cabernet. Mia notes the red smudges of Primo

Bistro's famous homemade tomato sauce on her mother's white button-down as Liz reaches up and pulls out her high bun, unleashing a blond mane that tumbles halfway down her back and smells like another evening of hard work and sautéed onions.

As they do every night, mother and daughter sit at the kitchen table and Liz takes out the wad of cash from her server's apron and sets it between them. Mia grabs it and organizes the bills into Monopoly piles as her mother recounts the day's kookiest patients at the dental office. "You wouldn't believe this guy," Liz says. "Amy called me back to try to help him relax—I've never seen someone so scared to spit. He kept puffing his cheeks like this—."

Mia laughs at the impression but doesn't lose count of the money. There are several twenty-dollar bills, two fifties, and then a bunch of tens, fives, and ones. She counts the ones last while her mother stares into space. Nodding at the thick slab of singles in Mia's hand, Liz asks, "How much you got there?"

"Thirty-nine."

"It's all yours, my girl."

Since Mia took up the mantle of being Cricket's backup mom, the tradition has become just this: Sit at the kitchen table drinking water with her mother, catch up, and count the tip money. Mia is allowed to keep the one- and five-dollar bills that Liz makes at the restaurant as compensation for her unconventional extracurricular activity.

"My good night is your good night," Liz says, rubbing one of her knees as she stands up and hobbles over to the sink with their empty water glasses. Mia knows that her mom was a soccer star in high school. All the big universities and Ivy Leagues wanted her, and out of dozens of offers, Liz chose UCLA only to lose everything when she became pregnant. The worst thing Mia ever did in her life was exist, and she's been trying to make up for it ever since.

"The National Team is looking good this year," Mia says.

"Knock on wood! Right now!" Liz demands, rapping on the kitchen table herself.

Mia does as she's told and bangs on the table. Like her mother, she believes in good luck as much as she invests in hard work. For better or worse, their superstitions have rubbed off on Cricket, who refuses to wash her lucky—albeit rancid—soccer socks until the end of the season.

"What's more important," Mia asks, hungry to engage her tired mother for just a few minutes longer, "the World Cup or the Olympics?"

"World Cup," Liz answers as she limps back to the table. "More teams, more money, more coverage—although not as much as the men—at least not yet."

"But you think someday?" Mia asks.

Liz gives her a side glance. "You know what I'm going to say to that."

"Be positive?"

"Exactly."

Liz believes her sunny outlook is quite literally inscribed in her DNA. At the Red Cross annual blood drive, Liz rolls up her sleeve as her daughters look on, waiting for the day they're old enough to donate. They dutifully listen to their mother proselytize that the blood running through their veins—and the blood type they share—isn't just a double-helical polymer but an overarching life directive: B-positive.

"Do you think Cricket will really play on the National Team some day?" Mia asks as her mother turns off the kitchen light and follows her down the hall into the bathroom so they can brush their teeth, side by side.

"Only if she wants to, and only if she listens to Steve," Liz says, glancing at the Steve Prefontaine poster hanging above the toilet. "But do me a favor, just to be safe?"

Mia grins at her mother in the mirror and raps her knuckles on the wood window trim.

VISUALIZE TO REALIZE

"Again!" Coach yells from the eighteen-yard line through a pelting rain. As usual, Cricket is waiting for her mom, and so Coach makes use of the time by running her through extra drills. Paying for her mother's tardiness in the form of this additional exercise, Cricket allows her irritation to distract her. She lets in three easy grounders before Coach summons her over, Cricket's socks audibly sluicing with every step.

"Has anyone ever talked to you about visualization?" Coach asks. The wet soccer balls are as cooperative as greased piglets, and Coach has silently watched Cricket grow frustrated. She is used to the ball obeying her touch, a cooperative coconspirator in her aims. Not today. And where is her mom?

"Visualization?" Cricket repeats, trying out the word. "I don't think so?" Through the aggressive rain, she glances up at Coach, whose dirty blond hair is several shades dirtier now that it's sopping wet. Most of her teammates—and all their moms—have crushes on Coach, but not Cricket. He strikes her as a moody Muppet: tall and gangly with long arms that seem to go everywhere when he's yelling at the refs on the sideline of their games. But one on one, he's always patient, so even if Cricket doesn't think he's cute, she understands why her teammates doodle his initials in the back of their notebooks.

"Okay, cool, so before you strike that ball," Coach begins, "envision where you want it to go in your mind's eye." Using his laces, he flicks another ball up into his hands. "But also picture the arc you want the ball to take, how you want it to land, and at whose feet."

"But no one's here," Cricket says, pointing out the obvious. Every single one of her teammates, with their responsible, two-parent households, have already been scooped up, driven home, and fed a warm, home-cooked meal by now.

"That's the point of the exercise," Coach says. "Envision you're playing goalkeeper in a match, the ref blows the whistle, and you've got six seconds to clear the ball. Who do you see out there?"

Cricket looks out and sees their best forward. "Annabelle Fischer," she says.

"Let it rip. Put it right at her feet."

Cricket takes a breath, approaches the ball, locks her ankle, leans over, and looks out at her target—there's Annabelle, her long French braid chasing after her legs.

"Nice!" he shouts, jogging over to Cricket with his hand raised for a high five. "See how the visualizing helps?"

Cricket nods. She's pretty sure she's always visualized where to put the ball without necessarily knowing that what she was doing had a name.

"So a lot of athletes incorporate visualization into their training," Coach says. "It's like a meditation, with a goal in mind, to prime their brain and body for when the moment presents itself."

"Cool," Cricket says through chattering teeth. She looks past Coach at the headlights pulling into the parking lot, the windshield wipers waving frantically to convey her mother's message to hurry up, they need to go.

Spotting the car, Coach salutes Liz Lowe, and she responds with a double blink of the high beams. "Give it a try tonight," he tells Cricket, who is already halfway across the field. The water bottle in her blue

Stallions bag bangs against her hip as she runs, but her mother still rolls down her window to yell, "Let's go, Cricket Lowe! Move those wheels!"

And even though she's already sprinting, the sound of her mother's voice pulls her like a lasso, and the knowledge that Coach is watching makes Cricket lift her knees higher in a one-woman performance of athletic excellence. She is the best goalkeeper in the league and the fastest player on her team.

"Can I drop you on Main Street and can you hand me that shirt behind you?" Liz asks by way of greeting as she zips out of the parking lot before Cricket has clicked her seatbelt. They both understand that Liz is running so late that she will need to go straight from the Stallions' practice field to Primo Bistro. For this very reason, Liz keeps her black server's apron and several metal hangers of dry-cleaned white shirts in the back seat of her car.

As she zooms toward town, Liz blames her tardiness on Mr. Trott, who interrogated Liz about his molars before inquiring into her marital status.

"Typical," Cricket says with a sigh.

"Typical," Liz agrees. "Okay, get ready to run."

Normally, Cricket wouldn't mind the mile-long walk from Primo, but she's already freezing and this rain won't relent. Despite the ten full-field sprints she just did at the end of practice and the fact that she's still wearing her cleats, Cricket decides to run.

With each step toward home, Cricket feels the unforgiving sidewalk wear down the studs of her boots. This pair needs to last her all season, and she hates that they're taking such abuse as she makes a left on Main Street and charges the steep hill on Lavender Avenue, registering that the crashes of thunder are growing closer and closer together. Her left knee hurts and Cricket knows she will pay for this concrete mile on the soccer field, her studs failing her the next time she tries to make a hard cut, a sharp turn. How could she have left her sneakers in Hilary's mom's car? What was she thinking?

Then again, Cricket argues, if she were Hilary, it would have been fine to leave her shoes in her mom's car, because Hilary's mom, like every other parent of her Stallions teammates, picks up *and* drops off.

Only Cricket is expected to ask around for rides.

Only Cricket is forced to be prodigiously organized with all of her gear at all times.

Only Cricket is squinting through the pelting rain and running uphill between harrowing jags of lightning after a grueling practice, after a long school day, because only Cricket is expected to step up if she wants to play soccer at the most elite level. For everyone else on the team, the time required to be a Stallion—weekday practices, holiday-weekend tournaments three states and five hours away—is the sacrifice. But for Cricket, that time devoted to honing her craft is the reward, and it comes with responsibility.

She rounds the corner and sees her house a block away. Cricket sprints like her life depends on it, like every naysayer is chasing her, telling her she isn't fast enough, good enough, to become who she needs to become, which is an exceptional goalkeeper, an Olympic athlete, a World Cup winner. By the time Cricket opens her front door, it's impossible to distinguish rain from sweat as it drips off her fingertips and she shouts her sister's name from the threshold.

"Coming!" Mia yells, appearing behind a stack of folded bath towels she'd thrown in the dryer when she heard the rain, saw the clock, and did the transportation math. "These are still warm—take one now so you don't get pneumonia but then shower and get into dry clothes—and I made chicken noodle soup."

"Extra carrots?" Cricket asks.

"Extra carrots," Mia answers because she knows a keeper is only as good as her eyesight. That night, Cricket is too tired to tackle the reading homework for English so instead she lies in bed and practices visualization. First, she does what Coach suggested and imagines making a great save before clearing the ball up to Annabelle, who goes on to score.

But then Cricket imagines herself wearing the official kit of the U.S. Women's National Team and playing for a packed stadium at the World Cup. As she waves to the crowd, she sees Coach, and Mia, and her mom, all cheering for her in identical Lowe jerseys, but someone keeps saying her name, and that's when Cricket wakes up to the smell of fried garlic and her mother's hand on her cheek.

"You were smiling in your sleep," Liz whispers, beaming as she unties her black server's apron and sits on the edge of the bed. Cricket nods, still smiling.

After Liz leaves to brush her teeth, Cricket closes her eyes for another round of visualization. This time, she sees a future in which her mother quits her job at the restaurant—and at the dental office—and spends her days being the mother of superstar goalkeeper Cricket Lowe. She doesn't work a single night of the week. And when Cricket comes into town, Liz picks her up on time and drives her all the way home.

At the next Stallions practice, Coach asks Cricket if she had any luck with the visualization. When she answers yes, Coach throws his head in the direction of Annabelle, who is at the far end of the bench, solemnly applying deodorant. "You gonna get her a goal and yourself an assist on Saturday?"

Cricket nods. "Among other things."

"Oh yeah?" Coach asks, amused. "What else did you visualize?"

In her mind, Cricket clicks through the gallery highlights: the perfect playing fields, the sensation of stopping an unstoppable shot, the stadiums full of screaming fans, the locker rooms full of lifelong friends, the game-winning saves, the trophies, the sponsorships, hoisting up a World Cup with her teammates and bending down to receive an Olympic gold medal around her neck, the seven-figure contracts, the celebratory press conferences, the tropical vacations she'll take her mom and sister on, the big house she'll buy for the three of them to live in together, with a chef and a swimming pool and the original poster of Steve Prefontaine hanging in a gilded frame in their fancy dining room, right next to an orange Wheaties box with Cricket's face on it, because she's going to become the best goalkeeper in the world.

"Cricket?" Coach asks again. "What else did you visualize?"

"My life," Cricket says, grinning as she pulls up her socks. "It's gonna be awesome."

SUMMER CHAPERONE

"Remember who you are," Liz reminds Mia when she drops her off outside the coffee shop in Portland. Now a senior in high school, Mia is there to meet Ronald Cork, a Yale alum who has agreed to interview her as part of her college application.

After Liz drives away, Mia checks her watch—she has forty-five minutes to spare. Her mom had needed the car today, so rather than risk arriving on Liz Time, Mia lied to her about when the interview started. Better early than late.

Eventually, Ronald Cork arrives by bicycle. His long, white beard makes him look like Santa, especially when he smiles.

"Mia!" he says, extending one hand as he unsnaps his helmet with the other. "So good to see you!"

"Very nice to meet you, Mr. Cork," Mia says.

Still shaking her hand, he leans in and confides, "It's technically Dr. Cork." Mia's cheeks flush—she'd done so much research, and she knew he had a PhD in ethnomusicology, she just hadn't—"But please, call me Ronny," he says, interrupting her spiral. Peering through the coffee shop window, he tells Mia to grab the open table in the corner, and he'll order their Americanos.

In the last few days, Mia read on half a dozen websites not to let the alumni interviewer pay for anything but also not to come across as uptight. She freezes, conflicted, until Ronny gestures for her to hurry up and claim the table. Mia rushes to the corner and reserves their seats just in time, edging out a polished young couple. From his place in line, Ronny pumps his fist in the air and Mia snaps the hairband on her wrist to reset.

"So what are your plans for the summer?" Ronny asks twenty minutes into the interview.

Mia forces a smile to compensate for the embarrassment roiling in her stomach as she predicts his disappointment or, worse, his pity. Mia's AP classmates have either unpaid internships that require suit jackets or international volunteer trips involving dinosaur bones in Namibia.

"I'm chaperoning," Mia says, lifting her eyebrows to acknowledge its mundaneness.

"Chaperoning?" Ronny repeats. "Is that the new terminology for camp counselor?"

"Not exactly." Mia shifts in her chair, clawing for words that fail to come.

"Are you working at a sobriety house?"

"No," Mia says with a sigh, defeated. "It's just—"

"A retirement home!" Ronny suggests. "You're leading excursions for the elderly?"

"No," Mia says, her tone sharper than she'd intended. "I'm just taking my sister to soccer tournaments all summer so my mom can work."

"Really?" Ronny leans forward. "How old is she?"

"Thirteen," Mia answers, feeling herself land safely in familiar territory. "But everyone thinks she's going to be in the Olympics someday." Mia finds it easier to talk about Cricket than herself—her sister's talent is so obvious, so concrete. She would get into Yale no problem if she promised to play for the Bulldogs.

Ronny tugs on his Santa beard as he processes this, and Mia blushes, because he's probably wishing he were interviewing the soccer star right now, not the bland older sister with straight A's and glowing recommendations but unassorted mush for talent. Mia is just a responsible hard worker who happens to be naturally gifted in STEM. And while Yale isn't known for accepting future middle management, Mia agreed to apply to the Ivy because her college counselor had suggested it. *Your scores are remarkable,* Ms. Donilon had said on more than one occasion. Her mother had been ecstatic at the prospect of Mia attending an Ivy League school, especially one with need-based tuition, which in their case would mean free.

"I have an older brother," Ronny says now, apropos of nothing as he stares out the window at a skateboarder weaving between cars. "He's gone now, and I miss him terribly, all the time, and you know why?"

"Because he's your brother?"

"Precisely!" Ronny booms, slamming his fist into the table as if Mia has just answered the hardest question on *Jeopardy!* His eyes are bright as he explains, "My brother instilled a faith and a confidence in me, and a love for me, that made me who I am today."

Mia nods and tries not to stare at the crumbs of blueberry scone trapped in his beard.

"What you're doing, Mia, with this chaperoning business all summer"—Ronny downs the last of his coffee like it's a much-needed shot of something far stronger—"there's nothing interesting about it, or exciting, or the least bit academically enriching."

Ronny's observation rings all too true, but his need to say it out loud feels like he's swatting her on the nose with a rolled-up newspaper. Shame on her for taking up his precious time with her flimsy ambition. Mia looks down at her lap and tells herself not to cry, not to fall apart under any condition. *Remember who you are,* her mother had said.

"But it's also selfless," Ronny says, tapping Mia's coffee cup with his own. "What you're doing for your sister demonstrates maturity. Taking care of your family, sacrificing your summer for their benefit—it's noble, and it's refreshing, and I'm very, very impressed."

MIA'S BIG WIN

Six months later, when it is technically spring but still feels unmistakably like winter, Mia shivers on her bed, still wearing her heavy coat, and opens the email that determines her fate. There he is: Handsome Dan. Yale's famous mascot, the Olde English bulldog, smiles at her through his many wrinkles next to the only word Mia needs to know: *Congratulations!*

Like Handsome Dan's professionally lit face, her future looks bright. When Mia shows her mom the email, Liz kisses the computer screen and they are too overjoyed to acknowledge that she is already late for her shift at Primo Bistro. Instead, Liz grabs her apron off the kitchen counter and tells Mia to come to the restaurant to celebrate.

"But you'll be working!" Mia says.

"But this can't wait!" Liz wraps her black apron around her waist and gives Mia one more hug. She is already ten minutes behind but too thrilled to care. Or just too Liz to care.

That night, when Mia and Cricket arrive at Primo Bistro, they are greeted by Lucia the owner, who announces to the entire restaurant that their very own Mia Lowe has just been accepted to Yale University. She then leads her waitstaff and guests in an enthusiastic round of applause that inspires Cricket to whistle and makes Mia want to die before Lucia finally seats them in the front window.

When servers and patrons swing by the table to offer their congratulations, it is the first time their well-wishes are directed at Mia, not Cricket, who struggles to sit still, overwhelmed with admiration for her sister and giddy about being out so late on a school night. Liz emerges from the kitchen with their favorite entrées, which they usually eat at home, reheated in the microwave and still in their plastic to-go containers.

"Chicken marsala for my baby," Liz says, placing the hot dish before Cricket. "And tonight's special—Timballo di Maccheroni—for my college girl!"

"This is so beautiful," Mia says, admiring the entrée. She knows from her own efforts in the kitchen just how complex this dish is to make—all the steps and patience required to make such different flavors and disparate textures sing together.

"It tastes even better like this," Cricket says, using her fingers to lower a ribbon of pasta into her mouth. "Eating it here, I mean."

Lucia approaches the table with five small plates balanced on her forearms, up to her elbows. "This is how I express my love," she says, setting down each indulgence as the Lowes stare, agape. The honey-browned focaccia. The shrimp scampi. Roasted carrots and beets stacked like a game of Jenga. The award-winning pot roast. The mouth-watering bluefish.

"Save room for dessert," Lucia says, planting a kiss on Mia's cheek before rushing back to the host stand to answer the phone.

"This is amazing," Cricket says to Mia, reaching across the table to grab a hunk of focaccia. "You're amazing."

Mia grins as she spears a macaroni. For the first time in her life, she considers this possibility—that she, too, is amazing. Going to Yale is a big deal for anyone, but Mia's acceptance feels like a win for everyone—her mom and sister, the whole home team.

"So Coach taught me how to visualize," Cricket says before taking several deep gulps of water. "And I've been doing it, and I visualized you getting into Yale weeks ago, so I'm going to keep visualizing, and that way our lives will always be totally awesome."

"Totally awesome?" Mia repeats, chuckling as she folds her napkin on her lap. Cricket nods, empowered by her prophecy. Lucia arrives at their table and hands Mia an envelope from the older couple at table 10 who just left. Inside is a hundred–dollar bill. Lucia beams as she explains, "They said to tell you, 'Go Bulldogs!' "

"Oh my God, see? I told you!" Cricket says, bouncing in her seat. "Totally awesome!" She is kinetic energy in kid form, her sister, but on a night like tonight, Mia can't help but believe it, too. Their lives will always be totally awesome.

FAMILY MVP

The morning the three Lowes plan on driving the four hours to Yale, Liz asks Mia if she'd mind taking the bus instead.

"Today?" Mia manages.

"I'm really sorry but Dr. Green called and she has emergency back-to-back root canals," Liz explains. "So now I have to call all of her scheduled patients who are going to be so upset and—"

"I can't go, either," Cricket says through a mouthful of toast. Ignoring Mia's wilting soul, she adds, "Sitting for that long is so bad for circulation and preseason starts next week."

"What about my stuff?" Mia asks, pointing to the six green storage bins she has already packed, labeled, and staged by the front door. She swallows hard, too shocked to think beyond logistics. "Would they let me bring all of those on the bus?"

"Maybe you could drop me off at work early?" Liz suggests. "Then you drive down to New Haven in my car, unload your stuff, and then drive back here, and then take the bus back down there?"

Before Mia can formulate a response, or at least a snarky remark about a four-hour car ride turning into twelve, Cricket volunteers to load Mia's bins to make sure they fit.

"They fit," Mia says flatly, watching her younger but now significantly taller sister deadlift a green container up over her head and kick open the front door. "I already measured—four go in the trunk and two go in the back seat."

When Cricket returns moments later, she's shaking her head. "Don't get mad at me, but there's no way they all fit."

"Of course they do."

"No, they don't."

Too angry to argue, Mia storms past Cricket to show her what a little spatial reasoning can do. She should have known a weekend devoted to her college departure—not an expedition in the name of soccer—would be an impossible sacrifice for her mother and sister. Also, screw the emergency root canals, and all those patients with all their teeth who have ruined her plans for the weekend: a family jog in East Rock Park, pizza at Pepes, a ghost tour in Grove Street Cemetery. Mia was going to make the trek so fun that her mother and sister would be excited to visit regularly. Now they aren't bothering to come at all.

Mia stomps off the front porch, down the stairs, and into the driveway, where she confronts Liz's car but can't get in. "It's locked!" she calls out, fury bubbling in the pit of her stomach. Peering through the window, she adds, "And the bin isn't even in here, Cricket!"

"Wrong car," Liz says, floating onto the porch and into view. She nods straight ahead to the silver minivan parked across the street.

"A rental?" Mia asks, her blood pressure skyrocketing as she estimates this unforeseen expense. She still does her mother's accounting. "What's wrong with your car?"

"Nothing," Liz says dismissively, taking her time walking down the steps.

Cricket, who has always best expressed herself through physical spectacle, leaps off the front porch, skipping the stairs altogether, holds out a key fob like a wand and incants, "Open Sesa-Mia!"

The minivan door slides open.

"It's yours," Liz says, her sled-dog eyes sparkling. She is thirty-six now but has retained an air of youthful mischievousness.

"She got it for you!" Cricket shouts, unable to contain herself. "Mom got you your own momvan! A mini-Mia-van! A mama-Mia-minivan!"

"Wait, what?" Mia asks, unable to discern the truth from the chaos of the moment.

"Listen to me," Liz says, walking toward Mia. "I wouldn't miss dropping you off at college for all the emergency root canals in the world." She wraps her arms around her firstborn daughter, who decides to laugh because crying would be too embarrassing.

"What about your legs?" Mia asks, turning to Cricket.

"What about 'em?" Cricket shouts with her feet over her head. She is mid-cartwheel in the middle of the street. "We're taking the train back, so I can walk around as much as I want."

"Oh cool," Mia says, forcing herself to keep smiling. Already, she can feel the onset of Lowe family FOMO, and she hasn't even left yet.

But then her mom's arm cinches around her shoulder. "What am I going to do without you?" Liz asks, and Mia doesn't have to force the grin that spreads to her eyes. It's a fair question.

"I helped Mom make a playlist for the drive," Cricket volunteers, now cranking out push-ups in rapid succession.

"Ask me what I titled the playlist," Liz says.

"What did you title the playlist?" Mia asks obediently.

"The only thing that makes sense," Liz says, squeezing her tight. "Family MVP."

NEW HAVEN

Yale is beautiful in the fall. The professors are brilliant. The assigned reading is fascinating. And, as Mia tells Liz after her first full day on campus, not only are the meals insanely good but every bite tastes especially transcendent when enjoyed in the high-ceilinged and deeply historied dining halls.

Every time she leaves her dorm room in Silliman College, Mia feels like she's stumbling into the opening number of a musical about the ideal learning environment. Or growing up. Or Connecticut foliage and Gothic architecture.

And yet, two weeks into her undergraduate career, Mia is convinced she should go home. Texting with her mom between classes and talking each night on Liz's drive back from Primo Bistro, Mia knows her time would be better spent ferrying Cricket to school and soccer so Liz could head straight from one job to the other. Instead of contributing directly to her family's success, Mia's days on campus feel like sitting in a warm bath, navel gazing between classes, meals, and her part-time job in the archival library. It's so solitary—*so easy*—it feels wrong.

During office hours, Mia's academic adviser insists her homesickness is normal. "You've never been on your own before," Dr. Peters says. "Every first-year grapples with living independently, but trust me, you'll settle in and realize you belong here." Mia fingers the moth hole on the hem of her sweater. She's too self-conscious to disagree with Dr. Peters, but the professor has misdiagnosed her.

Rather than a maiden voyage into independent living, college feels like reattaching the long-discarded training wheels of Mia's youth—hot dinners she doesn't need to shop for, prep, or cook; bathrooms she never has to clean; countless free hours to read or mull over homework that isn't due for a week. She can physically and academically meander in whichever direction she pleases because here at college, her wants are the only wants that matter. The design of the curriculum is so intensely focused on each student's individual performance that it strikes Mia as a breeding ground for narcissism.

"I'm here to connect with people I might not otherwise meet," another first-year from Silliman says over dinner. His name is Landon and, from the first day of the semester up until exactly now, he has come across as the fourth-generation legacy from Andover that he is. But now, touched by this sentiment, Mia smiles at Landon, grateful for the reminder that engaging her intellectually-curious peers could and should be one of the most enriching pieces of college.

With a newfound fondness, Mia watches Landon dip a wedge of baguette into his crock of French onion soup. "Look, education as we know it is dead," Landon says, scooping up a glob of Gruyère while simultaneously puncturing the hope in Mia's chest. "We're all just here to expand our networks."

"Gross," balks Nell, Mia's roommate, from across the table. She half-jokingly accuses Landon of being part of the problem while allowing her eyes to linger on his mouth. The two of them hooked up last weekend and now there's a detectable crackle of flirtation in their public discourse.

"What do you think, Mia?" Nell prods. "Is college just a four-year tutorial in douchebaggery?"

Mia stirs her tea in contemplative circles, thinking of the four students in her eighteen-person seminar who showed up to class this morning still reeking of whiskey. One of those students shares a surname with the looming biology tower, and another is known for speeding through campus in a matte black Range Rover with the vanity plate SUCKIT. When the inebriated party of four were kicked out five minutes into class, none of them seemed concerned. In fact, they were overjoyed by the professor's instruction to go sleep it off.

"I think it should be easier to get in and harder once you're here," Mia says. "And I think everyone should have to volunteer off-campus or be held accountable for something other than their own transcripts."

"Really?" Nell asks, surprised. "That sounds a touch like socialism."

"Of course we do stuff outside of class," Landon says indignantly, pushing away his empty crock. "Otherwise, we wouldn't have gotten in."

"And I think we should have to clean our own bathrooms," Mia adds, ignoring Landon's point and instead thinking of the knotted clumps of hair Nell leaves on the wall of their shower.

"You're an odd duck," Landon says, tilting his head as if appraising Mia for the first time. And with that, he and Nell stand up to clear their places, leaving Mia alone with her thoughts. She doesn't mind. Rather, Mia idles there for another thirty minutes because she is plagued by so much burdensome free time.

Three nights a week, Mia works in the often-forgotten archival library, which knowing students frequent for handsy make-out sessions. Sitting behind the checkout desk, Mia gets paid to do her homework during these shifts—and to look the other way when a couple emerges from the stacks with swollen lips and flushed cheeks.

Except for the sporadic moans and gasps emanating from the back wall, Mia relishes the peace of the library. At home, her sister is a clomping, yelling, singing, chewing, ranting human sound machine permanently set to shuffle. Cricket needs the TV on to do homework, her pregame playlist blasting in the car before soccer, a podcast to fall asleep, and a P!nk song to destroy in the shower.

It took enrolling at a school with fifteen thousand strangers for Mia to find her sanctuary. Here, in the underutilized archival library, Mia can concentrate without interference and becomes even more efficient with her time. For the past two hours, she has read Dublin headlines for her world history seminar without a single interruption. The professor had emphasized the use of primary sources, requiring a minimum of five for their upcoming paper. But Mia enjoys the elite access to the periodicals and has skimmed at least fifteen different papers from the period.

After completing her research for class, Mia still has time to kill before her shift ends. She stares at the magnifying glass on the computer screen. Delving into a foreign past inspires Mia to research a far more local subject: her mother. If primary sources can ground Mia in 1919 Dublin, what color will they provide of Elizabeth Lowe from Warren High School in 1999?

Mia types her mother's name into the database's search bar.

It begins as a hopeful expedition to see photos of Liz at Mia's current age and read up on her storied, if blunted, soccer career. She unceremoniously taps Return with her pinky.

The documentation propagates immediately. All the could-haves and should-haves and would-have-beens if not for Mia. The proof is right here, pages of her mother's life before Mia arrived to ruin it all. Headlines compete for her attention but nothing pulls in Mia like her mother's young, jubilant face, so she clicks on the first image that pops up, attached to an article from the *Richmond Times-Dispatch*. She zooms in and leans forward to inspect the slightly blurred and discolored photograph from the late nineties.

There is her mom, front and center and grinning behind a state championship trophy, surrounded by her teammates. Mia doesn't realize she's beaming as she stares at the monitor, already blindly feeling around for her phone to send a screenshot of the image to her mom and Cricket. The photo is too fuzzy so she zooms out again when suddenly her stomach constricts.

It's him.

Standing at the far edge of the photo with two other men, his hands tucked professionally behind his back, is the mustachioed man Mia instantly recognizes as her father. The caption beneath the photograph reveals his other identity: Coach Richard Quimby.

Just as it took living among fifteen thousand strangers for Mia to find a few hours of silence, it required moving several states away from her family for Mia to learn her mother's secret. There in the archival library, Mia stumbles upon the truth of her existence, and it's too late to unsee how it all started because there he is.

Mia takes a long, slow inhale and counts to four in her mother's voice. During the morning training sessions of her childhood, Liz taught Mia how to breathe through any minor injury she incurred on the beach—slicing her foot on a rock, tweaking her ankle, breaking a fall with her face. Mia exhales and waits to feel the sharp agony subside. When it doesn't, when the throbbing in her head and gut persists, she inhales and counts to four again, her mind reeling for an answer that doesn't come.

Her father was her mother's high school soccer coach.

Mia shouldn't be here. Or rather, if the world were a better place, she wouldn't be here.

Mia exes out of the state championship photo. The headlines celebrating her mother's talent stare back at her, but she is no longer interested. Liz Lowe, the once-promising soccer player, no longer fascinates Mia. Instead, she clicks on the Search bar and types "Richard Quimby + Warren High School Soccer Coach." This time, her pinky hovers over the Return key. She knows enough to fear what she's about to learn, and still, it's much worse:

> *High School Senior Alleges Sexual Relationship with Soccer Coach*
>
> *Former Players Say Warren High School Ignored Sex Abuse Allegations*
>
> *Three Women Accuse Soccer Coach of Inappropriate Conduct*

It goes on for pages. The allegations, the lawsuits, transcripts of the cases that traveled all the way to the state supreme court. After the third page, Mia puts her head down on the desk, her hand still gripping the mouse, ready to click on another disturbing article, but her head is about to explode and her jaw is set, expecting to vomit. She closes her eyes. The reminder to breathe comes in her mother's voice.

Her mother.

Liz has always pitched her relationship with Q as a tragic love story, but Mia now understands it's all a lie her mother has been telling herself and selling her daughters for nearly twenty years. It's an actual crime. Richard Quimby should be in jail.

Mia lifts the mouse in her hand and slams it against its pad as hard as she can. Her mother let that creep into their house, she'd encouraged Mia to spend time with him, fall in love with him, imagine a future with him as her father. How delusional must her mother have been when she was clearly just a number to Richard Quimby, a malignant tumor of a human who now must be either in hiding, in prison, or deceased.

Mia decides it doesn't matter. He was a predator then, so he's dead to her now. She vows she will never search his name again, never look for him, never wonder "what if" about a grown man who preyed upon young girls and derailed countless lives.

The library closes at ten p.m., but Mia can't bring herself to move until half past eleven. She makes sure to erase her search history before shutting down the computer, turning off the overhead lights, and locking the doors. Mia usually clutches a small bottle of pepper spray when she crosses campus alone in the dark, but tonight she dares any man to emerge from the shadows and try her. She even imagines it, how she will scratch out his eyes, use her teeth if she needs to. She has worked too hard and come too far to allow any man to change the course of her life. Even if it kills her, she will not be a victim.

And here they come now.

A whole group of stumbling silhouettes. Drunk men, goofy and gangly and fearless.

She will take them all if they so much as whistle at her.

"Mia!" someone shouts from the pack. It's Nell, staggering toward Mia with the ambulatory finesse of a newborn giraffe. Under a streetlamp, Landon's grinning face floats behind Nell's, along with a few other familiars from Silliman. "You're coming with us," Nell says, linking arms with Mia and spinning her back in the direction from which she came. "We're not taking no for an answer."

In the past, Mia has pitied her classmates for wasting precious time humiliating themselves after drinking too much, but who is she to decide what's worthwhile in college when her very existence is not only mortifying but criminal? She is done being her mother's best friend and MVP. From now on, Mia Lowe is just a regular college student and it's Saturday night.

Landon offers her the plastic Poland Springs water bottle filled with brown liquor that burns as she takes it down. She resists the urge to say that Poland Springs is in Maine, not far from where she grew up. None of it matters. She's here now. Mia tilts the plastic bottle up toward the sky. She drinks with the abandon of someone who has long denied her own thirst.

Landon reaches out for the bottle and they both laugh because it's empty. Mia is at Yale because she is smart and makes good decisions—better decisions than her mother ever made. She understands choices and consequences, can decipher wrong from right, and, starting now, she is here to connect with other people.

By midterms, Mia is an expert at so-called independent living. College is far more fun—and debauched and liberating and excruciating and enlightening—than she could have gleaned from reading any number of primary sources in the archival library. When she's out, Mia ignores her mom's calls and her sister's texts. Instead, she stays up late with Nell, Landon, and their burgeoning group of friends, roaming parties until someone demands they go to Yorkside for slices.

It's there, eight of them impossibly smushed in a booth, that opportunities are passed around like paper napkins from the metal dispenser at the end of the table. Internships in New York and spring break at someone's aunt's house on Tortola and a group study session tomorrow night on the lower level of Bass with a borrowed copy of the exam.

Mia bites into her pizza and says hell yes to all of it. She has four years to capitalize on this opportunity. These are her shots to take and her glory to seize. She nods along to everything that her mom was forced to turn down as a result of her own foolishness. Because Mia is not her mom and she is not the sum result of her mother's mistakes.

She is Mia fucking Lowe. When she orders a round of tequila shots for the table, she understands this is how an intelligent, capable woman of limited means expands and strengthens her networks. This is how she fits into this booth with Nell and Landon and everybody else, giggling as they lick salt and approval off each other's open palms.

A GOOD NIGHT IN TIPS

Home for the summer, Mia hears the brakes screech in the driveway and a car door slam just after midnight. She turns off the reading light next to the pink floral couch and sneaks into her childhood bedroom to avoid seeing her mom. It's the same thing she's done every night for the past week since she returned to Victory.

The misadventures of Mia's first year of college already seem like a different life, a hazy dream sequence on some cutting-room floor. But that one grainy image from the archival library still nags at her with unparalleled clarity. Behind Mia's closed eyes, she sees her mother in that high school photograph, smiling a state championship smile with a growing secret in her body.

Every day, Mia considers asking Liz about Q—or rather confessing what she now knows about their relationship—but instead, she finds herself walking out of the room. In the past, Liz has always referred to Q as her "great love" and "the one who got away." It's enough to make Mia sick.

Thankfully, circumventing her mom is just one of many activities keeping Mia busy. She threads her own marketing internship through Cricket's dizzying summer soccer schedule, which includes her high school, club, and Youth National Team obligations. Mia quickly reestablishes herself as Cricket's stay-at-home parent, although they are barely home. Instead, Mia and Cricket gas up the momvan and drive up and down the East Coast for tournaments.

After a year apart, it's the same but different between the sisters. Their days, as ever, revolve around Cricket, but the keeper has evolved in her chauffeur's absence. "Thank you for doing this," Cricket always says as they buckle up for another road trip. She is keenly aware of how much she missed Mia while she was away at school. "The drives are only fun with you," she confesses. "You're the only person I can spend so much time with, you know?"

Mia nods, because she does know, even though she doesn't feel the same way. The most exciting development of this summer—besides Cricket's dramatic uptick in gratitude—is that Mia now has a serious boyfriend. Ben is someone Mia can spend a lot of time with, which she's done since February, when Landon paired them up late one night for a round of beer pong. Despite the sloshy introduction in the dingy frat house basement, Ben's quiet maturity—a rising senior majoring in microbiology—rattled Mia almost instantly.

"Are you comfortable with this?" he'd asked, holding up a red Solo cup.

"With winning?" Mia responded, feeling that particular kind of clever that arrives after the third drink.

"Sharing the same cups, I mean," Ben clarified. "Because I can drink from a separate set if you're concerned about the spread of virals."

It was the most romantic thing anyone had ever said to her. She'd kissed him on the spot and they'd gone on to win the next two games, sharing the same red cups.

The only downside to dating Ben is that he's on the other side of the country for the summer. Unlike Landon, who has made his parents' Nantucket cottage the headquarters for his online poker LLC, Ben is spending his last college summer interning for the Doctors Without Borders office in Oakland, California. His absence but frequent Face-

Times are the trickiest but also the most thrilling part of Mia's summer juggling act. Ben's texts throughout the day make her ache for the privacy and freedom of her life on campus. Cricket found out about him when he called while they were driving to Connecticut, but Mia has intentionally and successfully kept Ben a secret from her mom.

The car door slams, the house keys jingle, and the doorknob squeaks. "Guess what I have!" Liz shouts, bursting into Mia's dark bedroom with a pungent gust of garlic and onions. She is backlit by the hallway light, her blond bun illuminated like a thick halo and three distinct paper rectangles in her hand.

"Tickets?" Mia guesses. She sits up and tries to remember which bands she saw were coming to Portland but can't imagine who would have her mother this animated.

"Yes, tickets!" Liz shouts, dancing maniacally. "But tickets to what?"

Mia scrunches her eyebrows as her mom shimmies in her doorway. "Disney World?"

"Try again!" Liz trills before spinning on her toes and floating down the hallway. "Let's wake up Cricket!"

Mia follows and watches her sister's eyes go from slits to saucers. "Are they real?" Cricket asks, jumping out of bed to examine the tickets. Her new pajama pants already look a little short after Cricket's second insane growth spurt in May. "Are these really real?"

Liz nods vigorously. "I waited on these two guys and I guess they were bored of each other because—"

Mia and Cricket roll their eyes at each other. Their mother blames "boredom" for crazy moments at Primo Bistro when what really happened—as has happened multiple times in the past—is that one or both men fell in love with Liz. While on the clock and wearing her black server's apron, their mom has been proposed to not once but twice.

"Anyway," Liz continues, "I ended up telling them about you, Cricket, and then when they left, these tickets were on the table with a nice note—apparently they're high up in FIFA!"

"Can we go?" Cricket asks, turning the tickets over in her hand like bars of gold.

"I think we have to, don't we?" Liz starts her maniacal dancing again, and now Cricket joins her, and it's like an uncoordinated octopus has taken over the room.

"Where are we going?" Mia asks.

"The World Cup!" Cricket shouts, waving the tickets in the air. "The World freakin' Cup!"

QUARTER-FINALS

With three expedited passports, two connecting flights, and a backlog of good luck, Liz Lowe has forever changed the trajectory of her daughters' lives. From now on, Mia and Cricket will understand that anything is possible. No one from home will believe what they've done or what they're currently doing, which is driving through the streets of Paris before sunrise. They are here to cheer on the U.S. Women's National Team against the home team of France.

From the pitch black of the back seat, Liz holds up her phone screen to the cabdriver, who takes them to the only available bed in the only hostel with what seems to be the only vacancy left in the city. Mia almost asks Cricket to pinch her, to prove it's real, this is really happening— *they're in Paris!*—but decides against it. She'd rather see what happens next, even if it's only in her mind. Besides, her little sister is already asleep again, comfortably slumped against Mia's shoulder.

Yesterday morning, they'd taken a bus from Portland to Boston, a small plane from Boston to New York, and then a big plane from JFK to CDG, where they have arrived at two a.m. on the day of the game that justifies this trip they can't afford. They will fly out the following night so Liz doesn't have to miss more work, but the breakneck schedule doesn't intimidate them—not here, not now, because no one anticipated this for them.

Collapsing into their shared hostel bed just before dawn, they are giddy with disbelief and the infinite possibilities that ride shotgun to hope. The drunk German boys abusing their guitars down the hall do not bother the Lowes. The thin mattress with scratchy sheets and questionable stains cannot dampen their euphoria.

Nor can the distinct sound of retching that wakes them five hours later. Just a couple of inches of plaster separate their pillows from the row of urinals in the communal bathroom. The unframed print of the Seine hanging above their bed shakes with yet another toilet flush.

"Perfect timing," Liz says, yawning cheerfully. She kicks the sheet off the bed and hums as she gets dressed. Mia watches her mother through slitted eyes and remembers this is not Liz's first time at a World Cup game: She was at the Rose Bowl in 1999 with her high school soccer teammates and with—

Mia snaps the hairband on her wrist to shake off the thought. She deserves to enjoy this day. Q isn't here and Q doesn't matter. Neither do her mother's past decisions. Mia is in Paris for the first time in her life and she will savor every second.

Pulling over her head the white linen dress she wears every Fourth of July, Liz ties one of her old red game ribbons around her high bun. Both girls watch their mother apply ruby red lipstick, using the camera lens of her phone as a mirror since the puking in the communal bathroom has continued, now with different voices cursing in German but still at steady intervals.

"Can I have some?" Cricket asks.

Liz shakes her head. "You're too young for makeup."

"What about me?" tries Mia.

"You're too—this lipstick got me pregnant when I was your age—no, younger, actually."

"Mom!" Cricket squirms, embarrassed by the thought of her mom's sex life. Mia bites the inside of her bottom lip so she doesn't ruin the mood.

"Okay, I'll tell you what," Liz says, blotting her lips with the back of her hand. "We'll compromise."

Mia sits down on the bed beside her mother, closes her eyes, and puckers, but instead of painting her daughter's mouth, Liz draws a heart on Mia's cheek.

"What are you—"

"Trust me," Liz says.

"Oooh, me next!" Cricket chirps over her mother's shoulder. "That's perfect!"

At the Parc des Princes Stadium, the Lowe women keep close as they move through the metal detectors, the bag checks, and the ticket collectors. Amid the ear-piercing screams of French and American fans alike, they find their seats, which are right at center field and just twenty rows back. Cricket squeals as both teams jog onto the field for warm-ups. "We're so close I can see Alex Morgan's blue fingernails!" The team benches face them from across the pitch, and so Cricket can study every single French and U.S. player on and off the field, especially when she uses Liz's phone to zoom in until their faces turn granular.

Five minutes before the game begins, the teams leave the field and return to their locker rooms for last-minute pep talks and superstitious pregame rituals. In the stands, Cricket stares at one of the empty goals, mesmerized by something Mia cannot see. The air in the stadium is already changing, the barometric pressure rapidly dropping before the hurricane that is the match.

"Someday," Cricket says, hypnotized by the swirling atmosphere, "I'm going to play here."

"Of course you will," Liz says, throwing an arm around her younger daughter. "And when that happens, can I ask you a big favor?"

Mia looks over with curiosity. Their mother rarely asks anything of Cricket.

"When you're a famous soccer star," Liz says, "can you make sure we get the very best seats to all your games? Like, seats as good as these?"

"Front row, every time," Cricket beams, sticking out her hand for her mother to shake. It's a deal. She is well on her way to becoming a professional player—her mother tells her so all the time, and even her club soccer coach offered the same prediction last month, after Cricket made the U-16 Youth National Team roster.

A vendor walks by selling cotton candy. Liz digs into her wallet for euros and buys three sticks of spun sugar. Mia gawks as her mother hands over the crumpled bills. "When in Paris!" Liz declares, reading her daughter's mind. "Besides, other people paid fourteen thousand dollars for their tickets and we got ours for free!"

Mia takes an oversize chomp of her overpriced cotton candy. She resists mentioning the credit card Liz opened to pay for their flights and reminds herself that her mother's financials are not her problem. As she learned this past year in college, Mia Lowe is only responsible for Mia Lowe, and right now, Mia Lowe is in Paris watching the World Cup Quarter-Final. Ben and Landon and Nell have all expressed their envy in the group text.

Holding up her phone, Liz flips the camera to selfie mode. "Lean in, girls." On each daughter's cheek, a ruby red heart competes with Liz's Siberian blues for the lens's attention. Mia kisses Cricket's cheek, as her sister lifts her chin and smiles proudly for the photo.

Since her return home, Mia has found herself guiding Cricket through the murk of early adolescence with a wisdom she didn't know she'd accrued, like scraping the change from the bottom of her purse only to discover she has a stockpile of serviceable cash. On car rides to and from soccer, Cricket has asked why her friends are obsessed with boys and she isn't, and why their mom hasn't found someone new, and why anyone would wear a pad instead of a tampon during a soccer game if they didn't have a gun to their head, and why Mia is dating Ben when Cricket hasn't even vetted the guy. It's been an entertaining and surprisingly fun summer for Mia, even if she has kept the knowledge of Q to herself—or, rather, it's been a great summer only because she has kept Q to herself and her mother at arm's length.

"It's starting!" Cricket squeals, hopping on her tiptoes.

As the players jog out from the tunnel and take the field, the stadium feels ready to ignite. More than forty-five thousand fans rise to their feet, desperate for their team to win and hungry to see where the story goes from here. For reasons beyond the pitch, this quarter-final game between France and the United States boils with the intensity of a final match.

Two days earlier, the president of the United States tweeted three times at the purple-haired American forward, goading her to engage, provoking her when she needed to focus. Megan Rapinoe did not respond to him then but delivers her answer now, in the form of a free kick she converts into a goal, just five minutes into the match. She runs to the corner of the field and transforms into Lady Liberty, a moment that makes her an icon forever.

Mia looks over to see her mother wipe tears off her face as she screams her approval. Cricket throws her arms around both of them, about to combust from the thrill of it all. The Jumbotron finds them just then, and for a moment they are famous together, the three Lowe women who have traveled all the way from Victory, Maine, on the wings of Liz's smile to witness greatness in person, history in the making.

That day, the Americans prevail over France, 2–1, knocking the host country out of the tournament and advancing the United States to the semifinal. Mia, Cricket, and Liz join the thousands of fans in celebration and then book it directly to the airport where they manage to just barely make it to their gate. Boarding the plane, the three Lowes look over their shoulders as a crew member locks the plane door behind them and it feels like a portal shutting, like they've just lost access to Narnia.

Four hours into the flight back home, the main cabin lights are off, the attendants are elsewhere, Cricket's asleep with her head against the window, and there's a long enough lull in row 33 that Mia almost wills herself to speak the words burning on her tongue. She wants to release the secret thumping in her chest.

"Did you have fun?" her mother asks, interrupting her thoughts.

"That was amazing," says Mia from her aisle seat. "Like, truly unbelievable."

Sitting between her daughters, Liz struggles to origami her long legs in the middle seat. She spools a dark ringlet of Mia's hair around her own finger before pulling Mia's head onto her shoulder. Mia doesn't fight it.

"So how serious is this boyfriend?" Liz whispers.

Mia leans forward and glares at her sleeping sister, who clearly betrayed her confidence. "I don't know," she says. "But I like him."

"He'll be a senior?"

"Mm-hm."

"And that's okay?" Liz's voice strains as it climbs an octave. "He's not too old for you? Because at that age, some guys will really pressure you and—"

"Seriously?" Mia asks, barely suppressing a torrent of sudden rage.

"Never mind, sorry," Liz says, putting her hands up to imply no foul. She redirects her attention to Cricket, who has conveniently just woken up. "Hey, Cricky, was today the best day of your life?"

The gangly fourteen-year-old picks up the World Cup program she'd tucked into her seat pocket. "For now."

Knees pressing into the seat in front of her, Cricket traces the face of each player in the U.S. team photo with her finger. She is excited to go home: back to her Stallions teammates and her upcoming training camp with the Under-16 Women's Youth National Team.

"It was the best day of my life so far," Cricket says after several moments of consideration. "But not forever." Mia and her mother exchange amused looks. "Because someday I'm going to be the goalkeeper for the National Team," Cricket says quietly. Mia strains to hear her sister over the plane's engine. "And we're going to win the World Cup, and then *that* will be the best day of my life."

"Something to drink?" a flight attendant asks, holding out cocktail napkins. When Liz asks for a glass of red wine, Mia asks for the same. Her mom is clearly surprised but says nothing, and Cricket is too busy quoting her Stallions coach to notice.

From her aisle seat, Mia half-listens to Cricket recite the supposed MAP to excellent goalkeeping. She misses Ben. And parties. And the way her room remains just how she left it when she comes back from class, never pilfered through by little sister paws.

But it's not only that she misses her life at college—she misses her mom. That's it. That's what it is. Mia downs her plastic cup of wine in three deep glugs. She misses her mom, who is sitting right next to her, their arms touching on their shared armrest, but this huge lie cratered between them, it's too much, and it's not fair, and it's—

"I know Q was your coach," Mia confesses, lifting up her tray table so she can turn to face her mother.

"Huh?" Cricket asks, leaning forward.

Mia stares at Liz, who stares straight ahead, either strategizing or recovering from the blindside. In Liz's stunned silence, Mia tells Cricket, "Our dad was Mom's high school soccer coach—like, when she was in high school."

"What?" Cricket makes a face that Mia has only seen once before and that was yesterday, when she learned what escargot was.

"Mia—" their mother tries.

"You should have told us," Mia says, energized by molten anger. "The so-called love of your life was a fucking predator."

"Language!" Liz hisses. "Where is this coming from?"

"I found out at school," Mia says. "In the fall."

"Mia—" Liz tries.

"I searched your name and saw Q in a team photo."

"Okay," Liz says, looking down and spreading her long fingers on her lap. "Okay. Wow. Let me just—" Liz snaps the hairband on her wrist and closes her eyes. Mia and Cricket watch her four-count inhale and wait for the exhale. The Lowe family reset. "Okay," Liz says, taking a small, slow sip of wine. "What do you want to know?"

MOMFESSION

"What did your teammates do?" Cricket asks, but Liz shakes her head to dismiss the question. There are many places to begin, but her teammates' reaction—their collective excommunication—isn't where Liz wants to start, and this is her story. She brings her hands together because what is a prayer if not a concentrated plea for help. Beyond the plane's window, the dark horizon stretches across the Atlantic and into the unknown.

"As I've told you before," Liz says, her eyes still closed, "Mia was conceived the night of the 1999 Women's World Cup and—"

"Did you think about an abortion?" Mia interrupts. It's a question she's had since seventh-grade health class, when the teacher referred to abortions in a lesson called "Family Planning." Mia has always wondered where she'd be if her mom had gone that route—would she be with another family right now? Would she be at all?

Liz nods. "I did. Of course I did—I had signed with UCLA, and Q was—it was complicated. And my parents told me I'd be on my own with a baby."

"So you gave up everything to have Mia," Cricket says, cobbling together the facts.

"I loved Q so much," Liz deflects, "and I knew I was going to love Mia even more than I loved him, because she would be the best of both of us."

"But how'd you fall in love with your soccer coach?" Cricket asks, her lips curled back in fear. It seems to her that love must be some kind of airborne disease you could catch just about anywhere, from anyone, and she does not want to fall in love with any of her coaches, ever.

"Well, he was a very good coach," Liz jokes, hailing the flight attendant for another glass of wine.

"He should be in jail," Mia growls. "He ruined your life."

"Oh, Mia," Liz whispers under her breath. "I was in love with him. It was consensual."

"But you were underage," Mia points out. "And you weren't the only one." Mia thinks of those pages on the internet, all those women coming forward, confronting society's scrutiny by telling the truth.

"I learned about the others much later on," Liz confesses. "At the time, I believed we were soulmates." She sighs, resigned to her own ignorance. "That, of course, proved to be wrong." The flight attendant hands her a tiny screw-top bottle and Liz refills her own cup. "He was sick, in more ways than one, not that it excuses his behavior."

"Sick how?" Cricket asks.

Liz refolds her legs and turns to Mia. "Remember the summer he came to visit?"

Mia nods.

"So he shows up, tells me he's told his wife about me, and that he wants to move up here, and start all over. With me."

"And you said yes."

"I said, 'Let's try it,'" Liz says with assertiveness. "We talked it over that first day, after he showed up on the porch, and it seemed promising, and we were so happy that summer." She tilts her head and pierces Mia with those ice-blue eyes. "You were so happy that summer."

Mia can see him now, Q driving her home from the fancy plant store in Kennebunkport, the shared Mexican Coke between them. The knowing she'd felt at the time. The understanding that he was the piece they'd been missing, but he'd found them. They could finally be a family.

"And then he left," Mia says, a detached coldness in her voice. "I guess he was excited to get back for preseason and start grooming the next star player."

"No, I kicked him out," Liz says, reaching up to open the air vent above her seat.

"No, he left," Mia argues. "And you spent weeks crying in bed."

"After I kicked him out," Liz insists.

"So why'd you kick him out?" Cricket asks, cutting through the tension.

"Because he was an alcoholic and I had no idea," Liz says, unfazed, delivering a blow Mia did not see coming. "It turns out he was drunk the whole summer, and even driving Mia around totally wasted while I was at work."

Mia's breath snags as she remembers all the silly road swerves. The loud bragging to strangers. Falling asleep in the middle of the day. Lumbering up the Skee-Ball lane.

"That last night he was here, we'd had a damn near perfect day," Liz continues. "We tucked Mia into bed and went downstairs, and I had this great idea to play a board game."

"But you hate board games," Cricket says.

"Now I do," Liz corrects her. "So I go to the basement and start looking around for them and I find them tucked away in the back of that narrow closet, next to the washer and dryer, and when I reach up to grab the stack, something falls, and it's an empty beer can."

"Uh-oh," Cricket says, captivated, and Mia looks at her sister with contempt. This is not just some scary story told in the dark at a sleepover; this is their family history.

"So then I decide to explore what's on top of all the board games, in a big sparkly gift bag I'd saved from Mia's fourth birthday, and it's filled with crushed beer cans."

"Silver," Mia says, suddenly remembering. "They were in his glove compartment and in the center console. He called them his hockey pucks."

"That's right," Liz says, sighing loudly. "His fucking hockey pucks." She surprises both daughters by wiping at her eyes, but the tears fall too fast to catch them. She hadn't even seemed upset until right then. "It was one thing that he was secretly drinking, that he was sick and had lied to me every which way, but then I realized that all those drives with you—I could have—you could have—" She shakes her head to finish the sentence, and then takes several long pulls from her water bottle. Mia watches her closely, sees her mother thinking of a different world in which they weren't together right now.

"Here's what I need you both to know," Liz says, clearing her throat. "When you're young—and I know I sound old starting out with that—but when you're young, it's impossible to understand the permanence of your decisions or their ripple effects. Because at the time, I truly thought I could do anything, and I thought your father was a good man, and I was very, very wrong."

"Neither of us is ever going to sleep with a coach," Mia says.

"Or an assistant coach," Cricket adds helpfully.

"Or a professor," Mia says. "Or anyone in a position of power over us."

"And that makes me happier than you could ever know," Liz says, covering Mia's fist with her hand. "But someday it might be trickier to avoid than it seems right now."

Mia scoffs as she looks at Cricket for camaraderie, but Cricket has turned her attention back to the view outside her window. Mia recognizes her sister's visualization face. Cricket isn't dwelling on their mother's poor choices, or Mia's fury, but on her own future.

Picking at a scab on her knee, Cricket swears to herself that wherever her father is, he will hear her name someday and learn that she has become a world-class soccer player. She will avenge her father's wrongdoing with her own stellar career.

Liz drinks the rest of her wine, exhausted but determined to push her point home. "Even though I didn't make great decisions—when I was younger than you are now, Mia, I think it's fair to point out—I'm grateful that I ended up in this life, with you two."

Once again, the flight attendant appears, rustling a fresh trash bag in the aisle. Liz reaches over Mia to dispose of her plastic wine cup. "He was a bad guy, and it was a terrible time, but without him, I wouldn't have you," she says, lifting Mia's chin and making her elder daughter look at her. "And I'm so proud to be your mom."

"What about me?" Cricket asks, abruptly leaning in from her window seat. "Aren't you proud of me?" She smiles sheepishly at Mia, as if waiting for her sister's response as much as their mom's.

Liz laughs and Mia, as always, softens at Cricket's raw desire to please her—the warm sensation of being worthy of impressing, especially by someone whose own talent has been deemed so impressive so publicly; her little sister's budding soccer career has been featured in *The Boston Globe* twice and in the *Portland Press Herald* too many times to count.

Maybe it's the altitude, but Mia feels her head lighten and her shoulders relax. It's like she's been clenching her teeth since that night in the archival library, pushing down on what needed to breathe free. No more dirty secrets. She and her mother are back on the same team.

Her father—a terrible, albeit sick, man—can be laid to rest. It's Mia's choice how to handle him from now on, and she decides to banish him from her mind. He's irrelevant. His chapter is closed. From now on, this is the epic adventure of the three Lowe women.

FIFTY VS. FIVE

I t's a chilly November morning but the sunlight streaming through the windshield is strong enough to warm Liz's hands on the steering wheel. Outside, the bare trees wave to her from either side of the street. After dropping Cricket off at her teammate's house, Liz imagines Sarah Compton's Toyota Highlander heading to Massachusetts stuffed with adolescent Stallions and feels overwhelmed with gratitude for her own empty car.

Liz opens her window, lets her left hand ride the breeze. The town is still sleeping and Liz has a whole hour to herself before she's expected at the dental office. Cricket and Mia are both gone, busy living their own lives.

She is free. Free to dillydally. Free to daydream about the coffee shop in five blocks, the hot barista who flirts with her no matter the line. Liz wonders if it's time to start dating again. She finally trusts herself to make good romantic choices and in just a few years, she'll be an empty nester. The thought alone is reason enough to spring for a latte and some eyelash batting, so Liz hangs a last-minute left.

The lack of traffic is just one of several perks to getting up so early on a Saturday for Cricket's budding soccer career. That's how Mia describes it—Cricket's "budding soccer career"—when she calls Liz on her walk across campus. It's the same reverence with which Cricket refers to Mia as "the Ivy Leaguer" rather than the college sophomore. They take each other so seriously, her girls.

Amused by the thought of them, Liz calls Mia. When she doesn't pick up, Liz turns on the radio and switches from Cricket's favorite station to her own. She sings along to a pop song of her youth, only to grimace when the DJ refers to it as a "throwback." She is thirty-seven years old but still feels seventeen, still feels like her life is just beginning, and it is because she believes this to be true. *Be positive,* she reminds herself, and *poof!* The clock on the center console turns from 7:10 a.m. to 7:11. Liz follows her own standard protocol and makes a wish.

It is still 7:11 when she eases off the gas pedal several feet before coming to a complete stop at a red light. Liz watches a stray cat with a sagging stomach labor across the intersection, a pregnant female alone in the world.

When the light turns green, Liz doesn't look left.

She doesn't see the SUV running the red.

The SUV barreling toward her.

The SUV going at least fifty miles per hour compared to Liz's five.

She doesn't register the SUV, but as the impact T-bones her car, she does see herself, pigtailed and knobby-kneed at summer camp, dribbling a soccer ball as the counselors call her Pelé, and scoring the game-winning goal of her high school state championship match, and being right there in the Rose Bowl stadium when the '99ers won and Brandi Chastain tore off her jersey, and then receiving Mia in her arms, the nurse saying her features were heavenly, and driving all night to see the Maine state sign that read THE WAY LIFE SHOULD BE, and Dr. Green in the Hannaford parking lot telling her everything would be okay, and then five-year-old Mia in her favorite yellow dress holding a ridiculously long-legged Cricket for the first time. Liz sees the three of them chasing down an ice-cream truck on the Eastern Promenade, and decorating Mia's dorm room at Yale, and hugging at the World Cup in Paris, and so she is spared the unspeakable horror that occurs just before her heart stops beating.

WAKE UP

Four states and four hours away, Mia sits in Sterling Memorial Library, no longer studying the PowerPoint slides on her computer screen because her mother is dead.

"I'm so sorry," the police officer says a second time, her voice wet but her words continuing to thud into the receiver like falling logs. They're too big and heavy and moving too fast for Mia to understand, even as they flatten her. Hovering outside her own body, Mia notices the sunlight pouring through the stained glass windows and a couple of juniors flirting at the next table. It isn't even noon and campus is already abuzz with stories in the process of being created, revised, mussed, and unzipped.

How is this real?

Maybe it isn't, Mia thinks as the officer reassures her it happened in a flash, too quickly for her mother to experience any pain. *Wake up,* she tells herself. *Wake up. Wake up. Wake up.*

In shock, Mia unplugs her laptop charger, packs up her stuff, walks out of the library to the parking garage at the top of Science Hill, and begins to drive home. Speeding on 91 North in Connecticut, she worries about skipping her biology test so close to the end of the semester and pulls over to email the professor—"going home for a family emergency"—before asking, blood pumping fast with denial, if she can sit for the exam later in the week.

Wake up Wake up Wake up.

In Massachusetts, the sports complex is, indeed, complex, with an extensive parking lot that snakes around twelve fields, all in use. Mia scans each pitch in search of royal blue jerseys and there they are: the Stallions. Her eyes find Cricket in her neon pink goalkeeper jersey between the posts, standing tall and tense with anticipation, even as the ball moves away from her and up the field. A truly great keeper, Cricket likes to say, must always be ready for a sudden change in direction.

Over the years, Mia has only exchanged routine hellos with Coach, whom she finds intense to the point of intimidating. But she walks right up to him now, seventeen minutes into the first half, and doesn't apologize for interrupting his yelling. Mia regurgitates the police officer's words verbatim so that she doesn't have to synthesize what the words actually mean.

Coach steps back with his hands on his hips. The wind picks up and sweeps Mia's hair across her face. The bright sun of this morning has turned anemic, and the thin residue of light that speckles the field threatens to disappear entirely. November in New England is a predictable slow dance with winter; one can expect the early frosts, the hours of daylight lost, and the familiar faces that disappear under wool hats, which is what Coach tells himself when he scans the bleachers in search of Liz and can't find her. She must be hiding under a new hat or cocooned beyond recognition in a scarf. Because she can't actually be dead.

Coach stares down at Mia and then out at the Stallions' goalkeeper, who just returned from a Youth National Team Camp and can't stop smiling when she talks about it. His eyes slide from Cricket back to Mia, who seems too collected, too poised. Her stoicism unnerves him until he realizes it isn't stoicism at all—it's the marbled sheen of raw shock.

Mia explains she just drove up from Connecticut because she thought Cricket needed to know. "But now that I'm here . . ." Her voice drifts off. It feels both critical and unthinkable to tell her sister that their mother is gone. Mia feels her car keys in her pocket and considers driving back to school. If she leaves now, she can protect Cricket from the thing she won't be able to undo, unknow, unlive.

"I can be there when you tell her," Coach says, wiping his eyes with the sleeve of his Stallions windbreaker. "If that's helpful—or I can—whatever you want." Mia looks away, afraid that his tears will elicit her own. This guy barely even knew her mom and he's losing it, and his reaction is making the impossible mutate into something otherwise. Something real. Something permanent. Something so horrific that she can't feel it yet, even as she senses it speeding toward her like an SUV going too fast.

Coach flags down a ref, who jogs over with lips pursed, head cocked with self-assurance because this guy has a reputation. But Coach doesn't yell or throw his arms in the air. This isn't about her recent offside call. Instead, Coach leans into the ref's shoulder with a hand-covered whisper. She pulls back, scans his stricken face, and blows her whistle for a time-out.

Mia stands with her back to the field so that Cricket can't see her, can't guess that she's here to ruin her life, even if she can only protect her for a few more moments. The ball is still in play, still consuming all the players' attention, so the ref blows her whistle again and sends both teams to their respective benches. Only Mia sees the ref steal a glance at Cricket, rubbernecking the wreck about to occur.

The Stallions' assistant coach directs the players to take a knee. Coach calls Cricket by name, beckons for her to join him away from the group. The opposing team looks over with interest as they squirt water into their mouths and catch their breath.

"Mia!" Cricket shouts, recognizing the familiar if inexplicable silhouette off to the side of the bleachers, halfway between the pitch and the parking lot. "Mia!" she calls again, piecing together that Mia has shown up as a surprise, and what a perfect day since she's playing so well.

Coach nods his release, and as Cricket runs toward Mia, they will both recall this moment in slow motion, the severing of their lives into before and after, mothered and orphaned.

"Mia!" Cricket shouts a third time, and Mia turns toward her sister, grief tattooed across her face like winter's shadow. She is the messenger of death. She is the ruiner of lives. She is familiar but unrecognizable, and so Cricket searches the stands, looking to their missing piece for an explanation, eyes seeking to disprove what her body already knows.

SOGGY BREAD BOWL

"As young as she was, your mother was more responsible than most parents," Clint says the next day upon entering the house. Behind his back, Cricket makes an obscene gesture while rolling her eyes at Mia. This is going to be a terrible morning after the worst possible day.

Clint the lawyer is married to Amy the dental hygienist, which is why he is working on a Sunday even though, as he has already pointed out multiple times, his office is technically closed, and even though Mia had tried to push this off until Monday. It was Clint who'd insisted. "Friends and family get me on my day of rest," he jokes, making himself comfortable in the living room. "And trust me, it's much better to get this part over with."

"For us or for you?" Cricket asks. She has never been one to hold back, especially with men. In her mind, they are all unnecessary—or almost all of them.

Coach is also here, enduring the legal logistics of hell because Cricket asked him if he would. He is the one man—aside from Steve Prefontaine—who serves a clear purpose in Cricket's world. His presence lends a sense of security to this nightmare, an emotional anchoring as Cricket's entire life vanishes before her eyes.

But Clint sucks. Mia and Cricket know their mother never liked him—Liz would come home from the office Christmas party every year complaining about how Amy's husband told tacky jokes and gave sloppy hugs. Now he's in their house and Liz isn't. He's here because their mom is gone, and it's so unfair that Cricket wonders if Amy the hygienist would stand to benefit from Clint's life insurance policy if he were to, say, trip over his athleisure pants and land on a tragically misplaced and upturned meat cleaver.

"This is it," Mia says, handing Clint an old Primo Bistro menu, a faint ring of cabernet just above her mother's loopy signature.

"It's a good thing she thought to have this notarized," Clint says, flicking at one nostril as he reviews the wine-stained document.

"Of course she did," Mia snaps defensively. In truth, Mia had been the one to research the basics of estate law after reading *A Little Princess* in fourth grade and consequently suffering a string of orphanage-related nightmares.

"You okay?" Coach asks, leaning forward to look at Mia on the other side of Cricket. Seated at the far end of the pink floral couch in a royal blue Stallions pullover, his five-o'clock shadow barely hiding his discomfort, Coach appears profoundly out of context. Nevertheless, Mia finds herself nodding back at him—yes, she's okay.

Coach matches Mia's solemnity, but he is confused about his role in this moment and desperate to extricate himself. He's here because he believes that the best teams show up for each other as family, but on a more tactical level, he's here because he can't figure out an appropriate time to leave.

The day before, when the ref blew her whistle and the Stallions returned to the field to resume their game, Coach gave his own car keys to his assistant coach and drove Mia and Cricket back to Maine in Mia's car. On the ride, the sisters oscillated between full-body sobs and an excruciating silence that made Coach itch to be back in his apartment, away from an agony he couldn't fix, or stop, or shout into submission.

When he pulled into the driveway of 125 Knickerbocker Avenue, both girls burst into guttural wails that robbed him of his flight impulse. He went inside, ordered them dinner, and, as he was trying to decide what to do next, Amy called Mia on her cellphone about the will. She said Clint would review it pro bono, but did Mia know where Liz kept it?

Yes, Mia knew. She had been the one to purchase a lockbox to store important family documents in after she found her own Social Security card stuck to the back of a Thai take-out menu with what appeared to be peanut sauce.

"Such an attractive woman," Clint says now, grabbing one of Liz's throw pillows as a bolster for his back. "And surprisingly smart for a high school dropout—I mean, look at this." He holds up the one-page will. "Efficient!"

"Unlike a bread bowl," Cricket says, and Mia hears herself guffaw uncontrollably. The men stare at her, but she doesn't care. Laughing suddenly feels as critical as crying.

"A soggy bread bowl," Mia enunciates, wiping the corners of her eyes and grinning at her sister. She'd forgotten all about Liz's nickname for Clint—or, more specifically, her description of his intellect.

"Sure, so you two share all assets," Clint continues, unwrapping a Werther's Original as he speaks. "Which will be helpful in covering the cost of the funeral because, yikes, those do not come cheap these days." He pops the hard candy into his mouth, sparing no sound effects but quite a bit of spit as droplets make landfall on Liz's will. "And just to be explicit," Clint says, "Mia, you're Cricket's official guardian from now until she turns eighteen, and what's—oh, this is sweet." He holds up a second, smaller paper and, in her distinctive handwriting, Liz had instructed: *Take care of each other, my girls.*

"Not to toot my own horn," Clint says, "but I encouraged your mother, as a single mom, to take out a robust life insurance policy, and she did just that. So you girls have a financial bumper that will cover the mortgage and living expenses for—I'm not an accountant, but you'll be okay for a while, as long as you don't—"

"But Mia can't be my guardian," Cricket says, cutting Clint off. "She lives in Connecticut."

Mia takes a steadying breath and closes her eyes. She sees the road back to New Haven, mile after mile, state after state. She feels the pages of old books, the taste of cold beers, the silence of the archival library. But then, just as viscerally, she hears the voice of her mother, yelling from the sidelines of a windswept soccer field: "Get back on defense! Protect your keeper!"

Mia adapts, just like she learned to do all those years ago, on the beach with her mother. She straightens her shoulders and turns to face her sister. "I live in Victory now," she says. "You and I are going to stay here until you graduate high school." Her strength steadies them both. Cricket nods. Staying here makes sense. Home makes sense.

"Everything stays the same," Mia announces to the living room, keeping her eyes locked on Cricket. "It's what our mom would have wanted."

"What about you?" Coach asks, exhaling at the relief he feels in Mia's authority. "What will you do?" At twenty-eight years old, he is not so young, but he isn't old enough to be responsible for Cricket. And yet, he really needs his keeper if he wants to win the upcoming club championship. Coach gets a hefty bonus for a championship, plus more name recognition and professional status within the coaching world. His success is only possible with Cricket in goal.

"I'll get a job," Mia says simply. "And then I'll go back to school when Cricket goes to college." She cracks a smile before adding, "Who knows? Maybe we'll both go to Yale?"

"But Yale isn't one of the top soccer programs," Cricket says, horrified by the prospect.

Mia tousles her sister's topknot. "We've got time to figure it out, and it's what she—" Mia's voice breaks.

Clint coughs over her stifled tears.

"Everything happens for a reason," he says, reaching over to pat Mia's hair. "I have it on good authority that she's staring down at you from heaven right now."

"Soggy bread bowl authority," Cricket says, unceremoniously removing Clint's hand from her sister's head.

Finally, Clint leaves. Coach follows suit, but only after promising the sisters he'll be back with groceries and takeout around dinnertime.

Then it's just Mia and Cricket. They scan the floors and counters, the walls and bookshelves in the quiet of their motherless home. They are not looking for clues but still lifes to store in their memories: Liz's scuffed restaurant clogs kicked off haphazardly beside the couch, her running shoes still double-knotted by the back door. A green ceramic mug next to the sink, her faint kiss of ruby red lipstick on the rim and a few mouthfuls of cold coffee still patiently waiting in the pot. Her orange cardigan on the coat hook, a quart of her favorite tomato soup from The Dutch Oven Duchess in the refrigerator.

"She couldn't find her car keys," Cricket says, staring at the front door. "I yelled at her because we were making the whole carpool late."

"It's okay," Mia says.

"I said 'I love you'—when I got out of the car, I told her I loved her."

Mia nods. "That's good." She'd ignored her mom's call yesterday morning because she was already caffeinated and studying. "That's good."

Slouched together in the living room, dazed and nauseated, Mia and Cricket imagine Liz walking in any second, asking for help with the groceries, reminding the girls to carry the bags from underneath using both hands. Their mother is supposed to text them from the dental office break room, ask how Mia's exam prep is going, how Cricket's soccer game went, wonder if they think the preview for that new movie with those old Hollywood stars looks any good, and complain about how Cherry Garcia is never on sale anymore. But their mother is not texting any of those things.

"How is this real life?" Cricket asks. Outside, a neighbor starts up his leaf blower, ignorant of the world's loss.

Before bed, Mia emails her professors and Dr. Peters along with the director of financial aid, the dean of residential life, the president, and the provost to cover all her bases and create a robust trail of correspondence should her student status ever be questioned down the road. Unsurprisingly, all the adults write back that they are deeply saddened by the news. They offer their thoughts and prayers and encourage Mia to take off as much time as she needs. In their Reply Alls, they each assure Mia that her spot will be waiting for her when she is ready to return to campus. It is the last email she ever receives from any of them.

BACK TO THE BEACH

They haven't been here together in years, but now Mia and Cricket come every morning, just as they did as girls. And like any destination mythologized in youth, the beach strikes the Lowe sisters as less impressive now—instead of the ten-foot waves they remember, the ocean's surface is glassy enough to host a slew of bobbing seagulls, mallards, and great cormorants. The rocky shoreline goes on for maybe a half mile, which contradicts their elementary school estimate of forever and ever.

Nevertheless, walking along the water's edge and allowing their eyes to comb the sand for worthwhile shells is a welcome distraction from the grief eating them alive at home. The beach appears smaller now but no less beautiful. Especially at sunrise. "It's like she's here, and also so obviously not here," Cricket says, staring into the orange blaze consuming the eastern corner of the sky. "Like, I keep waiting for her to pass me the ball."

Mia smiles, nods. It's an impossible reality, being here. Being anywhere, really—existing has felt like such a chore since last Saturday—but being at the beach, in Liz's favorite place, feels especially impossible. Impossible and maddening and profoundly reassuring.

It's been eight days since the accident and forty-eight hours since the funeral, which Sally Green organized with Mia and Cricket's permission. The service had been fine. The day of their mother's funeral was never going to be a good day so much as something to shower for and get through. But everyone felt compelled to tell them afterward, at the reception Lucia hosted at Primo Bistro, that it was the best-attended funeral they'd ever seen, including the retired police chief's.

"Liz would have loved that her service was standing room only," Lucia told the girls in Primo's kitchen as she covered extra trays of manicotti and stuffed shells for them to take home. Mia had nodded, catatonic. Cricket looked stoned. But it was true, what Lucia said, her mother would have appreciated the great turnout.

Over the years, Liz had accrued many admirers, and they'd all shown up to pay their respects: The entire crew of mechanics from Victory Auto had made an appearance, along with the team of technicians from Cute Nails and the hot barista Liz liked to flirt with when she thought Mia and Cricket weren't paying attention. All the volunteers from the swap shop, and several tellers Mia recognized from the bank, and even her high school assistant principal who'd tried to ask Liz out multiple times but failed because Liz was a black belt in romantic jiujitsu.

But even after the funeral home director had turned on the ceiling fans to accommodate the crowd, Mia understood they would be on their own. Because despite her friendly waves and infectious smile, Liz had kept everyone at a distance—at first because being a single parent didn't afford her the luxury of a social life, and then, when the girls were older, out of habit. At her core, Liz was a lone wolf, even if the dozens of sympathy cards crammed into the mailbox suggested differently.

"We're going to be okay," Mia says now, threading her arm through Cricket's as they walk toward the far jetty, where Liz used to hold their morning training sessions.

"How do you know?" Cricket asks, picking up a stone larger than her fist and hurling it into the ocean. The rock makes a satisfying splash. Cricket turns to Mia and the bright sun forces her to squint, making her look even more like their mom. "How could we ever be okay?"

"Because we have to be," Mia says. "She'd want us—I don't know—I feel like she'd say something annoying about B-positive."

The sisters climb out on the jetty, aware of the slick seaweed, the incoming tide. All the things their mother would point out. All the warnings they always chose to ignore, they now wish to hear one more time. In Liz's absence, the sisters are careful on the rocks, her voice in their heads. The sun continues to rise, carving their silhouettes into the horizon.

This is where they feel closest to her and the most like themselves.

"I can't live without her," Cricket says, the tip of her nose pink from the cold.

"Neither can I," Mia agrees. "But we've got to try. She'd still want you to play soccer. I think she'd actually be pissed if you didn't—at you and at me."

"I was thinking, Mom would have played at UCLA if—"

"So you'll go to UCLA," Mia says matter-of-factly. "If that's where you want to play, then that's where you'll play."

"And you'll graduate from Yale and become a super successful therapist," Cricket decides, because Mia was planning on declaring a major in psychology.

"Yeah," Mia agrees with far less conviction. Ben's sweet face flashes behind her eyes but it wasn't that serious, she tells herself. Nothing at school was real life, as best proven by the stilted condolence messages Mia received from the people she considered her best friends. No one had even called, they'd all just texted. Ben didn't come up for the funeral, or even offer to come, and he was supposed to be her boyfriend.

Mia's college friends had never met her mom—except for Nell on move-in day their freshman year—so how substantive could their connection have been? Six months ago, Mia valued her pregame social circle above all else. But now, abandoned at the intersection of loss and crisis, she sees Nell and Landon and Ben as loose bonds of convenience, strung together by proximity and alcohol, lust and ambition.

"Or a sports psych!" Cricket shouts suddenly, interrupting Mia's thoughts and startling a nearby seagull, who rebukes her with a ragged *caw!* before flying off. "Or just, like, a famous doctor to the stars, and you'll treat so many celebrities that you'll get your own show."

Mia laughs. "We'll see," she says, turning away from the ocean to appreciate how the sun has started its daily transformation of Victory. The boughs of their neighborhood oaks and pines and hemlocks glow golden. At this time of day, from this particular beach, even the wonkiest rooflines and ugliest additions look majestic. Despite the cold, everything the sun touches wears a crown of warm light. "I think the key for now is to stick together."

Cricket nods. Her plan has always been to stay as close to Mia as her sister will allow. Liz often said Cricket learned to walk so early and then run so fast because she was born trying to catch up to Mia, as if closing in on a five-year gap were possible.

"If you don't want to be a sports psych, you can be my manager instead, and then once I become rich and famous, we'll build soccer fields all over the world and name them after Mom."

"I love that idea," Mia says, dragging her heel through the sand, only semiconscious of the *L* she is creating. "Although I'm probably better suited to be your accountant."

"Be both!" Cricket offers magnanimously, stopping to watch Mia. She jumps ahead and uses her heel to draw a five-foot *Z*.

Walking toward the entrance, Mia and Cricket relish the sun on their faces, the lapping waves, this place they've been lucky enough to know their entire lives. She is here, and they will be okay. When the Lowe sisters leave the beach, they have a plan for the present and a vision for the future.

CAT LIVES AND DOG YEARS

In December, Mr. and Mrs. Tupper's twenty-foot-tall Santa lawn ornament across the street trolls Mia and Cricket through the kitchen window. It's been six weeks since their mother's accident. The sun set hours ago and now, with growling bellies, they excavate the neglected remains of their refrigerator.

"I don't think we should eat this," Mia says, gagging at the mold growing on top of a tuna fish salad.

"If you don't think we should, then we definitely shouldn't," Cricket responds, chugging another glass of water. She wants to trick her stomach into feeling less empty.

The moldy tuna fish salad is the last of what Cricket refers to as the pity food. Dazed by the slow drip of reality, the sisters have steadily eaten their way through the disposable trays of macaroni and cheese, ravioli, lentil soup, and spinach casseroles that friends, neighbors, and acquaintances have dropped off since Liz's death. It didn't matter whether it was Lucia's homemade pasta from Primo Bistro or Dr. Green's chicken enchiladas or the gourmet black and white cookies from New York that everyone else from the dental office sent over—it all tasted like globs of sawdust to the Lowe sisters. But now it's all gone and they're starving.

"I kept meaning to go to the store," Mia says absently. While she has bravely tackled the shoeboxes full of her mother's unopened bills and dialed hundreds of 1-800 numbers to ask for extensions, she has tried to avoid face-to-face interactions as much as possible. Other people's blissful ignorance of the world's incomparable loss strikes her as deeply offensive.

"Let's go together, right now," Cricket says, tossing Mia her van keys.

With ten minutes before the store closes, they race through the aisles of Hannaford, frantically grabbing random items in record time: pickles and barbecue chips and a frozen shrimp tower that's on clearance but looks fancy. It feels inevitable that the sisters will see someone they know, so they go faster and faster. But it nevertheless happens in aisle 7, when they bump carts with the red-bearded Dr. Wilkins, Victory's trusted veterinarian.

"Listen, I know it probably doesn't mean much, but I'm so, so sorry about your mom," he says, reaching out to put a hand on each of their shoulders. Mia flashes to seeing him at the funeral and feels an unexpected wave of warmth for him. Dr. Wilkins and his husband kept a standing reservation at Primo every Thursday at seven p.m. Mia remembers they tipped exceptionally well. "How can we help? Dinner? Gift cards?" Dr. Wilkins asks. Looking into their cart, he adds, "Do me a favor and check the sell-by date on that shrimp tower, okay? But seriously, what do you need?"

Mia demurs, even though all three of them smell desperation wicking off her. "Reach out anytime," Dr. Wilkins says gently with a parting smile.

"Mia needs a job," Cricket calls after him, suddenly inspired. If her mother landed her first job at the Hannaford, then it's where Mia might secure a job, too. "Can she work in your office?" Cricket asks with enough assertiveness that it feels more like a command than a question.

This boldness, according to Coach, is Cricket's superpower on the field.

This boldness, according to Mia, is humiliating in real life.

This boldness, according to Dr. Wilkins, warrants an immediate "Yes! Of course!"

The paperwork takes an hour and the training takes three days. The return to society, however, requires a bit more time, but not as much as Mia expected. In fact, she likes the job. She enjoys the distraction of helping Dr. Wilkins and his menagerie of patients.

Compared to fighting with the automated messaging of her mother's homeowner's insurance, Mia finds greeting pets and their human companions a far more enjoyable way to spend the day. Seated at the front desk of Oceanside Animal Hospital, Mia checks in furry guests, records their weight, bills their adoptive parents, and considers an alternative future for herself, one that might not involve a return to Yale.

Amid the meows and hisses, the Labrador barks and the hound dog bays that mark the passage of hours and weeks, Mia feels the straight, rigid arrow of her ambition curl in on itself like a sleeping cat. Rather than strive to become as extraordinary as her mom could have been, Mia feels a growing desire to be entirely ordinary. The predictability feels safe, and the safety feels good.

Sitting on the floor of exam room 3 with a white-faced golden retriever and a little girl dressed in purple corduroy pants, Mia feels she's in the right place. "I lost my best friend, too," she tells the girl, Abby, whose father sits across from them in a visitor's chair, preoccupied with his phone. He is the first person Mia sees wearing a face mask, his glasses fogging up every few minutes above his N-95.

As Mia watches the girl and dog lie nose to nose, the capacity to love strikes her as cruelly beautiful. At birth, each person unwittingly signs a contract to say goodbye to everyone they're about to meet. Life is merciless in that way, in its promise to end.

Why invest what uncertain amount of time she has left somewhere new when her whole world is here? She has nothing to prove. Without Liz around to witness Mia's academic milestones, the conventional sense of academic achievement and pursuit of socioeconomic status seems laughably trivial. Because Liz hadn't gone to college, she'd raised Mia to think it was everything, and Mia had bought in, never pausing to question the price of such an endeavor until she tallied up the cost per minute of her freshman seminar on twentieth-century literature.

What Mia has gained in the loss of her mother is perspective. She understands she is on Earth for such an indefinite amount of time and that the only guarantee is that life is short and unreliable and that it is easy to get waylaid in daily stress that doesn't ultimately matter. Her gift, if she has one, is simple: She is at her best when she is supporting others.

As the front desk caregiver, Mia dotes on her fluffy patients and smiles at their human companions as they swipe their heavy credit cards. When Dr. Wilkins rubs at his eyes, Mia leaves a fresh cup of coffee and a glass of water by his computer. When one of the vet techs says she'll die if she has to perform one more glands expression, Mia gloves up because she learned all of the tech duties in the first few months at Oceanside. She is the unsung hero, the first line of defense, the understudy and the fill-in, and she finds comfort in the familiarity of a low profile. It reminds her of her childhood, forever the sweeper to her sister's keeper. Sacrifice has felt like love, and love like sacrifice, for as long as Mia can remember.

It's March 2020 now, more than four months since Liz sent her last group text reminding both daughters to replace the heads of their electric toothbrushes. If she were still alive, she'd text them about the coronavirus that's all over the news. The World Health Organization declared it a pandemic this week. For the world and the Lowe sisters, life has only become more unrecognizable.

Stationed at the front desk, Mia answers Oceanside's ever-ringing phone.

A dog needs his teeth cleaned. Mia books the appointment and walks the owner through different payment plans for such an expensive procedure. It isn't rocket science, and it doesn't require a degree from Yale, but it's worthwhile.

A steady, ordinary life can be extraordinary so long as it's centered around family and community and filled with love. On a freezing Friday night, just before closing, an older woman arrives at Oceanside with her ancient cat, who is rail thin and missing large patches of fur. It's impossible to say who looks more stricken as they approach the desk, and so Mia gives them her most reassuring smile as she reminds herself: The only way to use your head is to keep your eyes wide open.

BEEP TEST

Cricket doesn't miss school.

Not yet.

As a sophomore at Victory High, she's enjoyed the two weeks that school has been closed on account of Covid-19, especially because outdoor activities are still allowed. It's kind of the ideal life—no school, and more time for soccer. Besides, the current president says the pandemic will be over by Easter, which is only a week away.

On the turf in downtown Portland, everyone groans when Coach announces the beep test. It's the end of a long training session, and the players had assumed it was time to scrimmage. Instead, Coach is subjecting them to a competition he describes as 50 percent conditioning and 50 percent mental training, or, as Liv puts it, "100 percent torture."

The beep test starts out easy enough, providing plenty of time between beeps to hit the twenty-meter mark, turn around, hit the mark, turn around, hit the mark. Along with her teammates, Cricket jogs and pivots, jogs and pivots, toeing the line with her cleat, anticipating the hell underway. Level one is just the warm-up, but everyone knows what's coming. This is a battle of psychological toughness as much as it is an assessment of physical endurance. Pain is inevitable, but dreading that pain is a choice. Cricket has decided to relish the discomfort required to achieve her dream.

BEEP!

"Your mind is your strongest muscle!" Coach yells from the sideline as the beeps speed up, the pace becoming less and less sustainable. Cricket digs deep, then deeper. She hits the mark before the beep, pivots, hits the mark, pivots, hits the mark. Around her, teammates gasp, curse, drop out, but Cricket refuses to submit. Her chest is on fire, her quads are trembling, her entire body feels like it's been cranked through a meat grinder multiple times, but she will not quit. The beep test will not beat her. This is an invitation to challenge the limits of her being. It even feels good, for her outsides to hurt as much as her insides—a kind of perverse homeostasis, a distraction from the distraction that is her life without her mother.

BEEP!

Teammates begin to drop. There are fewer bodies in motion now, fewer mouths audibly panting, reminding Cricket of her own labored breath. She is giving her everything and barely hitting the line in time. She puts her head down, gives more. Because love always requires more than you think you have.

BEEP!

There are only a handful of Stallions still running. At this point, especially as a goalkeeper, Cricket knows she could give up with dignity, but she is trying to cultivate the grit required for a life of professional soccer. On either side, Cricket's teammates choke on air until Coach calls their names, points out they didn't quite hit the mark in time. Cricket hears the players croak with relief as they join the chorus of sideline support. She keeps going, trying to outrun time. The beeps cluster together but she is faster. Hit, pivot, hit, pivot. She is the only one still on the field now, but Cricket is not alone—not now, not ever.

Because she's here.

BEEP!

Cricket doesn't stop until Coach calls her name, tells her that's enough, grab some water. The stunned applause of her teammates set-

tles in like heavy rain because *holy shit, that was level 13*. Cricket stands
still while her legs shake. The beads of sweat that race down the sides of
her face disguise the tears.

Until Mia drove Cricket to her first Stallions practice after the funeral, Cricket had thought that she'd lost her mother forever. Lacing up
her cleats, she'd endured the dramatic blather of her teammates whin-
ing about the cold snap because they didn't know how to acknowledge
her mother's death. During warm-ups, Cricket found it impossible to
care about who was hooking up and who got a spray tan but lied about
it, and she thought about quitting the Stallions altogether. Maybe,
without her mom, soccer wasn't worth it.

But then Cricket had jogged to her position at the far end of the
field, and there she was, waiting for her between the goalposts.

"Welcome back," Liz said, beaming with her arms crossed over her
red winter coat, glacier eyes sparkling. She'd always loved a surprise.
"Let's see what you've got."

Everyone says goalkeeping is the loneliest position, but the end line
is the one place where Cricket can commune with her mother. It is the
only place where Liz shows up, day after day, with her magic smile and
her nails painted royal blue to match the Stallions uniform, screaming,
"Wheels, Cricky!" and quoting Billie Jean King's "Pressure is a privilege!"

After that first practice, Cricket realizes she can never give up
soccer—not until she is ready to say goodbye to her mom. She arrives
to practice early and stays late. Failure is not an option.

Liz is the reason why Cricket just outlasted her teammates on the
beep test. Liz is the reason why Cricket operates with a newfound fear-
lessness that spooks her opponents and draws the ball into her possession almost supernaturally.

After every game, Coach pulls Cricket aside and applauds her quick
decisions and even faster reflexes. "Your confidence is an asset," he says.
"If we keep building your game—mentally, tactically, and physically—
you'll be unstoppable."

Cricket beams from his approval and says what she always says when
she has his attention: "I want to be on the National Team."

Coach heeds the familiar call-and-response. "You're on your way, kid." It's how he answers her bold ambition, mussing her topknot but careful not to agitate the red ribbon tied in a bow. He knows the significance of that ribbon, knows to whom it originally belonged.

Together, Cricket and her mother are going to make their dream come true. All Cricket has to do to see Liz is devote her life to soccer. It's more than just visualization. Her mom still exists between the goalposts, and that makes every sacrifice for the game worth it.

While Cricket's teammates might complain about the early-morning games or the mandatory practices over spring break, Cricket understands that dedication is imperative to get where she wants to go. Commitment is not the same thing as sacrifice. But every time she sees Liz leaning against a goalpost, casually examining her freshly polished fingernails while commenting on the opposing team's lackluster performance, Cricket imagines telling Mia. She fantasizes about the release she'd feel, the liberating gush in her core and the gobsmacked look on Mia's face as Cricket described their mom in every detail, down to the colorful mismatched socks she still wears.

And yet, Cricket instinctively knows she can't share these interactions with anyone, even Mia. *Especially* Mia. At first, she thinks she's just being superstitious, but it goes beyond Cricket's own fear of losing her mom again. It's less of a jinx and more of a test: Can she keep this miracle to herself?

And so the biggest sacrifice Cricket makes for soccer is not choosing an optional practice over Addie Lim's Sweet Sixteen at the best restaurant in Portland. It isn't the pair of cracked ribs Cricket obtains from an attacker's cleat, which requires sleeping upright for a week and walking around school with a large bag of ice under her shirt, giving her a very embarrassing, very lumpy third boob. No, the greatest sacrifice Cricket makes in the name of soccer is keeping her mother a secret from her sister.

OWN THE WIN

"**B**ig day," Corinne says at the cash register, eyeing Mia's purchase as she rings her up.

"Big day," Mia grins in agreement.

Today, at 7:38 a.m., Mia Lowe is purchasing her first toilet seat. She is surprised by her own delight but nevertheless delighted. It had been Cricket's idea, in the form of a complaint, that the one they'd been sitting on was probably from the 1960s. And so not for the first time, Hammer It Home Hardware has provided Mia with support she didn't know she needed in the form of a gleaming white toilet seat.

So pleased is Mia with her purchase, so empowered with the knowledge that comes from having already YouTubed the installation process, that when she swings open the glass door to leave, she doesn't notice the man to her right until he calls her name through his Covid mask. Even then, she doesn't recognize him until he asks if Cricket is with her.

"She's at school—on Zoom," Mia says, finally identifying him as Coach. She's never seen him dressed in anything other than royal blue Stallions gear.

"Oh, right, Zoom," Coach says. "Yikes." As he talks about how well

Cricket played in the game last weekend, Mia notes his faded jeans and gray zip-up hoodie over a white T-shirt. Mia judges him for the flip-flops—it's only in the mid-forties—and then registers the gigantic bag of kibble tucked under his arm.

"You have a dog?"

"My neighbor," Coach says. "She's gotta be close to eighty, so between Covid protocols and Trevor still being a puppy and—"

"Trevor!" Mia shouts. "Your neighbor is Bitsy Beedy?"

Coach cocks his head. "You know Miss Bits?"

They laugh with a shared appreciation for the diva-and-dog duo, and Coach sets down the heavy yellow bag of kibble on the sidewalk. Mia fights the urge to check her watch; she doesn't want to be late for work. And then she remembers what she's holding at the same moment Coach spots it.

"Nice," he says, nodding at the toilet seat.

"I know!" Mia agrees, holding it up for him to admire. If Coach were her own age, she would be mortified, but he's an adult. She can only assume he gets it. "Who knew you could just buy a toilet seat?" Mia says. "I feel like such a grown-up."

Coach takes a step back. "You are the legal guardian of a teenager," he says with a raised eyebrow. "I'd say you're definitely a grown-up."

"How old are you?" Mia asks. Her mind is still trying to negotiate the shaggy man in front of her with the clean-shaven Coach on the sidelines of her sister's games.

"Twenty-nine," he answers. "But in guy years."

"What's that mean?"

"It means I'm not ready to have my own dog," he says. "And I've never experienced the joy of purchasing my own throne."

Mia laughs uneasily, surprised by the heat pooling in her cheeks. "It was Cricket's idea."

"No, no, don't do that," Coach teases, taking two steps closer and wagging a finger. He is tall. Mia didn't realize just how tall until now, as he looms over her, a glint of mischief pulling at the corners of his green eyes. "You picked this baby all on your own," he says, patting the seat. "Own the win."

"My win is a literal toilet seat," Mia says, staring down at her purchase. "That's embarrassing."

Coach picks up the bag of dog food. "Mia," he says. "Adulthood is constantly embarrassing." Under her mask, she smiles at the sound of her name in his voice, and from his squint Mia can tell he's grinning underneath his, too. "Same time next month?" he asks.

Mia makes a note of the date and wonders if Coach is serious, if he really does come here on the first of every month. But no, of course he doesn't, so Mia feels free to joke back, "You're on, Coach."

"Right," he says, shifting the gigantic bag of kibble to one arm. "About that." He clears his throat as if he's about to deliver a verdict, but what he says instead hits Mia like her new favorite song. "I'm Oliver," he says, adjusting his weight and sticking out his hand to properly introduce himself seven years after they first stood on opposite sidelines. "Please call me Oliver."

THE WORST KIND OF ANNIVERSARY

In lockdown, there's no hiding behind busy schedules or routine. The Lowes' shared Google calendar is just a grid of vacant real estate, and in the absence of distraction, they've learned that the gut punches of grief hit hardest when they least expect them, and the only way to survive the pain and anger is to surrender to it.

So they do.

Masked up at the grocery store, Mia and Cricket cry openly when they confront Liz's favorite spicy mustard. They yell at the sky on morning beach walks and curse every silver SUV on the road. They say, "I miss her," at least once during every meal and think it to themselves too many times during an episode of *Friends* to keep count.

And yet, even in quarantine, time still manages to rip Mia and Cricket away from their mother like muscle tearing from the bone. They have been unwilling participants in the forward march of minutes, sickened by how the months seem to pick up speed, even as they remain frozen in place.

"How is this real?" Cricket asks in the kitchen on the morning of November ninth.

"One year without her," Mia says, searching the kitchen cabinets for the coffee filters she just bought. The shock of the trauma has lifted, and in its place anger, depression, and profound sorrow have surged. In the days leading up to the worst kind of anniversary, Cricket and Mia have both felt themselves getting pulled under by a riptide of resentment: *Why her? Why them? Everyone is so scared of this virus, but we already lost everything.*

"But how?" Cricket asks. "How has it been a year?"

"All the grief books say it's supposed to hurt less from now on," Mia says, relieved to find the filters and choosing not to reprimand Cricket for putting them under the sink with the cleaning supplies. Instead, she measures coffee beans for the grinder and looks out the window to see if she needs to grab her raincoat. A gray, overcast sky promises another wet day—the kind of damp cold that penetrates bones, making it impossible to keep warm. Appropriate grieving weather.

"Give it one full year," Mia says, quoting from one of the dozen books she borrowed from the library. "Go through all the holidays, birthdays, and voilà, it won't hurt as much as the first time around."

"The grief books didn't know Mom," Cricket says as she plucks the last two eggs from the carton and sticks the empty container back in the fridge.

After the funeral, it was like Mia and Cricket were forced onto the Gravitron—that terrible carnival ride—and have been stuck on it ever since. Life has become a circular blur of centrifugal force that lasts forever and is apathetic to their screams.

The truth is, Mia and Cricket don't want to move on, but the more they fixate on the clock, the faster it moves away from the moment where they need to stay. They want to remain right there, with their mom, in the center of the open wound, because the pain is entwined with the love, and the love is what conjures the stories and the jokes and that one time Liz went on a date with a ref because he asked her out just before the Stallions' first playoff game so it seemed like bad luck to say no. When the Stallions won the tournament, Coach awarded Liz her own trophy. *For your sacrifice,* he'd said with a deep bow during the team's end-of-season banquet.

"How am I supposed to Zoom like this?" Cricket asks, her face blotchy, her eyes swollen and red.

"You don't have to," Mia says. "I can email Ms. Hayes."

"No." Cricket rests her forehead on the kitchen counter. "I have to go."

"I was thinking—would you want to do a New Year's Eve party tonight?" Mia posits tentatively. "And a polar plunge?"

Cricket looks up at her with surprise. "You want to reset from Mom?"

"No," Mia says, pressing the button to start the coffee machine with unnecessary force. "I want to establish a ritual with you, in honor of her, to help us both get through today, and all the November ninths in the future."

"There's no resetting from Mom," Cricket says with an indignant sniff. She stands up, a pink half-moon on her forehead from the counter. "There's no restarting."

Mia crosses the kitchen to hug her sister. "I agree, but I think she'd like us having a tradition with her, and with each other—unless you have a better idea?"

"I don't want to have any ideas," Cricket mutters. "I just want her back." Her body starts to convulse in Mia's arms.

"The books say you don't move on from grief," Mia murmurs in Cricket's ear. This only makes her sister cry harder. "They say that, to accommodate all the love and loss and loneliness, your heart has to grow bigger."

"But I don't want a bigger heart," Cricket whimpers into Mia's shoulder. "I want to have a normal-sized heart and for her to be right here."

That night, as she wriggles into her swimsuit for the midnight polar plunge, Mia thinks back to all the past New Year's Eves with her mom. She can already feel the freezing sand between her toes, the surprising weight of those sequined dresses her mom liked to rescue from Goodwill. All those times she took for granted, or even complained, as they walked toward the ocean, bathed in turquoise sparkles and ivory moonlight.

"Ready, set, go!" Cricket shouts, and as they race to the sea, they yell the opening lines of "Get Low, Fly High." When the water hits their ankles, then above their knees, Cricket curses up a storm of *holy fucking hell*s that zing around them in echoes, making them laugh through chattering teeth. Their mother hated when they cursed, but they hate that she's dead, and that this ocean is ice cold, and that this New Year's Eve polar plunge was Liz's idea of a good time. "Why couldn't she just bake cookies like a normal mom?" Cricket yells to her sister, who cackles with her head back, the luminous white flesh of her neck offered up to the stars.

Mia emerges from the Atlantic and the November air feels like a million beestings, like wrestling a rosebush. But there is Cricket jumping like a lunatic in the sand and insisting they do this every year, that she can feel their mom's energy coursing through her veins. "Be positive, Mia!" Cricket shouts with her arms outstretched like a cheerleader, impersonating the woman they miss most. "Be! Fucking! Positive!"

HEART STAMP

Mia forgets about running into Cricket's coach outside of his soccer-field context until it happens again in the last week of December. This time, she sees Oliver inside the post office. He is two people ahead of her in what quickly proves to be an exceptionally slow-moving line. When Oliver gives up his place to join her, Mia balks.

"It'll go faster talking to you," he says. "And if I stayed up there, I'd have to keep wondering if you think the back of my head looks too big for my body."

Mia laughs and it rings out in the contentiously hushed post office, everyone barely keeping it together as their lunch hour ticks down to nothing.

"What are you in for?" Oliver asks.

"Stamps," Mia says.

"Same." He smiles and holds up a pink envelope. "My mom's birthday." The address reads South Carolina and is printed in clear, clean capital letters. "As the prodigal son with no plans of returning, I figure this is the least I can do."

"Do they ever visit?" Mia imagines Oliver's parents with his same green eyes. She wonders if he's the carbon copy of his father, the same dirty blond hair and blocky head, or if he inherited his high cheekbones from his mother. "Do they ever come up for games?"

"No way," Oliver says without hesitation. "That would require missing Bible study, or a fellowship meeting, or a pancake breakfast in the name of Jesus Christ our Lord and Savior."

Mia rocks up on her toes, uncertain how to respond. Religion was never a thing in the Lowe household, unless she were to count their weekend lip syncs to Madonna's "Like a Prayer" or their annual Christmas viewing of *Sister Act*.

"I think everyone is entitled to their faith, obviously," Coach volunteers. "But I wish they'd said something other than to 'pray on it' when I was diagnosed with diabetes."

Mia does a double take. "You have diabetes?" she asks, unable to hide her shock. "But you're so"—she almost says "fit," but it seems borderline inappropriate that she's noticed his physique. Then again, how could she not have when at least one mom makes note of it during every Stallions game? Mia mentally scrambles as they move up another person in line and ultimately lands on "active" rather than "fit."

Oliver holds her gaze and Mia worries he can read her mind. "Yeah, this is Type 1, so it doesn't matter how active I am. It's why I wear this." He lifts his shirt ever so slightly. Mia barely trusts herself to glance down, but he's waiting for her to look, so she does and sees a black insulin pump clipped to the waistband of his khakis. She also sees a flash of flat stomach.

"Anyway, we get along great," Oliver says, looking down at his pink envelope. "As long as we don't speak." It seems like a far too personal conversation to have while waiting in the post office line, but here they are, still four people away from being able to purchase stamps. Mia asks Oliver what he does for the holidays.

Oliver shrugs. "Play it by ear," he says. "I probably don't buy into the holidays as much as other people."

Mia thinks of her mom, and their New Year's Eves that rarely happened in December. "I get that," she says.

"I thought you might," Oliver says, nudging her with a conspiratorial elbow. Mia has seen him do this with Cricket and the rest of the Stallions. It's just a show of camaraderie, Mia knows this, so why is the spot on her arm where he touched her now tingling like she rubbed a whole jar of Cricket's Tiger Balm on it?

"After you," Oliver says, motioning for Mia to approach the available clerk's window.

Because stamps.

She is here for stamps so she needs to move her feet, but she is also a little lightheaded.

The postal worker gives her a choice between a book of hearts or the two hundredth anniversary of Maine statehood. Mia chooses the sheet of familiar rocky coastline and glances left to see Coach adhere his single heart stamp to the pink envelope. He meets her eye.

"I'm sorry to complain about my parents," he says. "I just realized how insensitive—"

"No, it's okay," Mia insists. "All good."

"See you on Saturday?" Oliver asks, holding open the door for her. For a moment, she wonders what he might mean.

"Saturday," she repeats. Is he asking her out? No, the Stallions have a game on Saturday, and he is her sister's coach.

He is her sister's coach.

On the sidewalk, Mia's mind reels.

Oliver is her sister's coach, just as her father was her mother's coach.

Feeling suddenly ill, Mia tries to calm herself down by calculating the bivariate data because math always makes sense.

Unlike her mother and father, there is no imbalance of power between Mia and Oliver. But there is an undeniable correlation. Two sets of values, different but related. A pattern on a slant.

Mia remembers the flight home from the World Cup in Paris and vowing she would never date a coach. She puts herself back at Yale, promising herself not to repeat her mother's mistakes. And then she thinks of that heart stamp on the pink envelope, those green eyes finding her at the back of the line, the flash of stomach behind the black insulin pump, her elbow, still tingling. This is why surprises are upsets.

As Oliver walks Mia to her van, his hands in his pockets, poised for more conversation, Mia abruptly steps off the curb. "I have to work this weekend," she says. "But good luck!"

For an instant, his face falls, but he collects himself quickly and offers a bright grin that stretches beyond the edges of his face mask. "I'll take all the luck we can get against those New Hampshire girls," he says. "Have a great day, Mia." Before she can respond, Oliver is halfway down the block, heading to his own car.

Watching him walk away in her rearview mirror, Mia thinks of Cricket's evolution as a goalkeeper since joining the Stallions. She no longer pouts when a ball gets past her in a game but instead hustles to retrieve it from the back of the net, and once she passes it up to center field, she pulls up her socks and claps three times as a physical and emotional reset. *Coach says it's about using your body to trick your mind,* Cricket has explained to her more than once.

At a red light, Mia rubs the heat of Oliver's touch out of her arm. As ridiculous as it may look, she claps three times, right there in the driver's seat. Because he is her sister's soccer coach. Because he is off-limits. Because whether or not he is aware of his effect on her, or how twenty-nine in man years compares to twenty-one in woman years, none of it matters, because Oliver represents a very specific history threatening to repeat itself if she isn't careful.

But she is Mia Lowe.

She is always careful.

BLACK ICE

C ricket knows the name long before she plays against Sloane Jackson at a showcase in Rhode Island. The Florida native, also a high school junior, is rumored to be the best goalkeeper in the country. Even if she weren't an impressive six feet tall and wearing a bright red goalkeeper's jersey, Sloane has received enough national media attention and online fame for Cricket to recognize her during warm-ups.

Her celebrity has drawn an impressive crowd to Kingston. Dozens of college scouts clutch their iPads as they watch the game between Cricket's Stallions and Sloane's Hurricanes. Photographers from reputable news outlets steady their cameras while journalists take notes, jotting down questions to ask Sloane after the final whistle. They want to capture her in print now to reference when she's world-famous later.

At sixteen years old, Cricket is hardly immune to the proximity of such attention. All weekend, the hot edges of Sloane's spotlight burn Cricket at an angle, distracting her from her role on the field.

"Focus on this play," Liz says, appearing by the goalpost just in time for the first whistle. "Never mind the noise from the sidelines."

But Cricket can't shake off her nerves or the fact that everyone here thinks Sloane is the better keeper. She gets so in her own head that she doesn't even notice when her mom vanishes. Sloane's existence, her potential superiority in goal, consumes Cricket entirely as she allows questions to nag at her for all ninety minutes of the match. Because what if she isn't good enough? What if her best simply doesn't measure up to Sloane's best, and UCLA doesn't offer her a scholarship? What if she fails at the one thing she's supposed to be good at, and her mom and sister sacrificed everything for nothing? Then what?

That afternoon, the Stallions lose to the Hurricanes, 1–0. The match itself feels stilted, as if every player thinks a lens might be trained on them. Cricket lets in the one goal of the game at the start of the second half. Most of the match's action, however, happens at the other end of the field, giving Sloane ample opportunities to demonstrate her talent.

After the final whistle, Cricket jogs to the bench disappointed in her performance. An unfamiliar self-doubt persists on the long drive home, questions buzzing like mosquitoes in her ear: How many goalkeepers stand between her and the National Team? Did any of those scouts notice her? Did all of them write her off after that goal?

As if to further punish herself, Cricket keeps replaying the shot she let in, which she could have blocked if she'd only—

"Stop thinking about it," Mia says, interrupting Cricket's spin cycle. "Everyone's rusty after not playing together for a year."

"But I played like shit."

"It's one weekend," Mia says, trying for a nonchalance that immediately backfires.

"So you agree I played like shit." Cricket's chest constricts with terror as she awaits Mia's response. Her sister has given up so much, and Cricket has only just realized there is a chance, a sizable possibility, that she won't be good enough. That she already isn't good enough and everyone has just been lying to her, feeling sorry for her because her mom is dead, which is exactly why she needs to carry her mother's legacy between her shoulder blades, her last name and lucky number on the back of a National Team jersey someday.

But what if Cricket never makes it that far? What if her father was just a bad man, and she is just a mediocre keeper, and she fails to ever redeem her mother's almosts with her own golden achievement?

"Actually, no," Mia sighs. "I don't think you played like shit." She flicks on her turn signal and wishes for the hundredth time that day, for the billionth time that week, that her mother were here to go on a Be Positive rant long enough to pacify Cricket. "But if that's what you think, I'm just reminding you it was one showcase. It doesn't matter."

"It all matters," Cricket says, ramming the back of her head against the headrest. "I need to impress UCLA." That's another thing she realized while she was standing in goal, getting eaten alive by questions she couldn't answer. UCLA is anything but a guarantee.

"Aren't they already impressed?" Mia asks.

"Barely," Cricket says, but Mia knows better.

Ever since June, Cricket has fielded interest from soccer coaches all over the country. College recruiting is little more than a shameless wooing of talented players—coaches start with generic questionnaires to gauge interest and then eventually offer an all-expenses-paid trip to campus so prospective student athletes can meet the team, view the training facilities, and imagine their life at that school.

At sixteen years old, Cricket has never been in a romantic relationship, but she has most certainly been courted by college soccer recruiters. Except for Stanford, where Sloane plans to go, every top-tier program has reached out to Cricket.

"You're our missing piece," one coach declared over voicemail.

"We're set up to go all the way this year," another divulged in a handwritten letter. "We just need you."

More than one coach has even DMed Cricket in a last-ditch effort to get her attention, and Mia almost feels sorry for those coaches because they have no chance. Cricket's heart is set on UCLA—their mother's would-be alma mater if not for Mia.

"I know they're impressed," Mia says. Without meaning to, because she is tired of driving and tired of this conversation, she makes a mistake: Mia exhales.

Cricket seizes on it. "What's with the sigh?"

"Nothing."

"No," Cricket says, sitting up, alert, a dog with a fresh bone. "You know UCLA's impressed but what?"

"You just need to play your game," Mia concedes. "I don't know how else to say it. You didn't look relaxed out there today, or like you were having fun."

"It was all those people there for Sloane," Cricket admits, leaning her head against the passenger window. She doesn't confess that it is bigger than the rival goalkeeper or the gaggle of reporters. Her entire life depends on hitting each of these upcoming milestones, one at a time but in rapid succession. Because if she doesn't clear the first hurdle of getting into UCLA, she can't earn the starting spot there, and that means she can't lead the Bruins to another NCAA championship, which brings more eyes and dollar signs to her name when she graduates and enters the NWSL draft.

The gauntlet continues from there. A long line of dominoes must fall in an unlikely, almost miraculous sequence for Cricket to ever make the National Team. It's damn near impossible but it's her destiny. Any other life path would be a forfeit, and yet, having seen the attention surrounding Sloane Jackson, Cricket is riddled with doubt about the reality of her dream.

"Don't worry about Sloane," Mia says, turning on the radio.

"I lost one of Mom's red ribbons during warm-ups and then I let in that stupid goal," Cricket mutters from the passenger seat. "So you know what that means?"

"What?"

"A third bad thing still has to happen today—bad things always happen in threes."

"Not necessarily," Mia argues, turning up the volume to drown out her sister.

"Mom said so."

"Should we stop for ice cream?" Mia asks, changing lanes and switching topics. "We're almost at the bridge."

"Ooh, the bridge," Cricket warbles with sarcasm. "A real cause for celebration." She glares out the window and curses the swirling hail, sleet, and rain. "This weather is garbage."

Elsewhere in the country, purple crocuses and other eager buds lend promises of spring, but Old Man Winter still reigns supreme in New England.

"The Hannaford bagger—the young one with the self-aware mullet—he told me we're getting a snowstorm," Mia says, a little too upbeat for Cricket's liking.

"Something to look forward to," Cricket huffs. "I can't let in a goal like that ever again, even if I couldn't feel my hands during the second half." Cricket cracks her window and forces herself to count her breaths. If she doesn't have soccer, she doesn't have anything.

"Are you okay?" Mia asks.

"Carsick," Cricket says. "You drive like Mom."

They stop at a roadside creamery in their big winter coats. When they get out, Mia keeps the van running, the heat on full blast. Even so, by the time they return, Cricket's sweaty hair crunches between her fingers, half frozen.

"I need to double down on my training," she says, unsheathing her straw with her teeth. "I've been taking it too easy if I want to be the best." Buckling her seatbelt between sips of her strawberry milkshake, Cricket elaborates. "Coach says he has a call scheduled with Teague, the head coach of the full National Team, not the Youth National Team, but, like, the actual full team."

"About you?"

Cricket nods. "He said he'd put in a good word."

"As he should," Mia says, face reddening at the thought of him. They cross the Piscataqua River Bridge and, upon reentering their state, pass the new blue sign in Kittery that says, "Maine: Welcome Home." Underneath, in smaller lettering, the board honors the decades-old slogan, "The Way Life Should Be."

Cricket scoffs as she stares at it. "That sign actually has icicles on it."

"It's March," Mia says defensively. "What do you expect?"

"But this isn't the way life should be. It's why half my grade is going somewhere tropical over spring break."

"You know Maine is why you're as tough as you are, right?" Mia looks over. "It's trained you just as much as Coach has."

"First you drive like Mom and now you sound like her."

"Thank you?"

"If we lived somewhere warm, I'd be as good as Sloane," Cricket argues, staring at the trees lining the highway, their bare branches shivering in the wind.

"How do you figure?"

Cricket holds up her hand to count off the reasons. "I'd be able to practice outside all the time, and the ground wouldn't be frozen for half the year, which means fewer injuries."

"But you're not injured," Mia points out, trying to disguise her fear. "Right?" She's not totally clear on how their health insurance works, but she knows that physically, financially, and spiritually, they cannot afford Cricket getting hurt.

"I'm fine." Cricket extracts a lock of hair from her high pouf and begins to weave a tiny braid in front of her nose. "We just need to get to L.A.," she says. "I'm sick of winter and I'm done wearing this stupid junk just to go for a run." She holds up a tangle of rubber and metal in her hand—a mysterious accessory to warm-weather dwellers but a ubiquitous necessity to Northerners everywhere. Indeed, one could measure a Mainer's life in Yaktrax.

"Blasphemous!" Mia teases, reaching over to snatch her spikes from the ungrateful naysayer beside her. In a slippery, unpredictable world, Mia appreciates a bit of traction.

Cricket, however, says she's going to throw out her Yaktrax the day she leaves for college. "Or maybe I'll burn them, just for the drama."

"But you'll still need them when you come home," Mia points out.

"Maybe I shouldn't come home," Cricket sasses. "Maybe we should sell the house and make a new home out there."

"Maybe," Mia says, humoring her sister for the ease of the moment although she can't imagine ever selling the house. It's a direct portal to their mother—the closest thing they have to her hugs is the roof over their heads. The spice drawer is still disorganized, but only because Mia now sees it as an homage, and Liz's bed remains in the exact same state of unmade mess that it was the morning of November ninth. "But still," Mia insists, "you can't underestimate Yaktrax—especially on black ice."

"Fuck black ice," Cricket says defiantly, challenging the gods of winter. And because Mia is her sister and not her mother, and therefore takes no issue with Cricket's casual profanity, she bursts out laughing. After everything they've been through, that they're still going through, this is the hill Cricket will die on. "I'm serious," Cricket growls. "Fuck black ice, and fuck Sloane Jackson."

What she really wants to say is, *I can't do this, I'm just going to let you down,* but she can't put that on Mia. Even if they've never discussed it, Cricket knows—and has always known—that Mia has given up her life to support Cricket's. She's given up soccer, Yale, and even her relationship with Ben all for Cricket's potential career, and Cricket isn't sure she even has a potential career after today's piss-poor performance.

"I get you're frustrated about Sloane," Mia says, glancing over at her sister before turning on the windshield wipers to their maximum output. "But can we please not pick a fight with public enemy number one until we get home?"

When Liz taught Mia how to drive, she repeatedly told her to take her foot off the gas as soon as Mia felt the car begin to slide on ice. "Jamming on the brakes is the most dangerous thing you can do," Liz lectured. "It's better to just turn your wheel in the direction of the tread and hope for the best."

"You mean give up control?" Mia had asked, clearly appalled.

"Mother Nature demands respect," Liz explained. "So if the tires slide, or you feel yourself start to lose your grip, it's safer to just go with it."

But right now, Mia forgets her mother's advice. She forgets that sometimes black ice will undercut the most vigilant Mainer. She forgets that sometimes the conditions make surrender necessary and that losing her grip can be inevitable. And so when the front right tire slides on a patch of black ice, Mia slams on the brakes.

The car bucks under her foot as other drivers honk and swerve to avoid a collision. It lasts seconds and it goes on forever and then Mia hears her mother's advice in her head and she releases the brake and follows the tread and allows the car and nature and the forces beyond her hands to guide the momvan off the highway and into a divot piled so high in snow that it isn't much of a divot at all. The snowbank acts as a bumper, and the van comes to a complete stop in the middle of the highway.

Mia looks over at Cricket and recognizes that her own arm has become a guardrail between her sister and the windshield. "You okay?"

Cricket nods. "What do we do?"

"Call 911?" Mia wonders, stunned, looking out her window and rubbernecking the rubberneckers. "Or I could just try to drive?"

"Um no. Call 911," Cricket insists. "What if something happened to the engine and it's about to blow up?"

The girls look at each other and then wordlessly evacuate the van, hearts thumping as their feet slide in the gray slush of highway snow. Mia calls the police from a safe distance away and within a few minutes, the girls hear sirens and see the emergency lights of a police car and an ambulance weaving through Sunday evening traffic.

"This is so embarrassing," Mia says. "Everyone is staring at us."

"Let them do their job," Cricket says, typing on her phone.

"But we're fine."

"We think we're fine but it might be the adrenaline rush," Cricket says, looking over at the abandoned momvan. "I want them to make sure the car isn't going to blow up."

"Fair," Mia admits.

"Coach is coming," Cricket says. "I texted him."

"What? Why?"

"Because I can't call Mom."

"But what can he do?" Mia asks, annoyed. "Yell from the sidelines?"

"What is your problem?" Cricket snaps, looking up from her phone. "He was ten miles behind us anyway."

"But what do you expect him to do that we can't do for ourselves?" Mia asks, not backing down. "He's going to think we're damsels, and we're not damsels."

"I know that," Cricket says, raising her voice. "But if the van is busted, how do you plan on getting home?"

The police and the EMTs are shockingly jovial as they approach the car and assess the situation. "It's always a relief to see something like this," one EMT tells Mia after asking her to wiggle her fingers and toes. They are okay and the van is, too. "You got very lucky," he says.

Mia looks over to check on her sister, who is talking to one of the EMTs with her hands about playing on the National Team. At times,

Cricket's confidence embarrasses Mia, but right now she takes pride in it, grateful that whatever just happened didn't compromise her sister's future. No shattered bones, no skull through the windshield, no reason to even go to the hospital. They were lucky. And before she can stop herself, Mia imagines her mom in those final seconds and clings to what the officer said—that it happened too quickly for Liz to experience any pain, any fear. Mia can only hope she was telling the truth.

The sun sinks lower. Mia finally relaxes just enough to experience the cold. Shivering, she watches Oliver pull up. He parks his black SUV a respectful thirty feet behind the ambulance, and he sprints through the snow in sneakers made almost entirely of bright blue mesh. Mia can practically feel his socks and toes getting wet, can imagine how miserable his drive home will be.

As Oliver runs toward them, the look on his face sends up a flare in Mia's chest. They stare at each other as the distance between them closes, both of them understanding something is happening, something is shifting with every step he takes.

Oliver brushes by one of the EMTs, then both police officers, and Mia notices the snow glittering all around him, and the highway on Oliver's left takes on that shimmer she's been trained to see as a warning, and no matter how much she wants to pump the brake, she can feel herself losing traction. She hears her mother's voice, encouraging her to surrender, so she goes with the tread and knows that what's about to happen is far more dangerous than black ice but just as slick with inevitability.

"Are you okay?" Oliver asks, reaching Mia in the snow-covered median and scooping her into a hug without gravity's permission. Her feet dangle in the air. His cheek presses against hers. When Oliver lowers Mia back down to the ground, he doesn't let go, and his hug feels so warm and sturdy that Mia suddenly wants to fall asleep right there on the highway.

"Home," she breathes into his neck, closing her eyes to shut out the rest of the world. This deep-seeded attraction, like any natural disaster making landfall, feels sudden but has been a long time coming. Mia's just been too busy carpooling for the Stallions, too bundled up in grief and Smartwool, too busy meal-planning on a tight budget to notice what's gradually taken hold.

"Home?" Oliver asks, his voice muffled against her snow hat. It sounds different, this close to the source. Intimate.

"I want to go home," Mia improvises.

"Yeah, I bet." Oliver swivels his head, looking for Cricket.

"She's in the back of the ambulance, talking about the World Cup."

Oliver laughs knowingly and takes Mia's hand, guiding her back to her sister. Through her gloves, Mia feels his long fingers, his tight grip, and wants to wrap herself up in him. How had she not seen this before?

After the EMTs clear them for injuries and the police file their report, Oliver insists on escorting the Lowes back home, just in case the van starts acting up.

"I told you he was the right person to call," Cricket says as the police direct them back onto the highway. Looking in the rearview mirror to wave at Coach, Cricket grins, pleased with herself. "Anyone else on the team would have made this about them and turned it into, like, content." Mia musters a laugh.

An hour later, the momvan rolls along the plowed streets of Victory without a problem. But Mia's heart flips over itself with the blind audacity of a kid practicing somersaults down a ski slope. Panicking, she loiters in front of her own driveway, engine running, window down.

"All good?" Oliver asks, pulling up next to them and offering a thumbs-up.

"Want stay for dinner?" Mia calls over, too loudly.

"Yes!" Cricket shouts from the passenger seat. "Do it!"

A pause. The van rattles, doubting itself. Oliver looks down at his lap, and Mia wonders if he's checking the calendar on his phone.

"Maybe another time?" he says finally. It strikes Mia as excruciatingly awkward. "I've got plans tonight."

"No, you don't," Cricket says. After the tournament, while peeling off her socks, Cricket had overheard Coach wondering aloud whether to order pad thai or pizza when he got home.

"I'm glad you're safe," he says, ignoring Cricket. Mia smiles mechanically before Coach drives off. At the end of the street, he turns right. She blinks and he's gone.

Unlocking the front door, Mia bolts straight for the bathroom. Staring down her reflection in the mirror, she berates herself for her impulsive invitation. She'd misread Oliver's chivalry for connection, and he'd flat-out rejected her, which is probably for the best because what was she thinking? Oliver belongs to Cricket the same way blue prewrap and sweat-stained socks and peanut butter protein bars belong to Cricket. They are her soccer things.

That night, as her sister flips through shows to watch, Mia sits next to her on the pink floral couch and tries logging in to her old Yale account. She needs to go back to school and be with people her own age, on a campus full of eligible men who will buy her shots on a Saturday night with one obvious goal in mind that has nothing to do with soccer. Unfortunately, her password has expired.

When Cricket finally lands on *Family Feud*, Mia decides to hell with Yale. Cricket is right—they just need to get to California.

"I'm going to apply to UCLA with you," Mia announces.

"HELL YES!" Cricket screams, jumping off the couch and dancing in front of the TV. The decision feels right. Obvious, even. Mia determines that UCLA is the best place for her next romantic relationship. And until then, she needs to save face by avoiding Oliver as much as humanly possible.

ALL THAT NOTHING

Carl is urinating in the middle of the waiting room.

"Our big boy is so nervous," his owner says, massaging the two-hundred-pound mastiff behind the ears. It's hardly the first time such disorderly conduct has occurred at Oceanside Animal Hospital—it's not even the first time this week—so Mia abandons the front desk and, wielding an industrial-size bottle of Urine Destroyer, gets down on her knees in front of several panting dogs and wonders how her life came to this.

When Mia finally returns to her seat, she does a double take when she sees a missed call from Oliver. It's been forty-eight hours since she made an ass of herself by inviting him to dinner. Forty-eight hours since she vowed to steer clear of him.

"Sorry to bother you at work," he says when she calls him back. "I was just thinking about you and wanted to see how you're doing." His voice on the line makes Mia instantly dizzy—unless that's just the residual fumes of the concentrated cleaning solution affecting her brain.

"I'm good," Mia says, not trusting herself to elaborate. *He was thinking about her?*

"Well, that's great to hear." A beat. And then another. "I guess I'm really calling because I was rude on Sunday," Oliver says, and here he takes a deep breath. "It's just—I didn't think it would have been a good idea to have dinner with you and Cricket."

"Oh," Mia manages, looking around for her water bottle. All at once she is desperately thirsty. "Why?"

"So I've—" Oliver starts, and then cuts himself off. "Sorry, let me think of a good way to say this." He clears his throat and then, instead of speaking, he clears it a second time. Finally, he says, "I didn't think it would be appropriate with everything going on right now."

"Yeah, of course." Mia flips through world events and Stallions gossip but comes up empty. "Wait, sorry, what's going on right now?"

"With the National Women's Soccer League—my bad, I assumed— it's just out of respect for—" Oliver interrupts himself several times before finding a way in. "A bunch of coaches, at every level of women's soccer, have been accused of misconduct by their players."

"Someone's accused you?" Mia asks, her stomach knotting. She almost hangs up.

"No. God no," Oliver says. "Definitely not, but I—this is what I didn't want to say, except now you're thinking—"

"What didn't you want to say?" Mia interrupts.

"Clear boundaries are the smartest course of action," Oliver states. He sounds like a lawyer reading out the terms of a restraining order.

"That's what you wanted to say?" Her heart plummets through her stomach and lands with a splat on Oceanside's laminate floors.

"No." Another long pause. "It's just—running into you—"

"I like running into you," Mia argues, emboldened by his incoherence. She is supposed to be avoiding this man, but he is not as grown up as she once thought, and he's so nervous right now, she can feel it through the phone. And it's because of her. She has the power to make him nervous.

In the silence that follows, Mia imagines Oliver running a hand through his dirty blond hair that curls when he goes too long without a haircut. All the Stallions mothers openly swoon over those curls, and according to Cricket, most of her teammates do, too.

"That's the thing," Oliver eventually says. "I like running into you, too."

Mia wills herself to stay quiet, to bait him into elaborating.

"See, this is where it gets tricky," Oliver admits. "Because it's—you probably—oh man, okay, so the truth is that I'm very attracted to you," he says, his voice dropping as he finds his footing. "And if Cricket weren't my player, I would have asked you out on a proper date months ago—"

"Well, *I'm* not your player," Mia says. Because she has already done this math, and her head is buzzing, her skin prickling, her entire body hot. Did he really just say he's very attracted to her?

"Right, but Cricket is," Oliver asserts, and the words land like cinder blocks hurled down a staircase. "And I can't pursue a relationship with you without it changing my relationship to her, which alters the dynamics on the team."

"Oh."

"Circumstances don't allow it, but in a perfect world, I would like to take you out," Oliver clarifies. "And not just because I know you've invested in a brand-new toilet seat."

Mia laughs. "You won't be her coach forever," she points out. "Right?"

"Through her senior fall," he says with a loud exhale, like senior fall is the new life sentence. "The championship is in November."

All the soccer talk makes Mia thinks of her parents, but Oliver is not Q and she is not her mother. For one, Mia is an adult with more life experience than most people her age. And while her father took advantage of her mother's naïveté, Oliver has gone out of his way to show Mia his hand.

He interrupts her thoughts. "Cricket said the two of you plan to go to UCLA after she graduates?"

"Yeah," Mia manages. "That's the plan." She holds up a finger to a woman trying to check in her rabbit, but Mia needs another minute to know where this is going, if anywhere at all.

"So given that timeline," Oliver says slowly, "coaching through November, you leaving the following August—I guess what I'm saying is, it's hard to justify the risk, you know?"

Mia does know. The cracked door of possibility slams shut with a bang. It's going nowhere because Cricket is going to the championships in November, and college in California, and Mia's life is in service to her sister. Once again, she will sacrifice her own desire for Cricket's destiny.

With Oliver still in her ear, Mia thinks of being fourteen and walking away from her own soccer team. She sees the stained glass windows of Yale's archival library, Ben's face on her pillow, Dr. Peters and Nell and Landon. All those well-rooted connections she let wither on the vine. Coach will join them as just another doomed husk of potential, a once-supple *what-if*—

"So I guess that's it," Oliver says, clearing his throat and summoning his professional signing-off cadence. "Cricket is lucky to have you."

"I could say the same thing about you," Mia says. "See you on the sidelines."

And that's it.

They hang up.

While checking in the rabbit, Mia rationalizes not telling Cricket about Oliver.

Nothing good can come from it, Mia reasons. Cricket will call the situation all too quickly like she is defending a penalty kick instead of supporting her sister. She will judge Mia harshly and boldly draw the inaccurate parallel to their parents. Even worse, if Cricket told her teammates, Oliver could face the exact consequences he's trying to avoid by not taking her out on a date, even though he said he'd "really like to." Just remembering his voice makes Mia blush as she answers an email inquiring about microdosing THC for an anxious parakeet.

She will not tell Cricket. Instead, Mia decides to keep this secret to herself because nothing happened. And nothing ever will happen. It's a mutual crush that can't go anywhere. She replays the moment when Oliver said, *"I'm very attracted to you,"* and then reminds herself that it's nothing, absolutely nothing, to counteract the levitating high of such an admission.

But it's nothing the way an empty soccer field is nothing. The way potential energy is nothing. It is white lines painted across a green rectangle and a ball suspended in midair. It is dirt and grass and sky and crisp air and low humidity with a 10 percent chance of rain. The field conditions are irrelevant until it's time to play, and then all that nothing becomes a match. Mia can't unsee the possibility, just like she can't wait to be in Oliver's presence again, because all that nothing has to add up. Even if she can't win the game, it's got to count for something.

CALIFORNIA DREAMING

In September of her senior year, Cricket receives the news she's imagined hearing for a decade: She's been invited to the full U.S. Women's National Team Training Camp in Carson, California. "The National Team!" she shrieks at Mia. "The full team! The real, actual National Team! I'm officially in the pool!"

Cricket knows there's no way she'll make the roster for any of their upcoming friendly matches or tournaments, let alone the World Cup next summer in Australia and New Zealand, but it's an honor to be brought into the pool of talent. Sloane Jackson is the only other goalkeeper still in high school to be invited, so Cricket's focus is on outperforming the towering Floridian.

"Just play," Coach tells her at the last Stallions practice before her departure. "Stay grounded and show up—you know how to do that."

The morning Cricket arrives in California, she recognizes Sloane from thirty feet away at LAX baggage claim. It doesn't matter that Sloane is dressed down to the point of incognito celebrity: black baseball cap with the rim pulled low, black zip-up hoodie, black leggings, white recovery slides on her feet. Even in the bad lighting, Sloane sticks out. She's a human exclamation point, and when she tilts her head back to watch another load of bags descend the silver slide, Cricket is hardly the only one to gawk. Online, Sloane is pretty; in person, she's a six-foot stun gun of gorgeous.

Cricket watches others clock Sloane, nudging elbows to ask each other, *Who is that?* They assume she's a model and Cricket smirks at their ignorance. They mistake Sloane for a fawn or some other leggy herbivore.

Just then, Sloane spots her, proving Cricket right. Predators always sense the competition. The two keepers are connected by a mutual respect as much as a high prey drive.

"Hey!" Sloane shouts from the other side of the room. She strides to close the space between them, giving Cricket just enough time to realize Sloane Jackson is the Tom Brady of women's soccer—too attractive to also be so talented, like her parents double-dipped in the genetic fondue of good fortune.

"Thank God you're here!" Sloane says, pulling Cricket into an unexpected hug. "Can we split an Uber to campus? I'm so nervous right now I want to puke." She smiles and Cricket notices the dimple in Sloane's left cheek, the sharp points of her canine teeth. "I've been waiting to meet you for so long—like, actually meet you, not just play against you in that Little Rhody tournament that suuucked. Also Meg Vinson says you're better than me—she says hi, by the way. I can't believe she tore her ACL again. Do you think they'll let us be roommates?"

Over the first twenty-four hours of camp, Cricket is shocked by how much she enjoys Sloane's company on and off the field. No one understands the pressure of being a goalkeeper quite like another goalkeeper. "That wasn't your fault," Sloane says under her breath during a water break. "You had to come out or she would have literally walked the ball into the goal."

Cricket repays Sloane's insights in kind, paying close attention when she's not in goal. "You narrowed the angle but you could have shut her down completely," Cricket says after Sloane lets in a shot. "You need to set quicker—I know, it was chaos in the box, but you've got to set first and then manage the chaos, not the other way around."

Sloane squints at her, debating whether to thank Cricket or tell her to piss off. Ultimately, she does neither. Instead, Sloane says dryly, "It's too bad you're better at coaching than keeping."

Around them, a few low defenders laugh at this, but none of them join in the banter. They are too worried about their own performance. This is called training camp, but everyone knows it's a tryout. On their iPads and in their exchanged raised eyebrows, the coaching staff takes copious notes on who exceeds, meets, and falls short of their expectations. Cricket understands that every field is an audition and that her top competitor over these ten days is also the closest thing she has to a friend.

"Did you see you that video of Messi rating his favorite power snacks?" Sloane asks at lunch, emptying a square packet of pumpkin seeds on top of her salad.

Cricket stares at the salad and then up at Sloane. "Did you bring those from home?"

"Sure did," Sloane says. "These were at the top of Messi's list—they're loaded with iron."

Cricket has never paid as much attention to what she eats as maybe she should—she's always just consumed whatever Mia threw together on a shoestring budget. But at camp, she copies what Sloane puts on her tray, and maybe it's just the placebo effect, but she's bursting with energy by day three.

"Do you always feel like this?" Cricket asks, taking a sip of water from one of the four glasses on her tray. For the first time in her life, she is properly hydrated, thanks to an electrolyte-tracking app Sloane shared with her. And despite the long, physically exhausting, and emotionally taxing days, her body is eager to push itself, which Cricket attributes to the protein shake that the National Team's performance coach custom makes for her each morning at six a.m.

"Do I always feel like what?" Sloane spools zucchini pasta onto her fork.

"Like the Incredible Hulk?"

Sloane snarfs, nearly choking on her pasta, and Cricket notices the veteran players look over with curious smiles. They know of Sloane from the lucrative endorsements she's already signed as a high schooler and the murmurs that she'll be the next Gatorade Player of the Year.

"My dad says the only way to play like a pro athlete is to eat like one," Sloane says. "He's such a nerd but really supportive."

Cricket nods, thinking of her own dad. Every day on the soccer field, she sets out to prove that she is not like Q, that she is the opposite of him. He may not be supportive like Sloane's dad, but Q is most certainly a source of motivation. Right there at the lunch table, Cricket nearly admits to Sloane that while she is sometimes scared of her own ambition, it's the possibility of failing that truly terrifies her.

Instead, Cricket says nothing. Camp isn't the place for such vulnerability; camp is a battlefield. Cricket swallows the truth of her father and uses it for fuel to fight for her spot on the National Team.

"Damn, Lowe!" Sloane catcalls from the sideline after Cricket lays out for a block in a warm-up drill. The intense flash of contact with the ball always feels like coming home to herself. Cricket slams her gloves together and even through the thick padding, she can feel the voltage of her own potential.

"She better watch out," Liz says, appearing at the left goalpost. The tails of her red hair ribbon reach for Cricket in the breeze. "Sloane is impressed by you—threatened, even." Cricket eagerly imbibes the mystical boost of maternal support as she visualizes her future on the National Team.

In the days to come, Cricket refuses to yield. She is smarter, more vocal, and more willing to come off her line, forcing the attacker to make a mistake. Her playing builds her confidence, and her confidence boosts her playing, and as she reaches new heights while deepening her flow state, Cricket becomes unstoppable.

"This is called training camp for a reason," Teague, the National Team head coach, tells Cricket on the sideline toward the end of the week. "This isn't the championship match; this is the laboratory, where you see what works and what doesn't, and let me just say, I'm seeing a lot of stuff that works. You should be proud of yourself."

"Thank you, Coach," Cricket says, squirting water into her mouth to hide her grin. In her periphery, she feels Sloane's envious gaze, but Cricket stares past her to the vast green field of her destiny.

THE DRAWBRIDGE

The bridge is up.

Of course it is.

The bridge is never up when Mia is running fifteen minutes ahead of schedule; it's only up when she doesn't have a moment to spare. It's only up at critical junctures like this one, when she is trying to do something big and has already been stalled by a flock of wild turkeys lollygagging across Route 77. And now she is going to show up late to meet a stranger who won't understand that, in a world without draw-bridges and turkeys, she is a Swiss watch in human form.

Mia takes a breath to reset. It's just an informational interview she intentionally scheduled while Cricket is at training camp. Everything will be fine. She snaps the hair tie on her wrist and reaches for her thermos.

The sudden knock on her passenger-side window scares Mia so badly that she jumps and spills a significant amount of coffee down the front of her blouse.

"Oh shit!" Oliver yells through the glass. "I'm so sorry!"

He opens the door and he's shirtless and the coffee burning Mia's skin is just confusing because the hot feels like cold, and the cold feels like hot, and who looks that good without a shirt on in real life?

"Are you okay?" Oliver asks. "I didn't mean to—sorry, I was on a run, and I spotted your van, but I'm so sorry about—" They both blush as he gestures to her coffee-soaked blouse, the stain spreading across her chest. "Give it to me and I'll dry-clean it—not now, obviously, but— shit, where are you going?"

"USM," Mia says. She can't believe she's running this late or that he's right here, just an arm's length away. Ever since their phone call four months ago, Mia has intentionally avoided him. She stays in the car when picking up or dropping off Cricket at practice. At matches, she arrives just in time for the first whistle and books it back to the parking lot after the final play. When Cricket asks why Mia didn't hang out after the game with the other parents, she says she was editing her UCLA application. She's never mentioned Coach, and Cricket has never suspected anything because there isn't anything. It's nothing.

"Do you want to sit down?" Mia asks through the passenger-side window, and before she can remove her notebook from the seat, Oliver is next to her and facing forward as they sit idling in the shadow of the lifted drawbridge.

"How are you doing without Cricket this week?" he asks, still breathing heavily from his run. Mia tries not to ogle his stomach, the faint trail of hair below his belly button, the insulin pump clipped to his shorts, the bead of sweat rolling down the side of his neck.

"I could ask you the same thing," Mia says.

"Our reserve keeper is definitely getting some good exposure and learning some tough lessons," Oliver says in his professional voice. His smile makes Mia swallow hard. She's suddenly aware that she's envious of the Stallions' backup goalkeeper, a high school sophomore named Alice with terrible acne and the SATs still looming ahead of her. But Alice gets to spend time with Oliver.

Mia's own interactions have been limited to a dozen *hey there*s and *see-ya*s yelled from afar. But even from across a soccer field, Mia has felt the pulse of connection between them, and now, sitting so close to him, it isn't a faint thrum like it was on the bleachers all summer but the same urgent, almost violent anxiety she experiences while watching Cricket in goal during penalty kicks.

"What are you doing there?" Oliver asks. At Mia's blank look, he clarifies. "At the University of Southern Maine?"

"I'm not convinced I'll get into UCLA," Mia admits. "Or that even if I do, the financial package won't be"—she pauses, self-consciously—"what it needs to be."

"I hear that."

"So I figured I should look into USM," Mia continues, bolstered by his sympathy. "I could take classes but live at home, still work."

Oliver nods, considering this strategy. "Cricket would be okay going to California without you?"

"She'd have to be," Mia says, sounding more defensive than she intended. "Even if it means sitting her down and showing her the numbers in our bank account."

"Right," Oliver answers supportively. And then, this alternative reality dawning on him in real time, he folds his hands in his lap and adds, "Interesting."

The bridge begins to lower, and with it, Mia's heart sinks because she doesn't want him to get out of the car. Not yet. Not after so many months of nothing. "Please don't leave," she says, surprised by her own impulsiveness.

"Mia," he says slowly, giving her goosebumps and red cheeks and a restless tongue.

"You're not my coach," she argues. "And you're not going to be Cricket's coach—"

"I'm hearing things about the Yates Report," Oliver says. "It won't officially come out until October, but there have been some leaks already, and it's disgusting—all the abuse that's just run rampant through every level of women's soccer, and I just don't—I don't want to be part of the problem."

"But you're not part of the problem," Mia says. The drawbridge security system dings and the sea of red taillights disappears as traffic begins to flow forward. "Don't you—or am I just—"

"No," he interrupts, looking over at her. "You're never just."

"What?"

"You're never 'just' anything," he emphasizes. "You're the opposite of that."

The car in front of them moves so Mia releases her foot from the brake and Oliver buckles up. Together, they drive off the bridge and into the city of Portland. Mia pulls over on the first available side street and puts the van in park before examining the coffee stain down her front.

"I need to cancel this informational interview," she says, picking up her phone and rapidly typing an email.

"I'm sorry about the coffee," Oliver says. "And everything else."

Mia presses Send and stares through the windshield, thinking of what she'd like to say, what she might say to change his mind without it sounding desperate.

"You're twenty-two and I'll be thirty this winter," Oliver says as if his math proves a point. "That's a huge age gap even without power dynamics—"

"I'm well aware of our age difference," Mia snips, agitated. For months, before and after every Stallions soccer game that she simultaneously dreaded and tried on multiple outfits for, Mia ran the numbers. They are seven and a half years apart, and still young enough that every year between them feels institutionally significant—collegiate years, and postgrad years, and then the not-so-young adult years. Mia has tried to add and subtract what she knows to see if she can change the equation, but just as crushes bend logic, they also defy math.

For example, how does one quantify the value of a man who brings extra hats and gloves to winter practices? Who can take a game so seriously but never himself? Who believes in grounding and visualization, but also alien conspiracy theories? Who talks with his hands and smiles with his eyes and, try as he might, cannot for the life of him, despite yoga four times a week, touch his toes? Who once took the entire team to an arcade in Maryland after their tournament was rained out, won a stuffed animal tiger from the claw crane, named it Carol Burnett, and now keeps Carol in his soccer bag at all times because he swears she's his good luck charm? Whose triceps are a triumph among men? Who regularly helps out the high-maintenance Miss Bits and her sociopathic puppy, Trevor? Who is a card-carrying member of Costco because his players swear Kirkland brand makes the best peanut butter pretzels? Who speaks to the Stallions about prioritizing joy and promotes tools for boosting mental health? Who knew Mia's mother—loved Mia's mother—and has learned to navigate life without his own parents?

"We are not the same age," Mia says now, regaining her composure. "But you are not my coach, and you hold no power over me."

Oliver laughs to himself as he runs a hand through his hair just like he does when the Stallions are down a goal. "But you've got power over me," he says to Mia with those sea-glass green eyes. "I know that sounds like a lame pickup line, but it's—"

With her seatbelt still fastened, Mia leans over and grabs Oliver's face with both hands. She kisses him because she'll die if she doesn't. She kisses him like she's needed to ever since she watched his mesh sneakers get soaked in the snow on that highway median. She kisses him until he gives up on his unfinished sentence. It's both satisfying and not enough after so many months of want.

"Mia," Oliver says when she finally pulls back. His eyes are still closed, lips hoping for more.

"Yes?" She likes how her name sounds when he says it, like there has never been a Mia before her, Hamm be damned.

Oliver's eyes flutter open as he laughs nervously, the tops of his ears prickling pink. He traces her bottom lip with his thumb. "This," he says dreamily. "Can we just—never stop?"

Over the next five days, while Cricket is away with the National Team, Mia and Oliver engage in their own intense training camp—bonding as teammates and learning to communicate as they become more themselves in each other's company. In Mia's childhood bedroom, they test their stamina in minimal clothing. During full recovery sessions, they hydrate, refuel, and stretch the limitations of new intimacy.

Mia tells Oliver about the summer Q came to town, and her mother's impromptu New Year's Eve polar plunges, and Mia's discovery in the archival library her first year of college. She tells him about the magical trip to Paris, and trying to give her mother a budget, and realizing only recently that her childhood felt like an adult partnership with a woman who was still a kid herself.

Oliver confides in Mia about becoming an angry teenager—first when he rebelled against his parents' evangelical beliefs, and then again when he was diagnosed with Type 1 diabetes and they said it was a sign from God. After they encouraged him to meet with their church's youth pastor rather than seek medical treatment, Oliver moved out, living at a teammate's house for the rest of high school before earning a full athletic scholarship for college.

"I literally shipped up to Boston and never told my parents," Oliver says, twirling one of Mia's ringlets around his finger, just as her mother used to do. But the anger followed him to New England, he tells her, and after getting called a hothead and earning enough red cards to put him on team probation, Oliver started therapy. "Dr. Eiseman has really helped me," Oliver says. "And even though I only speak to my parents through birthday cards," he continues, "at least I'm no longer angry at them."

"You still yell a lot," Mia points out, propping herself up on a pillow.

"I'll stop now," Oliver says. "I was just trying to get your attention."

"By shouting at teenage girls?"

"Encouraging them!" Oliver insists. "And look!" he shouts with self-mockery. "It works!" he bellows over Mia's laughter. "Don't you feel encouraged?"

One morning at dawn, Oliver admits he initially resented coaching girls, but now he'll never go back to the men's side of the game. "Girls are just, I don't know," he says, searching for his socks and the right words. "More dynamic?" He then suggests they walk to the bakery so he can try the croissants that Mia claims are the best in the state. It's the happiest Mia has felt since her mother died, which seems like enough justification to not tell her sister what's developed in her absence.

Mia knows from the daily calls and texts she receives from California that Cricket is also thriving. She's competing against the best players in the country and having fun doing it. She is not only outperforming Sloane but also bonding with her, which Mia loves to hear. What neither of them says out loud is that Sloane is the first friend Cricket has made since November ninth.

And so three thousand miles apart, each Lowe sister flies high on the euphoria of self-discovery. They are sweating out grief. Having endured the worst few years of their lives, they are allowing themselves to revel in the 360-degree bliss of being exactly where they want to be.

AMBITIOUS WITCHES

O n the last night of camp and in full sweatsuits, Sloane and Cricket lie on the carpeted floor of Cricket's room with their legs up the wall.

"Can I cut your hair?" Sloane asks with her eyes closed, already half asleep.

"Why?" Cricket grabs her high bun protectively.

"Because I want it!" Sloane reaches over to palm Cricket's blond pouf, a sly grin across her face, her eyes still shut.

"But you have amazing hair," Cricket argues. It's true. In fact, most people would contend that Sloane has the nicest locks of anyone at camp—raven black tresses that cascade down her back like ocean waves at midnight. For training sessions, however, Sloane gathers all of that undulating silk into what's become her signature bubble ponytail, although their teammates are now calling it the "Sloaney tail" and trying to outlaw it because during drills that tail whips at them like a medieval weapon.

Sloane sighs dramatically, releases Cricket's bun, and stares up at the ceiling. "Isn't it sort of pathetic how we always want what we can't have?"

Cricket nods and allows her own eyes to close. There are so many things she wants that she can't have: She wants her mother to be alive, and she wants a verbal scholarship offer from UCLA. She wants to win the NCAA championship all four years as a Bruin, and then she wants to become the starting goalkeeper of the National Team without having to oust Alyssa Naeher or hurt Sloane's feelings. She wants to earn clean sheets in every match, and win the Olympics and the World Cup, and she wants to stay on this floor with Sloane Jackson forever because the carpet is like plush quicksand and she's so tired and also her right foot is asleep and she's scared to move it.

"I've thought about bailing on college," Sloane blurts out.

"What?"

"When I visited Stanford, everyone on the team seemed cool and the campus was sick, but for a couple of weeks I thought, What if I just went pro? You know Alyssa will retire in a few years—she's thirty-four now—so if I skipped—"

Sloane cuts herself short. What she doesn't say is that if she were to go pro now, she'd have a four-year head start on Cricket for Alyssa's starting spot on the full National Team. Friends or not, the competition between them is always lurking just below the surface. Rivalry isn't in the water—it is the water. It's what can buoy or drown them.

"I'm glad you're here," Sloane says, turning to face Cricket. "No one else gets it."

Smiling through a grimace, Cricket tries to wake up her right foot by rolling her ankle in the air. "How could they?" she asks.

"I know we need to compete against each other, but can we stay friends through it?"

"Totally," Cricket says. "Just don't expect me to take it easy on you."

"Seriously?" Sloane says with a theatrical scoff. "We only get along because we're both ruthless brutes."

"That might be the truest thing you've ever said." They both bring their legs back down to Earth and Cricket adds, "Although I'm more of an ambitious witch than a ruthless brute."

"Yes!" Sloane says. "Ambitious witches sound way cuter."

"You know," Cricket says, sitting up. "Unless one of us really starts to suck, we'll never get to play on the same club team because we'll both be starters."

"I think we should talk every Sunday," Sloane says, getting to her feet. "We review each other's game over the weekend and talk about it Sunday night."

"Why?" Cricket stays put on the floor and looks up at the only person who wholly understands what she wants and the only person who could stand in her way.

"To hold each other accountable and point out what no one else will," Sloane says. "Deal?"

"Deal," Cricket says, sticking out her hand.

Sloane shakes it but doesn't let go. Instead, she extends her other hand as well, offering to pull Cricket up off the floor. Cricket doesn't hesitate to reach for Sloane's open palms. Their crossed arms form an *X* as they find their footing.

They cannot yet fathom how far offtrack their careers will veer from their original design. They cannot yet know about the black eyes and bloody noses and stress fractures and ingrown toenails and black toenails and missing toenails. They cannot yet lament how prioritizing soccer means not pursuing other sources of fulfillment. They cannot yet appreciate how they will grow and improve, and how they will prematurely develop crow's-feet from double training sessions in the sun and deep worry lines from playing a game. There in Cricket's hotel room, they cannot yet imagine how soccer will unequivocally fill, torment, mend, and mangle both of their hearts.

GAME CHANGE

"How is homecoming still a thing?" the boy next to Cricket asks her as morning announcements play over the loudspeaker. Cricket shrugs as she continues a frantic search for her Spanish take-home test. At the bottom of her backpack, thousands of tiny black rubber pellets from the high school's turf field cluster together—enough to bury her house keys—but the test isn't in there.

Cricket doesn't care about homecoming for multiple reasons, not least because she has the New England Club Soccer League championship in Boston the same weekend. She won't be around for the dance, which she wouldn't necessarily attend anyway. But then she hears her name announced.

"Ah, Cristina!" Senora Vazquez says, clapping her hands. "Homecoming Court! ¡Muchas felicidades!"

Following their teacher's lead, the class applauds politely, so Cricket gives up her backpack probe and offers a campaign smile. She didn't see this coming, but a win is a win. As Cricket's competitive spirit embraces the fresh challenge, she remembers all too late that she left her take-home test on the kitchen table.

That afternoon, a coastal storm rolls in and lightning strikes halfway through soccer practice. Lucy, Cricket's co-captain for Victory High's varsity team, drops her off at home an hour earlier than usual. As they approach 125 Knickerbocker, Cricket mulls over her homecoming nomination. Her high school team—the Black Bears—will probably win another conference championship this year because no one seems able to score on Cricket. Everyone at school knows about Cricket's out-size talent, but it doesn't make her popular. Or at least, she hadn't thought so.

"I bet you win," Lucy says, pressing down on the brake outside Cricket's house. "Homecoming queen this year, and then Ballon d'Or down the road."

Cricket shakes her head in a show of modesty while imagining the homecoming crown on her head next month. She is surprised by her own excitement, the fact that her classmates have not only watched her but also seen her.

Cricket hops out of Lucy's car and notices Coach's black SUV in the driveway, with the royal blue Stallion sticker on the bumper. She takes the stairs up the porch two at a time, not bothering to wonder what's brought him to Knickerbocker on a Monday afternoon. Instead, Cricket finds herself delighted by the larger audience for her big news.

Floating in the haze of her own future celebrity, Cricket lets herself in, drops her bag, kicks off her slides. She follows the sound of Mia's voice in the kitchen. And there they are.

Leaning over the kitchen sink, Mia disembowels a chicken while Coach stands several feet away, chopping brussels sprouts into quarters. They aren't even speaking, but it's a depiction of domesticity so whole-some that it strikes Cricket as obscene. The familiarity between them fills in enough blanks for Cricket to understand what has happened, even if she doesn't know how, or when, or for how long.

"You're early!" Mia says, recovering from a double take, and Cricket catches the falter in her cheer, a nervous gleam of artifice behind her eyes. "Coach finally took me up on dinner."

"Hey, Cricket." Coach waves to her with the knife her mother used every Saturday morning to slice halftime oranges. Cricket keeps her eyes on the knife as she forces a smile. She would almost rather she'd walked in on them naked because then she could storm out of the room, justified in her disgust. This is worse.

"I'm on the homecoming court," she announces. But even as she says it, Cricket deflates, suddenly aware of how ridiculous she sounds. "I didn't, like try to—everyone just votes."

"Oh my God!" Mia abandons the chicken and rushes toward Cricket for a hug. "Careful of my salmonella hands, but oh my God! Cricket! Congratulations!"

"That's exciting," Coach says, although he doesn't sound particularly excited. Upon closer inspection, Cricket sees the knife wobbling over the cutting board. He's nervous, and this fact infuriates her, but if he and Mia are going to play it cool, then she will, too. She will play it the coolest.

"Yeah," Cricket says, a menacing heat growing in her core as she watches Coach continue to chop the brussels sprouts that her sister bought for them, not him. Or maybe Mia bought them for him and not Cricket. Maybe Cricket has no idea what's real if this has been happening behind her back. "But homecoming is the same weekend as New Englands," Cricket says, finding the hole in the defense and going on the attack. "So I'm gonna need to skip that."

Coach's knife hovers in midair.

Now she has his attention.

Cricket knows how important the New England championship is to Coach—he's already told the team that he plans to graduate from Stallions Soccer Club after this season; that he's reaching out to colleges and universities, and even some National Women Soccer League teams. Another win at New Englands won't make or break Coach's career, but it is one more feather in his cleat, and he won't get it without her in goal.

"You can't be serious," Mia says, letting go of Cricket and stepping back, hands glistening with raw chicken slime. "You can't just blow off the championship."

"Are you telling me to skip my own homecoming?"

Mia looks over her shoulder at Oliver, who continues to stare down at the quartered brussels sprouts as he calculates his words. This is

some serious backspin on the evening he and Mia have been planning—
the night they would finally come clean to Cricket.

"I think it's normal to want to go," Cricket says. "Even if it means
skipping Boston."

"Of course it's normal," Mia agrees. "But I thought we decided that
soccer comes first?"

"Who's we?"

Oliver puts down the knife, and both Lowes watch as he walks over
to the sink, rinses his hands, and dries them on their mother's favorite
purple dish towel. "I think I'm going to take a rain check," he says. On
the stove behind him, the onions and garlic begin to burn.

"Why are you here?" Cricket asks, standing in the doorframe and
blocking Coach's exit. She knows he is just barely keeping his cool, and
her skin itches to prod the fever out of him, to get him to yell the way he
yells during games when he disagrees with the ref.

"Because we have something to tell you!" Mia chirps. Oliver shoots
her a surprised look because timing is everything and now is obviously
not the right time. Mia responds to his scrunched nose with two raised,
Hail Mary eyebrows because it will never be a good time to tell Cricket,
who will see it as a betrayal, who will want to know all the details without
wanting to know any of the details.

"We're dating," Mia says.

"Not funny," Cricket replies.

"It's not a joke," Oliver says, lifting his eyes to meet Cricket's glare.
She grasps for words, reaches for something, anything.

Not this.

Not Coach.

"You can't be serious."

"We are," Oliver says, walking over and kissing Mia's cheek. "And
you two should talk without me." He pushes past Cricket and, in a flash
of Stallion blue, he's gone.

For a moment, the only sound in the kitchen is of the onions sizzling.
Over the high heat, they scream frantically, just like Mia wishes she
could right now.

"Okay, let's talk." Mia takes a deep inhale, walks over to the stove, turns off the flame, removes the pan, scrapes the charred onions and garlic into the trash.

"I can't believe you'd go behind my back—" Cricket begins.

"I never lied to you," Mia interrupts. This is true in a delicately threaded, defense-attorney's-opening-argument kind of way. There hasn't been any explicit lying, per se, but there's been a quiet, ongoing deception since Cricket returned from soccer camp more than a month ago. Pockets of time that Mia has failed to disclose to Cricket who, for the record, never asks Mia about her day as they sit side by side on the pink floral couch each night, sort of watching TV, sort of puttering around on their phones, comfortably spending their nights together.

Or at least, Cricket has been comfortably spending her nights with Mia while Mia has spent each evening pining for more time with Oliver. She hasn't lied to Cricket outright, but she's coordinated and executed a series of movements without her sister's knowledge, despite sharing a house, a car, a Google calendar. Mia and Oliver haven't gone ice-skating, or taken a sunset cruise around Casco Bay, or gone out to a movie at the old Nickelodeon in Portland—nothing montage-worthy. Instead, they have maneuvered around Cricket's schedule to avoid getting caught and allowed Mia's mundane needs to dictate the nature of their dates.

So for six weeks, they've been running errands. Every Monday at seven a.m., Oliver and Mia meet on the curb outside Hannaford to grocery shop. On Thursdays at three p.m., during Mia's afternoon break, they convene at Cumberland Farms to fill up the momvan with gas. They have mosied through every aisle of Hammer It Home and stood in line at the post office more than once. They are regulars at the fish market just off Commercial Street and the bottle redemption center on Broadway, and the Victory swap shop adjacent to the town dump. Although they don't plan on flying anytime soon, Oliver and Mia spent one afternoon at Staples applying for TSA PreCheck, and, despite the banality of all these excursions, they have nevertheless been tripping off their faces on the one illicit drug even TSA can't detect.

Looking at Mia from across the kitchen, Cricket reads her sister like a playback tape. She sees the evolution, frame by frame. It seems obvious now, checking the VAR, but she had not suspected that such a game was even being considered, let alone played behind her back.

"It's not like you ever asked to go to Target with me," Mia says meekly. She reaches for a bright yellow scrub pad and begins to clean the stovetop. Leaning against the doorframe, Cricket pinches the bridge of her nose and squints her eyes shut. Her two favorite people have made a fool of her. She's been emotionally nutmegged.

Cricket walks over to the sink and washes her hands for something to do. "This is bullshit," she says firmly, steam from the scalding water pluming in her face. There is nothing she hates more than being caught off-guard—and by Coach, of all people, who taught her to keep her head on a swivel at all times.

She storms out of the kitchen and down the hallway to her bedroom. Seething on her bed, Cricket presses a pillow to her face so she can scream into it. She wants to quit the Stallions just to spite Coach but knows she can't do that to her teammates or to him. After all, he turned her into the player she is and the professional keeper she dreams of becoming.

Mia knocks but doesn't wait for Cricket's permission to let herself in. When she opens the door, she is greeted by half a dozen all-too-familiar faces: Mia Hamm, Briana Scurry, Joy Fawcett, Kristine Lilly, Julie Foudy, and Brandi Chastain. Sun-faded posters of the 1999 Women's National Team line the walls—originals that Liz bought all those years ago at the World Cup Final in California. The best and worst origin story imaginable.

"No," Cricket says by way of greeting. It comes out muffled, her face in her pillow.

"No what?"

Cricket raises her head. "No, you can't date him."

"But I already am dating him," Mia says. She sighs in a weak attempt at a laugh, conserving her energy for what she anticipates will be several rounds of fighting. This conversation was never going to be easy, Mia reminds herself. There is a reason she kept it a secret for this long, and that reason is five foot eleven and scowling from across her soccer-themed bedroom. Ever since Cricket's eighth-grade growth spurt, her feet hang off the end of her single bed—it's usually a comical sight, but not now.

"Break up with him," Cricket says. Her gaze, now fixed on Mia, feels like that of a seasoned hunter. Poised but powerful, a tacit force, a deadly threat.

"I can't."

"If you keep hanging out with him," Cricket says, strategizing from her opponent's perspective, "he'll try to come with us to California."

"No, he won't."

"Yes, he will," Cricket insists. "And that will mess up every—"

"No, he won't," Mia interrupts. "Because I'm going to stay here." As Cricket wrestles with the shock, her face darkening, straining, Mia ekes out, "I can't even get into UCLA—"

"You wrote about Mom for the personal essay," Cricket protests, her voice thick. "You'll get in."

"No, I won't."

"Yes, you will."

"I never submitted the application."

Cricket screams into her pillow again and then falls silent. Mia waits. After several moments, Cricket chucks her pillow at the wall with notable force and sits up. She pushes the hair out of her face. "You can still apply," she says calmly. "The deadline is November first and I can help you—"

"I love him," Mia says, cutting off Cricket. "That probably sounds crazy to you, but I love him, and I know that he loves me—and he loves you, too—so why does this have to be such a bad thing?"

"Because this isn't the plan!" Cricket shouts, her eyes snapping open as she bolts upright. "We made a plan and you're screwing it up!"

"You have soccer!" Mia explodes, meeting Cricket's volume, her raised voice surprising them both. "Even if I got in, they're not going to give me a full ride, so why would I go into debt over there when the only thing I know for sure is that I want to be here?"

Cricket's mouth hangs open, unable to find words, so Mia continues, exploiting the hole in Cricket's defense. "Were we really just going to sell this house and never come back? There are so many real-life logistics we've been ignoring, not least of which is that I'd be going out there to be your security blanket." Mia leans in the doorway, exasperated, like she's already been over this a hundred times.

Only now does Cricket notice how tired Mia looks. Ever since No-

vember ninth, people assume there are more than five years that separate them. While Cricket runs out her grief on the field, Mia carries it
under her eyes and in the worry lines around her mouth.

"You can't do this," Cricket says with the same authority she uses in
team huddles. Winning not only means refusing to submit but also de-
nying the possibility of defeat. "You can't let him derail our plan just
like Mom let Q ruin her life."

"That was different!" Mia bursts out, her body hot with defensiveness, her arms suddenly desperate to swing. "Oliver is nothing like Q!
And I'm not like Mom!"

"How delusional can you be?" Cricket asks, leaping to her feet to
deliver the knockout punch they both see coming. "We grew up hearing
over and over again about how she gave up college when she got pregnant, and now—" Cricket shakes her head, coughs up a fake laugh. "I
mean, I miss her, too, but Jesus—do you really want to repeat her biggest mistake?"

"I already gave up college once," Mia points out. "To move back
here and take care of you, remember?"

But Cricket isn't listening. Burrowing deep into the hurt of Mia secretly dating her coach, Cricket manically tries to fill in the cracks of
their story, the reason behind Mia's devotion. "Maybe it's not a choice,"
Cricket posits. "Maybe you're—are you already knocked up?"

Mia's first instinct is to charge her sister at full speed, but she doesn't
chase impulses the way Cricket does. Instead, she stands there in the
entry of her sister's room and tries to wait out the hot tension pulsing in
her fists, begging for release.

"Well?" Cricket demands. "Are you?"

Mia's eyes rest on Cricket's neck and how she'd like to wring it as her
thoughts spill out in every direction. She can't talk, not yet. The mess
of love between her and Oliver—but also Oliver and Cricket, the girls
and their mother, the suffocating chaos colliding at her heart's center—
makes Mia unable to focus.

"Jesus Christ!" Cricket yells. "Say something!"

Between sisters, the only thing louder than a screaming match is silence. The only thing more maddening than a fight is the lack thereof.

"I'm not pregnant," Mia says, and her voice is as dangerously placid as an iced-over lake. "But I have spent the last three years choosing you, and now I'm choosing me."

"No, you're choosing him," Cricket punts back. "You're choosing a soccer coach, my soccer coach, and I'm sorry, Mia—" Cricket's voice goes high, on the verge of tears. "I'm sorry I called it a mistake, but—"

"Me," her sister corrects. "You called me a mistake. Mom was pregnant with me. Mom didn't go to college because of me."

"But you know what I—listen, if you're a mistake then so am I, but that was the past, and this is—he's going to stop you in your tracks, and you could be anything, and I can't just—you can't expect me to just stand by and watch."

"You're not going to," Mia says, crossing her arms. "Because you're going to California, and I'm staying here."

"No!" Cricket wails, doubling over like she's had the wind knocked out of her. Mia watches her and recognizes the opening for a surrender. She takes a step toward Cricket, and then another. Her proximity softens Cricket's shoulders, then her neck, as Cricket begins to relinquish control. "Please, Mia." Cricket's voice cracks on her sister's name, the captain's orders crumbling into a younger sibling's plea. "Please come with me. Please?"

Cricket waits for a response, but Mia just wipes her eyes, and Cricket can't help but wonder if women are not only destined to become their mothers but also doomed to repeat their mothers' mistakes. Cricket resolves to be different. She will reach her full potential. And in doing so, she will break the Lowe women's cycle of settling for less.

"You have a whole career ahead of you," Mia says, crossing the room and sitting on the edge of Cricket's bed. Deep down, she's as outraged as Cricket, silently roiling with her right to self-determination, but she is the adult in the room. She has always been the adult in the room.

And now she is also Cricket's legal guardian. Mia has no choice but to soften, to summon the compassion she can always find for her sister.

Pulling Cricket down next to her so they're side by side on the single bed, Mia reaches out and touches Cricket's arm. "You're lucky," she tells her. "You've grown up working toward such a specific dream, with the talent to pursue it, and I—I just need to see where this is going."

Cricket looks at her sister, her eyes apologizing, her bottom lip ripe with sorrow. This is about Coach, yes, but Mia now sees it's also about Cricket taking the next step without her, venturing into the unknown by herself. Going forward, Cricket's pursuit of their mother's dream—and whether or not she is successful in achieving it—will depend on Cricket alone.

A deep, mournful sob escapes Cricket, who slips off her bed and sinks all the way down to the ground. She rests her cheek on the wood floor. Mia kneels beside Cricket and hugs her. She squeezes her tightly, trying to absorb Cricket's fear and convey that this new plan is the best plan for both of them.

"I'll cheer for you always," Mia whispers. "But I'm staying here, and you can choose whether or not you root for me."

INTENT

Even though UCLA's head coach has been an enthusiastic pen pal for over a year, Cricket has barely spoken of their conversations to anyone. Not even Mia. She can't afford to jinx her future.

But now, in early November of her senior year, all the lofty promises, adoring emails, and flattering calls from phone numbers with a 310 area code pick up speed and rotate inward, creating a powerful cyclone of athletic courtship that finally makes landfall in a binding agreement known as the National Letter of Intent and this: National Signing Day.

Behind an eight-foot-long table in Victory High School's gym, Cricket sits at center court, tapping her lucky pen on the top of her leg, eager to sign already. She is not alone. Flanking her are four other seniors who have also secured full athletic scholarships.

A university banner hangs behind each student, broadcasting their new identity in bold colors and Latinate mottos. The five student athletes are dressed to coordinate with their school banners—crimson, purple, green, orange, blue, and gold. The resulting aesthetic is that of a discombobulated rainbow.

At this special all-school assembly, the principal refers to the National Letter of Intent as a contract, but Cricket views it as more permanent than a binding document and more profound than legal jargon. The NLI is an oath to everyone she loves: She hereby swears to give her best and never sacrifice the gift her mother gave her. The gift Mia has protected with her own sacrifice. The gift Coach helped her to hone before seducing her sister and ruining their plan.

Cricket shakes the thought out of her head. She fidgets with the zipper of her new Bruins pullover. This, too, was a gift, which means it came with a cost: acceptance.

Yesterday, a refrigerator-size cardboard box appeared on the front porch first thing in the morning. It was too cumbersome to move inside, so Cricket grabbed a knife and opened it right there on the front porch while Mia attempted to keep out of her way. In the weeks since Mia's decision to stay east, things had become slightly more civil. Cricket had implemented two rules: Coach was not welcome at the house, and Mia was banned from all Stallions events.

A note was taped to the top of the box. Someone had hand-delivered it before sunrise.

Cricket—

She froze, immediately recognizing Coach's clear, assertive handwriting.

"Did you know about this?" Cricket yelled into the kitchen, but Mia shook her head as she rushed over to see. In record time, Cricket hate-read the note and was appalled to discover a deep fondness spreading across her chest and creeping up her neck. Like a rash, it developed against her will and made her itch. And yet, it was Coach, her Coach, and so she read the note again and surrendered to the emotional fallout:

Cricket—

You have worked so hard for this. It's no coincidence that this special day falls on such a significant one. While your mom surely meddled with the calendar gods to show her support, mine is rep-

resented here. I look forward to watching your star continue to rise at UCLA. Congratulations, Keeper.

With admiration and respect,
Coach / Oliver

Inside the box appeared to be the entire contents of the UCLA campus store. Cricket couldn't help but laugh as she began to unpack the items while Mia came out to the porch and gawked over her shoulder. The man had lost his mind. Inside the box were four UCLA sweatshirts, eight T-shirts, five pairs of shorts, two pairs of sweatpants, six pairs of leggings, ten tank tops, two canvas totes, a Bruins water bottle, a hat, a visor, a vest, a glorified fanny pack, ten pairs of socks, a pair of blue Air Jordans with gold laces (what?!), and one—

"What the—" Mia marveled.

Cricket's eyes twinkled as she opened the golf umbrella. "Why would I need this in L.A.?"

"You don't *need* any of it," Mia pointed out.

Cricket nodded and turned her back so Mia couldn't see her face. She was still upset about the sneaking around, and scared for Mia if the relationship fizzled out, but right then, standing on the porch with a box full of Bruins gear she and Mia could never have afforded themselves, Cricket felt so seen by Coach that she began to cry. He understood better than anyone what Signing Day signified. After all, he had once signed a letter of intent himself.

Cricket texted Coach right then and invited him to the ceremony.

He responded a minute later with a meme of Alyssa Naeher, the current U.S. Women's National Team goalkeeper, making a great save with a message in all caps: *WOULDN'T MISS IT!*

Now, sitting at center court in her high school gym, Cricket looks down at her outfit and immediately thinks of an overdressed mannequin. She is decked out in her Bruins soccer T-shirt, zip-up, visor, leggings, socks, sneakers, and fanny pack. In fact, the only thing that isn't blue and gold is the lucky red ribbon tied around Cricket's high bun.

When Principal Tattersall gives Cricket the okay to sign her letter of intent, Cricket doesn't hesitate to scrawl her full name. She feels both an overwhelming sense of pride and an immense swell of relief. This is the next step. She is on her way.

In the overheated gym, Cricket sees her future gleaming in the freshly waxed hardwood floor—pristine fields and plane rides, ambitious teammates and double overtimes. She's heading toward a whole universe of possibilities, which only serves to highlight how tiny Victory, Maine, really is and how small Cricket's world has always been until now.

The ceremony ends with a thunderous round of applause from otherwise unenthusiastic teenagers. In the front row, Mia and Coach jump up to give a standing ovation as Principal Tattersall shakes Cricket's hand with both of his. A photographer from the *Portland Press Herald* prowls around the perimeter of the gym, snapping candids for tomorrow's front page.

"She would be so proud," Mia says, eyes filling as she pulls Cricket in for a hug.

"Congratulations, Cricket," Coach says. He is dressed up, having come straight from his new job as associate director of athletics and head coach of women's soccer at the University of Southern Maine. His tie might be for work, but Coach is here for her.

"Nice OOTD," he quips, because he does spend a large chunk of each day around adolescent females and is thus familiar with their favorite acronyms. Mia, however, is not, and shoots him a bewildered look. "Outfit of the Day," Oliver explains. *"Obviously."*

Cricket laughs because it's funny. And she keeps laughing because crying wouldn't be appropriate at such a joyous occasion. Even though today is also the hardest day.

Because out of the 365 days that comprise a year, what are the chances that Cricket's National Letter of Intent Signing Day would fall on November ninth? This morning, the universe—and the NCAA—and Title IX—promised Cricket a fresh start and a free ride exactly three years after her mother's life ended. Three years since Mia showed up at her soccer game in Massachusetts. Three years since her sky shattered and her world went black.

The timing is beautiful and devastating and a clear sign from her mom that this is Cricket's destiny.

After the ceremony, Cricket goes to fourth-period Statistics and finishes out the school day. That night, Coach and Mia surprise her with takeout from her favorite Japanese place and cookies from the best bakery in Portland. It's after eleven p.m. when Mia pulls out the trunk of frilly dresses from their mom's closet and asks Cricket if she's ready.

The sisters walk down to the ocean in silence, wind blowing against their bare legs and through their puffy, off-the-shoulder sleeves. They don't need a polar plunge to reset; their lives are already changing rapidly and heading in vastly different directions.

But this is for their mom.

A tradition for each other.

At midnight, Cricket and Mia jump in—not to move forward, but to hold still.

To hold on.

SLOANE'S CALL

In January, from the bench press in her high school weight room, Cricket doesn't hear the Google alert chime on her phone amid the teenage groans and mechanical clanks. Instead, she lowers the bar to her chest for another rep and envisions herself in goal next year, making a game-winning save while wearing Bruin blue and gold. Winter in Maine is the perfect time to dream about Los Angeles sun—she cannot wait to be tan.

Ever since Cricket signed her letter of intent, the UCLA strength and fitness coach has sent her weekly workouts, which Cricket follows religiously. Despite a wrestler impatiently waiting for a turn on the bench, Cricket stands and loads more weight to both sides of the bar. Not only does she want to impress her teammates on the first day of preseason, but she also needs to eliminate all potential reasons why the UCLA head coach might play another goalkeeper over her.

Because that's exactly what Teague did just last month, when she called to tell Cricket she would not receive an invitation to January Camp. "I've got to get eyes on other keepers," she'd said. "I don't need to tell you it's about team dynamics, and leadership, and finding that special sauce between players as much as it is about individual talent."

Cricket had tried to sound gracious as her cheeks burned with embarrassment and rage. It felt like a step back, like she was getting left behind before she'd even double-knotted her cleats. But then Sloane had texted and, between entire rows of expletives, reported having just had the same conversation. Despite their strong performances at previous National Team trainings, neither was invited to this year's January Camp. They agreed that the whole thing was trash, but at least they were getting left behind together.

Stretching on the mat, Cricket takes extra time rolling out her IT bands. On her slow walk back to the locker room, she takes pride in the lactic acid built up in her quads and actively enjoys her endorphins high as she checks her phone. But then Cricket reads the Google Alert again because it doesn't make sense. How could ESPN get this so wrong?

Cricket skims through the notices, confused as to how there could be such a huge misunderstanding—unless there isn't one. The truth congeals in her stomach like the oatmeal she ate this morning. Cricket reads each alert before she finally sees the text from Sloane: *Pray for me! Xoxo!*

Cricket closes Sloane's text without replying and clicks on the newest Google Alert from *The Athletic:* Sloane Jackson has entered the draft for the National Women's Soccer League.

Cricket grabs her stuff and slams her locker shut. Instead of catching the late bus, she walks the two miles home and allows her envy to get the best of her. While scrolling through the internet's reaction to Sloane's announcement, Cricket internalizes all the social-media enthusiasm around Sloane as a slight against herself. "Buying season tickets for whichever team you join!" wrote one eager fan in the comments of Sloane's post. "I'll move states if I need to!"

This was Sloane's response to the January Camp snub. Going forward, she would make it impossible for Teague to ignore her. And because Cricket had outperformed her at the last camp, Sloane was now outplaying her off the field. Coach was right: Strategy is everything.

The late bus speeds by and spits yesterday's runoff onto Cricket's sneakers. How could she have been so naïve? Sloane has always understood the underlying dynamics of their relationship. It's why she never brought up the possibility of skipping Stanford during all their Sunday calls. Maybe it's why Sloane initiated their Sunday calls in the first place—to keep tabs on Cricket, her biggest threat.

"I saw," Mia says, opening the door for Cricket. "But you're making the smarter decision. You know that, right?"

Cricket's eyes are glazed when she says, "We just talked on Sunday."

"And?"

"I had to talk her out of sending laxative cookies to the keepers invited to camp, but she didn't say anything about the draft."

Cricket starts to untie her soaked sneakers, then stops, then starts again, then stops. Tears she doesn't quite understand keep blurring her vision and landing on her laces. Mia watches her sister like she's a movie caught between Play and Pause, a girl stuck in a glitch. "I can't believe this is happening," Cricket says, her fingers finally unthreading her shoelace. She freezes, stunned all over again. Only her mouth moves as she whispers, "I'm so fucked."

"No, you're not," Oliver says, walking in the back door with a bag of groceries. He doesn't even knock anymore. If she's honest, Cricket doesn't mind his presence so much as Mia's starry-eyed preoccupation with his every movement.

"Anything could happen in the next four years," Oliver continues, gesticulating with a baguette in his hand. "But you're giving yourself the best shot, the biggest window for success."

"Not if Sloane becomes a star," Cricket argues. "And she basically already is."

Oliver shakes his head, unbothered. "An influencer isn't the same as a consistent player. And not to be callous, but she could get hurt or burn out," he says. "Nothing is guaranteed."

Sloane texts Cricket just then: *Where's my congratulations?!*

Cricket flips her phone over and hides her face behind her hands. "I thought we were friends," she says. "How stupid am I? I really thought we were friends."

"But you are friends," Mia argues. "You can push yourselves and still encourage each other."

"Hey, Coach," Cricket says, "can you tell Mary Poppins over here to get her head out of her carpetbag?"

As Mia opens her mouth for a rebuttal, Oliver cuts her off. "She's got a point," he says to Mia. "This does change things, at least for now."

Then, turning to Cricket, Oliver asks, "So what makes a great goalkeeper?"

Cricket rolls her eyes. It's the same question he asked when they first met.

"I'm serious," Oliver says. "Or did you forget?"

"Fuck off," Cricket says, mostly because she can get away with cursing at her coach now. Or rather, she can curse at *Oliver*, because he's no longer her coach—they won the championship the same weekend she lost the homecoming crown. Besides, he's in *her* house, dating *her* sister. "And fuck your MAP, too."

Coach wags a finger playfully, tells her to think about it. He's impossible to rile up these days and it's all Mia's fault. As much as Cricket tries to deny it, they are obviously, deeply, annoyingly in love.

"What map?" Mia asks, peeking her head out from the other side of the open refrigerator as she puts away a bushel of carrots.

"It's an acronym," Coach explains proudly. "Mentality, Adaptability, Patience: my MAP to being a goalkeeper."

"Yeah, and your MAP is bullshit," Cricket says, enjoying her profane petulance. She holds up her phone and walks over to Coach, shakes the ESPN news alert in his face. "Patience is overrated, brah. A sense of *urgency* is why Sloane is skipping college and why she'll get called up to the National Team before I do."

"You're playing the long game," Coach responds. "Focus on your own growth."

"That's exactly what I'm saying but no one listens to me!" Mia shouts before storming into the bathroom. She emerges with the Steve Prefontaine poster in her hands.

"I'm relocating him," Mia says, adhering the poster to the back of the front door. "From now on, every time you leave this house, you need to think about your gift. Not Sloane's strategies but your gift, Cricket Lowe. And you need to make sure you are giving your absolute best every time because that's the one thing in your control. That's what Mom would say, and that's what Steve would say, and that's all that matters."

Coach begins a slow clap. Cricket frowns but stares at the poster and the words that she memorized all those years ago. Mia is right. The only thing she can do is give her absolute best to soccer. Sloane's decision is just extra incentive for Cricket to stay focused on her own goals, to keep her friends close and enemies closer, especially if her enemies are her friends. She and Sloane are ruthless brutes, ambitious witches, soccer players vying for the number-one spot. If Sloane's strategy is to go pro early, that's fine, because Cricket's strategy is to never sacrifice the gift.

She's a Lowe, not a quitter.

COMMENCEMENT

After tossing their caps into the sky, the newly minted Victory High School graduates find their friends at the center of the football field. Parents rush toward them and let their camera shutters rip. In rowdy, weepy clusters, the graduates glom together, equally shell-shocked and ecstatic. It's all over.

Cricket is no different, throwing her arms around her teammates for their blood-related paparazzi. The senior squad reconfigures their faces every few seconds for a goofy picture, a normal one, a sexy one that makes Mia cringe, especially as the moms on either side of her seem to encourage it. "Ears forward, ladies!" one mom in a denim jumpsuit directs, walking in front of Mia to model what she calls her fail-proof pose.

Mia takes a step back. She wishes her mom were here, like she was for her own high school graduation. Together, they would admire how Cricket stands literally a head above the rest of her peers, shoulders back, head high, as steadfast as a lighthouse, unaware she is the landmark for her teammates. For a moment, Mia is back on that green metal bench on the playground, watching Cricket go down the big slide she herself feared. Today, Cricket gets a 10 for sticking the landing.

That night at Primo Bistro, Cricket spots their reserved table from the hostess stand and tells Lucia it's just the three of them; they don't need a fourth place setting.

"Actually," Mia says reticently, "we do."

She is still wondering if this was a good idea when the door behind them opens and twenty blue and gold balloons wedge themselves ungracefully into the restaurant.

"Surprise!" Sloane Jackson yells. "Sorry! I didn't realize these would take up so much space!"

Blinded by the balloons, Mia can't see Cricket's face, so she listens intently for her sister's reaction, but there isn't one.

"How festive," Oliver says, punching one gold balloon out of his way, and then another, until Mia can see him and the entire scene before them.

Cricket has thrown both arms around Sloane, but over her shoulder and between all the balloons, Cricket looks at Mia and asks with wary eyes, *What's this about?*

Introductions are made swiftly on their way to the table, even though Oliver and Mia feel like they already know Sloane, and vice versa. When Sloane sheds her jean jacket to reveal a bright blue UCLA soccer jersey, Cricket jokes that only a thin line separates fans from stalkers. From across the table, Mia watches with relief as her sister's armor melts in Sloane's presence; clever banter and obvious affection quickly replace Cricket's initial suspicion.

"You know, Sloane, you're kinda tied to our story," Oliver says, surprising everyone. "If Cricket hadn't been having such a good time with you at that first National Team camp, Mia never would have agreed to go out with me."

"You're welcome," Sloane says, slapping him on the back while grinning mischievously at Cricket, who pretends her laugh is a cough. Mia wants to ask them what's so funny, but the server appears just then and so they order two baskets of garlic bread, a blooming onion, a family-size salad, and four Shirley Temples. "It's a celebration," Mia informs their server.

"And celebrations call for gifts," Sloane declares, beaming at Cricket as she slides a small box across the table.

"But I didn't get you anything for graduating," Cricket says, sagging in her seat and tossing her napkin on the table. "You flew all the way here," she points out with genuine appreciation. "And I didn't even think to send you, like, a card."

The week before, Sloane had graduated from a private academy in North Palm Beach. For an undisclosed sum, Dwayne "The Rock" Johnson had given the commencement speech, and the photo Sloane had posted of herself pretending to arm wrestle him while wearing her graduation gown had garnered over thirteen thousand likes. The comments section was dominated by members of the current National Team and the Washington Spirit, which picked Sloane in the NWSL draft back in January. Now, Cricket flushes with guilt remembering how she had fixated on all those likes, and the chance to rub elbows with The Rock, instead of actually reaching out to congratulate her friend.

"Further proof I'm a better person," Sloane deadpans. "Open it!"

Cricket is still unwrapping the box when Sloane tells her it's a charm bracelet with a soccer ball on it. "Same as this one," she says, holding up her own wrist. "My mom got it for me when—" she says before stopping midsentence.

"Yeah, our mom would've loved this, too," Cricket says, putting Sloane at ease. She sticks out her arm and Sloane dutifully clasps the bracelet on Cricket's wrist. "Thank you," Cricket says. "And thanks for being here."

"Okay, me next then," Oliver says, handing Cricket an envelope over the blooming onion. "It's kind of a selfish gift, but I think you'll be happy to use it."

"Compelling," Cricket teases. She peeks inside the envelope and her whole face sweeps back as if blown by a high wind. "What the what?" she asks, pulling out the credit card.

"It's the best credit card for flying, so whenever you want to come home, we'll use that card. It'll help you build credit, and eventually you'll earn some free trips."

Cricket flings herself at her former coach, who pats her on the back and tells her it's no big deal, she's more than earned it.

"I guess I'm glad we didn't break you two up," Sloane says, just as their pasta dishes arrive. Cricket theatrically drills an elbow into her friend's ribs, who continues, undeterred. "On our Sunday calls, I came up with some pretty awesome ideas for how to drive a wedge between you—it usually involved fox piss or fake blood or both."

"I'm going to pretend I didn't hear that," Mia says as she laughs, leaning into Oliver.

"Yeah, but the important thing is that Cricket never followed through because she insisted you deserve to be happy," Sloane says, pointing her fork at Mia. Sitting back in her chair like a lawyer resting her case, Sloane adds, "and I think she's right."

"She certainly is," Oliver says, pretending to punch Cricket's shoulder.

"Last but not least," Mia says, reaching under the table to reveal her hidden gift. She gives Cricket a cardboard tube three feet long. "This is so you have a friend with you in California." Her voice breaks on "California" but everyone pretends not to hear it.

Cricket pops open the lid and sticks her hand into the tube. She only unscrolls an inch before she rolls it back up. "No way," she says to Mia, her face serious. "I can't take him—he belongs at home."

"No, he belongs with you," Mia says, blaming the blooming onion as she rubs her eyes.

"Who the hell is *he*?" Sloane asks through a mouthful of pasta. "Let me guess—Beckham? Is it young Beckham or current Beckham because I have thoughts."

"It's Steve," Mia and Cricket say together.

"Steve Prefontaine," Cricket elaborates, unfurling the tattered poster for Sloane to see. "I used to think he was my dad," she says, smiling at the memory. She is back there in the cramped bathroom, standing between her mom and her sister. "But yeah, anyway, this quote down here—it's what I've lived by since I was little."

"To give anything less than your best is to sacrifice the gift," Sloane reads aloud before looking at Cricket. "Wait, sorry, but how does that apply to you?"

Oliver chokes on his garlic bread as Mia stifles her laugh into her napkin and Cricket, hiding her own grin behind a scrunched nose and beady, indignant eyes, asks Sloane if she'd like to settle things in the parking lot. "To be honest, I'm not sure who's more vicious," Oliver says, clearly amused.

When the server comes around to offer coffee and dessert, everyone salivates before admitting they're stuffed. Nevertheless, Lucia comes by with a tray a minute later. "Your mother would want you to try one of each," she says. "And so do I."

Despite their full stomachs, the tiramisu, cannoli, homemade cinnamon ice cream, and raspberry cheesecake are all devoured quickly. Cricket and Sloane look like they're about to pass out at the table. As Oliver gathers up the gifts, Mia takes care of the bill—or at least tries to. In the black leather book, there is a blank receipt scrawled over with Lucia's tight cursive: *Tonight is your mother's and my treat. XOXO*

Mia looks up, and Lucia locks eyes with her from across the busy dining room and blows several red-lipped air kisses. "We love you," Lucia mouths with a comically dramatic enunciation, and Mia nods while biting down hard on the inside of her cheek.

"This was perfect," Cricket says. She thanks Sloane, Oliver, and Mia for their gifts. The bracelet, the credit card, the poster of Steve Prefontaine—they all serve as proof that everyone has bought into her dream. They're also a tacit reminder that Cricket's entire identity, and the dimensions of her destiny, fall within the perimeter of a soccer field. To focus on anything besides her own career would be to squander the only thing that makes her stand out.

"How long can you stay?" Cricket asks Sloane as they work to untie the twenty balloons from the back of Cricket's chair.

"Tomorrow morning," Sloane answers. "The Spirit has a bye this week," she yawns. "But Teague suggested I use the time to train with Anders, so I'm flying from here to Carson."

"Teague?" Cricket asks, agog and suddenly very much awake. "You're going to work with Anders?"

"Yeah, during my one free weekend," Sloane says, pretending to pout.

Mia hands the leather bill holder, now fat with a cash tip, back to the server and conveys to Oliver with a subtle eye flick that she had no idea. Tomorrow, they will have to weather Cricket's unfiltered reaction to this announcement.

Full-time employees for U.S. Soccer, Teague and Anders are expected to prepare the current and future U.S. Women's National Team for greatness. And they are investing in Sloane this weekend, at the official facilities in California, while Cricket just sits around, taking photos with her high school friends and figuring out where to hang her tassel.

She has been an idiot, resting on her laurels as Sloane continues to plug into the system. Smushed between Sloane's balloons on the car ride home, Cricket purses her lips to keep from laughing at herself: Maybe it's a good thing she's going to college, because she clearly needs to get smarter.

MIGHTY BRUINS

For Cricket, the only thing more grueling than UCLA's top-tier, Division 1 soccer preseason program is adjusting to life without her sister across the hall.

After saying goodbye to Mia at the airport, Cricket had to change her shirt twice on the plane because she couldn't stop crying. And then between the brutal three-a-day training sessions and sprawling campus, Cricket wondered if she could survive the West Coast without her sister's support. But during that first week of separation and despite the three-hour time difference, Mia picked up the phone whenever Cricket called and always offered a positive spin lifted directly from their mother's playbook. "No pain, no gain," Mia reminded her in every conversation. "You've got this, I promise."

And now, after only a week on campus, Cricket understands on a molecular level that she is where she is meant to be. As usual, her sister was right. With her feet firmly planted on the Pacific plate, Cricket's clear blue eyes not only reflect rows of palm trees but are also focused on what's next. Today, it's learning the UCLA Eight-Clap.

While Cricket feels as self-conscious as everyone else in her orientation group—half-heartedly fist-pumping and chanting, "*Fight! Fight! Fight!*"—she appreciates the major advantage of being a fall athlete. Arriving to campus early and landing in the open, sweaty arms of her teammates means she's already earned a sense of belonging.

Thanks to the returning players who have taken her under their wing, Cricket knows the shorthand for different academic buildings and the shortcut between her dorm and the gym. She knows BPlate offers the healthiest meal options, which is why she eats there every day, except Sunday, which is her cheat day along with everyone else's on the team. Conveniently, it's also the one day of the week that they're most likely hungover and craving BLTs. "Obviously we're committed to college soccer," one of Cricket's captains told her between shots of beer during the team's Saturday-night power hour. "But we're equally committed to the college experience."

"*Fight! Fight! Fight!*"

When the enthusiastic orientation leader insists they practice the Eight-Clap one more time, Cricket's phone vibrates with a text. She isn't surprised to see it's her teammate asking for professor recommendations in the Geology Department. On the second day of preseason, Cricket's soccer captains established a text thread to communicate meetups, but it's quickly devolved into an open forum.

Even as a first year, Cricket feels comfortable seeking advice about classes and asking to tag along on Sunday sojourns to The Grove. And every time Cricket enters a packed lecture hall full of stone-faced strangers, the hyperactive text thread feels like a pack of sisters in her pocket, constantly abuzz with party invites, hot takes on pop culture, and comically predictable weather updates: *70 and sunny @4p—another perfect day for footie!*

When Cricket's phone vibrates on her walk to practice in early September, she assumes it's another team text but it's Sloane calling.

She picks up with the standard greeting of any Gen Zer answering the phone: "Is everything okay?"

"You tell me," Sloane singsongs. "Aren't you supposed to be at practice right now?"

"I'm walking there," Cricket says, basking in the autumn sun. "How's league life?"

Sloane sighs, and Cricket stops walking to make sure she hears what comes next.

"Honestly? It's so weird," Sloane admits. "Being an eighteen-year-old in the workforce is a dream but, like, the most intense dream ever, especially with playoffs coming up, which is why I wanted to call you."

"For advice?"

"Something like that," Sloane says, smiling through the receiver. Cricket can imagine Sloane's left dimple in full effect as she says, "I just needed to hear a joke, so I thought of you."

"I don't know any jokes."

"No, you *are* the joke."

"Oh! Then you're welcome!" Cricket says, because in her new SoCal bubble, Sloane is no longer a threat to Cricket's career but a funny sidebar, a goofy rival Cricket relies on for banter and constructive criticism after games. They still speak every Sunday.

Waving to her teammates up ahead on the path, Cricket quickly whispers to Sloane what no one else yet knows: "I'm starting this weekend," she gloats. "And I've got to go, but good luck with playoffs!"

After practice and recovery and team dinner, Cricket thinks of Sloane as she swipes her fob to get into her dorm. Now that she's here and immersed in Bruins life, she's not sure how Sloane ever decided to skip college. Passing through the common area, Cricket smiles at a group of sophomores drinking wine out of mason jars while working on a massive three-thousand-piece jigsaw puzzle, and enters her own suite to discover that Mathilda has left a plate of chocolate chip cookies in the shared kitchen with a note begging Cricket and Ayo to eat them.

Separated from everyone and everything she knows, Cricket has never felt more independent. She's learning so much, off and on the field, from her teammates and professors and even from herself, being out on her own without Mia helping her manage every little thing.

And as smart as her sister is, Cricket believes Mia, like Sloane, was a fool to forgo this opportunity. She was a martyr to leave Yale and move home for Cricket, but she was a fool not to even apply to UCLA this time around.

Sometimes, after texting with Sloane or reading up on Sloane's performance for the Washington Spirit, Cricket will have a fleeting thought about how Sloane gets paid an actual salary to play soccer in the NWSL right now. And occasionally, as Cricket shoves a protein bar into her mouth before an early class, she'll picture Mia baking her famous banana nut bread and offering Oliver a slice, still warm from the oven. But even as she envisions the Sloane and Mia highlights, Cricket knows there's nowhere in the world she would rather be than exactly where she is. It's never been easier to stay focused on playing sharper and smarter soccer.

On game days, Cricket dresses up for class and feels the eyes of other students looking at her with respect. She enjoys the local celebrity, appreciates how her classmates often show up at her matches holding signs with her name in gold bubble letters, and greet her at the next lecture with a congratulatory fist bump. In the locker room, Cricket dives headfirst into her own pregame routines—listening to her mom's high school warm-up playlist, dressing her left leg first, rolling out the perfect piece of prewrap. She tucks a lucky red ribbon inside her cleat.

And most importantly, when Cricket prepares to take her place between those pipes, she knows who will be there waiting for her. Siberian blue eyes shining with pride and a lipstick heart drawn on her cheek. No one else can see Liz Lowe standing by the goalpost, but whenever Cricket takes the field, her mother is impossible to miss.

DOMESTICATED

From a healthy distance, Mia revels in Cricket's success and openly marvels at the way all the states between them can bring them closer together in such unexpected ways.

When the sisters talk on the phone, Mia does not try to contain her shock at Cricket's newfound interest in academics, especially psychology. "I like how it ties into soccer," Cricket says. "I've been listening to audiobooks on sports psychology when we travel for games." It's the first time Mia has ever heard Cricket speak so enthusiastically about school. Actually, it's the first time she's heard Cricket speak about school, period.

"Oliver and Mom were definitely ahead of their time," Cricket theorizes from the other side of the country. While Mia returns to the house for lunch on a Saturday afternoon, Cricket walks to the dining hall for breakfast and explains how positive self-talk has proven effective on the soccer field. "And all those rituals, like Mom's hairband snap and Coach's obsession with visualization, his postgame grounding walks—they encourage mental toughness and are considered, like, legit sports psychology strategies. How cool is that?"

As Cricket continues her lecture, Mia watches Oliver unload the dishwasher in accordance with her system. If she's being honest, Mia would say it's a delight to have Cricket out of the house and Oliver using his own key to let himself in. She'll trade the emotional vicissitudes of a teenager for the balled-up socks of a recovering bachelor any day.

"Okay, I'm headed into class," Cricket says. "Love you."

After they hang up, Mia walks over to Oliver and takes the clean bowls out of his hands and sets them on the counter. She tells him the dishwasher can wait, but she can't. With her sister three hours behind and a plane ride away, Mia yanks off his shirt right there in the center of the kitchen.

"I love seeing you in the wild," she tells Oliver as she fumbles with his belt, his neck still salty from sweating on the sidelines. This morning, in unseasonable heat, he led the University of Southern Maine to victory over MIT in double overtime. It was exhilarating and hot in all the ways.

"Seeing me in the wild?" Oliver asks between clipped breaths as he pulls off her shirt. "We met at a scheduled place and time—I'd say it was more of a date."

"A date where you have your back to me the entire time?" Mia points out. "And then you give a speech to nineteen girls at the end?"

"Nineteen *women*," Oliver corrects her. "And I made sure to wear deodorant just for you." He traces her jaw with the back of his finger.

"What else do you do just for me?" She has never been a flirt until now, because now—she can't help herself, and she can't stop with Oliver. A trip wire of lust exists between them, insatiable and unrelenting, which is why Oliver has sort of, kind of—well, Oliver has moved in. Not officially, but when Mia pointed out how the commute from Oliver's apartment to Knickerbocker Avenue to his office on USM's campus was affecting the time they had together, and that Cricket was now out of the house, they had both agreed their highly specialized practice in nude calisthenics should be a top priority.

Mia pushes Oliver up against the refrigerator, and his shoulders make it rain magnets as he suggests they call Cricket, tell her about the plan for him to move in officially when his lease ends.

"Not yet." Mia bites on his bottom lip to convey why. She's told him before. "Let me be greedy," she says. "For once, let me just savor something I don't have to share."

"I know, but if she—"

Mia covers Oliver's mouth with her hand. "We'll tell her, just not yet. I want to enjoy the fantasy of you being here all the time."

"It's not a fantasy," Oliver says. "It's the real deal. You'll get sick of me." Mia shakes her head. It's hard to imagine such a thing, even as they hone their domesticity by offering and accepting constructive criticism about the best way to fold T-shirts. On a biweekly basis, Mia and Oliver debate which brand of toothpaste is best and agree to disagree about whether to hang the toilet paper over or under.

In the bedroom, Mia touches Oliver's forehead with her own. "Besides Cricket, you're the only person who's made me happy since my mom died," Mia says. "I know that sounds overwhelming but it's true."

Oliver nods. He holds Mia's face and kisses the tip of her nose. "That's what this is," he says, "overwhelming but true."

LOVE WALKS BACKWARD

A week later, Cricket calls her sister after class. This has proven to be their best window to catch up: As Cricket sunbathes outside of Haines Hall at three p.m., Mia sets up her phone in the kitchen and talks while preparing dinner.

"You know we wish we could be there for the game, right?" Mia asks over FaceTime, eyes pleading from three thousand miles away. Cricket does understand: Flights are expensive and this is just the beginning of her time in California. From here, her career is only going to get bigger and grow more global.

Cricket reassures herself that in just a few years, she'll be able to pay for Mia and Oliver's tickets to follow her all over the world. Soon enough, she'll be a professional athlete with a dozen endorsement deals. But for now, or at least for this weekend, Mia and Oliver will watch the live stream of UCLA's home opener from their own home on Knickerbocker Avenue.

"We'll be cheering for you," Mia says. "Last night we taught ourselves the Eight-Clap!"

"You didn't."

"We sure did!" Mia insists, raising both arms and wiggling her fingers to demonstrate just as the smoke alarm goes off. "Oh no! My broccoli!"

They hang up and, still laughing at the expense of her sister's charred broccoli, Cricket applies sunscreen and visualizes her performance at practice, which starts in an hour. She is too focused on her upcoming training session to notice the gossamer strings that tug at her as she stands up and heads toward the athletic center. Cricket doesn't sense the sudden pull or question the inexplicable gravitational force yanking her in the opposite direction. Instead, she simply looks right, indulging what feels like a random urge, an innocuous itch, that proves to be anything but.

Because there she is, smiling broadly from across the green.

The world moves backward.

Or rather, just the girl—the girl is moving backward.

Cricket blinks once, then twice, but the girl is definitely moving backward, at a clip, parting the crowded sidewalk behind her like a backpedaling Moses.

She strides in rewind while addressing a gaggle of overattentive parents and prospective students. Her long dark hair is pulled up into a high ponytail, with a thick strip of neon pink streaking down the middle like the tail of a punk-rock skunk. The girl tilts her chin up to better project her voice to her captivated audience.

Before she can stop herself, Cricket moves across the green at what she hopes looks like a casual pace and not the emergency that it is. But after just a few steps, she realizes she's doing that nervous, stiff-legged walk-jog of the lady in that commercial about bladder control.

"Hey there, interloper," the young woman says, giving Cricket a friendly wave like they know each other. Cricket catches her glance like a boot in the chest. The yards and milliseconds close between them, even as the tour guide continues to walk backward. Behind her, the skunk tail swishes left to right.

"Glad you could make it," the girl says. Her voice is deeper and richer than Cricket would have anticipated, like the woods after a summer rainstorm, a verdant lush. Cricket just nods, as if she's trying to respect the flow of the tour, and not because she's violently choking on her own tongue. The dozen people in the group turn to look at Cricket, who at five foot eleven sticks out even when she doesn't impulsively hop on a college tour halfway through touring a college at which she's already enrolled.

Pulling out her phone and miming a reaction of shock, Cricket turns and runs away, fleeing the group. Even when she's well out of view, Cricket continues to sprint, keeping up the charade of an emergency. She has no idea what just happened, what's still happening now inside of her, so she runs to the safest place on campus.

When she pushes open the door to the athletic center, Cricket remembers to breathe. In the foyer, her hands shake as she refills her Bruins CamelBak at the water fountain and watches the growing number of plastic bottles she's apparently saving from a landfill slowly tick up. She times her inhales to each hypothetical bottle saved, but her heart continues to thump so violently that she lurches forward. This might be her first California earthquake, but Cricket is pretty sure it's only happening to her.

She snaps the hair tie on her wrist, but it does nothing. This is not a championship game. This is not a National Team camp, or a beep test, or a timed mile. She can't reset from that woman walking backward across the green.

"Cricky, baby!" a teammate announces, entering the locker room. "You're here so early!" Cricket smiles and resists the urge to tell Ellie what's just transpired. Instead, she reaches up and touches the top of her head as if a hot pink stripe might have appeared there, branding her and simultaneously splitting her heart in half between who she has always been and who she's about to become.

Cricket begins to dress her left leg and realizes she's been wrong. All this time, she has been so wrong, and Mia has always been so right, because a sudden change in expectations is indeed upsetting. Love isn't a decision or a game one willingly plays; it's a straight-up ambush, and Cricket already knows she's too late to be saved.

PUNK ROCK SKUNK

Hours after making an ass of herself on the campus tour, Cricket lies in bed, her face aglow from the light of her phone as she scours the UCLA admissions website for the punk rock skunk. She learns the school hosts thirty-two thousand undergraduate students spread over 419 acres. That's a lot of people over a lot of land, but at least Cricket knows her person of interest is a guide. She will not sleep until she finds her.

Scrolling down the page, Cricket vows to search the admissions website from top to bottom, even email the office from a burner account if it comes to that. But there she is. Sitting pretty under the banner: MEET OUR TOUR GUIDES. For Cricket, however, the banner may as well read, STALK THE LOVE OF YOUR LIFE.

Name: Yasmine Frankel
Nickname: Yaz
Pronouns: She/her
Hometown: Seattle, Washington
High School: Choate Rosemary Hall

Major(s): Public Policy and Studio Art double major
Fun Fact: I'm fluent in Arabic, French, and Italian.
Favorite Place on Campus: Franklin D. Murphy Sculpture
Garden

Beneath a flattering photograph, Yasmine's profile is meant to impress prospective students and their parents, not enchant a first year or single-handedly awaken her heretofore dormant sexuality, but this is exactly what happens. And oddly enough, Oliver's MAP to goalkeeping springs into Cricket's mind—*Mentality, Adaptability, Patience.* Success relies on executing a winning strategy, and so Cricket commits to spending every free moment she doesn't have in the Franklin D. Murphy Sculpture Garden. Destiny will meet her there, Cricket determines, knocking on the wood of her bed frame.

The next morning, egg sandwich in hand, Cricket spreads a blanket next to Gerhard Marcks's seven-foot-tall bronze statue. "Good morning, Maja," she says to the imposing sculpture. Over the next six weeks, Cricket becomes a loyal and knowledgeable devotee of Hans Arp, Barbara Hepworth, and Deborah Butterfield—artists whose works keep her company as she becomes a sculpture garden regular between classes, meals, and practice. Cricket waves to the grounds crew each morning, and a sophomore named Cliff who arrives every Friday afternoon to meditate. The only people who know what Cricket is truly up to are Gus and Judy, a retired couple from the neighborhood, who give her an encouraging thumbs-up as they stroll through on their daily constitutional.

A month goes by and Cricket still hasn't seen Yasmine. She begins to grow impatient in her wait, and with the students who skulk through the sculpture garden, oblivious to the art with their hoodies up because *sixty-three degrees is so fuckin' frigid, man.* If not for Yasmine's profile on the admissions website, Cricket would wonder if that afternoon back in September was an extended daydream, a visualization gone rogue. How has she not spotted the beautiful sophomore with a hot pink stripe of hair, who could do the Eight-Clap in Arabic or lead a campus tour in Italian?

In late October, they do not bump into each other near *Maja* or Rodin's *The Walking Man* as Cricket envisions. Instead, destiny finds them at an on-campus coffee shop, during midterms, on the one day Cricket is too stressed about her upcoming exam to shower or even change out of her mustard-stained sweatpants. An angry cluster of pimples conspires on her chin.

But amid the buzz, Cricket feels that gravitational pull once again, the air humming with an electric current, and there she is, Yaz, scrolling through her phone as she pulls open the glass door and joins the back of the snaking line. She is a goddess among mortals, and no one else has even noticed.

"Hi," Cricket says to Yaz before realizing she can't hear her. Yaz's dark hair is down this time, the hot pink streaks framing either side of her face and hiding the fact that she has AirPods in and music blasting. But she must feel something, too, because she looks up.

"Interloper!" she beams, warmth exuding from her dark brown eyes like trapped sunlight. "I was wondering if I'd see you again."

Cricket forces words through a dry mouth. "Can you drink the coffee here? With me? Together?" In their exaggerated retellings of this interaction, Yaz admits to wondering whether the baby blond Amazon had learned English only recently.

"Now?"

Cricket nods, distrustful of her love-drunk brain to deploy proper syntax.

Yaz shrugs. "Who can say no to the star soccer goalie?"

"Keeper," Cricket musters. Ever since Coach differentiated goalie from goalkeeper when she was nine years old, Cricket has, too. "I'm a keeper," she tries to clarify. "Not a goalie."

Yaz laughs and it sounds like sleigh bells, like a snow-driven Christmas in the middle of the desert. "Don't I get to decide that?" Her smile lingers in a flirtatious tease, and Cricket stares at her, trying to pretend that she's not stroking out.

"Cricket!" the barista announces. "Medium hot chocolate!" But Cricket stays right there in line with Yaz, afraid that the girl she's been looking for will disappear again, or that Cricket will wake up from yet another dream of her, or that there will be a fire drill and they will have to evacuate the building before exchanging information. As Yaz orders her matcha, Cricket pulls out her card to pay.

"Slow down, puppy," Yaz says, giving the cashier a twenty-dollar bill with one hand while nudging Cricket's card back with the other. Their fingers touch, and by the time they find vacant seats by the windows, they both understand this is the first of many coffees together.

What the admissions website could not tell Cricket during her on-line investigation is that as impressive as Yasmine comes across on paper, her résumé does not come close to capturing the power of her presence. Instead, what Cricket learns for herself in the days and weeks ahead is that when Yaz focuses her attention on her, which is often and yet never enough, Cricket is overcome with a euphoric peace she has never experienced. Like she would give up soccer tomorrow if it meant she could spend every second with this woman whose lightest touch sends Cricket into a blissful blackout.

Also not included on Yaz's tour guide profile: She has a sardonic, inexhaustible sense of humor she attributes to her dad, and an equally relentless empathy she credits to her mom. Yaz was eleven, swimming in a pool in Bora Bora, when she realized her family was not upper middle class but "legit rich," and she was in the middle of her own Bat Mitzvah, singing in Hebrew, when she decided she was "zealously ag-nostic." She is lying next to Cricket in her off-campus apartment when Yaz notices for the first time how much she loves Cricket's pronounced deltoid muscles, and it's in this same romantic moment that Cricket ac-cidentally, but with quintessential Cricket impulse, tells Yaz she loves her. They have been together for nine days.

Yaz replies without hesitation: "I love you, too, my gigantic puppy superstar."

Their catalog of differences is a source of endless intrigue: While Cricket feels most comfortable wearing whatever she can play soccer in—or actively recover from playing soccer in—Yaz selects clothes she refers to as *pieces* that speak to her soul in sustainably made fabrics she calls *textiles*. In giving Cricket a tour of her studio space, Yaz explains she prefers working with oils over watercolor and stoneware to porcelain, which she accuses of being fussy, and she'll take sturdy over fussy any day. "You're example A," she says, grinning at Cricket. "Sturdy and no fuss."

Cricket laughs and decides to go along with it. Sure, she doesn't care too much about what she's wearing, or which sushi place they pick to celebrate their two-week anniversary, but she's undeniably particular—Mia calls her obsessive-compulsive—when it comes to soccer. Beginning with her morning routine, and going through her pregame rituals, midmatch resets, her postgame grounding walk, Cricket is fussy straight through her nighttime stretches, right up until the moment she falls asleep, only to wake up and begin all over again.

Every single game day, Cricket makes the same protein shake, eats the same healthy meals, and consumes the same snacks. Hydration is a top priority at all times, so Cricket tracks her intake on the same app Sloane introduced her to back in the day. Before warm-ups, Cricket consumes three pumpkin seeds like she's taking holy communion. Each ritual is grounded in what's worked in the past, which is why Sloane herself has become another fixture: She and Cricket speak within twenty-four hours of every match, debriefing about who played well, who shanked an easy goal, who lost their head but somehow didn't get carded. It doesn't matter that Cricket is playing collegiate in the Pac-12 and that Sloane is competing professionally in the NWSL—their dogged quest for excellence is identical.

"Yeah, I guess I'm not fussy," Cricket agrees tentatively in Yaz's studio. "But I've got my quirks." Yaz leans over and pulls out Cricket's hair tie, freeing the shiny knot of blond pouf. Her fingers massage Cricket's scalp and it would be relaxing if it weren't so sensual.

"Everybody has their quirks," Yaz says just before kissing her.

Under the sheets and upon closer inspection, Cricket finds Yaz to be a committed truth-teller with secrets mapped across her skin. She has an inked sun hovering above her pubic bone, an iguana holding a balloon at the top of her left thigh. A cluster of white circles on the back of her neck, just below her hairline, linger still from her grandfather's lit cigarettes.

"You're the first to notice those," Yaz says quietly, the two of them hiding from daylight.

Cricket holds her, listening closely as Yaz tells her everything, and at some point, the conversation turns to Liz and the car accident. "She was driving home from dropping me off for a tournament," Cricket confesses. "The only time I feel absolved is when I'm playing soccer, because that's what she wanted for me."

They do their best to kiss away the pain of each other's past and plan for a future together. Under Maja's steady gaze, Cricket and Yaz spend every free moment they don't have in the sculpture garden or in Yaz's apartment.

There is no question what this is. Like that first time from across the green, Cricket still senses the molecular pull of Yaz just before she walks into any room. In every soccer-related injury Cricket has ever incurred, Yaz goes there and heals her but also pushes her. Because despite all the demands Cricket has put on her body through over the years, it's Yasmine Frankel who teaches her the discipline of surrender.

GRAY OWL

"I can't believe we get to live this way," Mia tells Oliver as he clicks out of the spreadsheet and closes his laptop.

"We can live any way you want," he says, picking Mia up, tossing her over his shoulder, and carrying her out of the kitchen and into their room.

Tonight, they have created a budget, and in graphing their financial caps, the future seems limitless. Each month, if they stick to the plan, they'll be able to take trips, try new restaurants, and still save for the future. Mia believes that looking ahead means worrying less, and unlike her former financial partner—her mother—Oliver heartily agrees. Systems and discipline, not whims and superstition, will guide their trajectory.

Flinging Mia on their bed, Oliver hops in after her, his hands running up her sides with obvious intentions. "Is this where I make that joke about being a tiger in the spreadsheets and the bedsheets?"

"You just did," Mia points out, breathing him in. "And yet I'm still attracted to you."

Almost immediately after Cricket left for UCLA, Mia realized she had no interest in going back to school. Instead, she wants to keep working at the animal hospital, in a job for which she is technically under-qualified and overcompensated. Dr. Wilkins pays Mia what he would pay a college graduate, and Mia reimburses him with her unwavering competence. There's no reason to leave Oceanside; it's predictable, with cute, loveable patients and plenty of opportunities to offer care and support to those in need. For Mia, it's everything a job should be: one designated piece of her life, not an all-consuming, wholly defining existence.

Because unlike Cricket, Mia doesn't want to be wedded to her occupation. Rather, Mia wants to marry Oliver. She knows she's still young—only twenty-three—but she also *knows*. Since November 9, 2019, Mia has understood that life is fleeting and dangerously unfair. And since meeting Oliver, she believes her life is both steadier and more exciting with him playing a starring role. It's Oliver. Every single day, Mia chooses Oliver.

Together they are making 125 Knickerbocker feel like theirs: blending silverware, donating spaghetti pot redundancies, and filling a raised bed with seedlings purchased from the farmer's market. Everything is moving forward—or almost everything.

"Can you explain to me how I haven't officially moved in," Oliver says the morning after creating their budget spreadsheet. He asks this with his back to Mia as he FrogTapes the window casings. Their current project is repainting Mia's bedroom—now their bedroom—a soothing gray over a garish purple she chose when she was seven. "I gave up my apartment and I sleep here seven days a week."

"Right," Mia agrees, using a screwdriver to remove an outlet cover. She loves that they are taking the time to properly prep the room. When she and Liz last painted these walls, sixteen years ago, they did two coats in under two hours—Liz had timed their performance, as usual. They didn't even mix the cans or paint a sample strip. If they had, Mia would have realized that what appeared pretty on a tiny square didn't look the same when it saturated four walls. But Mia had endured the purple for all these years, until she had complained to Oliver and he'd insisted they pick out paint that same day.

At Hammer It Home, Mia found Benjamin Moore's Gray Owl soothing but sophisticated. Unlike her mother, who deemed all neutrals boring, Mia appreciates how the gradient subtly changes with the sunlight, evolving with the day's weather. There is a measured acceptance of ambiguity in Gray Owl, a flexibility to let the room transform in its own time.

"So for example, these were delivered here," Oliver says, interrupting Mia's thoughts by holding up a paint roller, "because this is where I live, right?"

"Mm-hm."

"So why did I hear you tell Dave the mailman that I don't live here?"

Mia freezes. "You heard that?"

"Yep."

Standing up to buy herself a moment, Mia shuts her eyes and cracks her neck one way, then the other—a bad habit she picked up from sitting at a desk all day. Keeping her eyes closed, she tells Oliver the truth: "I haven't told Cricket yet," she confesses. "And I'm scared of her reaction."

"What? Why?" Oliver asks, genuinely surprised. "She's in California having an amazing time." It's moments like these when Mia wishes Oliver weren't an only child, wishes he could innately understand a sibling's shared sense of ownership over everything, from phone chargers and sweaters to DNA to, most definitely, family real estate.

"Because this is our house," Mia says, spreading her arms wide. The room is small enough that with her full wingspan, Mia's fingertips can almost graze the primed walls. "This is her house."

"It's as much yours as it is hers," Oliver argues.

"Not Cricket's," Mia says. "My mom's."

Without a word or a second's hesitation, Oliver takes the two steps required to cross the room, over the meticulously distributed drop cloths, and enfolds Mia in the same all-encompassing, claustrophobia-inducing hug as the ugly purple paint that surrounds them.

"I know I'm biased, but I truly believe she would support my moving in," he whispers in her ear.

Mia laughs as she feels her tears wet the front of Oliver's painting smock, which is an old Stallions T-shirt, soft and thin with a nickel-size hole in the shoulder. She's long since stopped wondering why she cries when she does because it's ultimately always the same reason—she misses her mom. It's impossible to hold all the sorrow when it blindsides her like it did just now, this tremendous ache of not getting to talk to the one person she really, desperately needs to.

"Liz is as excited about us getting together and living here as she is about Cricket playing at UCLA," Oliver posits.

"How do you know?"

"Because I would have already been struck by lightning or swallowed by one of those sinkholes if she had any doubts."

Mia snorts her agreement, and Oliver remembers aloud that her mom was also a laugh-snorter. He has been trying to help Mia live with her grief by speaking often and fondly of Liz. Last week, when the sisters were apart for the first time on the anniversary of Liz's death, Oliver joined Mia on the beach for the New Year's Eve polar plunge. He held the phone up while Cricket and Mia FaceTimed at midnight Eastern Time, screaming, freezing, cursing, crying, and laughing together through the dark and distance.

"Call Cricket and tell her I'm moving in," Oliver says, putting down the roller and crossing his arms. "The paint can wait."

As Mia calls from the privacy of the front porch, she hopes this will be one of those times that Cricket is in class, or at practice, or just in the middle of a good old-fashioned college shenanigan that makes answering the phone impossible. No such luck. She picks up on the second ring, impish giggles in the background of her hello.

"Honestly? I figured he already had," Cricket says calmly after Mia reluctantly shares her news. Listening to the intermittent smacking sounds on the other end of the line, Mia can picture her sister taking too-big bites from her pretraining peanut butter and jelly sandwich. "I figured you guys went straight from dropping me off at the airport to the U-Haul rental place."

"Huh?" Mia asks, squinting to discern how many people are with Cricket. The giggling has returned to full volume. "So you're not mad?" she asks.

"I guess I'd say I'm resigned," Cricket answers. "And on that note, I wanted to tell you I'm dating someone—she's a girl, by the way, and her name is Yasmine, but everybody calls her Yaz."

A pause stretches between them before Mia asks, "She's sitting next to you, isn't she?"

"Uh-huh."

"Am I on speaker?"

"I didn't say you were, and I'm not a sociopath, so no."

"Wow!" Mia is beyond relieved that Cricket is okay about Oliver moving in, but it comes out as clumsy enthusiasm for someone she's never met as she gushes, "I'm so happy for you—tell me everything!"

"Can she visit over winter break?"

"Absolutely!" Mia says, rushing back into the bedroom and trying to mouth to Oliver the big news. "This is so exciting!"

"I know," Cricket says. "And I'm sorry I was such a dick about Coach, but now I get it."

"Get what?"

"Love," Cricket says, without an ounce of self-awareness. Mia scrunches her eyes shut from the immediate bout of secondhand embarrassment. Her sister is besotted.

"It's crazy, but I really get it now," says Cricket, sharing a laugh with the woman next to her, this stranger Mia is suddenly dying to know. "And the nice thing is, now that I get it, I feel like we can be on the same team again."

"We're always on the same team."

"Yeah, but it's like what you said before I left—now it feels easier for me to cheer for you, too."

After Mia hangs up with Cricket, she smiles at the purple walls and realizes that life has begun to right itself. With Oliver by her side and her room extensively prepped, they roll out the first coat. The Gray Owl provides the perfect backdrop to make Oliver's green eyes pop as Mia fills him in on Cricket and Yaz.

"That's fantastic!" Oliver says, stepping back to examine his work. "I thought she seemed different on our last FaceTime—like a different kind of happy than I've seen."

Painting over what was, Mia listens to Oliver sing along to her playlist and imagines him as her husband, as the person to whom she'll always be bound. In her mind's eye, she sees him become more vivid in this new form, as will she, a partner for life, and then co-parents, a family of their own, kids her mother will never meet, never kick a soccer ball to, or polar plunge with, or shop for at Goodwill. The speed of her racing thoughts suddenly makes it difficult for Mia to catch her breath.

"Deep inhale," Oliver says, crouched down beside her and rubbing her back. "I'm right here. Let's do it together."

Ever since the ninth of November four years ago, Mia has struggled to keep her footing in the chaotic tornado of heartbreak, financial stress, Cricket's adolescence, and a pandemic. If she'd known what she would be forced to endure, Mia isn't convinced she'd still be standing.

But here she is.

What good fortune to be spared one's fortune.

On the floor of her childhood bedroom, Mia breathes with Oliver. She is coming to understand that love and loss live on the same coin. It's never heads or tails but joy and agony, grief and delight, spinning in the air, waiting on time and luck to determine not when this chapter ends but how the next one begins.

WINTER BREAK

S now falls in fat, packable flakes the morning Oliver and Mia pick up Cricket and Yaz from their red-eye flight. It's the sticky kind of snow that children deem perfect for forts and snowball fights, and the type adults curse while hunched over their shovels. This had not been in the day's forecast.

For Cricket and Yaz, the unexpected precipitation only enhances their dramatic entrance into the winter wonderland of Maine in December. Amid the wool-and-flannel crowd, it could not be more obvious that these two have arrived fresh from Southern California. Suntanned and stylish, they vacuum up every set of eyeballs at Portland Jetport. Cricket looks notably fashionable in an outfit that, given the clear lack of elastic, Mia highly doubts her sister assembled herself.

"Wow," Oliver says, peering over his sunglasses.

"Double wow," Mia agrees, taking in the self-possessed, full-lipped bombshell next to Cricket. "Soccer Barbie has met her match."

When Cricket spots Mia across the parking lot, she runs toward her screaming, "I didn't even think I missed you!"

"I knew I missed you," Mia says, hugging Cricket tight and noting the new muscular thickness of her sister's neck before holding out her hand to Yaz.

Staring at Mia's hand like it's some local dish no one in their right mind would eat this early in the morning, Yaz takes a step toward her. "Mia," she says calmly, "you may not know this, but we are most definitely on a hugging level."

When they pile into the car, Cricket demands they take the scenic route back to Victory, stopping by Portland Headlight, the iconic lighthouse at Fort Williams where tourists binge on buttery lobster rolls and breathtaking views of the ocean. "Do you guys want a photo together?" Mia offers from the passenger seat.

Yaz and Cricket shake their heads in unison. They're too cold to get out of the car.

"California has made my toughest keeper soft," Oliver teases.

"Excuse me, did you see UCLA's record?" Cricket protests from the back. "We only lost one game in the regular season."

Turning around in her seat, Mia asks the new arrivals if they want to nap or stay awake.

"Stay awake," says Yaz.

"Nap," Cricket counters.

"Becky's it is," announces Oliver, breaking the tie by steering them toward the famous diner on Commercial Street in downtown Portland.

Cricket grins her consent and explains to Yaz, "My mom's favorite place."

Like Liz, the owner of Becky's Diner single-handedly supported her kids while balancing hot plates up her forearms and still managed to greet each stranger as a friend. On the special occasions when the Lowes would go to the diner—birthdays and snow days—Liz and Becky would paw at each other like bear cubs, celebrating the fact that they'd both defied the odds stacked against them.

Now, Liz's grown daughters and their significant others follow the hostess to a booth and pile in while inhaling the promise of a hot breakfast and bottomless caffeine.

"I'm so happy," Mia says, distributing menus.

"I'm so tired," Cricket yawns, staring at her sister to see what she thinks of Yaz. To anyone else at the table, even Oliver, Mia's expression remains the same, but Cricket translates her held gaze as a seal of approval.

"Waffles for the table?" Mia suggests, shooting Cricket a knowing smile, who fires it right back. It's the classic Liz move.

"I like your style," Yaz says, examining the laminated menu with the discerning eye of a forensic scientist. Cricket watches her, mesmerized, as Yaz puts her hair up in a ponytail and the strands of hot pink reappear as that middle stripe.

Even as she witnesses it from point-blank range, Mia can't believe how smitten her sister is. She stares at Cricket, who stargazes at Yaz, who takes a sip of her coffee and then says to Oliver, eyes shining bright at a joke only they seem to know, "That was me."

"Oops!" Oliver smiles, embarrassed. "My bad—I wanted to kick one of these clowns so they snapped out of it."

"Sorry," Mia says, shaking her head and sitting up straight. "Yaz, tell us everything about you—I've been looking forward to this for months."

"I have, too," Yaz says, putting her hand on the table and reaching for Mia, seated diagonally from her. "There's not much to tell—I guess the most relevant thing is that I'm in love with your sister. Is that weird to say? But it's true, and school is way more fun with her there."

"Have you seen her play?" Coach asks, unable to hide his desire to talk soccer.

"Hell yes!" Yaz says, slamming down her coffee mug. "And, oh my God, you guys missed some killer games! That first playoff game against Irvine was such a bummer but still amazing—the atmosphere was like nothing I've ever seen—not that I'd been to a lot of sporty things before Cricket, but still. Unbelievable."

"We streamed all of them—all the games," Oliver says, massaging Mia's shoulder to remind her that flying out to California for Cricket's matches would have obliterated their budget. They'd been strategic in their decision-making, and between the mortgage and paying for Cricket's living expenses, including her flight home for this visit, and everything they envision in their five-year plan, a bunch of quick trips to the other side of the country was too hard to justify.

"Yeah, but could you really get a sense of the crowd through the screen?" Yaz asks before her eyes skate past Mia's to their server fast approaching with five huge plates. "Amazing timing—I'm starving."

For a solid two minutes, no one speaks as fork tines plunge into omelets, waffles, pancakes, bacon, and English muffins fresh off the griddle and loaded with butter. Eventually, Yaz picks up where she left off. "So could you hear everyone doing that chant for Cricket? When you streamed the games?"

Mia nearly spit-takes her coffee. "No! Cricket, what? Seriously?"

Cricket blushes and takes a huge bite of toast to avoid answering.

"It's incredible," Yaz says. "Everyone knows her and it's like dating a celebrity, but in the best possible way—like every time they won, which was all the time this year, people came up to congratulate me in class, as if I had something to do with it."

"Because you did," Cricket beams, leaning into Yaz and openly swooning.

With full stomachs and jittery coffee legs, they leave Becky's and head for the woods, where the narrow path forces them to pair up. Yaz takes off with Mia.

"What do you think they're talking about?" Cricket asks Oliver as they move at a significantly slower clip. She worries about tripping over a snow-buried root in her Birkenstocks and Oliver indulges her. They both know that, all too often, an embarrassing story from the offseason can lead to a career-ending injury.

"They're talking about you," Oliver says matter-of-factly. "Just like I want to talk to you about Mia."

"What about her?" Cricket asks, with no small amount of little-sister safeguarding.

Oliver lowers his voice. "We want to get married," he says, eyes darting over to catch Cricket's. "But before I propose, I was hoping to get your blessing?"

"She's right there!" Cricket hisses, pointing to her sister, who is still visible through the trees but certainly out of earshot. "And she's so young!"

"True and true," Oliver acknowledges, bending down to scoop up a handful of snow he now molds into a ball. "But I'm not that young, and

I know she's my person, and my health insurance through USM is so much better than what she's got through Oceanside, and we really want to save as much money as we can."

"How romantic." Cricket looks up at the white-capped pine trees, the gray sky beyond the boughs. The snow keeps coming. How did Mia let her get out of the car in Birks? The woods were a bad idea and now Oliver is talking nonsense, unless—

"Is she pregnant?" Cricket asks, feeling her pulse quicken.

"No," Oliver says, tossing his snowball into the air and catching it while clearly mulling something over in his head.

"Tell me."

"She's not pregnant, I swear," Oliver insists, "but she does—she's pretty set on having a baby, and it seems like she wants one sooner rather than later."

"MIA!" Cricket shouts. Breaking into a run, screw the shoes, she needs to talk to her sister. Oliver reaches out, grabs her arm, catches Cricket mid-step.

"Hold up," he says. "I'm serious about proposing." Cricket shrugs off his grip but doesn't run ahead. "So do I have it?" Oliver asks. "Your blessing?"

Cricket looks at this man, her coach, Mia's Oliver, the closest guy she's ever had to family—some weird blend between a father and a brother. He makes Mia happy, that much is obvious, and he's proven his loyalty time and again. Now that Cricket is really thinking about it, she has to acknowledge that Coach's presence helped anchor them during the worst time of their lives. And ever since.

"Of course you do," she says, pulling Oliver in for a hug. Thanks to Yaz, Cricket can appreciate the healing power of love, the freedom that comes with fully trusting another person, bearing witness to the struggles and triumphs of their existence. "You have my blessing and, more importantly, you also have my permission."

"Oh, thank God," Oliver says dryly, keeping his arm around her shoulder as they trudge forward, "because we want to do it soon."

"How soon?"

"I guess it depends on your schedule," Oliver says, winding up and pitching his snowball against a white pine. Through the stand of looming trees, Cricket watches Mia's red coat bob out of sight. She deserves happiness more than anyone—of this Cricket is certain.

"Would tomorrow work?" Oliver asks. Registering Cricket's stricken eyes and hanging jaw, Oliver backpedals. He offers a far more rational date. "Okay, fine, the day after tomorrow."

SOMETHING RED

The next day, after Oliver proposes to Mia on the beach, Cricket helps her sister choose a dress from their mother's closet to wear to the courthouse. Although the winner is not seasonally appropriate, it is the one Liz loved most—a white linen halter dress laden with summer memories. It's the dress Liz wore every Fourth of July and to the World Cup quarter-finals in Paris.

"I'm pretty sure she found it in the dollar bin," Cricket says, standing behind Mia to tie the straps in a bow.

"It doesn't fit me right," Mia says, staring at her reflection in the full-length mirror.

"Really?" Cricket squints, trying to find a problem. "You don't think so?" She's hardly a bridal consultant but the dress looks great. "Let's show Yaz," Cricket says, steering Mia toward the living room, where Yaz is curled up on the pink floral couch, scrolling through her phone.

Oliver has gone out in search of a bouquet for Mia to hold during the ceremony. He purchased the wedding rings months ago—two matching gold bands Mia had admired through an estate jeweler's store window in Ogunquit.

"Yeah, no, it fits you perfectly," Yaz insists, covering a jet lag yawn as she stands up to inspect the situation more closely. "You look stunning," Yaz says definitively, pulling Mia back into the moment with a slow, graceful nod of assurance. "It fits you, and more importantly, it suits you."

"Thank you," Mia says, throwing back her pale shoulders and lifting her neck with confidence. "Which shoes?"

"Let's take a look." Yaz follows Mia back into Liz's room, and Cricket trails after them, heart swelling that her two favorite people are bonding in her mother's closet. It's almost as if Liz were a part of the festivities, especially when Mia digs out Liz's nicest pair of heels and Yaz declares them the clear winner.

On Mia's wedding day, Yaz helps the bride with her hair and makeup while Cricket documents it all on her phone with their mother's voice in her head. She would want to see all of this. Cricket takes a video of Mia applying Liz's ruby red lipstick in the mirror of their childhood bathroom. "Careful, Mia," Cricket teases. "Remember Mom said that lipstick got her pregnant?"

On the porch, right as they prepare to leave for city hall, Mia admires Oliver in his navy suit before her smile drops into a panicked droop. "You don't have a boutonniere," she says.

"This isn't prom," Oliver chides, but Mia, feeling fragile in her mother's dress on her wedding day, says it isn't funny, he's supposed to have a boutonniere.

"No problem," Cricket says. "Hold on a sec." The others listen to her heavy-footed clip-clops as she runs down the hall to her room. They hear her opening and shutting drawers as if she might have misplaced a freshly cut floral arrangement in the back of her dresser.

"Here we go!" Cricket announces, grinning as she reappears with what looks like several short strips of translucent blue foam held together with a safety pin.

"Is that—packaging material?" Yaz asks, barely suppressing her dismay.

"It's perfect," Oliver says.

"It's prewrap," Mia scoffs, shaking her head at her feet in amused resignation. Even on her wedding day, soccer must play a role.

"Not just any prewrap," Cricket corrects her. "Stallion blue pre-wrap."

"Like I said, it's perfect," Oliver asserts, taking the strips from Cricket's hand and fastening them to his left lapel.

"Also, this seems imperative," Cricket says. She holds up the ribbon, slightly frayed and still knotted, and Mia knows it's the one Liz wore to watch the U.S. women win their World Cup quarter-final match in 2019. It's been on Liz's bureau, memorialized and collecting dust ever since. "I know the saying is all about blue and new, but in this family, I think you need something red and from Paris."

"But she's wearing her hair down," Yaz points out.

"Give me your wrist," Cricket demands.

Mia holds out her arm and watches her sister tie the ribbon. "I wish she were here," Mia whispers. She tries not to cry—Yaz has warned her that her mascara isn't waterproof.

"She is," Cricket whispers back. "Don't you ever—" Cricket watches Mia's face, searching for a sign of recognition, some hint that some-times Liz appears to Mia, too, the way she shows up at Cricket's goal-post on game days. But Mia squeezes her eyes shut, and when she opens them, they are trained on the momvan in the driveway.

"Let's go," she says, her voice steady once more. "I don't want to be late."

At nine-thirty a.m., Oliver drives them to city hall. On the marble curved staircase, Mia's heels clack so loudly that they echo, and the foursome giggles self-consciously, bodies and hearts on full display as they navigate bureaucrats with coffee breath to find the State of Maine Room.

The ceremony lasts fourteen minutes. As Cricket watches her sister and Oliver promise forever to each other, Yaz squeezes her hand to imply that someday it will be their turn. Cricket squeezes back but keeps her eyes fastened on Mia. She tries to ignore her dry mouth and the tight knot in her chest. Growing up, Cricket never dreamed of a wedding day or a gold ring. Instead, she fantasized about gold medals and the five Olympic rings.

But Yaz will want this. She already does. And Cricket—although she can hardly believe it—she can imagine wanting this, too. Someday. Not yet.

A World Cup win, Cricket tells herself as she kisses Yaz's cheek in the State of Maine Room. A World Cup win for her and then one hell of a wedding for them.

1-2-3 JINX

"It's *not* a babymoon," Mia insists on the phone. In the fall of Cricket's junior year at UCLA, Mia is seven weeks pregnant. To celebrate, Oliver books a trip to Key Largo over Christmas, when Mia will have just entered the blissful second trimester. "And because it's *not* a babymoon," Mia emphasizes, "I'd love for you to come."

Cricket knows Mia is terrified of jinxing her fertility luck this early in the game, which is why she's refusing to call the trip what it clearly is. She considers the offer before asking, "Are you still puking all the time?"

"It should stop soon," Mia answers. "I think."

"And the Airbnb is a one-bedroom?"

"With a pullout couch in the living room."

"Sounds delightful," Cricket jokes. And then, because she loves mentioning it at every opportunity, Cricket adds, "I need to focus on training for camp."

After Cricket's third tremendous season with UCLA, Teague has once again invited her to the National Team January Camp. Sloane is also invited, and so Cricket wants to show up in the best shape of her life. She can't compromise her performance at camp—or her lower back—with a week on a pullout couch.

Yaz plans to spend the entire break at her conservative grandmother's in Laguna Beach. "I would say come with me," Yaz says, taking out her diamond studs before bed, "but our love would literally kill her."

And so Cricket is just beginning to entertain the idea of spending Christmas alone in Victory when Sloane calls, freaking out about camp and talking way too fast.

"Hi!OhmyGod!Youhavetocomehereandstaywithmeeeee!"

This year's January Camp is being held in West Palm Beach, not even thirty minutes from Sloane's childhood home. "We can train together ahead of time," she says. "We'll run fartleks on my high school track, and my parents will totally love having you here for Christmas. Oh my God, they will actually, truly die from happiness."

Without hesitation, Cricket says yes, because only Sloane will understand the importance of pre-camp training. Only Sloane won't ask her why she'd rather do sets of box jumps than drink rounds of eggnog on Christmas Eve, or skip New Year's altogether to wake up at five a.m. for an endurance run. When Cricket calls back to confirm her flights, Sloane expresses her joy by singing so loudly and poorly that Cricket, out of respect for her ears, hangs up.

Yaz, however, is less thrilled. "Wow," she says, scrolling through Sloane's online presence as they lie side by side on her bed. "She's really pretty." Skimming Wikipedia, Yaz adds, "She's taller than you?"

"By one inch, if that," Cricket says dismissively, pulling Yaz into her arms. "You know I'd much rather go somewhere—anywhere—with you," Cricket adds, gathering up Yaz's hair to kiss her on the neck, and then the collarbone. She lifts Yaz's shirt over her head and gazes admiringly at Yaz's body. "Goddamn," Cricket sighs, enjoying the warmth of Yaz's skin on her lips. "I'd face off against ten homophobic grannies if it meant getting to spend winter break with you."

Two orgasms later, Yaz gives Cricket her blessing for West Palm Beach. "The internet says Sloane only likes brunettes anyway," Yaz smirks, pulling her shorts back on.

"Brunette *runway models*," Cricket corrects, lacing up her sneakers. She is relieved to have Yaz on the same page and excited to see Sloane in her natural habitat.

And here she is now: Sloane Jackson in a turquoise tank top, practically falling out of a white Escalade that's fast approaching the curb at the Palm Beach International Airport.

"Ambitious witches unite!" Sloane yells. Behind the wheel, Sloane's mother, Bonnie Jackson, honks the horn with abandon.

"Ho ho ho!" Sloane shouts, hopping out of the SUV and smothering Cricket in a hug. "Merry Christmas Eve!"

Cricket ignores the crunch in her chest as she thinks of the Christmas Prelude in Kennebunkport, where Santa arrives via lobster boat. This is the first time she won't be there. It's the first Christmas in Cricket's life that she won't spend with Mia in Maine.

"Merry Christmas, darlin'!" Bonnie says, pulling Cricket into a hug. "We're so glad you made it!" Cupping her mouth and lowering her voice so Sloane can't hear, Bonnie adds ominously, "If you don't like your room, just let me know."

"Of course I'll like it!" Cricket says, loading her suitcase. Bonnie shoots her a look that can only be translated as: *You don't know what you don't know.*

"Close your eyes and hold out your hands," Sloane instructs after Cricket buckles. She does as she's told and is rewarded with something cold. "Iced vanilla latte with oat milk," Sloane announces, visibly proud to know Cricket's caffeinated drink of choice. "It took you long enough," Sloane says as they exit the airport, "but I'm glad you're finally here."

After a thirty-minute drive up I-95, the Escalade pulls up to a high wrought-iron gate and Bonnie types a code into the kiosk that blends into a twelve-foot hedge. The gate ceremoniously opens. "Almost home," Bonnie says, reaching back to pat Cricket's knee.

If only that were true.

But if Cricket were really almost home, there would be a taxidermized moose in the airport, and snow in the weather forecast, the smell of sugar cookies in the oven, and Mia reciting all the words to *It's a Wonderful Life* along with the movie. There would be Canada geese trying to cross the icy street, not three girls in bikinis speeding past on a golf cart.

Sloane had warned Cricket that her family lived in a gated community, but she hadn't said her house consumed half a city block and abutted a golf course. She'd also failed to mention that her house was technically on the grounds of the Pelican Country Club—as they drive by the clubhouse, a member of the grounds crew operates a chain saw to tidy up the hedge that spells out PELICAN just in case anyone forgot.

"You have a pool across the street?" Cricket asks, staring in disbelief. The pool is actually several interconnected pools with two hot tubs and a mile-long lazy river, but all of it somehow understated amid the remarkable gardens. Sloane explains that the Pelican hired a Harvard graduate of landscape architecture to design the "community campus" and Cricket nods along as if she hasn't just landed on another planet.

At the top of a long driveway, Bonnie parks the car and Sloane skips up the steps to the largest house Cricket has ever seen, which includes the governor's mansion in Augusta. "And to think this is where the greatest goalkeeper in soccer history spent her formative years!" Sloane announces.

"When did she sell it?" Cricket quips.

Standing in the marbled foyer of the Jackson residence, Cricket takes in the grand staircase, the framed art, the absence of mail or keys, shoes or coats. It feels more like a hotel lobby than a home. Cricket thinks of the old Smiling Hill Farm milk crate overflowing with sneakers by her own front door. She suddenly wants to go home, but without Mia there, it doesn't exist.

"There's a gym in the basement that my dad modeled after the Carson training facility," Sloane says, speaking quickly as she leads Cricket up the staircase. "And I know my mom made a bunch of reservations for us while you're here, but just tell me if it's too much and I'll get her to dial it back."

Cricket nods. She feels like crying for a hundred reasons and no reason at all.

"I hope you know you can change your mind," Sloane says, stopping halfway up the staircase and turning around to stare at Cricket.

"Yeah, no, it all sounds great," Cricket says, forcing a smile.

Sloane leans back on the banister and drops her head over the railing, exposing her stomach. She does this when she's thinking, a mini-inversion to promote blood flow to the brain. Cricket has witnessed this move at camp but also over FaceTime—when she gets an unflattering view up Sloane's nostrils.

"I didn't mean whether or not you wanted to eat at Elisabetta's," Sloane says from upside down. She rights herself and grabs Cricket's shoulder, holds her gaze for a moment too long. "Give me some credit," she says before spinning on her toes to continue up the stairs. "I meant about you being here. Since Yaz feels weird about it."

Cricket's skin prickles with defensiveness and so they move on in silence. Anything she might say will sound like a betrayal. Yaz doesn't get it because she's never met Sloane. She doesn't understand that they are friends, yes, but also fierce, ambitious-witch rivals. Yaz wants Cricket to continue to be a star goalkeeper without necessarily realizing that earning a top spot requires competing against the best. And Sloane Jackson, even if Cricket would rather self-immolate than say it to her face, is second to none. Yaz can't understand because she's not a keeper.

Upstairs, Sloane walks down a corridor as long and wide as the drive-way outside, and Cricket realizes that this is the kind of house that is divided into wings. "My mom wanted to put you in the guest room, but I vetoed that because it's all the way down there"—she gestures behind them—"and I told her you're the one person I don't care about sharing a bathroom with."

"I'm flattered, I think."

"You should be," Sloane says, opening the door. The bathroom is all white marble and the size of the UCLA locker room.

"Are you serious?" Cricket asks, eyeing the two-headed shower, the infrared sauna. There is a television embedded in the wall across from the freestanding bathtub. Its gleaming hardware winks condescendingly at Cricket.

"I have the best soaking tub in the house," Sloane says, nodding at the modern whirlpool. "And I know how nuts you are about your baths." Over the years, as part of her pre- and postgame routine, Cricket has developed an elaborate bath ritual that requires more ingredients than most cocktails. In her suitcase is a bath-designated toiletry bag that tends to raise eyebrows at airport security: Epsom salt, lavender oil, jojoba oil, olive oil, a travel candle, and an eye mask.

"Is this a joke?" Cricket asks. Her jaw isn't the only thing unhinged on this tour. Tucked on the other side of the sauna is a cold plunge pool that she knows costs north of fifteen thousand dollars.

"No, but hold on, because this is your room," Sloane says, opening a connecting door. "Ta-da!"

Cricket squints, her eyes adjusting to the sharp spike in sunlight as she steps inside. Only it's not sunlight. Or rather, it's not just sunlight. It's the afternoon sun refracting off glass and gold, silver and bronze. Four-foot-tall display cases line the walls and are filled with medals, trophies, and cups. Above the cases hang frame after frame of memorabilia—gloves, soccer jerseys, American flags, rally towels, and photographs of Sloane standing with famous figures, from former National Team keepers Briana Scurry and Hope Solo to former Presidents George W. Bush and Barack Obama.

"You're staying in my trophy room," Sloane says, barely suppressing her mirth. "So to answer your question, yes, this is a joke." She nods to the twin-size mattress shoved in the corner. A single prison pillow serves as the cherry on top of this well-executed stunt.

Cricket looks at Sloane. Sloane stares back. It's not clear who cracks first, who lets out that initial burst of devilish delight, but they don't stop laughing for a long time.

That night, however, as Cricket tries to get comfortable, she wonders if she's really in on the joke. Because in this moment, and by the light of the moon bouncing off Sloane's medals, it feels more like the joke is on her. *Why did she agree to this? What is she doing here?*

"Good morning, sunshine!" Sloane says, jumping on top of Cricket the next morning. "How'd you sleep?"

"Terrible," Cricket says, squinting in the sunlight. Once she started questioning Sloane's motives, and if they were actually on the same team or just pretending to be, she couldn't stop. Now Sloane is ready to go and Cricket is exhausted.

"Oh no." Sloane frowns. "Do you want to sleep in the actual guest room? I liked the idea of you being so close by, but not if it compromises your rest and recovery."

Cricket nods, confused but grateful for the sympathy. Sometimes Sloane felt like two different people with two sets of competing motives, but maybe Cricket had just been paranoid last night. She shakes off her groggy concerns, gathers her stuff, and together they carry her things down the long hallway to the guest room.

After that first restless night, Cricket sleeps soundly in the creamy linen oasis that is the Jackson family's guest room. She chalks up her suspicions to Sloane just being Sloane and taking a prank too far. Luxuriating in a privacy she's never experienced, Cricket cannot believe she has her own bathroom, or that the hamper she assumed was for dirty clothes is actually designed to warm her towels.

Training with Sloane is so much better than being home alone in Maine or cramped at the Airbnb with Mia and Oliver and all their expecting-parents anxiety. As Cricket and Sloane fall into an intense training routine and equally strict recovery program, the days pass quickly. They are determined to crush January Camp, and here at Sloane's house, they have all the tools and resources they need to do just that.

"Who has two pairs of these?" Cricket asks, sitting next to Sloane in the family den on a decadently oversize leather couch. Their legs are elevated and encased in cutting-edge compression boots.

Sloane shrugs. "My dad kept stealing mine so I told him to get his own."

Bruce Jackson is a burly man with thick black hair on his forearms and oil-funded privilege in his blood. Cricket has never seen him not smiling. At four p.m. each day, Bruce arrives home. Like clockwork, he collapses on the leather couch between Sloane and Cricket, offers his take on the weather, the Dow, his swing if he played golf that afternoon, and then asks to hear about their day of training.

"You two are going to go all the way," he says, delivering each of them a tall glass of his signature ginger-and-lemon restorative iced tea. "Mark my words: No one works harder, plays better, or deserves to wear the crest more than you two."

Bruce is so supportive, so enthusiastic, that his presence underscores everything Cricket's father was not. Each day spent with the Jacksons reminds Cricket that she must counterbalance her dad's sins with her own greatness to honor her mother's legacy. She has so much more to prove on and off the field than someone like Sloane, who has a mom who's still alive and a dad like Bruce, who's always had everything.

Not that Sloane considers any of this, or would ever agree if she did.

And so, as usual, an electric current of competition buzzes between them at all times: in goal, in Sloane's basement gym, at the Jacksons' dining room table. When Cricket and Sloane elbow each other while loading the dishwasher, Bonnie tells Bruce, "They're more like brothers than sisters."

"More like prizefighters than brothers," Bruce says, chuckling.

Despite their rapid-fire trash talk during their thirty-minute skin care routines, Cricket and Sloane benefit from the constructive criticism and hard-won compliments they offer each other. A mutual respect toggles between them in equal measure for ten days straight. Thriving on each other's determination, they drive to camp feeling confident and prepared. And thanks to the Jacksons' Costco membership, they also arrive with a ten-pound bag of pumpkin seeds.

"Sloanie!" someone shouts from across the field as soon as Cricket and Sloane arrive. Because Sloane already plays for the Washington Spirit in the NWSL, she knows nearly everyone at camp. Teague teases Sloane incessantly and Anders constantly pulls Sloane aside to share his observations on her performance. They do not do this with Cricket, who feels the frost even in the debilitating humidity.

When Yaz calls from her grandmother's house, Cricket tells her it's going well. But when Mia calls from the Airbnb in Key Largo, she sounds concerned, as if she already knows how camp has panned out, how Cricket is once again wilting in Sloane's shadow.

"You doing okay?" Mia asks.

"Yeah," Cricket says, her own voice faltering. "It's just—hard, you know? With everyone already obsessed with Sloane and joking around with her all the time. Like the roster is already set."

"Just be patient," Mia says, her tone tight, almost sharp. "Just try to be patient."

"Are you okay?" Cricket asks, sensing something else. Mia remains quiet for so long that Cricket assumes the line has gone dead. "Mia?"

"I'm here," she whispers. "But I lost it."

"Lost what?"

"The baby," Mia confides, her voice breaking. "I lost the baby."

"Where are you?" Cricket leans forward, determined to fix the unfixable, because Mia has already been through enough, they have both been through enough. "Send me the address and I'll borrow Sloane's car, I'll leave—I'll come to wherever you are right now."

"No, stay there," Mia says firmly. "None of us can do anything. We just have to be patient, too." She sounds hollowed out, and Cricket yearns to be with her. She should have gone to Key Largo. Her presence would have prevented the jinx of a babymoon and this devastating loss.

"I want to be there for you," Cricket tells her, an all-too-familiar grief tightening its grip around her neck. "Tell me where to go—"

"Cricket," Mia says in her stern professional voice. "There's nothing you can do. Just focus on soccer."

It lands like a slap.

Mia doesn't need her.

Mia has never needed her.

"Okay," Cricket says slowly, trying to eliminate the hurt from her voice. She tells herself this isn't about her, but Mia has just made it abundantly clear what she values in Cricket, and it's the same thing their mother valued, and what Yaz values, and what UCLA values. It's what Sloane and Bonnie and Bruce Jackson value, why she was invited into their home, and why she was invited to this camp. Her worth begins and ends with the ball at her feet, so Cricket hangs up and gets dressed for afternoon practice.

That day she plays with such ruthlessness that the coaches exchange looks and crack jokes about what she ate for breakfast. They call her fearless and out of her mind and gunning for Alyssa's starting spot. Cricket ignores their cheers as she adjusts her gloves. If she's only good at soccer, then she damn well better be great.

NO-TRY VALENTINE

S ince her fertility journey began two years ago, Mia has learned to avoid certain sections of her local Hannaford. The deli counter. The wine and liquor aisle. The cheese section. The coffee section. The candy section. The cereal section. The snack section, with its deliciously ultra-processed cheese puffs and shelf-stable pretzel rods.

As ever, love demands sacrifice.

But today is Valentine's Day, so Mia has allowed herself to trespass down the baking aisle. She scans the ingredients on the side of the brownie box, justifying her breach with the vague argument that chocolate's aphrodisiac properties might counteract the added sugar that fertility websites so puritanically frown upon. Besides, she and Oliver deserve a treat for their extreme efforts in reproduction. Because that's what it feels like these days: zoological attempts at breeding. Their time in bed is no longer about attraction and love but syncing ovulation cycles with rounds of successful insemination. They are mating in captivity, and as Mia and Oliver often commiserate, sex has never been less sexy or more fraught.

Mia tosses the box of brownie mix into her cart, where it lands between the bag of walnuts and six cans of sardines (both full of baby-making omega-3 fatty acids). She's rounding the corner to the dairy aisle to compare the prices of organic plain yogurt when she sees the woman and freezes.

Slurping from what appears to be a venti caramel Frappuccino, the woman bounces the baby strapped to her chest. Tiny, doll-like arms and legs dangle on either side of the infant carrier, hitched snug above her obscenely pregnant stomach. With her Frappuccino-free hand, the woman pushes her cart, which not only brims with wine bottles and frosted animal crackers, but also a toddler standing up in the designated seat, his face stained an unnatural orange as he vrooms a Cheeto through the air.

Appalled, irate, and so, so sad, Mia walks past them at a clip, and as she does, she realizes she's been doing this whole thing wrong. Oliver, of all people, should have figured out the holes in their strategy, their weak line of attack, their utter lack of dynamism. Snapping the hairband on her wrist hard enough for it to sting, Mia does not proceed to the yogurt section but instead turns her cart around and starts again from aisle 1.

"What's all this?" Oliver asks that night when he walks into the kitchen and sees the table. He has arrived home with a bouquet of overpriced lilies wrapped in Valentine-heart paper, a pound of salmon, and a bottle of Perrier because he knows that he is little more than the quality of his sperm these days, which is why he drinks twelve ounces of pomegranate juice each morning.

The spread before him looks like a cross between a police drug raid, a college dorm room, and a child's lunch. Stretched across the kitchen table is a landscape of small plates, each one presenting an illicit temptation: a tuna-avocado roll; a turkey and cheese sandwich; lime wedges next to shots of tequila; a gigantic cup of hot coffee; a fat pinch of what appears to be magic mushrooms; a thick, gloopy triangle of brie; a can of Diet Coke; an expertly rolled marijuana joint; a bowl of M&Ms; seven pornographic slices of rib eye; a package of Dunkaroos; and a canister of Cheez Whiz.

"I'm scared," Oliver says, staring at his wife.

"New game plan," Mia tells him, setting down a brownie barely visible under an avalanche of whipped cream. She wipes her hands. "No more trying."

"But we said—"

"No," Mia interrupts, making room on the table for more plates as a timer goes off. "We've been trying so hard for so long and it's not—we need to take a break and enjoy the freedom that comes with not being pregnant and not having a kid."

"Like red wine?" Oliver says, examining the bottle on the table. "Wow, this looks nice."

"Like red wine," Mia says, pulling a small hunk of swordfish out of the oven. "And everything else."

"So you've rounded up all of fertility's archenemies."

"Ha!" Mia laughs, throwing her head back for high drama. Oliver notes the bowl of chocolate-covered espresso beans and wonders how many Mia has already eaten because how did she pull this off? There must be twenty small dishes, overlapping and fighting for space on the table.

"It's like what you tell your goalkeepers," Mia says. "Stop thinking and just play."

"How'd you get the mushrooms?" Oliver asks, investigating the table. "And the—Mia, is that cocaine?"

"I know people," Mia answers, baffling her husband. "Want to try it?"

Oliver eyes her. "You okay?"

She nods vigorously. "I'm in love with you and I missed out on three years of college so I think this needs to happen. We gotta cut loose, man."

"Where's that steak from?" Oliver asks, visibly salivating. He hasn't had red meat since Mia said it compromised the quantity and quality of his semen. Two years of deprivation and yet his soldiers are still underperforming.

"Primo Bistro."

"Can we eat it?"

"Absolutely."

Oliver pulls a steak knife out of the drawer as he continues to take in the wide-ranging contents on the table. "Is that brownie normal or special?"

"What do you think?" Mia asks, hands on her hips. "And just to be transparent," she says slowly, "I'm ovulating, but we're definitely not having sex tonight."

"Really?"

Mia nods.

"Oh, thank God," Oliver says, allowing his shoulders to slump as he pulls her into a grateful hug. Whenever she's ovulating, Mia has insisted they have sex three times a day, and it's been the least erotic thing they've ever done. At this point, Oliver would rather floss than copulate.

"Let's be wildly irresponsible," Mia declares now, swooping her finger through the dollop of whipped cream and inserting it in Oliver's mouth.

"I love this," he says. "And I love you, and I love—is this Pez?" He picks up a tiny purple skull candy.

Mia shakes her head, grinning mischievously. "Ecstasy." Oliver laughs because there's no way, but Mia just shrugs. "Toby's brother has a side hustle," she explains.

"Who's Toby?"

"One of the vet techs," Mia says. "He promised on a blind shih tzu's life that his brother only sells the best product."

Oliver drops the skull back into the dish. "Okay, so I appreciate the lengths you went to," he says, "but I'm gonna say no to the ecstasy. And the coke. And the magic mushrooms."

Mia shrugs, unfazed by his rejection. She nods to the brie on the far end of the table. "What about unpasteurized cheese?"

"Oh yeah, I need that," Oliver says, reaching for a cracker.

"So we're on the same page?" Mia asks, fixing him with a penetrative stare. "About not trying for a while?"

"Absolutely," Oliver says, pulling her in for another hug. Mia already feels more relaxed, her body melting into his. "But I've got to admit," Oliver continues, "not being forced to have sex with you makes me really want to—almost."

Mia cackles as she twists around and grabs the closest plate. She shoves the piece of maki into her mouth. God, she's missed raw fish.

Oliver leans past her and helps himself to another slice of rib eye. "This steak is unreal," he says, feeding her a forkful. It's been five minutes and they are already giddy with freedom, spry with youthful disregard for anything beyond the goodies in their direct line of sight. Not trying has never felt better.

"You are brilliant, Mia Lowe," Oliver says, taking a sip of Diet Coke. Mia beams at him, her eyes bright and dilated, and not just because she consumed a sizable marijuana gummy an hour ago. "This is a brilliant idea."

Mia kisses Oliver, his mouth full of artificial sweetener and hers savory with saturated fats—all of it horrible for fertility, all of it delicious. Mia doesn't need Oliver to tell her this is a brilliant idea. She knows it's genius, just like she knows it's already working.

ON TRACK

Still catching her breath and dripping sweat from her sprint workout, Cricket would bet good money that never in the history of her high school's football field has someone laid topless at its center in the middle of the day, wearing only the bottoms of her yellow string bikini. But Yaz does what she wants, including coming here to surprise Cricket. She looks like a bronze sculpture installed on the fifty-yard line.

"I feel like I still don't totally get how the draft works," Yaz says, sitting up as Cricket approaches.

"Or Victory," Cricket says, watching the middle-aged walkers and joggers register Yaz's bare chest from the outside lanes.

After she graduated from UCLA this past spring, Yaz secured a job in the Los Angeles Mayor's Office. She then promptly asked for a week off to go to Maine, and her boss had said okay, probably because there was no precedent for such gall. So now Yaz is here, with Cricket, at the expense of the Mayor's Office but not her tan lines, to see her exhausted and overworked girlfriend.

Just like she has every summer since her mom died, Cricket has booked herself for back-to-back soccer camps, clinics, and individual goalkeeping tutorials. Thanks to Oliver and his extensive network, she knows which opportunities are the most lucrative and has lined them up accordingly. These ten weeks coaching soccer pad Cricket's slush fund through the school year, and even if her days are long and hot and usually end with a headache from girls screaming about one more round of Power and Finesse, Cricket absolutely loves it. There's no better place than Maine in the summer. Except on a soccer field, in Maine, in the summer.

"The NWSL draft?" Cricket asks, thankful for the endorphins from running, and thus the patience to explain her postgraduate plan for the ten-thousandth time. Somehow, after four years together, Yaz still claims not to understand it.

"The one you'll be in."

"The NWSL," Cricket says, untying her sneakers and peeling off her socks. "It stands for the National Women's Soccer League."

"I know that," Yaz says.

Cricket takes several sips of water, trying to see around the corner of this conversation to what Yaz is really thinking about. "It's in January."

"And it's for another team?"

Cricket smiles so she doesn't scream. How many NWSL games have they watched together? Denial is a powerful thing. "Yes, the professional team I'll play for after I graduate."

"But you already play for the National Team—"

"I'm in the National Team *pool*," Cricket interrupts, correcting her. "Teague, the head coach of the National Team, has invited me to some of the National Team training camps, but I've never made a National Team roster, so I'm not technically on the team, just in the pool."

And there in the pool, Cricket reminds herself, she has been treading water, which isn't to say she's been doing nothing. Because treading water means consistent, whole-body work, and actively deciding not to drown, and staying calm about not drowning, and continuing to push in one place even as fatigue settles in and threatens to pull her under or push her out.

Cricket mentally pivots. She needs to be positive and she just crushed her sprint workout. She's putting in her days, and keeping her head down, and she will make the team soon enough. Never mind that Sloane has already made the roster and even played in three games for the United States, earning her first three international caps.

"Okay, fine," Yaz says, plucking one blade of grass at a time as she thinks. "But why don't you just pick a team?"

"Hopefully someday I'll get to," Cricket says. "Players are working on a collective bargaining deal to replace the draft with free agency, but for now I'll play for whichever team picks me in January." She almost says that NWSL preseason begins at the end of January, that her career will become her priority six months ahead of her college graduation.

"L.A. has a team," Yaz points out, looking over at Cricket as if this is groundbreaking news and not a known fact, as if Cricket isn't already praying that Angel City FC will draft her so she doesn't have to uproot her life.

"Yeah, but I don't get to choose."

Yaz turns to swat a mosquito on her back and inadvertently flashes an older man in black knee socks. "But what if a team on the East Coast picks you?"

"Then I go east and we figure it out." Cricket tries to sound nonchalant as she squirts Yaz's expensive sunscreen on her hand and rubs it into Yaz's shoulders. For a moment, birdsong fills the silence, and then a ride-on lawnmower huffs along the adjacent soccer fields, where the records Cricket once set still stand. "Can we not worry about this right now?" she asks. "I still have my entire senior season to play, and you're here, and now we have the rest of the day to just chill."

"What's your end goal?" Yaz asks. "With soccer, I mean."

Cricket homes in on a knot under Yaz's right wing bone and applies deep pressure with her thumb.

"Cricket?"

"Hm?"

"You can't play soccer forever."

Cricket releases the knot. She isn't in the mood to fight—not here, not now, not when they have such limited time together and she has so many secret beaches she wants to show off to Yaz, and so many different places where she wants to show off her girlfriend.

"Answer me," Yaz says, reaching for her bikini top and tying the strings behind her neck. "How long?"

"As long as I can," Cricket says, stating the obvious.

"And then what?"

"And then we'll see." Cricket wipes her hands on the grass. Life after her professional soccer career is inevitable but also seems impossible. It's too terrifying to fathom. The clear track of her life as she knows it ends in a chasm she's not yet prepared to face.

Yaz's crocheted top is tugged to the left, but Cricket dares not fix it. "You missed my graduation because you were with the National Team," Yaz says. "And now you're telling me you're not even on that team, you're just in the pool."

"Okay?"

"And you can't come to my cousin's wedding in September because UCLA is playing against Santa Cruz."

"Right."

"You're just missing a lot," Yaz says, standing up suddenly. Cricket watches an elderly woman in a pink visor nearly faint at the sight of Yaz's minuscule bikini bottom. The woman then takes out her cellphone and Cricket knows it's entirely possible she's calling the police.

"I'm missing the same stuff I've always had to miss," Cricket says, indulging in a sudden surge of defensiveness. "I didn't go to my homecoming or senior prom because of soccer, and if I get drafted, I'll probably miss my graduation." Cricket plucks a blade of grass and twists it between her thumb and pointer. "The only thing that's different about my schedule this year is that you're working a real job."

"So this is my fault? For graduating?"

Cricket reaches for Yaz's hand. "Come here," she says. Yaz reluctantly accepts and falls to her knees, wriggling closer to Cricket until their foreheads touch. The world disappears. "My punk rock skunk," Cricket whispers, even though Yaz got rid of her pink streak six months ago when she began applying for civil service jobs. "We're going to be okay," Cricket whispers.

Yaz pulls back. "What if I have the mayor write a letter to Angel City demanding they draft you?"

"Do it!" Cricket laughs. "I love that you've been there a month, already taken vacation days, and now you're going to muddy the waters between sports and state."

"Too much?" Yaz grins, her teeth a dazzling white against her golden skin, the green grass, the infinite blue sky.

"You're always too much," Cricket says, taking Yaz's left hand and kissing each fingertip. "It's what makes you just right."

THE DRAFT

"Should we order a bottle of prosecco?" Oliver asks. Seated at a high top, he continues to scan the drink menu while Cricket and Mia roll their eyes in synchronized disdain.

"No, we should not *order a bottle of prosecco*," Cricket hisses with clear irritation.

Mia places her hand on Oliver's knee. "We should see where Cricket is going to spend the next year of her life," she translates. "Before we celebrate with prosecco."

"*If* we celebrate," Cricket corrects.

They have driven more than eight hours, through every type of precipitation, to attend the NWSL draft held in the Philadelphia Convention Center. The three of them are hangry, nervous, and tired of Cricket's phone vibrating every five minutes with a text from Yaz, who decided not to come. Honoring the Lowe mantra of "Be positive," Yaz admitted to Cricket that she couldn't trust herself to be supportive if the draft didn't go the way they hope it will.

But it should go our way, Cricket reminds herself now for the hundredth time, adjusting her feet on the rungs of her barstool. Because this past fall, the Bruins won the NCAA championship and ESPN made Cricket's game-winning save their play of the week. As if that weren't enough, Teague called her last month to invite her to the National Team's January Camp. From every angle, Cricket's star continues to climb higher.

"Wedding?" the server asks, taking in their formal attire. Cricket and Mia are in rented cocktail dresses, and Oliver wears his navy interview/marriage/only suit.

"The National Women's Soccer League draft," Mia says slowly, with unabashed pride, grabbing Cricket by her topknot. "My sister is going to be the first goalkeeper picked."

"In the fourth or fifth round," Cricket adds, not out of humility but in mental preparation for the long night ahead. Historically, teams prioritize field players for their first several draft picks.

"Well, that's exciting!" the server says, swatting Cricket on the shoulder with her order pad. "Your drink is on me, Miss Fourth or Fifth Round. What are you having?"

Cricket laughs, bashful. "Thank you, just water."

"Even better," the server jokes. "How about you two?"

Mia orders a glass of red wine but then Oliver orders the same, so they decide to split a bottle before open-mouthed kissing.

"Unnecessary," Cricket says, flagging their behavior. Since she arrived home for winter break, they've been so handsy. But whenever Cricket asks Mia what's going on, Mia says they're just in a good place, no longer trying to get pregnant and simply enjoying their youth instead. Cricket is happy for them so long as she never again catches them making out during *Jeopardy!*

"We should leave here in an hour," Cricket says, checking the time on her phone and ignoring a slew of texts from Yaz. "There's a red-carpet thing and then the draft itself and then there's, like, interviews and stuff if I get picked."

"*When* you get picked," Oliver says emphatically.

"We'll see." Cricket knows the odds are in her favor, but only slightly. More than four hundred young women have registered for the draft and schlepped to the City of Brotherly Love with their friends and family in tow, hoping to be picked and not publicly humiliated. Tonight, fewer than 25 percent of them will hear their name announced. The rest of these big fish will return to their small ponds and put on a brave face as they consider alternative routes forward, both inside and outside the world of professional soccer.

"Be positive," Mia says. "Mom would tell you that. Be positive: It's in your blood, this is your destiny, this is what you've sacrificed for."

"But this is like getting picked for gym class in public," Cricket says. "And on television, with contracts, and sponsorships, and the rest of my life on the line."

"To draft night!" Oliver intones, raising his glass before remembering the rules. No toasts until Cricket has been selected to a team. "Sorry, I'm just excited," he says. "Anything can happen."

Inside the convention center, Cricket, Mia, and Oliver stick close together as they navigate draft hopefuls, camera crews, and famous retired players. Team owners speak in low tones, emanating the power that comes with deep pockets, while head coaches wear official gear from head to toe. They look like cartoonish mascots compared to all the young women in six-inch heels and eyelash extensions.

When they are asked to take a seat, Cricket turns her phone off because Yaz keeps texting and she needs to be present. Onstage, men and women in suits take turns behind the dais to speak about progress and promise and honor, and then the draft itself begins. Cricket takes a sip of her ice water, then downs the glass and refills from the carafe in the center of the table. She has never been this thirsty.

It's only the second round when the coach of the Chicago Red Stars announces his team's pick into the microphone. "Cricket Lowe," he says, looking straight at her. And so Cricket waves to him, curious what he could possibly want to tell her in front of such a huge crowd because it's way too early for teams to draft goalkeepers, and the Chicago Red Stars are way too middle America—*way too not Los Angeles*—to pick her.

"Cricket Lowe," he says again, waving back at her like this was a funny game and not her real life. "The Chicago Red Stars select Cricket Lowe from UCLA."

WHEN IT RAINS

Within six months of moving to Illinois, Cricket suffers a roach infestation in her building, tendonitis in her rotator cuff, a losing season, and an increasingly resentful long-distance girlfriend. Yaz has tried to be supportive of Cricket's Midwest career move, but the relationship feels as tender as Cricket's shoulder injury. By the end of May, the daily wear and tear of disparate schedules and missed FaceTimes has created an undeniable strain between them.

"Do you like it?" Yaz asks, emerging from Cricket's bathroom modeling a wide-brimmed straw hat and a white one-piece bathing suit only she could pull off.

When Yaz first told Cricket she'd carved out a weeklong trip to St. Thomas with her former college roommates, Cricket burst into tears. In response, Yaz added a two-day stint in Chicago to the front end of her vacation to try to make things right. But now that she's here, it just feels wrong.

"What do you think?" Yaz delivers a sultry pout over her shoulder meant to lure Cricket off the couch. "Cute or too much?" she fishes again, arching her back so the swimsuit strains to cover her curves.

"I don't know," Cricket answers, continuing to look down at her phone. Yaz arrived this afternoon, and she leaves in twenty-six hours, not that Cricket is keeping track of the minutes (approximately 1,532). Rain sloshes against the drafty warehouse windows by the bucketful. Cricket still hasn't received an invitation to the June National Team Camp, which will be the last one before Teague decides the roster for the World Cup this summer in Brazil.

"Um, hello?" Yaz says. "Eyes up here, staring at my tits, please."

Cricket forces herself to ogle her girlfriend, who does, in fact, have perfect breasts, but then she checks her phone again to make sure she didn't somehow put it on silent or airplane mode because Teague should have called by now.

"Are you going to be like this the whole time I'm here?" Yaz asks.

"You mean the whole time until tomorrow?"

Yaz walks over and stands in front of the TV in a starfish pose, the floppy brim of her straw hat hiding her eyes. She is adorable and sexy and abandoning Cricket for the Caribbean.

"Come on," Cricket says, exasperated. "I'm trying to watch this."

Yaz pushes up the brim of her hat, sticks out her chin. "Since when did you care about baseball?"

"Since that ridiculous hat."

"Should I just leave?" Yaz asks, throwing her arms up to signal the official start to this fight. "Because not to sound like an asshole, but I don't know why I used up my last two sick days to be here if you're just going to sit around, hate-watching ESPN."

Cricket checks her phone yet again, which is fully charged with the ringer on top volume and airplane mode off. Despite having given up everything to be alone in Chicago, she's still not good enough for the National Team.

"I'm serious," Yaz says, her voice its own ultimatum. "Why am I even here if you're going to be like this?"

"Like what?" Cricket asks.

"Like this!"

Yaz throws her hat on the floor and paces in front of the windows, but when she glances over at Cricket, she stops. Their fate is written all over Cricket's face, and so Yaz walks toward her and perches on the arm of the couch, wearing an expression that is no longer belligerent so much as defeated. "I'm just going to say what we're both thinking."

"Don't."

"Let's take some space," Yaz forges on. "Then you can figure out what's important to you, because it definitely doesn't seem like I'm even in the running anymore."

Cricket reaches for Yaz, but when their hands touch, she only feels inevitable disappointment.

"I'd rather quit now and keep loving you," Yaz says quietly. Outside, the rain pounds harder, and Cricket wants to jump through the window rather than live through this moment. The thought of goodbye seems impossible, but maybe one goodbye is better than all the ones they'd have to suffer through in the future.

They don't sleep. They try to talk but mostly kiss with the salt of each other's tears on their tongues. In the morning, Yaz books an earlier flight and leaves Cricket's apartment red-eyed and ragged, a single woman on her way to starting over in St. Thomas.

Cricket doesn't move from her bed. She has the day off from soccer, which only makes things worse. A whole day to drown alone in self-pity. At some point, she googles "Saddest Movies of All Time" and sets to work with her laptop under the covers. She's halfway through a film about star-crossed cowboys when her phone rings.

It's her.

"Hi there, Cricket," she says with seasoned casualness. The head coach of the U.S. Women's National Team, Teague Rollins, has earned the respect of her players. With short gray hair and wire-rimmed glasses, she presents like a college professor but runs camp like a four-star general. Teague is clearheaded, calm, and positively cutthroat.

"So there's no good way of saying it," Teague says. "We're not taking you this time."

No June training camp.

No World Cup this summer.

Cricket has tried to prepare herself for the possibility, but she didn't actually believe it would happen. Her trajectory has been up, up, and up, but Teague just shot her out of the sky like a hapless pheasant. In a World Cup year. After so many almosts.

"Are you sure?" Cricket hears herself say in a voice so threadbare that she envisions Teague wincing at her weakness. A goalkeeper must remain poised, even when she's down. "Sorry, I didn't, sorry—" Cricket blathers, and then, in a scramble to recover for her blunder she adds, "I mean, thank you for the opportunity."

"It was a difficult decision," Teague says. "But it's the right decision for right now." Her curt tone seems more appropriate for announcing a drone strike than a camp cut. Then again, the news that Cricket isn't going to the World Cup does indeed feel like a missile exploding her life.

"Get in your days," Teague says. "I'll be checking in. Keep working."

It takes thirty seconds on social media to find out who Teague deems more promising—Sloane, of course, who has been starting for the National Team ever since Alyssa announced her retirement, along with Emma and Des.

Her phone rings again.

"You're better than Emma," Sloane says. "And it's actually insulting to me that they're bringing Des." Cricket can hear the angry smack of Sloane's gum and imagines her chewing with her mouth open. She is the most credible and least enjoyable person to hear from at this moment. "I'm pissed—for your sake, obviously, but also for me," Sloane continues, barely coming up for air. "They don't work like we do—not because they don't want to, but unlike us, they just don't have that fourth gear, or the consistency, you know? Are you listening?"

"Yeah."

"Get it together," Sloane says. "This is only the beginning of our careers."

"Maybe," Cricket says. "For you."

"Can you stop feeling sorry for yourself? Please? I'm going to need you."

"I don't exist to be your ego boost," Cricket snaps.

Sloane responds with more gum smacking. "Okay, so, never in my life have you boosted my ego," she says with contempt. "Which is fine, because that's not why I need you."

Sloane waits for Cricket to ask, but she doesn't.

"I need you because we make each other better and that's the whole fucking point, so get off your pity potty and start training like your life depends on it. Okay?"

"You realize this means I'm not going to the World Cup," Cricket feels the need to point out. "I'm not going to Brazil."

"Yes," Sloane concedes. "So do you want to just quit? Or do you want to make sure you're at the Olympics in L.A. next year?"

HIGHLIGHT REEL

Sitting alone in the back row of the Chicago Red Stars' screening room, Cricket redoes her topknot and silently questions the purpose of a highlight reel. Scrubbed clean of its context, the seeming effortlessness of each play feels adjacent to a lie. It's propaganda and it's patronizing and it's a complete waste of time. A highlight reel serves the same purpose as a children's bedtime story: to soften the edges of the real world so everyone can sleep at night.

The Chicago Red Stars did not make the NWSL playoffs. They finished in last place in the league. As commentators are quick to point out, the Chicago Red Stars went from first to worst. Just like Cricket.

What a godforsaken year. Ever since going pro, the work has felt like work. Playing soccer has become a grind and the dream has warped into a never-ending obligation. The sum dumped into Cricket's checking account every other week doesn't compensate for living such an isolated existence in the middle of the country. Thanks to Instagram, Cricket knows that Yaz and her new girlfriend are spending their winter break in Maui while Cricket shivers alone in Chicago. In the seven months since their breakup, Cricket has tried to go out more and date online.

This has only resulted in a substantial uptick in Cricket's alcohol consumption and an equally clear decline in her confidence.

Yaz has forgotten all about Cricket, and apparently so has Teague. The National Team coach has not invited her to join a training for such a long time that Cricket can't even summon the energy to be disappointed about not getting called up for January Camp next month. She's just here, shivering alone in Chicago with nothing to show for her sacrifice but this losers' highlight reel.

Finally, the lights come on, the team applauds their own unsuccessful effort, and the coaches wish everyone a happy holiday. Cricket cleans out her locker and walks to her snow-covered car with a trash bag of gear in each hand. Waiting for the defroster to kick in, Cricket calls the only person who might understand why she thinks a losing team is undeserving of a highlight reel.

"Okay, so let me get this straight," Sloane says from the D.C. Metro. The Washington Spirit have not only advanced to the playoffs but are ranked first in the NWSL. "You think sending everybody home without any motivation would be a better idea? That a low-light reel would get them horny for circuit training in their stepdad's basement?"

Cricket laughs and the physical sensation feels odd in her throat. It's been so long since she's laughed. Entire weeks. "Yeah, maybe."

"You're sick," Sloane says, and in the background, Cricket hears Sloane greeting someone with a dramatic *mwah!* "Okay, I gotta go," Sloane says. "But if you need to escape the lovebirds over break, my trophy room is always available to you."

That evening, as Cricket descends the Portland International Jetport escalator, she spots her sister standing in front of the taxidermied moose. The sight of Mia cracks something open she's bolted shut for months. Cricket is halfway down the escalator when she finally allows her heart to give way to all the pressure, all the disappointment, and by the time she steps back on solid ground and into her sister's arms, she is a blubbering mess.

Without a word, Mia pulls Cricket into a tight hug with no plan of letting go. "I'm so sorry about—everything."

Cricket nods into Mia's shoulder as more tears flow. It is everything.

Her entire life—it's either going down the tubes or already gone: Yaz. The Red Stars. The National Team.

They walk toward baggage claim and as they wait for Cricket's luggage, Mia grabs her sister's elbow. "I want to tell you something," she says. "You're doing everything right, okay?"

Cricket stares ahead, searching for a black suitcase with a Chicago Red Stars sticker on the front, a red ribbon tied on the handle.

"Listen to me," Mia says with uncharacteristic force. "What you're trying to do is so, so hard. If it were easy, everybody would do it, but to get where you want to go means enduring disappointment along the way. Use it as motivation because you're going to play for the National Team. You're going to do it, okay, Crick? And we're going to help you in any way we can."

Cricket steps forward to retrieve her bag, but Mia knows her sister is paying attention from her set jaw, the focus in her eyes, so Mia keeps going, determined to get this out now. "You are going to make that team because you're extraordinary, Cricket, and just because it's been a tough year, it doesn't make you any less extraordinary. It just means you've got to double down and fight, okay? No matter what happens, double down, because you're extraordinary and you've earned the extraordinary life you want."

Cricket silently wipes tears away. The sisters have always been close, but Mia has never given her a pep talk like this before, like she's channeling Vince Lombardi. Cricket doesn't trust herself to speak. Instead, she drapes her arm across Mia's shoulders and touches Mia's head with her own.

They emerge from the revolving doors of the jetport and there's Oliver, pumping his fists in celebration of Cricket's arrival. She forgives his tone-deaf excitement because somewhere, buried deep, she's happy to be back in Maine, too. Or not exactly happy per se, but relieved. Like the flu, absolute demoralization is best suffered from the comforts of home.

The sisters watch as Oliver darts across the street. He is exuberant as he runs toward them and then, upon seeing the wet trail of Cricket's recent tears, visibly perplexed.

"Did you tell her?" he asks Mia, his mouth falling into a cartoonish droop.

Cricket looks at her sister. "Tell me what?"

As Mia struggles to remember the particular words she planned to say at this exact moment, she compulsively touches her stomach.

"Oh my God!" Cricket screams, because that touch says it all, and Cricket drops her suitcase to tackle Mia. Outside the jetport, surrounded by snow, they are yelling and laughing and shrieking and causing a scene because, after all this time, Mia is finally pregnant.

"I just reached the second trimester a few days ago," Mia volunteers, and Cricket beams. Finally, some good news. Her sister is thirteen weeks pregnant and has never looked happier.

In the momvan, Mia hands Cricket the most recent ultrasound photo. Cricket rotates the picture clockwise, then counterclockwise, and swears she sees a penis.

"Well, that's interesting," Oliver says, "because the professionals told us it was a girl." Cricket can barely take all this good news. She hurls herself over the center console to kiss her sister's stomach. For good measure, she kisses Mia, and even Oliver. After the year she just had, she never thought she would feel this happy again, but here she is.

Before they've even left the airport parking lot, Cricket has reevaluated how she will spend her winter break.

"I'm going full Terminator," she declares from the back seat. "No parties, no relationships, no alcohol, and no cheat days. I'm going to double down to get my extraordinary life. No excuses."

"That's right," Mia says, turning around to grin at her.

"Let's do it," Oliver adds supportively. Mia plays "Get Low, Fly High" on repeat so it feels like Liz is in on their celebration and part of their plan.

As soon as they get home, Cricket chugs two glasses of water and stretches for a solid half hour to prepare for an early run the next day. Mia's pregnancy has not only surprised Cricket; it's also inspired her. The universe—and probably their mom—has reminded the Lowe sisters that anything can happen. Cricket can't control June Camp, or the

National Team roster, or the Red Stars' losing season, or Yaz—God, she misses Yaz—but Cricket can choose how she spends her time. The minutes and the days that add up to her life belong to her, and so it's on her to make them count.

When the alarm goes off the next morning, Cricket curses before rolling out of bed and layering up. The weather app on her phone says it's four degrees outside, but with the windchill, it feels like minus thirteen, and with the time difference it seems like four-thirty a.m. Cricket digs out her compression socks and puts new batteries in her old headlamp. She dunks her fingers into the tub of Vaseline that Mia keeps by the front door, just like their mom did, and slathers the petroleum jelly not just on her lips but across her entire face to protect it from a wicked windburn.

"This is ridiculous," she mutters as she laces up her sneakers, tired and resentful that she is back here, doing this, in the dark and all alone. But then Cricket remembers what her sister said at the airport—*You are extraordinary*—so she reaches into the old milk crate for a pair of loathsome Yaktrax to stretch over her running shoes. They are Mia's and purple and particularly hideous, but she is done complaining. It's time to grind.

Cricket is halfway down the block and praying the violent gusts of wind don't knock down a tree branch or telephone pole that then kills her when she hears the familiar sound of the front door slamming shut. Oliver's voice cuts through the bluster as he calls her name, and when she turns around there he is, head-lamped and Yaktraxed and ready to run.

"Morning," he grins, catching up to her.

"Morning," Cricket responds, too stunned to ask what he's doing, because since when did her still-groggy-at-the-ten-a.m.-game coach become a morning person?

"Here we go," Oliver says, punching the air as he matches her pace. "Full Terminator."

"What?" Cricket asks, pretty sure it's the wind that's making her eyes water.

"We believe in you," Oliver says. "You can make the National Team, and we're going to help you as much as we can, especially while you're home."

"But Mia's pregnant," Cricket says, stating the obvious. "You're going to be a dad. There are cribs to compare and baby showers to endure."

Oliver laughs what Cricket knows to be his genuine laugh, which is more like a seal bark, and Cricket sees the silver fillings in the back of his mouth. "Plenty of time for that in the months to come," he chuckles. They turn onto Spruce Street, thereby silently agreeing to do the big loop. "I thought we could train at USM," he offers. "I have twenty-four / seven access to the weight room, and the field house is great for our purposes—I know you're a professional now, but I've developed some strength-and-agility circuits that might be useful."

Cricket nods just as the wind dies down and the sky lightens from black to gray. She knows that by the time they hit the last mile of the big loop, which runs along the beach where Liz held her morning sessions, the sun will crest the horizon, hot pink and orange and beaming back at them as if to say the same thing the U.S. Women's National Team likes to yell in the locker room, and on the field, and wherever the game takes them: *LFG! Let's Fucking Go!*

"That sounds awesome," Cricket says, lifting her legs a little higher. "Thank you."

Over the next two weeks, Oliver's training is even more grueling than Cricket imagined: He brings in collegiate runners and has Cricket participate in their workouts—sets of 200-, 400-, and 800-meter sprints. On the track, Cricket gets routinely destroyed and deeply humbled, but she doesn't quit. Six days a week, Cricket performs agility drills in the field house until she can't see through the sweat stinging her eyes and throws so many medicine balls against the wall that she hears the rubbery *thwack thwack thwack* in her sleep. Cricket leaps and dives for shots she knows she won't get to, because the whole point is to extend her length, grow what she can do, and minimize what she can't. She devotes every waking hour that she's not training to active recoveries that require the same miserable discomfort as any speed workout. She ignores the voices that tell her she's not good enough. She listens to her body complain and says, *Okay, yes, but one more.*

"Again!" Oliver yells in the field house during an afternoon session. "Let's see some urgency in the distribution this time."

Tired and testy, Cricket wipes her face with the hem of her shirt and says, "I thought the *P* in your MAP stood for 'patience'?"

"Actually, it's for 'piss off.'" Oliver grins, jogging toward her. "Nah, in all seriousness, though, I've abandoned my MAP," he tells her. "It's too limiting; I realized it's better to ask questions than try to give directions."

"Questions?"

Oliver nods. "Are you making the most of this moment?" he asks. "What did you have to give up to get here? How do you want to leave the field after the game?"

"You've thought about this," Cricket says.

"It's my full-time job to think about this," Oliver agrees. "Opportunity, Monomyth, Legacy," he says, counting them out on his fingers. "On the first and last day of the season, I ask my players to reflect on all three."

"What's a monomyth?" Cricket asks.

"A hero's journey," Coach explains, casually balancing a ball on his laces. "What adversity have you overcome—or maybe you're still grappling with—on your quest to become a better player?"

"That's intense," Cricket says, jogging toward the closest ball. "I guess this is the opportunity right here, so let's go again." Only half mocking him she shouts, "This time with urgency in the distribution!"

Although she would never admit it to Oliver, Cricket can't stop thinking about his three questions revolving around her opportunity, monomyth, and legacy. Over winter break, she finds they're all in constant conversation with one another as she digs deep during training. After a week, Cricket actually befriends the physical suffering and embraces the moments of doubt. It's all part of getting stronger and smarter.

"Yes, Cricket, yes!" Mia cheers inside USM's field house. A few days before Christmas, Mia cups her hands around her mouth as she watches her sister struggle for power against a black resistance cable. Mia then turns to Oliver. "What's she doing?"

"Working on her deceleration," Oliver says. "She has to explode from one position to another in midair."

"Like a cat landing on her feet," Mia observes.

"Yes." Oliver agrees. "But also with the ball in her hands if she wants to make a world-class save."

"What about a world-class dinner?" Mia asks, tapping her watch. She stopped at the field house on her way home from work not only to show her support but also to keep them running on time. While Coach leads Cricket in agility, strength, speed, and technical training, Mia is in charge of scheduling and fuel. Left to their own devices, Oliver and Cricket would forget to eat and would forgo sleep to fit in an extra set of dead lifts.

Before, after, and even during her days at Oceanside Animal Hospital, Mia researches performance-optimizing foods with the same obsessive, academic mindset that earned her straight A's through high school and admission to Yale. Each meal and snack—every single calorie that Cricket consumes—should enhance her abilities on the field.

This morning, Mia made egg-white veggie omelets with a side of fruit. For each of their lunches, Mia packed a grilled chicken breast, sautéed spinach, a banana, orange slices, almonds, and a slow-roasted sweet potato. Tonight, they'll grill fish and asparagus—so long as the grill isn't frozen shut after yesterday's ice storm.

Teaching herself food science is an unexpected but welcome distraction from everything else Mia is learning these days—specifically, how this baby growing inside her is already changing her outlook. Mia's pants barely fit and she's forced to sleep on her side, but most importantly, she misses her own mother in a brand-new kind of way. She aches for Liz's insistent optimism and longs to ask Liz how she raised them all by herself, and which lullabies she sang, and if her feet grew a lot—because Mia's already jumped up half a size—and was she scared? Because Mia is so scared.

The enormity of motherhood—it's infinite, all-encompassing responsibility—terrifies Mia in her bizarre pregnancy dreams, and at work, and when she's brushing her teeth, and while she's swallowing her prenatal vitamin. It scares her everywhere and all the time except when she is standing at the two-hundred-meter line at USM's indoor track, stopwatch in hand, helping Oliver record Cricket in her sprint workout, or preparing the week's meal plan. The idea of being someone's mother seems too big a job except when Mia writes out notes of encouragement to hide inside her sister's running shoes, or her winter gloves, or her gym bag. It's in these moments of clear-eyed devotion to Cricket that Mia remembers the greatest lesson her own mother demonstrated on a daily basis was how to give with her whole heart.

On Christmas, Cricket and Mia nestle next to each other on the pink floral couch while Oliver cleans up from dinner, a mountain of dishes stacked high in the sink. The tree is decorated in their mother's hodge-podge collection of ornaments from Goodwill and, as always, Mia recites the words to *It's a Wonderful Life*. Traditionally, the Lowes have enjoyed eggnog while watching Liz's favorite Christmas movie, but this year, out of respect for Mia's baby and Cricket's ambitions, they have swapped out rum and heavy cream for honey and chamomile.

"Oliver!" Cricket shouts so he can hear her over the running kitchen faucet. "I love you!"

"Glad you like them," Oliver calls back. He and Mia splurged to give Cricket Normatec compression boots—an updated version of the ones Sloane and her dad had when Cricket stayed with them in Florida.

"Thank you," Cricket says, nudging Mia as she stares down at her booted legs with appreciation. "These are such game changers."

"So are those," Mia answers dryly, nodding toward the tree, at Cricket's Christmas presents to her: a foam roller and a fancy blender, two items Cricket complained about not having at home.

"And I can't thank you enough for my gifts," Oliver deadpans. "Nipple cream *and* hemorrhoid cream? You spoil me."

They were meant for Mia, of course, after the baby came, but Cricket had wrapped the gifts while watching a recent interview of Teague. In her distracted state, she'd mislabeled the presents.

"You all set for tomorrow?" Oliver asks Mia as he dries his hands and walks over to join them on the couch.

"What's tomorrow?" Cricket asks.

"Ultrasound," Mia says, touching her stomach. They've barely spoken about the baby, focused as they've been on Cricket. When she leaves in two weeks, Mia and Oliver are both anxious and eager to resume their new-parent freakout. Until then, and compared to the great unknown beating toward them, obsessing over Cricket's physical, emotional, and gastrointestinal well-being feels like a nice little staycation, a sense of control amid the chaos.

"You're not going?" Cricket asks Oliver with lifted eyebrows.

"He's been to all of them," Mia says. "They get boring after a while."

"Baby is moving, there's her hand, blah, blah, blah," Oliver says before taking a sip of his tea. In reality, he and Mia live for ultrasound days—the first time he saw his daughter's foot, he'd been so moved that he'd leaned down and cried into Mia's neck. *Those are her toes,* he'd wept. *Her perfect little toes.*

But the ultrasound is scheduled for ten a.m., which is right in the middle of Oliver and Cricket's first training session of the day. As much as Oliver would like to go, and as much as Mia wishes he could be there with her, they promised to prioritize Cricket's dream over winter break. It seems only right to help Cricket achieve her life goal now that they are well on their way to getting exactly what they want.

The next morning, Cricket texts Mia during a water break to see how the ultrasound went, and her phone immediately buzzes with a new message: *Got a minute?*

Before Cricket can process anything, her phone starts to ring. "Hello?" she answers, as if she doesn't have the caller's name saved in capital letters.

"Cricket, it's Teague." She sounds uncharacteristically ruffled. "Is now a good time?"

Cricket freezes in the field house, Oliver just a few feet away, looking over with concern. She gives him a reassuring wave so he knows it isn't Mia and then turns her back, trying not to hyperventilate.

"Here's where we're at," Teague continues. "Des is sitting out January Camp and I know it's not a ton of notice, but I'm hoping you'll come in her place."

Teague talks through logistics and expectations, but Cricket barely hears her. She is going to camp. She is being invited, right now, to January Camp, in an Olympics year, and she is ready. She is fit and fired up, and this is her chance. This is her time. And somehow, she already knows, before she even hangs up the phone, that this is the beginning of her highlight reel.

MOTHER AND CHILD

Squatting in search of her favorite skillet, Mia laughs at her own awkwardness as she tries not to get stuck. Her pronounced stomach and altered center of gravity have begun to make even the most mundane tasks comical, especially now that she's landed safely in the third trimester. "There should be an Olympics for pregnant women," she muses, pulling herself up with the natural grace of a walrus. "Pancakes?"

"Pancakes," Oliver agrees, his mind elsewhere as he peers out the kitchen window. It's a snowy Saturday morning—because it can snow in late April in Maine and it's considered unfortunate but not apocalyptic. He decides that right now is as good a time as ever to bring up what they've both been avoiding.

"So the baby needs a nursery," he says.

Mia nods. "I was thinking we could convert the attic." She throws a generous chunk of butter in her mother's pan and gives the batter one more vigorous stir. "We'd paint the ceiling white, get lots of floor cushions," she says. "Make it Bohemian cozy."

Oliver laughs before he realizes Mia isn't kidding. "The attic is a crawl space. It's not even insulated."

"I guess we could spruce up the basement?" Mia opens a drawer and roots around for the good spatula. "But would paint stick to—what are the walls made of?"

"Plaster."

"Does paint stick to plaster?"

"Sure, eventually," Oliver says, humoring her. "It'll take several coats, and then I guess we'd just wedge the crib between the pipe that drips whenever it rains and the dryer that randomly turns itself on."

"Ooh, next to the dryer is a good idea—I keep reading babies like vibrations."

"Mia!"

"What?"

"This is a three-bedroom house!" Oliver palms his forehead out of frustration. "We're not putting our baby in the basement. Or the attic."

"I promised Cricket we wouldn't touch her room," Mia says, adding more butter to the pan. "If we convert it into a nursery, she'll think we don't want her to visit."

"I agree, which is why I'm not suggesting Cricket's room."

"Oh." Mia waits to see bubbles before she flips the pancakes with an expert wrist.

"Mia?"

"Yeah." Mia tries to blink back the sudden sadness, the cold forward march of time, even toward something as beautiful as a baby.

"Mia?"

"Okay." Mia plates the pancakes and nods at the floor because she knows Oliver is looking at her with such gentle compassion that she will fall apart, and she is too hungry to fall apart right now. "Okay," she says again, softer this time. She wants to be in the past with her mom but also in the future with her family of three, and she wishes she didn't have to choose. Instead, life demands a constant compromise. What was that thing she'd read somewhere, before she was pregnant, when she still had a memory? A good compromise is when everyone leaves dissatisfied.

After breakfast and one more cup of coffee than she usually allows herself, Mia reties the sash of her robe as if she's dressing for battle. Outside, the snow has turned to rain. "Wish me luck," Mia says with a dramatic sigh.

"You don't need luck," Oliver responds. "You get to choose what happens next—what stays and what goes."

Down the hall, Mia holds her breath and turns the doorknob to her mother's room. It's exactly how Liz left it on November 9, 2019, only the shades are drawn. Taking a step inside, Mia realizes she never should have let this room sit in the dark when Liz so ardently lived for light— she often said it was the key to surviving a Maine winter. The first thing Mia does is pull up the shades. The bedroom has two south-facing windows and as the sun streams in, it exposes an inch of dust on every surface.

Motivated and caffeinated, Mia yells down to Oliver that she needs a bucket of warm, soapy water and a stack of rags. When he appears with the requested items, Mia dunks an old washcloth into the bucket of sudsy water and looks around the room, clocking the insurmountable work ahead of her. Where to start?

"Don't do it for me," Liz says, appearing on the edge of the bed. "Do it for the baby."

It's the first time Mia has seen her mother since the morning of November ninth, nine years ago. "Look at you," Liz says affectionately, tilting her head. "I know it's a cliché, but it's a cliché for a reason: You're glowing, Mia. You look beautiful."

Mia jumps at the sound of Oliver's voice shouting up the stairs to ask how she's doing.

"I'm good!" Mia yells back, unable to take her eyes off her mother. *Her mother.*

"You're going to be such a great mom," Liz says. "She's already so lucky."

Mia doesn't realize she's crying until Liz comes over, holds her hand, and she seems so real, more so than in any dream she's had—and she's had plenty of vivid dreams about her mom.

"Where have you been?" Mia asks. "Everyone says to look for signs, ask for a sign, but you—why now?"

"Because," Liz says softly, "this is the first time you've needed me."

"How can you say that?" Mia balks. "I've needed you every day for nine years."

Unfazed, Liz admires Mia's wedding ring. "Not the way I needed you," she says calmly. "You were always the rock—even when you were too young to be so steady."

"You were young, too," Mia points out through blurry vision.

"True," Liz says with a faint smile. "But I relied on you like a partner and it wasn't fair."

This acknowledgment shocks Mia more than the freezing waters of a polar plunge. She wipes her eyes with the back of her hand, swollen from pregnancy.

"But you're going to need me when the baby comes," Liz says, sitting up straight at the idea of being useful. "So what color for the nursery?"

"No." Mia shakes her head to try to stop the tears that keep coming. "This is your room."

"Don't be ridiculous. It'll be perfect for her—and look at all this light!"

In the living room, Oliver lies sprawled across the pink floral couch, reading his phone, when Mia comes downstairs carrying a box of her mother's black server aprons. The raccoon eyes suggest tears, but her face radiates hope. She grins at him like she did the day they found out she was pregnant.

"I'm making piles, so can you grab all the heavy stuff I'm not supposed to lift?"

"Absolutely," Oliver says, hopping to his feet. "I'll come up right now."

"And I think we should try lavender."

"Huh?"

"For the nursery—I'd like to paint it a super light, soothing lavender."

Oliver is not going to squander this step forward. He is already lacing up his sneakers and sliding his wallet into his back pocket when he asks, "Do you want to come with me to the hardware store? For the paint? Or should I just bring samples back here?"

"I'll go with you." Mia approaches Oliver and plants a forceful kiss on his lips. "You were right," she says. "It's the perfect room for a nursery—so much light!"

On the drive to Hammer It Home, Mia decides not to tell Oliver about seeing her mother. If this is some kind of pregnancy symptom, a temporary delusion that goes hand in hand with having to pee every seven minutes, so be it. She is grateful for this opportunity, even if the opportunity might also be a sideways brush with madness.

Two weeks later, Mia has transformed her mom's bedroom into a nauseatingly perfect nursery. The walls are painted a calming "Spring Iris," board books line the shelves in alphabetical order, tiny onesies are organized by season within the drawers of a new dresser, and the changing table is well stocked with diapers, wipes, and an assortment of ointments and creams. Rather than the holdover stillness of a shrine, the nursery is bursting with potential energy, like a classroom before the first day of school, right before life rips through it.

CLEAN SHEETS

In early June, Cricket lies on the balcony of her Chicago apartment listening to the birds welcome in summer with their song. A dreamy breeze from Lake Michigan rolls over her skin, and the savory smoke of a charcoal grill on the building's communal patio gives way to a severe cheeseburger craving, in which Cricket will not indulge. Instead, she checks the time and makes sure her ringer is on.

It's 12:43 p.m.

She is trying to wait patiently.

It's getting harder by the minute.

With her phone balanced on her chest, Cricket looks like any other twenty-three-year-old sunbathing on the first truly hot day of the year. Under a flat-brimmed hat and behind reflective sunglasses, an onlooker might assume she's daydreaming or even napping. But in reality, Cricket has never been more acutely conscious than right now.

After checking her phone yet again, Cricket wonders if Teague making her wait over an hour is a good or bad sign for what is to come. It's impossible to know. It's silly to guess. The fact of the matter is that it's Sunday afternoon and Cricket's stomach has been a mess all weekend from the nerves of anticipating this, because this is everything, and everything is happening any second.

And here it is. The cheerful ring of a FaceTime call when the theme music from *Halloween* would be far more appropriate because Cricket can't run or hide from what happens next. She instinctively gets to her feet before answering, as if standing might save her from ruin.

"Cricket," Teague says, her expression set in a professional neutral. "Congratulations."

That one word brings Cricket to her knees, and from hundreds of miles away, the head coach of the U.S. Women's National Team pauses to give Cricket a moment to collect herself. She is trying her hardest not to cry, but for several weeks now, Cricket has prepared herself for the worst, and so the sudden flood of relief overwhelms her system because *congratulations* can only mean one thing.

"You've been selected to the Olympic roster," Teague continues, sounding like an automated machine, like she is just the messenger and not the grandmaster of Cricket's fate. It's well known that Teague makes the heartbreaking calls first, telling the contenders from the most recent training camp that they did not make the squad. Now she gets to call twenty-two players and make their dreams come true.

Cricket Lowe is going to the 2028 Olympics in Los Angeles.

"I've obviously been watching you for years," Teague says. "And while I've always valued your talent, I've got to tell you, Cricket, your performance in the past six months has been nothing short of phenomenal. We're bringing you for your ability on the field, of course—it's you and Sloane, by the way, our two keepers for this tournament, with Emma as an alternate—but we're also bringing you for your attributes off the pitch."

"Thank you, Coach," Cricket musters.

"I see so much potential in you as a future leader of this team," Teague says in response. She is used to talking through players' tears—it's part of the job. "Starting at January Camp, you've made yourself an asset, and to be fully transparent, I'm interested to see you and Sloane compete for the starting spot this summer."

Cricket can hardly believe what she's hearing. As soon as Alyssa Naeher retired, Sloane stepped into her place, the natural heir apparent. But ever since Des dropped out of January Camp for mental health reasons and Teague invited Cricket to take her place, Cricket has felt like she's outperformed Sloane. Nevertheless, Sloane has still played every minute of every game in the smaller tournaments of the last six months. But now Teague is telling her, straight up, that the Olympics are up for grabs.

"Thank you, Coach," Cricket says again, wiping her eyes and waiting until they hang up to blow her nose. Teague may have several more calls to place, but Cricket only has one.

"Oh my God!" Mia screams as soon as Cricket tells her. "You did it!"

"Well done, Keep!" Oliver shouts, his gruff coach voice cracking with affection as he reminds her that this is her opportunity.

"You so deserve this," Mia says, and as Cricket grabs yet another tissue, she can tell her sister is crying, too. "You've worked so hard to get here, and Mom would be so proud—"

Cricket almost tells Mia it's okay, that she knows their mom *is* proud, that Liz was with her every day of the multiple training camps, and the Gold Cup and SheBelieves Cup, and that she'll come with her to the Olympics since Mia will be too pregnant to fly. They may be physically separated, but they're all in this together.

After she hangs up with Mia and Oliver, Cricket is too thrilled to keep still so she heads out for a run in the middle of the afternoon. She smiles the entire time, cranking out mile after mile despite the heat, and finds herself unwilling to stop. Walkers and other joggers wave to her, as if they know how her life has just catapulted in the direction of her dreams, thus justifying every hard decision she's had to make, even when it broke her heart. This is who she is and what she is meant to do. She will be an Olympian, just like her mom said she would be.

When Cricket returns to her building, dripping sweat on the marble floor of the lobby, Tony the doorman waves her over. "You've got a package," he tells her and then, seeing the small pool of perspiration collecting by her feet, he adds, "That must have been some run."

When Tony disappears into the mail room, Cricket considers telling him she made the Olympic team, but she also wants to enjoy this achievement on her own. In her world of professional soccer, there's little time to savor the highs, and Cricket knows today is the time to do so because tomorrow it's back to work. No one understands what she's sacrificed for the game. No one except maybe—

"Sloane Jackson?" Cricket says out loud, reading the sender's name on the package as Tony hands it to her. She rips it open right there in the lobby, only to be further perplexed.

Sloane picks up on the first ring. "Congratulations!" she shouts before blowing into what sounds unmistakably like a kazoo.

"You too," Cricket says. "Um, you sent me five-hundred-dollar sheets?"

"Yes," Sloane answers definitively. "But you can't open them, and you can't use them."

Cricket waits a beat for an explanation that doesn't come. "Huh?"

"You really don't get it?"

"I really don't get it," Cricket confesses, trying to scan her brain for the significance of expensive bed linens.

"We're competing for them," Sloane explains. "Whoever starts in the Olympics gets them—I'm guessing Teague told you the same thing she told me, that the starting spot is up for grabs—so do you want to Venmo me the five hundred bucks now? Or in August when you mail the sheets to my house?"

"What are you—"

"They're *clean sheets*, Cricket!" Sloane says, annoyed by Cricket's density. "Come on! Do you get it now?"

Oh. Wow. Yes, she does. A clean sheet is when a goalkeeper doesn't allow in a single goal. Lowering her voice so Tony won't hear, Cricket says, "You are out of your fucking mind."

"Ambitious witches forever!" Sloane sings in response, blowing heartily into her kazoo before hanging up.

Amused, bewildered, and a little bit ticked off that Sloane has already muddied what was supposed to be her day of pure celebration, Cricket waves goodbye to Tony, tucks the package under her arm, and takes the stairs up to her sixth-floor apartment. Sloane's joke is only kind of a joke; it's also a display of arrogance. Mailing Cricket these expensive sheets only she can afford is Sloane flaunting her inherent advantage. After all, Sloane is the team incumbent, the starting goalkeeper, and also America's sweetheart with several lucrative endorsement deals. She is the name and the face that everybody and their dad associates with the National Team. She's the new Alex Morgan, only probably more famous after her raunchy Bud Light commercial that played not once but twice during this year's Super Bowl.

Fishing out her key from the tiny pocket of her running shorts, Cricket unlocks the door and lets herself in as the realization dawns on her: Sloane sent the sheets because, despite her advantages, she is worried Cricket could steal her starting spot. Maybe, instead of it being a show of confidence, it's a sign of weakness. Sloane is desperate to knock Cricket off her game by messing with her head.

Cricket opens her hallway closet and is about to chuck the sheets into the back for some out-of-sight, out-of-mind peace, but then she thinks better of it. Instead, she cleans off her coffee table and places the packaged sheets in the middle, as a large, unconventional centerpiece.

Satisfied, Cricket smirks as she admires the new focal point of her living room. The clean sheets prove Sloane is nervous that her position on the National Team is in jeopardy.

Good, Cricket thinks. *As she should be.*

HAMMER IT HOME

In July, a much-needed breeze rolls through the open windows while Oliver and Mia sit on the pink floral couch with a hamper full of freshly laundered onesies wedged between them.

"Explain to me why we're washing brand-new baby clothes?" Oliver asks, attempting to fold tiny red pajamas that look too small for a chipmunk.

"To get rid of any chemicals from the manufacturer," Mia says matter-of-factly, as she hears her mom chuckle at the notion. *Not all chemicals are bad,* Liz says in her ear. *I raised you on bleach and Cheez-Its and look at you now!*

"I wonder if Teague has made her decision yet," Oliver says. This time tomorrow, the U.S. Women's National Team will play in their first Olympic match, the day before the Opening Ceremonies. In their week of practice leading up to the Olympics—and really, all year—Cricket and Sloane have been duking it out for the starting spot.

"Cricket's got this," Mia says knowingly. "She said she's been outperforming Sloane all week." In her calls and texts home, Cricket sounds calm and confident, like she not only knows that she's giving her best but that she also believes her best is good enough to earn the start. "She's got a winner's mentality," Mia says before bolting upright. "Oh my God! The baby just kicked! Literally right after I said *winner's mentality*—do you think she's already competitive?"

"How could she not be?" Oliver laughs, before an obvious reality hits him for the first time. "You know, Cricket and the baby are making their debuts the same summer," he says, shaking his head at the sneaky passage of time, the unexpected path of his life that took him from South Carolina and landed him here. He still remembers the first time he met Cricket, a mouthy nine-year-old at the Stallions tryout, and now she's at the Olympics, potentially starting. It's overwhelming enough to make him tear up, which has been happening more often recently, as if Mia's pregnancy hormones are somehow contagious.

"You okay?" Mia asks, putting her palm to his cheek.

"I'm just really proud of her," he says, leaning over to kiss Mia's bare shoulder. "That probably sounds ridiculous, but it's true."

"That's what this family is," Mia agrees. She illustrates her point by holding up a teeny-tiny U.S. Soccer onesie Cricket sent them just last week. "Ridiculous but true."

FULL CIRCLE

No one is quite sure how it started, but the week leading up to the 2028 Olympics in Los Angeles, every practice for the U.S. Women's National Team begins the same way: Spread across the field, engaging in various calisthenics, Naomi declares, "This ain't no disco."

The rest of the defenders reply in unison, "It ain't no country club, either."

And then everyone on the field, grinning in their lateral squat or backward lunge, shouts the next line together, "This is L.A.!"

The opening lyrics to Sheryl Crow's 1993 hit, "All I Wanna Do," has somehow become the call-and-response that serves as a shorthand for this team, a rallying cry to remind each of them that while the bumps and bruises are suffered individually, they are all here in the City of Angels together, hoping to win a gold medal for their country.

"I'm so confused," Teague says from the sideline, taking off her sunglasses to clean them. "That song came out before any of you were born."

"It's a classic," Sloane says. "Give us a little credit, Coach!"

"Pretty sure I give you plenty," Teague says without meeting Sloane's eye. "Okay, keepers are with Anders, everyone else down here."

Sloane glances at Cricket because *what was that?*

"She's just wound tight for tomorrow," Cricket reassures her as they grab their gloves from the bench and begin their jog to the far goal.

"All Teague will have to do at the game is stand on the sideline and yell," Sloane huffs.

"I could say the same thing about you," Cricket teases, but Sloane doesn't laugh. Competition between them has been fierce all week and what neither of them has said is that Cricket is playing better and more consistently. Despite Sloane's history as the starting goalkeeper, Teague has been explicit that tomorrow's lineup is still fluid, still dependent on daily performance.

"Now I have that song stuck in my head," Sloane whines.

"It's not such a bad one," Cricket argues before singing the next line. "*All I wanna do is have a little fun before I die* seems like a good thing to remember the day before we become Olympians, don't you think? Play with joy, et cetera?"

"You're annoying when you're happy," Sloane says, stopping abruptly to pull up her socks. Ahead of them, Anders waits with orange cones and a flexing jaw as he works over a fresh piece of electric-blue gum.

Cricket smiles because Sloane is right—she is happy. She's here. Against all odds and after so many detours, she's finally made it to the Olympics. Just like Oliver pointed out over winter break, this is her opportunity, and she's grateful for it. Also, not that she would risk jinxing it by saying it aloud, or even texting it to Mia, but she is pretty sure that Teague is going to start her tomorrow.

Halfway through the first drill, Liz appears by the goalpost. "Do you smell that?" she asks, wrinkling her nose. Cricket doesn't smell anything except her own body odor cutting through her coconut-scented sunscreen.

"It's the sweet, sweet smell of victory!" Liz shouts, raising her fists like she's Rocky Balboa. "You're going to start every game, and we're going to win gold! Be positive, baby!"

"Nice heart," Cricket says, noting the lipstick on her mom's cheek.

"A quality throwback," Liz says, beaming. "Just like Sheryl Crow." It was, in fact, Liz who first sang "All I Wanna Do" when Cricket arrived in Los Angeles the previous week. The pop song became a team-wide earworm within twenty-four hours, and now it is bugging Sloane, who is already in her own head about tomorrow, which delights Liz to no end.

"It's not that I'm rooting *against* her, I'm just cheering *for* you," she says. "Play well today, and that starting spot is yours tomorrow."

That night at dinner, the team is so mired in their own anxieties that, in the silence, Trinity wonders aloud when they all became such noisy chewers.

"It's true," Soph agrees, slicing up a pear. "Please, somebody say something."

But it's hard to come up with fresh material after a week of living and training with the same group. The pressure is intense and only mounting. Tomorrow, they begin their quest to win back-to-back Olympic gold medals in front of millions of viewers.

"Who is Teague meeting with first tonight?" Mal asks, and everyone looks around because *that* is an interesting question.

"Number one," Sloane says from the end of the table. "By which I obviously mean me." Maybe it's in Cricket's head, but it seems like more than a few teammates sneak glances at Cricket in response to Sloane, like reporters shifting their attention to the next big story.

As she does the night before every major international tournament, Teague conferences with each player after dinner to discuss their role for their opening match and, more explicitly, to tell them whether they're starters or game changers.

She meets with the players in one of the hotel's larger suites that the staff has converted to suit the team's needs. Her office is the bedroom, and what was once a cavernous living room has now become the 24/7 snack room. Players can grab fruit, granola bars, yogurt, bottled water, and hydration tablets at their convenience.

Just after ten p.m., a single banana—perfect in its slightly green pre-ripeness—tempts Cricket from an otherwise empty fruit bowl as she makes her way to Teague's office. She heard that more than three million bananas were consumed by athletes during the 2024 Paris Olympics. She can believe it. But Cricket walks by the fruit bowl because now is not the time for bananas.

"Come on in, Cricket," Teague calls through the open door. "Take a seat. How are you doing?"

"Great," Cricket answers, because she's never been entirely sure what she's supposed to say when someone asks how she's doing, and because, all things considered, she's truly feeling pretty great.

"Excellent, as you should be," Teague says, looking down at the open binder in front of her and scanning for something. She closes it and folds her hands, looks Cricket in the eye. "To be honest with you, I've wrestled with this decision quite a bit, but we're starting Sloane tomorrow, which means I'll need you to—"

Teague goes on about the role of a game changer, how integral they are to the success of a team. But Cricket isn't listening. Cricket is wondering how this can be, after the last seven months, when everyone from Gogo and Lindsey to Sam and Foxy have said that she's been incredible. Everyone has looked at her and all but told her that she earned the starting spot tomorrow.

It doesn't make any sense.

"Sloane has significantly more experience—" Teague is in the middle of saying, and Cricket wants to flip her desk over and throw that binder out the window, because how is Cricket ever supposed to gain experience if she isn't given an opportunity to stand in the goal and gain some fucking experience? She waits for the dismissal and when it arrives, Cricket says, "Thanks, Coach," before getting out of that office as quickly as possible, grabbing that perfect banana out of the fruit bowl, and throwing it in the trash.

Cricket returns to her room, body shaking, mind reeling. As she starts to run water for her bath, she tries to decide whether to text Mia when it's already past midnight on the East Coast or if she should just get in the tub and try to reset on her own.

But Cricket doesn't do either because someone knocks on the door.

"Hey, it's me," says a familiar voice. "Open up."

Cricket rolls her eyes but lets Sloane in, already aware this is a bad idea.

"Sorry," Sloane says, stepping past Cricket and into the room. "But also, obviously, not sorry?" She spins on her toes, a tone-deaf grin on her face, and Cricket realizes too late that Sloane is not even going to attempt sympathy, or diplomacy, or discretion. She came here to gloat.

"I've got to say, I'm a little stunned," Sloane admits.

"Congratulations," Cricket says, bending over and stretching her hamstrings to avoid eye contact. "But I need space."

"Totally," Sloane agrees emphatically. "It's just, I was thinking, these hotel sheets are pretty subpar, so could I get those nice ones? That I mailed to you?"

When Cricket doesn't respond, Sloane looks over at her. "What?" she asks.

"Are you serious?"

"This is all part of our friendship, Cricket," Sloane says, her smile faltering. "We compete to make each other better."

"But I'm better!" Cricket shouts suddenly, surprising Sloane with the boom of her voice and, if she's being honest, surprising herself, too. "I've been outplaying you! Everyone knows it! I don't know who your parents paid, but there—"

"My *parents*?" Sloane repeats, her face falling, then clouding over into game mode. "This is the Olympics and I have far more experience than you," she says. "Remember when you were at UCLA and constantly telling me that going pro after high school was shortsighted?"

"So?" Cricket says, aware that she is yelling and that the walls are thin but unable to stop. "Who cares what I said?"

"I do!" Sloane says with a derisive laugh. "I do, because every time we talked, you scared the shit out of me that I'd made the wrong decision and that you were having the best time ever, but now"—she lets out an exhausted sigh—"it's times like tonight where it seems like taking that risk paid off."

"Oh please," Cricket scoffs. "It was hardly a risk when you'd always have your parents backing you up and bailing you out."

"Bailing me out? Since when do you hate my parents?" Sloane asks, her voice high.

"I've been playing better than you," Cricket says, ignoring the question, because the answer is she loves Sloane's parents, she just hates how present they are, how supportive and rich and *alive* they are. "I should be starting tomorrow," Cricket states plainly. "According to literally everyone."

"Except Teague," Sloane points out.

"Which is bullshit!" Cricket shouts. She wants to throw something. She needs to punch something. If she kicked the wall as hard as she wants to, she'd shatter all the bones in her foot, so instead she bellows, "You don't deserve the start and you don't need it!"

"And you do?" Sloane asks, fuming. "You *need* it? Are you serious right now?"

"I've earned it—you know I have!"

"You've had a few good days of training," Sloane concedes, bringing each word to a simmer. "But years of experience trumps a few good days—"

"Months!" Cricket corrects her. "I've had the edge since January!"

"Your only edge is the chip on your shoulder!" Sloane snaps. "And I have to say, it's kind of funny how this afternoon, you could joke about me riding the bench, and now you're like—well, you're not winning any awards for sportsmanship, I can tell you that."

Cricket storms past Sloane and into the closet. She bends down, rummaging for something on the bottom shelf, beneath the small hotel vault. "Here," she says, taking long strides across the room and shoving the sheets into Sloane's stomach with the force of her rage. It knocks the wind out of Sloane, but she refuses to wince.

"I made that joke because you always start," Cricket says. "You always win, ever since we were sixteen, and you can buy five-hundred-dollar sheets on a whim, as a joke, and you know I can't. You know I don't have a single endorsement, let alone ten."

"Twelve."

Cricket rolls her eyes. "The fact is, you've been punching down on me for years, and you know it, and you enjoy it. You invited me to your house and then made me sleep in your trophy room, for Christ's sake."

Her words puncture the air. The only sound is the crinkling plastic around the five-hundred-dollar sheets. Wordlessly, Sloane backs away. At the door, she turns around.

"Maybe you think you've sacrificed more than I have, or deserve the start more," she says calmly. "But you haven't and you don't. I earned the experience I have now, just like I earned every one of my caps."

Cricket opens her mouth before realizing she has nothing to say.

Sloane drops the sheets on the ground by her feet. "See you at breakfast," she says. "From now on, I'll leave you alone."

After Sloane leaves, Cricket stares at the sheets on the floor for a full minute before realizing the bathwater has been running all this time. She turns off the faucet just before the tub overflows, the air so thick with steam that it hides her tears.

Over the next two weeks, as the National Team advances out of the group stage and survives the knockout rounds, Sloane and Cricket barely speak. When they cannot avoid each other altogether, they interact like business associates with an inconvenient but undeniable shared interest in gold.

Sloane plays well, like she always does. And Cricket watches from the bench, expertly performing the role of a supportive teammate. In the first round of the group stage, she cheers for Sloane with the other game changers but when Teague calls a time-out, Cricket avoids the starting keeper. Because that's all Sloane is now—the starting keeper. Not her friend. In the locker room before and after the first match, Cricket keeps her headphones on, her music loud, and her eyes down.

But as the United States advances in the Olympics, Cricket can't help but appreciate Sloane's poise under such immense pressure. In the second round of the group stage, Sloane blocks a penalty kick from Zambia in the fifth minute of the game, saving her team the burden of having to dig themselves out of such an early hole. On the sideline, Cricket remembers the tens of thousands of PKs she and Sloane shot on each other over the years, and they all just paid off.

Then, in the quarter-final against Colombia, Sloane steps off her line early to intercept a long ball. It's a bold move and one that Cricket and Sloane constantly debated when they reviewed game film together. The match ends in another victory for the United States, and Sloane's daring step feels like a win not just for Sloane but also for Cricket. That split-second decision to step off her line resulted from years of coaching each other to think fast in real time with huge stakes.

When the United States goes into overtime with Spain in the semifinal, Sloane comes up big with a save she converts into a clear, which then becomes the game-winning goal. As the stadium explodes with rapture, Cricket travels back to those ten days she spent with Sloane in Florida and how Sloane insisted they work on the accuracy of their clears after each speed workout. In the moment, it seemed insane and unnecessary, but it was that work ethic that was now taking the United States to the Gold Medal match.

And so before the final against the Netherlands, Cricket swallows her pride and goes out of her way to touch Sloane on the shoulder. "You got this," she says in the players' tunnel. Despite everything that's transpired between them, Cricket believes in Sloane. She believes Sloane deserves to win and, even if Cricket doesn't get to actually play, she'd still like to go home with a gold medal.

Except that in the eighty-third minute, Sloane's leg breaks. As she's wheeled off the field, expectations are shattered and then reimagined when Cricket takes her place in goal.

"Holy shit," Liz says, leaning against the left goalpost and staring up into the bright stadium lights, the stories of fans screaming her daughter's name. "You're here. We're here."

Cricket nods as she tries to warm up her cold muscles quickly. The announcers won't stop saying her name, and they keep repeating the fact that this is her first international cap like it's some dirty secret. In her head, Sloane reminds her to shut out the noise and just play. If he were here, Coach would tell her that this is her opportunity.

"Soak it in, baby girl," Liz says, lifting her hands toward the sky as tears roll down her cheeks. Their dream is finally realized. "Soak it in and play your heart out."

And that's exactly what Cricket does, stopping Mila Visschers's shot by making an unbelievable, game-winning save.

After the refs blow their whistles, the players dogpile on the field, relieved and euphoric to have once again won it all. It's the end of another grueling Olympics, sure, but it's just as clear to everyone in the stands and watching at home that this is Cricket Lowe's moment. This is how one opportunity can fling open the gates to a thousand more.

This is how the underdog becomes the hero.

LEGACY

2029

ON FIRE

Five months after winning an Olympic gold medal and learning Mia needed a kidney, Cricket finds herself sweating in Trilith. The air just hits different in Georgia.

At the new U.S. Soccer National Training Center, it's not yet eight a.m. and Cricket's jersey already clings to her body from the humidity. But January Camp is meant to be hard. Cricket is thankful it's this tough, this all-consuming, because it means she can't afford to think about anything else. Nothing like physical pain to make her excruciatingly present.

"Let's go," Anders says, blowing his whistle, and the keepers begin their circuit training. Cricket steps into the discomfort. She listens for her mother, but all she hears is the labored breath of Emma and Des on either side of her.

For the first time in her career, Cricket didn't spend the last month agonizing over whether she would make the cut for January Camp. With Sloane still rehabbing her leg, the starting goalkeeper position on the U.S. Women's National Team is Cricket's to lose.

This morning, she wears a tiny microphone to provide fans with a taste of behind-the-scenes candor from training camp. "Delay, delay!" Cricket shouts when they scrimmage. A minute later, "Stay! Stay!" she yells at her defenders. She does not worry if her audio is boring for the social media team; she knows it's working on the field.

While everyone else naps after lunch, Cricket partakes in three phone interviews because she is the newly crowned star keeper and, ever since she subbed into the Gold Medal match, her Cinderella status has piqued the media's interest. Cricket commends her manager, Paula, on the variety pack of today's inquirers: *The New York Times, Vanity Fair,* and *Bon Appétit.*

When the thoughtful young woman from *Bon Appétit* asks about her diet, Cricket credits Sloane for her daily pumpkin seed consumption. It is easy to be gracious from the number-one spot, and it seems as though everyone within the National Team bubble has signed off on Cricket's sparkling future. Teague wholeheartedly endorsed her during her latest press conference. Anders pays close attention to her during training, Cricket's performance overshadowing Emma's and Des's, just as Sloane's once did.

But there's also buy-in from the rest of the coaching and training staff, who go out of their way to check in on Cricket. And from the higher-ups at U.S. Soccer, veteran reporters, eager sponsors, and the well-groomed personnel that run the front office. In the parking lot of the training center, women in power heels and black blazers call her "Crick" on their way to investment meetings. Alyssa Naeher, her acclaimed predecessor, tells Cricket to reach out any time. And if that weren't rewarding enough, the contract Cricket signed last week with Procter & Gamble is her seventh six-figure endorsement deal.

That evening, after dinner and meetings, Cricket puts her legs up the wall as she runs bathwater and realizes she hasn't opened her mouth to speak in almost four hours—since the last training session when she shouted directions from the goal line. She didn't say a word all through dinner except when Rose asked her to pass the pepper.

Cricket tells herself she's just focusing, but she knows that's a lie.

The truth is this: Cricket has never been more alone.

Or more miserable.

As soon as Cricket steps off the field, the chambers of her heart echo with painful absences: Her mother hasn't appeared on the pitch since she left Mia in the hospital last August. Oliver hasn't replied to her texts since then, either. And hardest of all, Cricket hasn't spoken to Mia, even though it's Mia—more than anyone—who she wants to call right now and tell her that the captain, Gogo Garba, yelled from across the field and in front of the entire team that Cricket was on fire today.

Only Mia could wholly appreciate what it meant to Cricket when Megan Rapinoe showed up at dinner tonight, offering encouragement and a reminder that this team represents more than excellent soccer.

Did you tell her about Mom? Mia would ask. *Did you tell her about going to Paris in 2019?* And Cricket would say, *Of course I did!* But in reality, Cricket didn't say a word to their hero, because when everyone clapped for Megan, Cricket buckled with shame.

It's been nearly six months since Cricket spoke to her sister in Mia's hospital room. Six months since Oliver handed her the donor coordinator's business card, and Cricket said she would call, but life had come fast.

While Mia and Oliver went silent, Cricket's manager, Paula, kept reaching out. Endorsement offers kept flooding in, and then the Chicago Red Stars went undefeated and won the NWSL championship, which meant more notoriety, more interviews, more exhausting days that required an unnatural amount of smiling and lying through her teeth as Cricket insisted on live-recording podcasts and in front of ever-rolling cameras, "I'm so happy to be here."

THE CHAIR

Mia does her best—and worst—thinking in her dialysis chair. It's where she came up with Oliver's birthday present (running shoes), figured out the problem with her recent batch of tomato sauce (not enough nutmeg), and determined what she'll put in Betty's first Easter basket (bunny-shaped teethers and a pint of strawberries). It's also where she's dreamed the most realistic, horrific dreams about her sister.

The chair itself is simple, similar to one of those massaging recliners they have in nail salons. As Mia makes herself comfortable at the start of yet another three-hour session, she imagines that she isn't getting hemodialysis but a luxurious pedicure with all the expensive add-ons because spring is coming and that's the kind of thing other women do, even busy moms.

But not Mia.

No, Mia's spa day is spent here, shackled to a machine at the Kidney Care Center. The chair itself is dark gray. Mia refers to it as her loyal steed to the technician who checks her in, and the tech laughs politely, every time, which is now too many times to count.

"Mia!" Ro, Mia's favorite nurse, stands before her in Tweety Bird scrubs. "I feel like I haven't seen you in a minute."

"Wednesday?" Mia guesses, rolling up her right sleeve and making a fist.

Thumbing Mia's plump vein for the IV, Ro asks, "So you haven't heard about Mrs. Simms?" At Mia's worried expression, Ro clarifies, "No, no, it's all good—great, actually—her daughter said she'll be her donor."

The news knocks Mia sideways. No one deserves kidney failure, but Mrs. Simms just celebrated her eighty-fifth birthday last month and now her daughter is giving her a new lease on life. Everyone here should be so lucky.

"I'll check back in a bit," Ro says, patting Mia's shoulder before waving to her next patient from across the room. As the machine works to remove, filter, and replace Mia's blood, she closes her eyes and indulges in an alternative reality:

If her own mother were still alive, Liz would be a B-positive match and a willing donor, which means Mia would have a new kidney already, and she would never have fought with Cricket. If Liz were still alive, Mia wouldn't be here, tethered to this chair and dependent on dialysis for survival. If her mother were still alive, Mia would be at home with her six-month-old daughter, who would be content instead of bawling in the arms of whichever hungover college student Mia was able to nail down to babysit that day. And if Liz were still alive—

Mia is suddenly hot, very hot, which is weird because this process usually makes her cold. Sweating through her shirt, Mia checks the hemodialysis machine, but her levels are normal and it's running smoothly.

The problem is that Mia needs to set her chair on fire at this exact moment.

She needs to pour gasoline on the hemodialysis machine and watch it burn.

Because this is way too much and this is too damn hard and Mrs. Simms? *Really?*

"I'm done," she whispers to herself, testing out the sentiment. It feels good. An unfamiliar buzz tingles through her body and Mia realizes it's the rush of rebellion, the thrill of making a unilateral decision based on her own desire. "I'm done!" she says a little louder. "Done, done, done," she sings as she begins to detach herself from the machine.

Mia is twenty-nine years old. She is too young for chronic kidney disease, and Betty is too vivacious to have a mother so compromised. This isn't fair and she's not doing it anymore. Instead, Mia hums as she carefully removes the IV needle from her forearm and glances through the glass doors to her future. Outside, the next three hours beckon from the parking lot like a seductive stranger with a full tank of gas.

Mia slips her shoes back on and ignores the sounds of displeasure coming from her dialysis machine because she's done here, forever, and she's going to go get a pedicure like a regular mom, and she's also going to the mall, and the beach, and then she's going to drive to Montreal because in the grand scheme of things, it's really not that far, and—

"Mia?" Ro says, walking over. "What's going on?"

"I quit!" Mia announces, grabbing her bag from the side table. The other patients look over with a mix of curiosity and concern. Lowering her voice so only Ro can hear, Mia says, "I quit and I'm driving to Canada."

"What are you talking about?" Ro's eyes narrow, trying to understand. "I need you in that chair for the next three hours." But Ro has three exuberant kids and two healthy kidneys of her own, so Mia just stares at her because she doesn't get it. She can't get it.

"I need you to sit back down, please," Ro says calmly. "Come on, Mia, let's do this."

"No," Mia answers defiantly. "I'm leaving."

"Because this sucks?" Ro asks.

The answer surprises Mia. "Yes," she manages to say.

"And because this is unfair?" Ro continues. "And absolute bullshit?"

"Yeah," Mia says, her voice cracking as she tries to sniff back everything she's suppressed for six months. Everything she's told herself wasn't constructive in her effort to be positive.

"I don't know if anyone has mentioned this to you," Ro says. "But this is really hard."

Mia puts her hands on her hips and stares up at the fluorescent light, willing herself not to cry. "Yeah," she agrees. "It fucking sucks." And the expletive feels good as she releases it into the atmosphere, violent and transgressive, like the disease itself.

"Come with me," Ro says, steering Mia through a door with a sign that reads STAFF ONLY. Inside is a small office area with a mini fridge, a row of lockers, and a round table with two chairs. Ro pulls one out for Mia, then the other for herself. "Being a human is hard, and being a human mother is even harder," Ro says. "But being a human mother trying to care for her family while fighting CKD? *Are you fucking kidding me?*"

Mia laughs as she blinks back more tears. No one has said anything like this to her. Everyone has told her to stay positive, be strong, look on the bright side. Ro is the first person to express all the wretched feelings swirling inside her.

"Every time I see you, I hope it's the last," Ro says, offering Mia an opened box of Cheez-Its. Mia shoves a handful into her mouth. They taste like childhood and remind her of her mom. "You don't deserve this," Ro says.

Mia just nods, dazed by the staggering brightness of these neglected truths finally dragged into the sun.

"You're doing a phenomenal job in an impossible situation," Ro says. "Now do me a favor and get back in that chair."

Mia nods at Ro and they leave the staff break room. While Ro checks on another patient, Mia returns to her loyal steed. She stares at the chair, hesitating. She should sit down, she needs to. Instead, she walks out of the clinic without looking back. Because despite Ro's best efforts, Mia just can't do it anymore. She just can't.

MEDIA DAY

Backstage, Cricket can hear them talking about her. These reporters filing into the Mixed Zone are known for being particularly blunt and loyal only to the truth. It's time for Cricket to face them.

The communications director, Alix, hands Cricket a bottle of water before she goes on. "So just a quick reminder of the ground rules," Alix says. "No swearing, obviously, and only take questions from the center section—not from anyone leaning against the walls—they promised they wouldn't raise their hands, but you never know, and just have fun with it, they seem like a great group."

To help kick off the start of the seventeenth NWSL season, the Chicago Red Stars have invited journalists to participate in a whirlwind Media Day. Reporters have access to players, coaches, high-ranking members of the front office, and even Supernova, the fuzzy blue Martian who serves as the official Red Stars mascot.

After a morning of sit-down interviews, Cricket's voice is worn and her cheeks sore from all the polite answering and smiling. The number of times she's already said, "I'm just going to do my best to help my team" has tired her out more than yelling through a ninety-minute match. Playing soccer comes naturally, but today's production is as organic as a circus, and what she's about to do is the most absurd stunt of all.

This is what we wanted, Cricket reminds herself. But who is "we" without Mia?

Cricket still gets compared to Sloane constantly, but that's the cost of taking her position on the team and in the national spotlight. In the big picture, Cricket knows it's a small price to pay. Paula reaches out several times a week with a new opportunity—*Doritos wants to feature Cricket in a commercial! The Kellogg School would love for Ms. Lowe to speak at their Global Women's Summit!*

It is becoming more and more common for Cricket to be approached by fans when she's out running errands. Like Sloane, she says yes to every selfie request. All members of the U.S. Women's National Team, past and present, understand they represent more than a group of athletes. They embody a dream, and it is their responsibility to foster that dream with positivity, encouragement, and gratitude.

"Thank you for your support!" Cricket says at the end of every such interaction. If she and Sloane were on speaking terms, she would confess it can take a toll, walking through a world saturated in external expectations. With a newfound appreciation, Cricket finds herself recalling how Sloane always handled those situations with such tremendous grace.

"All set?" Alix asks Cricket now, and when she nods, they walk out onto the stage. As Cricket situates herself behind the dais, the journalists lean forward and clap politely, their sneakered feet dangling off the folding seats and their unabashed open smiles revealing crowded, crooked, and poorly spaced teeth.

They are children.

And this event is even more ridiculous than Cricket had imagined.

She looks out upon a sea of kids dressed in their best attempts to appear professional. Some wear blazers and most hold notepads. One boy in the second row shouts, "Cheese and crackers!" when his box of crayons clatters to the floor, and Cricket laughs as hard as the parents who line either side of the room.

"Hi everyone," Alix begins. "Thanks so much for being here. We're so excited to—"

In the first row, a hand shoots up.

"Okay, sure, let's jump right into questions," Alix says, gesturing to the girl. She's wearing a Naomi Girma jersey over sparkly red leggings. "How about you say your name and age before asking your question?"

"Hi, my name is Kelsey," the girl begins, "and I'm six, and I have a dog named Mango, and I'm wondering if you and Sloane Jackson are best friends? Or if you don't like her because she's better than you?"

Cricket feels all eyes on her, and she's pretty sure she can identify which couple are Kelsey's parents, given the scarlet mortification stamped on their faces, but all she can do is belly laugh and hope that Sloane is watching this. It's refreshing, the bald honesty of the girl's question. It's what adult journalists have asked her all day, but in dressed-up language that's harder to move through, like trying to swim in loafers.

"Hi, Kelsey, thank you for your question, and please give Mango my regards," Cricket begins. "So first of all, I love Sloane Jackson. And I cannot wait for her to recover from her injury because playing with her, and competing against her, not only makes me a better player but makes everyone on the National Team better players."

Kelsey nods, satisfied, so Cricket moves on to a boy in the last row, who decides to stand on his chair for better visibility.

"My name is Nicky," he shouts into the microphone. "I'm four and a half years old, I live at 93 Ashland Street in Chicago, Illinois, 6-0-6-3-1, and I have an older brother named Amos who still wets the bed, but I don't, and I want to know if you ever have accidents."

"Oh boy, Nicky," Cricket says, taking a sip of water to keep from cracking up. Poor Amos. "After many years of practice, I am good at making it to the bathroom in time," she says. "But I have other kinds of accidents, like when I don't save a shot, or I misjudge a player's speed. I think all accidents are trying to teach us the same thing, though, which is that we're human beings, which means we're still learning, and even if one night doesn't go our way, we can try again the next time."

The kids are already restless, fidgeting in their seats, turning their heads around to stare at one another and look for their parents, who are sneaking glances at their phones. Cricket doesn't blame them, even if she does think that was a pretty decent answer. The press briefing proceeds in this way as the room grows progressively hotter and the children more likely to rebel, until Alix announces they have time for one more question and calls on a girl in the center of the room with the thickest glasses Cricket has ever seen.

"Hi, Cricket," she says, her self-possession a little startling. "My name is Tasha, and I'm ten years old, and my question is, When you make a save or win a game, how do you celebrate?"

"Well, if it's a save during a game, I'll clap my hands—always three times, because I'm superstitious," Cricket says, modeling the behavior, careful to take a step back from the microphone. "But because I'm still in the middle of a game, I want to stay focused so I mostly just concentrate on doing well in the next play."

Along the walls, the parents nod along with her, and Cricket imagines them sitting in boardrooms, clapping three times when they nail their presentation. The image makes her grin before she continues: "If it's at the end of a good game and we've won and I'm proud of my performance, I'll celebrate with my teammates on the field and in the locker room."

"Excellent!" Alix says, sidling up next to Cricket behind the dais and thanking everyone for coming.

Tasha raises her hand again. "Sorry, but that's not what I meant," she says. "I mean, after you leave the stadium, how do you celebrate?"

"Oh, even better question," Cricket says, smiling as she stalls for time. "When I leave the stadium," Cricket says slowly, "I'll go out to dinner with a few friends, and then if I really want to celebrate, we'll go to Margie's Candies afterward."

"Yum!" Alix cuts in, nudging Cricket off the microphone and thanking her for her time. "Just talking about Margie's makes my mouth water—does that happen to anyone else?" Hands fly up and thus ends the PeeWee Press Conference and Cricket's participation in Media Day.

Tossing a Supernova T-shirt into her bag, Cricket waves goodbye to her teammates entering the press room and speed walks to the parking lot. She cannot wait to go home and do the same thing she does every day after soccer: collapse on the couch with her shoes still on and split her attention between the TV and her phone screen to ward off any deep thoughts. It's almost impossible to cry while consuming reality shows and deliberating what to order from which food delivery service. Almost.

Because the truth is that Cricket doesn't have any friends who aren't also her teammates, and, other than Sloane, she doesn't have any teammates who are aware of her family, or lack thereof. After a great game, they assume she is celebrating, like they are, with people who have watched her rise to the top—people who love her beyond the pitch.

But the people who love Cricket don't like her and won't speak to her. If Cricket had answered Tasha truthfully, she would have admitted that there are no celebrations after she leaves the locker room; that she has only experienced Margie's Candies while perusing the menu online. If Cricket had been honest, she would have said there hasn't been anything worth celebrating since the Olympics last year. Or, more accurately, in the seven months since she last heard her sister's voice.

TICKETS

After skipping hemodialysis and treating herself to a pedicure, Mia enters the kitchen to the delighted squeals of her daughter and the competing smells of macaroni and cheese, baked beans, and broccoli.

"Join us for dinner?" Oliver asks, just as Betty chucks her bottle at his head. As Mia and Oliver try to limit the number of broccoli florets that end up by their feet, Mia tries to act like she isn't debilitatingly nauseated. What she won't admit to Oliver is that the sight of food on the floor doesn't upset her nearly as much as the food on her plate. The baked beans are especially revolting. But Mia can only blame herself as she tries to eat without gagging. Acute queasiness is one of the more immediate side effects of skipping a treatment.

"You okay?" Oliver asks, wiping his mouth with his napkin and clearing his throat as if to speak. Instead, he takes a long drag of ice water. This gets Mia's attention, because Oliver is one of those people who "doesn't like the taste" of water and only consumes it in small, forced sips. But now, Oliver takes yet another deep chug.

"What are you not telling me?" Mia asks.

"I could ask you the same thing." Before Mia can formulate an answer, Oliver levels with her. "Ro called me," he says. "I'm your emergency contact, in case you forgot, and she considered you skipping your session an emergency, as do I—as does everybody invested in your wellbeing." His voice trembles, and Mia struggles to discern whether he's angry or upset before realizing he's terrified.

"You can't do that," Oliver says, crumpling his napkin in his fist. "Okay, Mia? You can't do that? People die from skipping treatment."

Betty, with a broccoli stem hanging out of her mouth like a green cigar, stares at her parents, rapt. She has never seen her mother scolded or her father scared.

"I love you," Oliver continues, reaching for Mia's hand as Betty smashes a fistful of macaroni into her own hair. Mia would stop her, but she is having a hard time sitting up as she imagines what's happening inside her body, how in the absence of clean blood, her kidneys are getting overwhelmed by toxins. Skipping dialysis, just wanting those three hours back, means her body is suffering fluid overload and electrolyte imbalances. There is urine in her blood now because she didn't feel like sitting in a chair. What was she thinking?

Oliver reaches into his back pocket and pulls out his phone.

"The National Team is playing Mexico at the Rose Bowl next month," he says, holding up his screen to display the announcement. "On May twenty-eighth."

Mia gives him the look he expects, the look every spouse receives far too often, especially after a baby arrives—the look that universally translates to, *What the actual fuck are you talking about?*

"I think we should go," Oliver says. He devised this plan weeks ago, but it was the phone call from Ro today that has empowered him to broach the idea with Mia tonight.

"She ghosted us," Mia sputters in disbelief. "She said she just had to think about it, and that she'd call us, and then she never did. I checked with Wendy for the first three months and Cricket never reached out to the donor coordinators, or even texted to see if I was out of the hospital."

The nausea is no match for Mia's anger at the mention of Cricket. "I am literally dying and she doesn't care." It's this interpretation of events, this version of the truth, that undoes Mia, just as it was this same conclusion she had drawn in the chair this afternoon that made her abandon the clinic, the plan, the regimen she knows she needs to stay healthy.

"Hear me out," Oliver says, pulling his chair closer to hers. "Okay, Mia? Listen to me: You have every right to be furious."

Mia wipes her eyes, unbuckles Betty from her high chair, and puts the baby on her lap.

"We both know your mom's ten-year anniversary is coming up in November—"

"What's that got—"

"I've been paying close attention, and given it a lot of thought, and then today happened, so now I'm that much more—look, your kidney may stop functioning." Oliver's voice breaks. "You might die. It's highly unlikely, a slim possibility, right?" Mia nods. "But what's not a possibility," Oliver continues, "what's an absolute certainty as far as I'm concerned, is that not speaking to your sister is killing you."

Mia bends down to retrieve her napkin off the floor only to reappear with glistening eyes. Oliver pulls both his girls toward him. Betty wriggles while Mia burrows into Oliver's shoulder. She doesn't cry so much as heave from the weight of his words. Diagnosing her unspoken affliction, giving the pain a name, a space, is a release unto itself.

"We don't have to go to the game," Oliver murmurs. "I just thought—"

Mia pushes deeper into his shoulder, the seam of his fleece a wet mess of her emotions. "How are the seats?" she asks, which makes Oliver laugh.

"Very good," he tells her, wiping Mia's tears with his napkin. Betty balks, so Oliver picks a broccoli tree off her plate and successfully airplanes it into her mouth. Like everything else her dad does, Betty finds his sound effects hilarious, which means spewed bits of broccoli fly across the table and down Mia's shirt, but her daughter's giggles are contagious and Mia doesn't care. The mess is worth it. The mess is always worth it.

From the same kitchen chair she has sat in all her life, Mia watches Betty and Oliver tickle each other and feels her lips separate like a stage curtain, a familiar warmth lighting her up. This is her family. So much of life has happened to her, but she did this. She chose this place, with these people.

Oliver is right.

"Let's go," Mia says, reaching for his hand. She feels exonerated, having finally admitted that Cricket's absence is killing her. "Thank you." She weaves her fingers through Oliver's and squeezes. Amid all the pain and loss and chaos of her past, every choice that was made for her, Mia looks at her husband and sees her best decision smiling back at her.

UP THE WALL

As she does every night before a match, Cricket dumps two cups of Epsom salt into the tub before filling it to the brim with hot water. On the edge of the bath, she has lined up a glass of mint-infused water and a bottle of electrolytes to maintain her hydration levels while she soaks. Next to Cricket's drinks, the delicate flame of a travel-size candle glows steadily, and next to the sink, a portable speaker plays meditation music. It's taken some time—more than two years of living on the road—but Cricket has learned how to make a hotel room feel like home.

And now she is in her second home, back in Southern California. This is the place where her life began, twice: first as a college freshman and then again in the eighty-third minute of the Gold Medal match. This afternoon, Cricket succumbed to nostalgia and walked through UCLA's sculpture garden, grieving the fact that Yaz would only ever be her ex-girlfriend. Cricket's wife—demanding, fickle, and often cruel— is soccer.

Adding a few drops of jojoba oil to the bath, Cricket undresses, turns out the lights, steps in, and lowers herself down. These next twenty minutes are as integral to playing well against Mexico tomorrow as sleeping and eating properly. She has already stretched and reviewed the defensive set plays on her iPad. Each piece of her preparation is equally vital. Every ritual is sacred. The heat pulls Cricket inward and helps consolidate her thoughts while the steam opens her pores, melts her anxiety. The bath is part of the process, and everyone knows to trust the process.

When she feels ready, Cricket begins her nightly visualization practice. She is fully present in the future as she watches herself emerge from the players' tunnel, sees herself dive for the first save of the game before clearing the ball to the midfield.

Cricket sees all of this with almost a three-dimensional clarity, but the only thing she hears is that all-too-familiar mosquito buzzing in her ear—the grating vibration of her phone on the marble vanity. She tries to ignore it, but only a select few are able to call through her do-not-disturb setting.

"You have a visitor," Paula says by way of hello. Cricket's manager prides herself on efficiency, word count included. "Visiting hours are over, but I checked with Teague and she has deemed this an exception to the rule."

"Who is it?" Cricket asks, trying to remain calm, but if Teague is making an exception, it must be Mia.

"She said she wants to surprise you," Paula says. "So it's okay to send her up? She's been waiting in the lobby."

"Okay," Cricket says, tasting the spaghetti squash from dinner. Mia is here. Finally.

The impatient knock on the door surprises Cricket—she expected more of a gentle rap, not the forceful pounding of a SWAT team bust. But maybe Mia isn't coming to make amends at all, Cricket thinks, wishing she had time to put on a bra, or at least take out her nighttime retainer.

More powerful knocking.

Cricket opens the door and steels herself.

"Hi."

Sloane Jackson stands in the hallway, arms crossed, lips taut, expression inscrutable. They haven't spoken in ten months, by far the longest they've ever gone, and just the sight of her makes Cricket smile because that's her friend. That is her goddamn pal of the last ten years, and only now, face-to-face, does she realize just how much she's missed her. She has missed feeling seen by someone who views so much of the world the same way that Cricket does: on her toes, with her head on a swivel, from the goal line.

Before she even considers stopping herself, Cricket envelops Sloane in a hug so tight they are both claughing by the time they separate, Sloane's left dimple on full display.

"What are you doing here?" Cricket asks, trying to comprehend the moment, ground herself in some context she must have missed. She's devastated not to see Mia but beyond thrilled—and more than a little relieved—that it's just Sloane.

"Isn't it obvious?" Sloane asks, sticking out her left leg to showcase the puckered-pink scar that runs down the side of her quadriceps, from the top of her thigh to the middle of her knee.

"You're done with rehab?" Cricket asks, even though she knows Sloane can't be. Everyone said it would take at least a year before she could even entertain the idea of training.

"Yep," Sloane deadpans. "And I'm starting tomorrow."

"Hilarious."

"Pretty soon it won't be a joke," Sloane says, crossing the room to investigate a large black gift bag. Cricket watches her, impressed with the fluidity in Sloane's movements. She expected a dramatic limp, or at least a hitch, but Sloane has returned to her panther-on-the-prowl silken gait.

"You're moving well," Cricket acknowledges with genuine awe.

"I miss this," Sloane says in response, rooting around the gift bag until she comes up with a box of truffles from Mignon Chocolates. "Being on the team and playing, obviously, but also swag bags."

Cricket stares as Sloane helps herself to a truffle. She hasn't allowed herself to consume simple sugars for over a year now, since before she went Terminator over winter break in Victory. A lifetime ago. When Oliver and Mia were still on her team. Before she'd let them down, and they'd stopped speaking. Cricket shakes the thought from her head and focuses on Sloane, who is now opening a bottle of Perrier she's plucked from the minibar.

"So what are you actually doing here?" Cricket asks.

"I saw your interview on YouTube," Sloane says, lifting her shoulders. "The one with the little kids, and when you got that last question, I knew you were lying."

"No, I wasn't." Cricket watches Sloane pop another truffle into her mouth.

"Yes, you were," Sloane says while chewing. "But I wanted to come see you even before that because—gah, I practiced this so many times and it's still hard."

"What?"

"I'm sorry," Sloane says. "I'm really sorry."

Cricket stares at her as twenty different alarms go off in her head. This is a prank. Sloane is once again messing with her, the night before a match, after ten months of not speaking.

"This isn't—I'm not—this is real," Sloane says, reading her thoughts. "I'm sorry for all the times I said one thing and did another."

"What do you mean?" Cricket asks coldly as she flashes back to Primo Bistro the night of her high school graduation and the sad twin mattress on Sloane's trophy room floor. The five-hundred-dollar clean sheets.

Sloane lets out a long sigh. "Upon deep reflection—and after many sessions with a surprisingly militant therapist named Barbara—I can now see how I used our friendship as a smoke screen for some pretty bad behavior over the years."

Cricket stares at the carpet near Sloane's left foot. Is this really happening? Right now? She feels simultaneously vindicated and insane. So it hadn't just been in her head. All this time, Sloane had known what she was doing. "And the thing is," Cricket says, forcing herself to meet Sloane's gaze, "you were punching down."

Sloane nods. "I can see that now, and I'm—look, this whole injury"— she gestures to her scar—"it put a lot of stuff into perspective. I thought I'd miss soccer, and I do, but I've missed talking to you so much more than the sport itself, you know?"

Cricket glances at Sloane, expecting to see her eyes twinkling facetiously, but Sloane has never looked more serious. "I got so depressed—like, so depressed—and everyone assumed it was the lack of exercise, but it wasn't just—and I was so mad at you last summer, for saying those things about my parents and me, but it's also true. I came from a lot, and achieved a lot, but you came from a little and still managed to do a lot, and then I felt threatened enough to really mess with you, like some gross bully shit while disguised as your friend, and I'm really, really, sorry."

They stand there for several moments before Sloane whips her head up and scans the hotel room, clearly looking for something. When she spots the dresser, she approaches it like it's offended her. Bending her knees and using all her strength, Sloane shoves the dresser into the corner.

"What are you doing?" Cricket asks as Sloane performs a deep squat to lift the hotel desk and its accompanying chair on top of the dresser in the corner, creating a small tower of industrial furniture.

"We need the space," Sloane answers, sliding down the exposed wall, where the dresser and desk had been, their heavy outlines still imprinted in the carpet. She kicks off her slides and spins around. Now Cricket gets it.

"Seriously?"

"Seriously." Sloane pats the vacant patch of carpet next to her. "Also, I brought contraband." She pulls a packet of pumpkin seeds out of her sweatshirt's kangaroo pocket and dangles it in front of her face, wriggling her eyebrows. "Ready to get into it?"

"I'm sorry, too," Cricket says, feet grounded in place. "I could've handled it better, especially right before your Olympic debut."

"Thank you," Sloane says. "But what else?"

"What else?"

"I broke my leg and you never reached out."

"We were in a fight!" Cricket says, far too loudly.

"Who cares!" Sloane yells, meeting her volume. "If something bad happens to someone you love, you check in. It doesn't matter if you're in a fight, you set aside your ego and you fucking check in."

"Well, then, I've blown it twice," Cricket mumbles. "With you and my sister."

"Mia?" Sloane asks. "What's up with Mia?" Just hearing her sister's name spoken out loud brings Mia to the forefront of Cricket's consciousness in a way she hasn't allowed in almost a year. And Sloane has met Mia. Sloane knows Mia, which means Sloane knows Mia has never asked for anything.

"It's a long story," Cricket says.

"And this wall is calling your name."

They put their legs up, just as they did when they were sixteen.

"It's like I finally get everything I wanted—or at least I'm on track to get everything I wanted—no offense—and I've never been more alone." Cricket turns her head, looks at Sloane's profile, backlit by the hotel lamp behind her. "Was it always this lonely for you?"

"I guess," Sloane says, keeping her eyes on the ceiling as she thinks through her answer. "But we're goalkeepers—we're lone wolves by design."

"But what's the point if she's not here?"

"Maybe there isn't one," Sloane says, rolling her right ankle clockwise, and then counterclockwise. "Or maybe—and I've thought about this a lot since getting hurt—but maybe soccer—or I guess sports in general—is just a relatively healthy coping mechanism."

"For what?"

"Being human."

Cricket huffs at the sentiment but Sloane continues. "Like, in a game, the only way to play well is to be totally, completely grounded in the moment. But if you're—maybe you've given all you can—"

Cricket shakes her head. "I know I haven't."

"Yeah." Sloane agrees. "Then maybe you have to decide if the cost of the dream is worth the price of playing."

"I'm not even sure it is my dream anymore," Cricket admits. "Mia hates me, and my mom—she's gone, too."

Looking over to meet Cricket's eye, Sloane asks delicately, "But she hasn't been around for a while, right? Almost ten years?"

Cricket stares into the recessed lights as tears slide off the sides of her face. She shakes her head. "This is probably going to sound so crazy."

"Then it will sound like every other conversation with you."

"After she died," Cricket begins, using the back of her hand to wipe at her tears, "she would show up at my games and hang out by the goalpost. I've never told anyone this, not even Mia—"

"It's okay," Sloane says. "Tell me."

Cricket sniffles hard and takes a few deep inhales. "Okay, so, all through high school, all through college, even through that first awful season with the Red Stars, when we couldn't string two passes together, she was always there."

"Your mom?"

Cricket nods.

"And then what?"

Cricket starts to answer but suddenly she can't breathe, not with this anvil in her chest, this shame lodged in her throat. She takes her legs off the wall and brings them down to Earth, rolls over onto her hands and knees, tries to catch her breath, but the harder she tries to swallow air, the more she craves it in gulps and the harder she cries out in uncontrollable sobs. Somewhere in the thick of it all, Sloane is there, drawing slow circles between Cricket's wing bones, counting seconds to inhale and exhale, her voice as steady as her hand on Cricket's back.

"She disappeared," Cricket manages. "She disappeared and she hasn't come back since I left Mia in the hospital, even though this is what we all agreed to, this was everybody's dream for me."

"Yeah, but Cricket," Sloane says, gazing at the carpet, processing, "dreams can change."

"Not this one." She feels another wave of agony beginning to crest and doubles over.

"Yes, it can." Sloane pauses mid-circle, her hand still on Cricket's back as she points out the obvious: "Because circumstances change."

"But this is who I am," Cricket argues. "This is all I am."

Sloane sucks in her breath, as if this level of armchair therapy is above her pay grade. "Okay, so, two things right off the bat. One, you are not just a goalkeeper. And two, priorities shift. That's okay. Dreams can change. You just have to be brave enough to step off your line—"

Cricket's laugh interrupts Sloane's pep talk. "Are you really throwing out a goalkeeper metaphor right now?"

"I thought it was pretty apt, but fine, let me ask you this instead." Sloane sits up so she can make clear eye contact as she posits: "Are you having fun?"

Cricket stares at her. It feels unfair, and almost irrelevant. Fun isn't the point.

"When I come back," Sloane begins, "which is a lot sooner than you'd think, I'll play from a place of joy."

"But this is what I'm good at," Cricket insists, whispering it like a confession. "It's the one thing, and Steve Prefontaine said that to give anything less than your best is to—"

"—sacrifice the gift. I know, I know," Sloane says, speaking over her. "But maybe Steve didn't have a sister like Mia? And maybe your gift isn't what you think it is."

Cricket twists her head to look Sloane in the eye. "I can't tell if you're trying to inspire me or sabotage me."

Sloane keeps her focus on the ceiling, as if the truth hovers up there, under the paint, between the cracks, where heat gathers first. Without looking at Cricket, Sloane reaches for her hand. It surprises Cricket— the action itself and also how sweaty Sloane's palm is. "I'm not trying to do either," Sloane says earnestly. "But I know that winning a World Cup in two years—assuming we win, which is a big assumption—but winning a World Cup will not bring you peace." Sloane shudders, as if reliving a bad memory, and lets go of Cricket's hand. "Think about it: You already have an Olympic gold medal, and that isn't enough. Waiting for the next World Cup will only make you want more, because there's always another cup, and another lump of prize money, and more endorsement deals."

Cricket watches Sloane stand up and brush the pumpkin seed dust off her hands. "You have to accept wanting more. We all do. I'm probably the most guilty when it comes to that, the greediest little piggy of all."

"How so?"

Sloane crushes the empty pumpkin seed bag into a ball, takes a fadeaway jump shot. Behind her, Cricket hears the elegant *swish* as the bag hits the bottom of the trash can. Nothing but net.

"That's for another time," Sloane says. "The point is, ambitious witches always want more. But right now, you need to get some sleep, so you can give everything you've got tomorrow."

"And then what?" Cricket asks.

"And then you need to reach out to Mia."

RETURN TO THE ROSE BOWL

Thirty years after the 1999 Women's World Cup shattered records in the Rose Bowl stadium, a ten-month-old baby with startling blue eyes and visibly sleep-deprived parents arrives in California. They are here to cheer on the U.S. Women's National Team as it takes on Mexico in a "friendly" match that promises to be anything but.

"You have everything?" Oliver asks Mia for the fifth time since landing.

Mia pats her bag as they walk up the aisle of the plane. "All good," she says.

This cross-country trip revolves around Mia's dialysis schedule, which means it is only thirty-six hours long and both flights are redeyes. Dialysis, as her doctors are quick to remind Mia, is the only thing keeping her in stable condition. The process is critical for Mia to experience any semblance of a normal life.

It's a relative term—"normal life"—especially since officially giving up her job at Oceanside. Dr. Wilkins had floated different ideas about how Mia might do her job remotely after maternity leave and around her treatments, but Mia bowed out. Between Betty and dialysis, Mia's dance card is filled with diapers and needles, milk-encrusted pump parts and infuriating phone calls with the insurance company. Giving up Oceanside was imperative from a logistical standpoint, but Mia misses her furry patients, and her sense of utility, and the security her paycheck afforded her family. It had been Mia's decision to leave; however, it had hardly been her choice.

"I'm glad we're here," she says, holding out her finger for Betty, who bounces from the carrier strapped to Oliver's chest. "It feels—I don't know, hopeful."

"Maybe it's your mom's influence," Oliver suggests. "Be positive."

Mia's nephrologist had urged them to stay home, deeming the cross-country flight "unnecessarily dangerous and, in no uncertain terms, inadvisable." Oliver had been in the room to hear the doctor say this, and afterward he'd held Mia's hand in the elevator and out to the parking lot. On the drive home, Oliver said he would support whatever she chose to do.

Now, as the family navigates LAX for the first time, the rising sun chases them from one window to the next. The airport in Los Angeles is full of people wearing black baseball caps and smooth expressions of cultivated chill. It is a well-hydrated, trim, and wrinkle-free group. "Everyone is so good-looking," Mia says, rubbing her eyes. "Even at six a.m."

"They're just tan," Oliver counters, unimpressed. "You're the prettiest one here—or at least in Terminal B."

Their hotel room is conveniently located near the Rose Bowl and contains two queen beds with plush down comforters, crisp white sheets, and, best of all, a Pack 'n Play already set up. Oliver successfully transitions a sleeping Betty from the carrier to the portable crib and looks at Mia with wide, *can-you-believe-it* eyes. She mouths back, "Is this a dream?" because absent are the baskets of dirty laundry and stacks of sticky dishes and the general sense that the walls are closing in around them. The peace of a luxurious hotel room and slumbering baby lures Oliver and Mia into bed and they crash hard as the sun continues its daily climb.

When Betty acts as an alarm clock a few hours later, Mia ties a red ribbon in her daughter's tiny blond pouf of hair and pulls on her own lucky jersey—the one Oliver wore during the Olympics after she puked down the front of his. At 11:11, Mia kisses her watch three times. She is here to somehow move past her own disappointment and make peace with Cricket's decision, which means Mia needs all the luck she can get.

When purchasing the game tickets, Oliver intentionally did not go through the National Team's front office. He didn't want to raise any false white flags or faulty olive branches in case Mia changed her mind, or if her kidney function dropped enough percentage points to make it impossible for them to travel. As a result, they are not sitting in the designated Friends and Family section, and Cricket has no idea they will be at the match against Mexico. Instead, Oliver and Mia agreed to reach out to Cricket only after the game. It gives Mia the freedom to watch Cricket play without feeling like she, too, must perform.

Before they leave the hotel for the Rose Bowl, Mia grabs a tube of hydration tablets from her suitcase and shoves them into the clear bag she's bringing to the game. In the mirrored elevator, surrounded by somber versions of herself, Mia takes a small sip of water and holds it in her mouth to make it last. As thirsty as she is after the cross-country flight, she can't put herself at risk of hypervolemia, especially when she is so far from her treatment center.

Oliver examines the art on the side of their daughter's face and compliments Mia. "It's some of your finest work," he says, kissing the tip of her nose. In the mirror, a family of three in matching U.S. jerseys smiles back at them, a lucky red heart drawn in ruby red lipstick on each of their cheeks.

SOONER OR LATER

In the locker room before warm-ups, each player mentally prepares in her own way. Music blasts from a tiny but powerful speaker and some women dance. Others meditate with the help of noise-canceling headphones. A few pray. One player reads her horoscope while holding butterfly pose, because it's what she's done since ninth grade and look where it's taken her.

Cricket sits on the bench in front of her locker, reciting the lyrics to "Get Low, Fly High," just as she always does at this point in her process. She shoves a piece of her mom's lucky red ribbon into her sock. Near the showers, Gogo and Speedy execute choreography they've been working on for months. It seems like they're just messing around, but everyone here knows this is how they get ready to ball out. Cricket watches them while visualizing her own saves.

"What's up, party people?" Sloane says, making a characteristically dramatic entrance that instantly changes the molecules in the room. The team greets her with shrieks and *oh my God*s because they haven't seen her in person since she looked like roadkill Gumby, writhing on the ground and screaming to the sky in the eighty-third minute of the Gold Medal match.

"How's your leg?" Gogo asks, and Cricket tries not to take the polite inquiry as a slight, as an implication that Gogo wishes Sloane were tending goal today.

"Which one?" Sloane answers, improvising a series of Rockette-inspired high kicks. Everyone laughs and someone tells Sloane the team isn't the same without her, which begs the obvious question several people call out at the same time: *When are you coming back?*

"Sooner than Cricket wants me to, that's for sure," Sloane says, walking over to Cricket and jostling loose her topknot.

"Bring it," Cricket responds, tucking her gloves into her waistband.

"You want to get in on this huddle?" Gogo asks Sloane.

Through the stack of fingers, Cricket swears she can feel an electric current pulsing. It *tick, tick, ticks* like the clock on the wall behind her teammates' heads. It's the *tick, tick, tick* of Cricket realizing she's running out of time. Sloane is coming back, and anything could happen, and sooner or later, her last game will be behind her.

It might be in ten years, or two weeks, or today.

And when that happens, who will be waiting for her? Who will she be without soccer?

Only forever is long enough to be a part of this team, Cricket realizes in the huddle. Only forever is long enough to feel the way she does right now. She needs to exist here, surrounded by promise, on the verge of something great and so much larger than herself. Nothing less could ever be enough, impossible as that may sound. To keep things the same, she'll need to change her dream.

Sloane is right: It's time to step off her line.

Gogo counts them in, and Cricket cries out with all her heart:

"Oosa-Oosa-Oosa-Ah!"

THE DREAM

"Wanna hear a fun fact?" Mia asks Oliver as they enter the stadium. "The National Team stole their cheer from the Italians."

"The Italians?"

Mia nods knowingly. "In 1985, Italian fans were impressed with the American team, which was making its international debut," she explains. "So the Italians actually started chanting 'U-S-A' but they pronounced it 'Oosa,' and it's been around ever since."

"Your mom tell you that?" Oliver asks.

"She sure did." Mia grins, resting her head on Oliver's shoulder. Liz told her the history of the chant on their flight home from Paris, nearly a decade ago, and then again on the flight here, while Mia was dreaming of her.

Because this was always the dream.

It's all upside down, but this was the dream and they're here. For so long, Cricket in a USA jersey was what all three Lowe women worked toward, and for a moment, Mia tells herself this is good enough. They are Lowes, and so they don't quit on each other.

As unfair as it is, being the older sister has always meant brokering peace. This trip is already helping Mia understand Cricket's reluctance to give it all up. The career of a professional athlete, at best, is extremely brief. Before even getting to see her sister emerge from the players' tunnel for warm-ups, Mia knows in her bones that this trip was worth ignoring her nephrologist's warning.

Fisting a soggy hot dog bun in one hand, an American flag in the other, Betty yells "Oosa!" from Oliver's lap. Or at least, that's what Mia hears amid the ricocheting energy of the packed Rose Bowl stadium as she tries to soak up every detail, every memory as it happens. Her daughter, despite having more leg rolls than lexicon, seems to understand how special today is, her "Lowe" jersey dangling past her feet.

"It's so nice here," Mia says to Oliver, lifting her face to the sun. "Maybe I really should have gone to UCLA with Cricket."

"You could have married a surfer," Oliver agrees wistfully. "Opened a chia seed café."

"This was a good idea," Mia says, grabbing him by the elbow, overcome with gratitude. Before she even sees Cricket, Mia knows she will forgive her sister. They will be okay. Mia has been on the donor list for almost a year now, and her donor-transplant coordinator feels certain that she will get a new kidney before Betty's third birthday. She just has to hang on until then.

"Here it comes!" Oliver yells, lifting the baby up for The Wave. Betty claps and squeals, and as the three of them throw their arms up in unison, their world—ever so briefly—becomes perfect.

But despite Mia's best efforts to balance her hydration levels on the cross-country flight, the long plane ride was too much. Mia tries to tell Oliver that she can't catch her breath. Only the words suddenly elude her. She can't speak and she can't get Oliver's attention. Black spots speckle her view. The blue sky dims.

Mia collapses. From the depths of where she's landed, she can't hear Betty crying out or Oliver shouting for help. Instead, she hears the ocean waves crashing back in Victory and her mother's voice promising a reset. Mia knows she needs to dunk her head under the water for it to count, but she's so scared.

As medics weave through the crowd, Betty's cries turn into terrified wails. She screams, reaching for her mother, for the one person she believes to be part of herself.

But even through Betty's pleading howls, Mia remains unresponsive. Crumpled on the ground between the row of seats, she is gone. And somewhere down below on that lush field of green with clearly drawn lines and agreed-upon rules, a whistle bleats for a game to begin.

OTHER PLANS

When the Rose Bowl security team radios in that a woman has collapsed, Sloane Jackson is standing next to a bearded guard in the players' tunnel, signing a program for his daughter.

"Does Cricket Lowe have a sister?" he asks Sloane, forefinger pressing into his earpiece.

"Yeah," Sloane says. "She lives in Maine."

"They're saying she's here and she's unconscious—they're transporting her to the hospital now."

Sloane doesn't respond because she is already running, a slight limp in her gait but determination in every step as she sprints toward the locker room, scanning the sea of familiar faces for a boppy blond pouf, but Cricket isn't in the locker room, or getting taped up by one of the team physios. Instead, Sloane finds her in a bathroom stall and calls out her name.

"I'm surprised they let a civilian back here," Cricket teases before flushing the toilet.

"You have to go to the hospital," Sloane says, catching her breath. "Your sister passed out, I'll tell Teague—"

The stall door flies open. "That's not funny," Cricket says, pushing past Sloane to wash her hands. "You always take jokes too fucking far."

Undeterred, Sloane grabs Cricket by the shoulders and pins her against the wall. Her dark brown eyes are dilated with urgency. "You need to go. Right now."

"What are you—" Cricket stops, recognizing the truth in Sloane's face. "But I would have—they would have told me—"

"I don't know anything except she was here," Sloane says. "And now she's not."

"Where do I go?"

"This way," Sloane says, grabbing her hand and guiding Cricket through a maze of hallways.

The Uber driver speeds through greens, yellows, and even one red light while Cricket hovers over his shoulder, ignoring the ding of the seatbelt reminder as she grips the neck of the headrests and tells him to go faster. FASTER. She is fourteen years old again, playing well at a tournament in Massachusetts, when the ref calls a time-out and Mia appears to tell her in no uncertain terms that their mother is gone, even though she can't be, because Cricket still needs her, and her mom still needs Cricket.

But Mia has never needed Cricket. Mia has never needed anyone. For Cricket's entire life, Mia has crunched the numbers, made the calls, and figured out the answers. Mia has always been the adult in the room. But now, on the way to the hospital, Cricket understands that acting as the adult in the room means just that—acting—and so she pretends that she is in control, that she is not too late.

ALL IN

On the second floor of Huntington Hospital's East Tower Annex, a nurse leads Cricket down the hall of the Critical Care Unit, to a dark room where Mia lies prone, eyes closed, skin sallow, attached to multiple machines. Cricket rubs her eyes but the tears just keep coming.

"We gave her fluids, and the doctor wants her to go through a round of dialysis before she leaves—the cross-country trip wiped her out, but she's okay," the nurse emphasizes. "And if you talk to her," she nudges, "I bet she'll listen."

Cricket wipes her face with the sleeve of her bright green gameday jersey. She assumes Oliver is nearby, with Betty, speaking with a doctor, and Cricket feels a shameful pang. A child should never have to fear for her mother, or spend time in a hospital, but because of her own decisions, her own inaction, Betty is here.

"Mia," Cricket says, leaning over her sister. "I'm so sorry."

The monitor acknowledges Cricket's apology with a noncommittal beep.

"I just thought—you've always come up with what you've—what we've needed, you know? You just always found a way—"

"She tried," Oliver says, entering the room with Betty strapped to his chest. Facing outward in her carrier, Betty proudly crinkles the plastic sleeve of vending machine peanut butter crackers in her tiny hand. She waves both arms at Cricket, and Cricket waves back, dazed at the sight of her own mother's sled-dog eyes. Betty is no longer the newborn she met ten months ago but a little person whose outlook hinges on Cricket's choices.

"It's been hell," Oliver continues. "Also: Hi."

"I'm sorry," Cricket says, turning to Oliver. "I just—"

"The worst part is that she really missed you," Oliver interrupts. "In spite of it all, she missed you, and the fact that you were suddenly everywhere, brazenly having the time of your life while we—"

"No, I wasn't," Cricket sniffs, using the hem of her game jersey to wipe her nose. "I thought I needed to finish what we'd started, win enough games and make enough money to—"

"Cricket?" Mia croaks from the hospital bed, her small voice drawing all attention to her as she opens her eyes and lifts her head ever so slightly.

Betty reaches out for her mother so Oliver places their daughter on the bed.

"Hey," Cricket says, taking her sister's hand and leaning in close, until their noses are a millimeter apart. "I'm sorry," she whispers. "I'm sorry and I'm here and I'm all in."

"All in?" Mia asks.

Cricket nods. "For the last—I thought—I mean, I get it now."

"What?" Mia rasps, her voice sounds painfully dry.

"You finally need me," Cricket says, fresh tears falling.

"I've always needed you."

"Not until you needed a kidney." Cricket tries and fails at a smile.

"No," Mia interrupts, slow and deliberate. "I needed you—and I still need you—because you're my sister."

A knock, and Oliver stands while Mia and Cricket try to compose themselves.

"Excuse me?" the woman says, craning her long neck around the door and into the room. To their surprise, she is not a doctor or a nurse. "Sorry to interrupt, I just wanted to—"

"Sloane," Mia announces from her hospital bed. "Get in here."

Cricket feels the room simultaneously expand and shrink as Sloane steps into it. "The nurse told me you're okay," Sloane says, smiling at Mia.

"She's okay," Cricket confirms, beaming and feeling oddly whole, like Sloane isn't an intrusion so much as a completion.

It's then that Betty decides to test the laws of gravity by diving head-first off the hospital bed. Cricket rushes to catch her, but Sloane gets there first and swoops Betty midair. Hugging Betty to her chest, Sloane raises one eyebrow at Cricket to silently point out that she got there first, that her reflexes are still second to none.

"Nice hands," Oliver says, reaching out for his fearless daughter.

"More!" Betty demands, and everyone laughs. Cricket is relieved that the attention remains on her niece because she feels a tingling in her ribs and a buzzing through her limbs that she's never before experienced. She is still wondering if this sensation is just what absolute relief feels like, or if such an extreme physical reaction might be indicative of something else entirely, when Sloane walks over and hugs her.

But the embrace does not provide any comfort. Nor does it convey a sense of peace.

At all.

In fact, Sloane's hug terrifies Cricket, because it electrifies her, spelling out the answer to her heart's question in high-wattage lightbulbs too bright to face alone:

It's her.

It's always been her.

UNDER THE LIGHTS

From the hospital room in the Critical Care Unit, Oliver calls their nephrology team in Maine and puts everyone on speaker. Mia's organ-donor coordinator, Wendy, explains every step ahead of them, from the tests Cricket will need to take, to the timeline of the surgery, to the extent of the recovery process. "It makes the most sense to formally begin the process with your established health care provider," Wendy says. "Give me a ring when you get back to Chicago and, until then, enjoy the time you have left with your team."

After that intense conversation, Cricket steps outside to make an even tougher call.

"You sure?" Paula asks, forever economical with her words. "Want to sleep on it first?"

"I've been sleeping on it for almost a year," Cricket says. "I'm sure."

"I'll circle back." The call lasts under a minute. It took twenty-four years to build the career she'd always dreamed of, and less than sixty seconds to shut it all down. In breaking the news to Paula, Cricket's decision takes on another dimension of reality. Her manager is now tasked with the unpleasant job of figuring out how to breach Cricket's contracts with as little financial and legal fallout as possible.

Next, Cricket calls Teague to apologize, and then Gogo the team captain, and then Emma, who'd stepped up and played in her stead, consequently earning her first cap and first clean sheet in front of ninety thousand people. They'd won, 2–0, and now everyone was back at the hotel, celebrating at the rooftop bar. Their jubilation doesn't make Cricket feel sad or envious or angry; she's too drained to feel anything at all except relief. She wasn't too late.

When visiting hours end, Cricket escorts Oliver and Betty back to their hotel.

"I'm sorry," she tells Oliver in the dark, as they both hover over Betty in her Pack 'n Play.

"I know," Oliver says, putting his hand on her shoulder.

By the time she returns to her own hotel room, Cricket is practically sleepwalking. Nevertheless, she packs up her suitcases, along with the life she knows. It's the first time she's been alone since this morning, the first time she can try to wrap her mind around what she's done, what she's doing, and what she's signed on to do next. Maybe Sloane is right: She has to make peace with wanting more.

Ambitious witches always want more.

All evening, Cricket's teammates have texted her their condolences about Mia, but now, as the night wears on and the drinking continues, they beg her to come join them on the roof, come celebrate, come blow off steam, so when Cricket hears the incessant knocking, she knows it's them.

"I'm too tired," Cricket yells to her drunk teammates as she shoves her bag of Epsom salt into her suitcase.

"That's okay!" one of them yells. "Open the door!"

Cricket rolls her eyes but does as she's told.

"Hi," Sloane says. "I'm kidnapping you." She is alone. And sober. Down the hallway, a door slams and music starts up.

"Good, you're still dressed," Sloane says, taking in Cricket's bright green game jersey.

"I don't feel like seeing anybody."

"Perhaps you misheard me," Sloane says, shoving her foot against the hotel door so it stays wedged open. "I'm kidnapping you, so your consent is not of my concern." Sloane speaks like nothing between them has changed. Because nothing has changed. But her being here, right now—Cricket feels a magnetic pull in her fingertips, a voltage humming between them.

Before leaving the hotel room, Sloane ties a blindfold over Cricket's eyes and guides her along the empty hallway, down the staff elevator to the loading dock, where several employees on their smoke break recognize Sloane and ask for her autograph, oblivious to or disinterested in the hostage situation they're witnessing.

"Unbelievable," Cricket mutters, which makes Sloane laugh as she helps her abductee buckle her seatbelt.

On the highway, Cricket relaxes enough to recognize the smell of sweat embedded in the seatbelt strap across her chest, and the vehicle's poor shock system that makes Cricket bump her head every time they drive over a pothole.

"How'd you get a team van?" Cricket asks.

"Don't you know who I am?" Sloane answers.

When they park, Sloane takes Cricket by the hand and leads her through darkness with pockets of light bright enough to see through her blindfold. Cricket hears a key card swipe, a confirmation beep from a security system, and then the artificial arctic blast of air-conditioning. They are inside but it is silent, and then back outside, swaddled in the stillness of a cool summer evening in Southern California.

"How scared should I be?" Cricket asks.

"Not at all."

Several more steps and Cricket suddenly smells her favorite smell.

"We're here," Sloane says, unknotting her blindfold.

Cricket looks up and her mouth drops open.

The Rose Bowl is beautiful any time of day, but it is majestic at night. The field is empty save for a cluster of soccer balls in front of the opposite goal. Cricket moves so quickly it looks like she's flying as she sprints across the field and fires a shot at the open net.

Under the lights, Cricket's legs are convinced they've never been heavy, or tired, and her ankle has never been sprained, her rotator cuff never strained. She is an invincible, rubber-boned kid with keys to the kingdom. She is an ambitious witch dancing at the height of her power. She is an extraordinary keeper playing on a perfect green pitch at midnight.

Nudging one ball away from the rest, Cricket allows her momentum to carry her through the release. The soccer ball takes flight and finds the upper right corner with unapologetic audacity. She is meant to be here. She was born to be here. A part of her will always live between these pipes.

"Nice one," Sloane calls from midfield.

"I wish I had my gloves!"

"Check the left post," Sloane calls back. There are Cricket's gloves, swiped from the locker room and begging for action. She has never belonged anywhere the way she belongs on a soccer field. She has been appalling at so many things, all to get here. It has required everything to be extraordinary in this one particular space, but it wasn't for nothing.

Cricket is still Velcroing her left glove when Sloane rockets a ball past her.

"That was your one," Cricket says, bouncing in ready position. She watches Sloane's face as she concentrates on the ball and can't help but appreciate what she has always appreciated about Sloane: Her force and foresight. The liquid in her movement, how Sloane's hips do not shift or tilt like other players' but flow, pouring from one motion into the next. A body of rivers.

"Ready?" Sloane asks, setting up another ball for a penalty kick.

Cricket nods and moments later the ball sails directly into her arms. Sloane curses.

"Don't you know who I am?" Cricket yells and they both cackle with delight.

They collect the balls and go again. And again. And again.

At some point, they switch out, and Sloane hops in goal.

"You're rusty but not horrible," Cricket tells her.

"That's so funny," Sloane says, "because you're horrible but not rusty."

Even as it's unfolding, Cricket tries to archive the details of this night in her memory—how the stadium lights stretch out their arms in every direction and appear like supernovas against the black sky, how her legs feel like pogo sticks, desperate for that spring of release, how Sloane grins at her every time she sneaks in a grounder, and how Cricket has never been more in love with the game, because tonight is the essence of what soccer can be: Fun. Liberating. An invitation to run up to the future and kick it as hard as she can.

"You're looking a little tired," Sloane yells from eighteen yards away.

"I'm not tired," Cricket shouts back. "But if you're tired, we can call it."

"Me?" Sloane doesn't try to hide her indignation. "I could go all night."

"Great, because I'm not calling it."

"Neither am I."

"Then shoot already."

They play for another hour. By the time they silently agree to bag the balls, Cricket looks like she's been swimming, her clothes glued to her, steady drops of sweat dripping from her high bun, which is now comically lopsided.

"I'm not a medical professional," Sloane says, bent over at the waist and tenderly massaging her quad muscle, "but I'd say my femur is back, baby."

"That was impressive," Cricket agrees. "Maybe you should return as a striker."

"Maybe you should—" Sloane starts to fire back a joke and then catches herself. The truth ripples between them: Cricket is giving up her spot just as Sloane prepares to seize it.

By the time they arrive at the hotel, Cricket shivers under a layer of cold, dried sweat.

By the time she says good night to Sloane in the elevator, it's nearly three a.m.

"Hey," Sloane says over her shoulder as she steps off the elevator. "Can I make one suggestion? About your future?"

Cricket nods, her heart thumping wildly.

But before Sloane can offer her advice, and before Cricket even realizes what she is doing, she is already stepping off her line and leaning through the elevator doors, taking the biggest risk of all by kissing the greatest keeper she's ever known.

TEN YEARS

The night before their operations, Cricket waits impatiently in front of the teakettle. Oliver removes two bottles of Martinelli's from the refrigerator and tells her that they need to get going.

"You're not the boss of me," Cricket chides.

"You can only consume fluids until midnight." He taps his watch. It's almost eleven p.m.

Mia drops a large cardboard box full of sequined dresses in the middle of the living room floor. "We should go in the next five minutes," she says. "We don't want to be late."

The kettle whistles just as Sloane appears from the basement with a stack of towels, still warm from the dryer. "I think you need a bottle opener for those," she tells Oliver, who is struggling to twist off the caps of the sparkling apple cider.

Mia helps Cricket pour the boiling water from the teakettle into two hot-water bottles. They then wedge the bottles into the stack of folded towels. It's exactly what their mom used to do for them.

It is no coincidence that the Lowe sisters booked their kidney surgeries for the day after their mother's ten-year anniversary. Tonight, they honor her, and tomorrow, they reset their own lives to move forward.

Sloane and Oliver are hanging back with the sleeping Betty, and so it is just the two sisters who walk down to the ocean under a sky that glitters almost as much as they do—they wear sequins from head to toe.

"Hey," Mia says as they approach the beach. "Thank you for doing this."

"It was my idea!" Cricket feels compelled to point out.

"Not tonight, ding-dong," Mia says. "Tomorrow."

They set down their bags in the cold sand. Cricket digs out her portable speaker and presses Play before daring to look at her sister's face in the moonlight. It's the first song off their mother's high school warm-up playlist.

"Get Lowe," Mia sings along.

"Fly high!" Cricket booms, mimicking the backup singer's deep bass.

"Ready?" Mia asks.

"Always."

The sisters scream as they forge ahead, voices banging against the waves and rocks. They get low to fly high and they risk death to celebrate being alive.

Diving in, the freezing cold lifts them to a higher plane of consciousness, which is how they know she's not a mirage. They've never experienced such clearheaded thinking or superb vision as when their mother appears just after midnight, barefoot and way down the beach, past the jetty where she held their morning training sessions. It's the first time the sisters see her together, but it will not be the last.

MATCH DAY

"Count down from ten," the anesthesiologist instructs Mia. She is asleep before she gets to her lucky number.

Out in the waiting room, Oliver checks in with the neighbor who is watching Betty and then texts Sloane with updates as they trickle in: Mia is under, they've begun, everything is going well.

Sloane texts back a thumbs-up and lets Oliver know that down the hall, in OR 2, Mia's donor is just beginning to wake up.

Five days later, Oliver flips on his turn signal and Mia eagerly watches 125 Knickerbocker Avenue come into view. When they pull into the driveway, Mia is already unbuckled, desperate to hug the people waiting on her front stoop.

Cricket, Sloane, and Betty wave and yell like they are welcoming home a war hero. The car is still running when Oliver sprints around the hood to help Mia with the door and here's Betty, face-planting into her mother's lap as Mia bends over to greedily inhale the back of her baby's head.

Her girl.

Mia's incision is no longer sore, and while it's too early to deem the transplant a success, Dr. Landwosky and his team are optimistic. He called Cricket's kidney, now in Mia's body, the most beautiful kidney he'd ever seen, and reported with elation that it had "pinked up immediately." So far, Mia and Cricket have both fought off infection. Equally promising, Mia's new kidney began producing urine immediately and was fully functioning within twenty-four hours of the operation.

"I made you dinner," Cricket announces proudly, helping her sister out of the car.

Mia grimaces.

"Taste it first!"

The four adults and one tottering human make their way back into the house. Betty shows her mother all the new toys and shiny, breakable gadgets she's received from friends and neighbors while Mia was in the hospital, including a signed soccer ball from the U.S. Women's National Team.

In the living room, Oliver hands Mia a tall glass of water and gestures to the pink floral couch, but Mia is sick of being sedentary. Her legs are restless, begging to be used. Her brain, too, is hungry for fresh stimulation after five days in the hospital. Mia slowly raps her knuckles on the wood bookshelf. It's time to make a plan for what comes next.

"What do you want to do?" Cricket asks, already knowing the answer.

"The beach," Mia says. "Let's go to the beach."

EPILOGUE

2031

THE GIFT

I t's a global frenzy.

A pageant of madness.

The Richter Scale records it as a 2.7 earthquake, but everyone will remember it as the 2031 Women's World Cup Final.

In the players' tunnel, Cricket watches Sloane bend down and whisper something to the little girl white-knuckling her hand as they wait to step onto the pitch. Through the sea of American and Spanish women standing shoulder to shoulder, Sloane turns around and finds Cricket, just as she always does. Their eyes catch and they flash their matching grins before reassuming their gameday faces.

The journey to this match was circuitous. "We took the scenic route," Sloane likes to tell the press. But they've made it. Together. Finally.

After Cricket and Mia's kidney operations, it took a year of rehab, a dozen daily medications, and routine check-ins before Mia's care team declared the transplant a success. During that time, Betty took her first wobbly steps. And Paula, Cricket's manager, reached an agreement with U.S. Soccer, the NWSL, and Cricket's sponsors to bring her back here, in the tunnel, with her team.

Back where she belongs.

It would have taken even longer had Sloane not tipped the scales of power with her own team of heavyweights, her own savviness with the spotlight. Cricket has never felt luckier. Ever since the surgery, she has experienced an undeniable lightness—and not just because of the half-pound kidney she gave up. It's loving Sloane, and living this dream with her, but also reuniting with Mia after those ten agonizing months of silence. It's recognizing her life for the one-take miracle that it is.

To make it to the final, the U.S. Women's National Team beat their opponents in every match of every stage of the World Cup. As individuals and as a collective, however, they've endured far more defeat and heartbreak to ultimately arrive here. A key part of winning, Cricket likes to point out, is simply refusing to quit.

Out in the designated Friends and Family section, Oliver and Mia sit among the spouses, partners, parents, and children of the players. Sloane's mom and dad, Bonnie and Bruce, compliment Oliver and Mia on their matching JACKSON jerseys before they all put their arms around each other for a photo. No matter the outcome of the game, they already know they want to remember this day.

Even in the height of the moment—*especially* in the height of the moment—Mia misses her mom. And yet, Liz is everywhere. She is all around this stadium—among the screaming kids with the face-painted cheeks, and the women in their thirties wearing Abby Wambach jerseys, and the men donning pink wigs to honor Megan Rapinoe, who is also in attendance with so many of her former teammates, including the entire roster from the 2019 World Cup. The '99ers have come out in full force, too, including the Lowe sisters' namesakes, Mia Hamm and Kristine Lilly. A far-reaching coven of living legends are here to support the next generation, and the generation after that. They have gathered to celebrate the Beautiful Game, the contest that helped them find their best friends and true selves both within and beyond the sharply drawn lines of the field.

Oliver wipes the tears off Mia's face, taking care not to blur the red heart on her cheek. Each of them wears one of Liz's lucky game ribbons around their wrists. "I miss her," Oliver says, and Mia knows from the downy softness in his tone that he isn't talking about Liz.

"She's in good hands," Mia assures him, just as they see Cricket emerge from the tunnel.

Crossing the pitch with the substitute players, Cricket now understands that the reserves truly are game changers. She sees how their performance on the sideline affects their teammates in real time. But Cricket is not a game changer.

As Anders's assistant, Cricket will take over as head goalkeeping coach when he retires at the end of this year. It had been Sloane's idea in the elevator that night—her suggestion for the future—right before Cricket kissed her. Several hours later, with their legs intertwined rather than up the wall, Sloane finally had the chance to voice it.

And so thirteen months after Cricket's surgery, the National Team announced their newest hire with a press release featuring a familiar face and signature blond pouf. Sloane followed it up with her own glowing endorsement: "It's simple," Sloane had posted on her social media platforms. "She makes me better." Above her words, she'd shared a throwback photo of the two of them from their first January camp together, sixteen years old, sweaty and serious as they stood next to the net and watched Alyssa Naeher in goal.

Cricket is quick to tease Sloane that all the support—and the several million "likes"—she garnered for that statement made Sloane creatively lazy. It's hard to dispute. After all, less than a year later, Sloane recited the exact same sentence in her wedding vows.

Cricket had been open to a destination wedding, with just her immediate family by her side. But Sloane wanted to celebrate—*really celebrate*—with everyone she'd ever played with, or maybe ever met, based on the staggering number of RSVPs. And rather than asking everyone to fly to some tropical paradise, Sloane insisted they wed in the one destination they'd always shared: Victory.

And so on a blustery day in the offseason, Cricket and Sloane stood next to each other at the far end of the beach, in the spot where Liz once held those morning training sessions. Betty served as an easily distracted but nevertheless dazzling flower girl. Oliver officiated with the poised generosity he'd cultivated through coaching and the expansive humility he'd acquired from parenting.

It wasn't easy to herd almost three hundred people into chairs that were sinking in wet sand as the tide came in, but Cricket had wanted to marry at sunset, so everyone took off their shoes and hiked up their hemlines to bear witness to a soccer love story.

Of all people, it had been Mia's idea to start the ceremony five minutes late as an homage to Liz, and it had been Cricket's firm insistence that the string quartet play "Get Low, Fly High" when it was her turn to walk down the aisle, a red ribbon tied around her topknot.

And then they were a married couple. Mia had warned Cricket ahead of time that it felt totally the same but also entirely different, and Mia was once again right. The Monday morning after their wedding, Sloane put bread in the toaster while Cricket cracked eggs for their omelets, and everything seemed normal except for the unforeseen media frenzy surrounding their nuptials.

The feast of possibilities kept them busy through the winter as they pored over glitzy invitations that arrived as regularly as Hannaford coupons. They were, apparently, a power couple, and so they spent the spring harnessing their influence into tangible support for women with fewer opportunities. Together, Sloane and Cricket founded a nonprofit that offered resources to single mothers looking to restart their lives. They called it New Years and asked Mia if she would serve as their executive director. It was scheduled to launch the upcoming fall, on Liz's birthday.

But this summer, Sloane and the Lowe sisters have devoted all their attention to winning the World Cup, and now they're here, at the final. Standing on the sidelines in front of the U.S. bench, Cricket turns around to find her family and there they are—Mia and Oliver, Sloane's parents, and everyone else she does and doesn't recognize. She loves and appreciates them all for being here tonight. Every women's World Cup breaks records in attendance, viewership, and revenue because of the fans, who not only show up but speak out about the need for equality in pay, exposure, and distribution.

A high school team dressed in their green uniforms scream Cricket's name so she turns around and waves to them, makes a heart from her two hands. On the Jumbotron, her gold band reminds the fans of their queen and so there is a sudden surge of screaming just as the starting lineup emerges from the tunnel and the true show begins.

Sloane Jackson crosses the pitch and her loyal subjects create seismic waves with their applause and approval. Here is the woman who snapped in half but came back stronger than ever, with a gleam in her eye, a strut in her stride, and a dimple in her left cheek.

"There she is!" Mia yells from the stands, but Oliver already sees their daughter, grinning under all the lights as she holds her Aunt Sloane's hand. The three-year-old is oblivious to the underlying stakes that make this a night to behold. And yet, just by being here, Betty absorbs the magic of this community, the power of the crowd. As a witness to all this, she will never doubt what's possible on or off the pitch. She will grow up knowing she comes from a line of women who ignored the rules to chase their dreams out of bounds.

What good fortune to share our fortune.

And so tonight, before she lets go of Sloane Jackson's hand, Betty doesn't wish her aunt luck, and she knows better than to tell her to break a leg. Instead, Betty reminds the celebrated goalkeeper of what her mother likes to say on especially beautiful mornings when they walk down to the beach in Victory. Hand in hand, sometimes with a soccer ball but usually with just a shovel and pail, Mia will take a deep breath, close her eyes, and remind Betty of the truest thing she knows.

Crossing center field, Betty squeezes Sloane's hand to get her attention. Ahead of them, Cricket waits with open arms. And above her, standing in the best seats, Betty's parents wave with frenetic pride. The energy continues to swell, gathering power in a mounting haze of patriotic cheers and ferocious hope that can never be effectively simulated or properly communicated, only lived.

Betty smiles and the stadium lights catch her bright eyes as she tugs on Sloane's hand one more time and yells above the roar, "What a gift!"

ACKNOWLEDGMENTS

Long before this book was complete, I dreamed about writing these acknowledgments. Maybe it was the isolation of the pandemic, or moving to Maine by myself, or the identity crisis/temporary lobotomy that accompanied the miracle of becoming a mother, but man oh man did I lean extra hard on others as I slowly made my way back to myself. Thank you, reader, for enduring the long game with me. We've only arrived on these final pages because of the wise, generous, and sublimely spectacular humans mentioned here.

Thank you to my literary agent, Becky Sweren, for supporting my dream to write about women's soccer. One bright spot over the past several years has been watching you bloom from a reluctant sports person to a slightly less reluctant sports person. Another bright spot has been continuing to have you in my corner every step of the way.

If only LED lights could harness Whit Frick's energy because she is the brightest AND warmest bulb in the box. Thank you, Whit, for your singular brand of brilliance and for assembling the illuminati over at Dial Press, especially Talia Cieslinski, whose support on this project cannot be overemphasized, as well as Rachel Parker, Madison Dettlinger, Emma Caruso, Avideh Bashirrad, Debbie Aroff, Maria Braeckel, Aarushi Menon, Donna Chung, Muriel Jorgensen, Maggie Hart, Rebecca Berlant, Andy Ward, and the genteel Ted Allen.

Thank you to Andrew Macara for the beautiful artwork that graces the cover. I truly love it.

Thank you to Poet Laureate Ada Limón for all your work and especially the poem "Dead Stars," lines from which not only inspired the title but also serve as the epigraph. Consequently, thank you to everyone at The Permissions Company for the green light to reprint Ms. Limón's work.

Here seems like the appropriate place to thank my dear friend Nick Hiebert, who sent me a card with several lines from "Dead Stars" years ago. Since its arrival, the card has stood on display in our kitchen, to the left of the sink, and serves as daily motivation. As if that gift weren't enough, Nick also read an early draft of the book and encouraged me all the way here, so it's easy but still worthwhile to point out that everyone needs a pal like Nick.

Thank you, Lori Lindsey, for sharing your time, insights, and memories of the U.S. Women's National Team with me. Your willingness to talk on multiple occasions speaks to your generous spirit and commitment to the game. It's because of you that Cricket always dresses the same leg first, and even though she prefers a different song in the locker room, I appreciate your openness to, as Kenny Loggins would say, "Meet Me Halfway."

Thank you, Dr. Colleen Hacker, for the psychological insights into professional athletes, particularly those on the USWNT. Visualizing loved ones in the Friends & Family section, utilizing mistake rituals, committing to a positive outlook, and reframing pressure as an opportunity—these are all lifted from your toolbelt and proved essential in building this story. Thank you.

Thank you, Aaron Heifetz, for entertaining my enthusiastic inquiries about the USWNT. The specific color and logistics you provided about training camps, matchdays, and what makes a great goalkeeper all proved integral to this project. Furthermore, your emphasis on the culture and future of women's soccer beats at its heart.

Thank you, Dr. Helena Kurniawan, for answering all my frequent, random questions about kidneys with such thoughtful professionalism. Anything accurate about CKD is thanks to you; anything otherwise works in service of the narrative or, let's face it, reflects my own failure as an amateur nephrologist.

Thank you, Dr. Charlotte Hastings, for talking me through various aspects of pregnancy and childbirth throughout this project. We've come a long way since Swann, and I'm so grateful we've come all that way together.

Thank you, Caitie Whelan, for the enlightening but all too few walk-and-talks on loss and womanhood and mental loads. Mia and Cricket's conversation about needing a larger heart to house their grief is a great example of writer thievery. Thank you.

Thank you to Becky Cohn, May Paterniti, Devin Moore, Peggy Stewart, Jen Scott, Ana Martinez, and the devoted teachers at Chickadee—especially Chloe, Katija, Gabbie, and Alex—for loving on Hank while I worked on this project.

Thank you, Elsa Bertlesman, for taking such great care of Hank and for helping me get through the first two years of motherhood/figuring out how to write as a new mom.

Thank you to my cousin, Stacy Goldate, for swooping in last summer and injecting my life with encouragement, enthusiasm, and obscenely helpful edits.

Thank you, Kerry Rose, for being an early reader during the first year of Sal's spectacular life.

Thanks to my older brother, Zach, and my sister-in-law, Shilpa, for their steadfast support and earnest encouragement.

Thanks to my younger sister, Caroline, for the steadfast support and earnest criticism.

My mom's sister, my Aunt Caroline, whom I called Iyi, unexpectedly passed away last year. I want to honor her and my Uncle Murphy here because they have always been so deeply supportive of my writing.

Thanks to my parents, now better known as Papa and NeeNee, for everything along the way. I have no idea how you kept three kids alive, but I'm so glad you did.

Finally, thank you to the boys at home. Hank and Daddy Deane, it's not easy living with a writer, but you guys are my champions. Thank you for loving me and letting me love you.

What a gift indeed.

ABOUT THE AUTHOR

BECK DOREY-STEIN grew up in Narberth, Pennsylvania. Her first book, *From the Corner of the Oval*, was a *New York Times* bestseller and her debut novel, *Rock the Boat*, was a *New York Times* Editors' Choice selection. She now lives in Maine with her family but will always root for longer summers and Philly sports teams.

Instagram: @beckdoreystein
Facebook: @BeckDoreySteinAuthor

Books Driven by the Heart

Sign up for our newsletter
and find more you'll love:

thedialpress.com

 @THEDIALPRESS

@THEDIALPRESS